THE NOISE OF WAR

THE SERTORIUS SCROLL BOOK II

VINCENT B. DAVIS II

THIRTEENTH PRESS, LLC

For Scott Pratt and his family

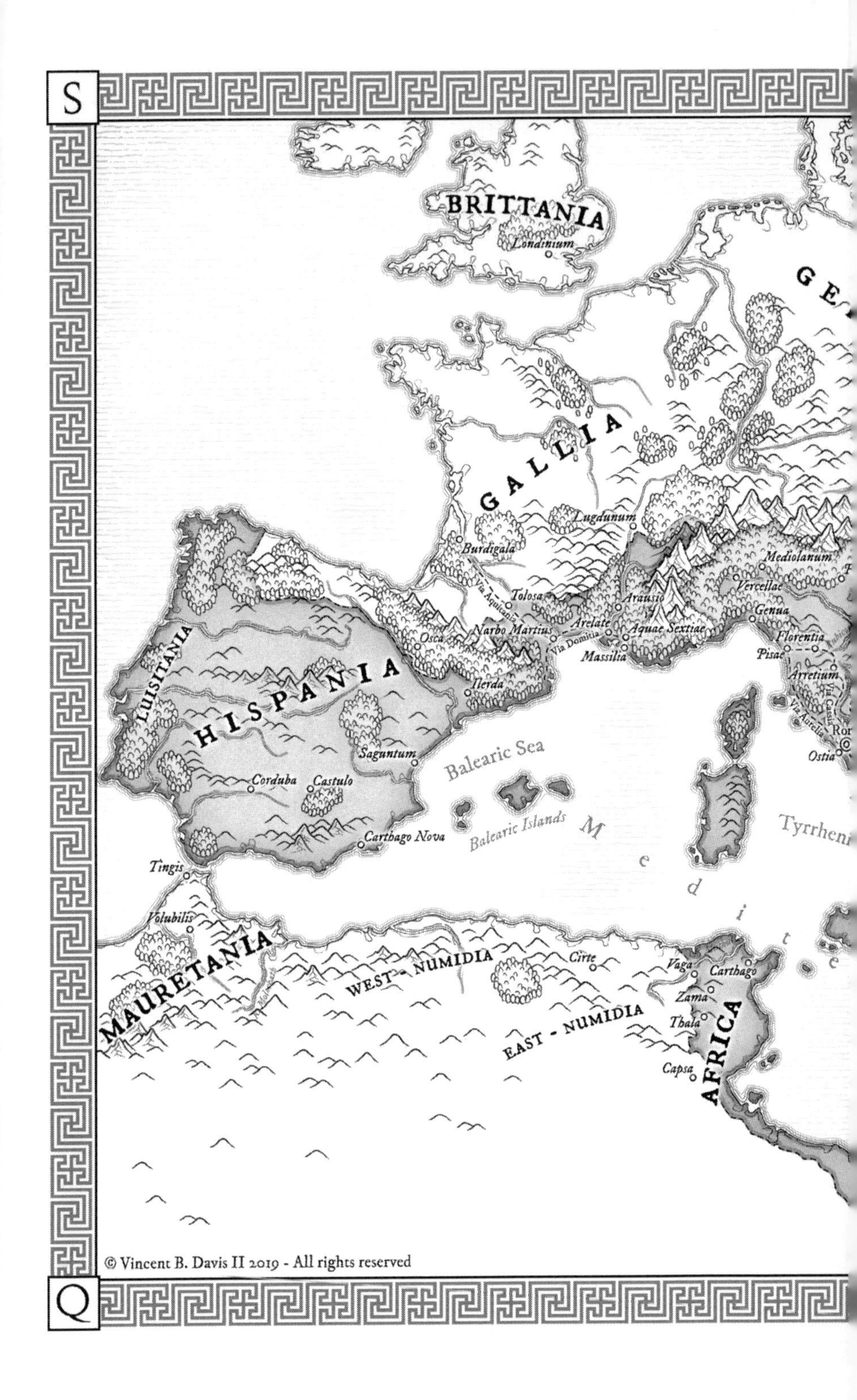
S
BRITTANIA
Londinium
GALLIA
Lugdunum
Burdigala
Tolosa
Via Aquitania
Narbo Martius
Arelate
Arausio
Aquae Sextiae
Via Domitia
Massilia
Mediolanum
Vercellae
Genua
Florentia
Pisae
Arretium
Via Cassia
Via Aurelia
Ostia
HISPANIA
LUISITANIA
Osca
Ilerda
Saguntum
Corduba
Castulo
Carthago Nova
Balearic Sea
Balearic Islands
Tingis
Volubilis
MAURETANIA
WEST - NUMIDIA
EAST - NUMIDIA
Cirte
Vaga
Carthago
Zama
Thala
Capsa
AFRICA
Q

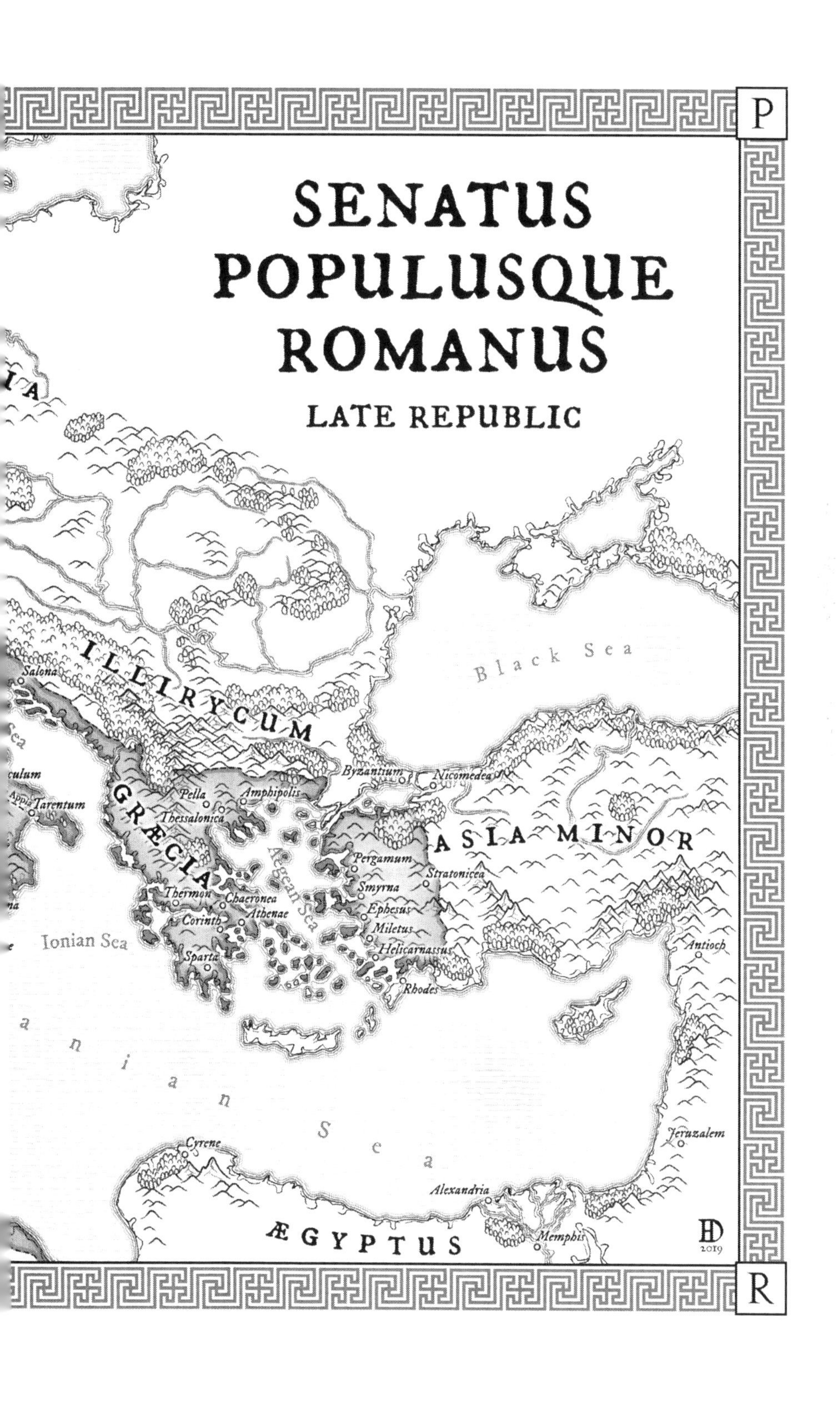
P
SENATUS
POPULUSQUE
ROMANUS
LATE REPUBLIC
ILLIRYCUM
Salona
Black Sea
Tarentum
Pella
Amphipolis
Thessalonica
GRÆCIA
Byzantium
Nicomedea
ASIA MINOR
Pergamum
Stratonicea
Smyrna
Ephesus
Miletus
Helicarnassus
Aegean Sea
Thermon
Chaeronea
Athenae
Corinth
Sparta
Ionian Sea
Rhodes
Antioch
Jeruzalem
Cyrene
Alexandria
ÆGYPTUS
Memphis
HD
2019
R

READING ORDER

1. The Man with Two Names: The Sertorius Scrolls I
2. Son of Mars: The Marius Scrolls I (FREE via link)
3. The Noise of War: The Sertorius Scrolls II
4. Blood in the Forum: The Marius Scrolls II (FREE via link)
5. Bodies in the Tiber: The Sertorius Scrolls III
6. Whom Gods Destroy: The Sertorius Scrolls IV preorder for **.99c** *limited time*

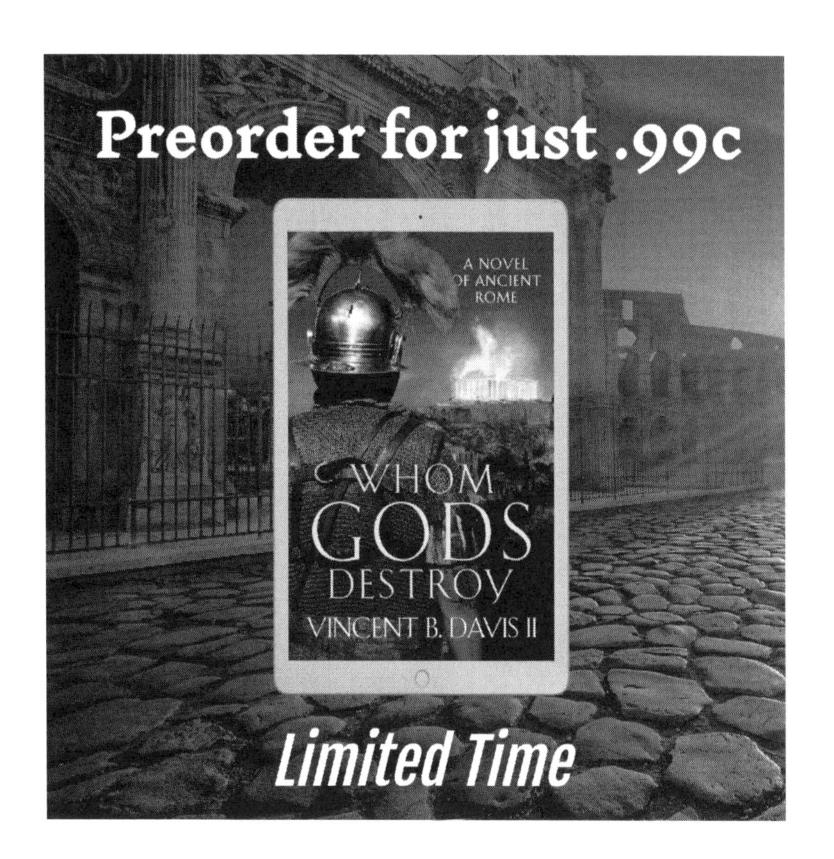
Preorder for just .99c
A NOVEL
OF ANCIENT
ROME
WHOM
GODS
DESTROY
VINCENT B. DAVIS II
Limited Time

This story is based on a real man and real events

After any battle, a soldier must check himself to see what he's lost and what remains. Has he sustained any injuries? Does he have any major hemorrhages? Lost any fingers? Any toes?

After Arausio, we who survived were forced to do the same with our very souls.

Had we lost our sense of humor? Our love for one another?

What possibly could have survived the great loss of Arausio, where ninety thousand Romans were slaughtered? The bodies of my brothers covered the earth for miles. The treetops of the aged pines shook with the ascension of their ghosts.

I apologize, reader, for not writing in so long. It has been almost a year since I wrote the final chapter of my last scroll, detailing my first years in the Colors. It was much more difficult to relive than I had previously anticipated. In that one day, when our numbers marched against the vicious and boundless forces of the Cimbri and Teutone armies, I lost my only sibling and all of the men I had served with. They were butchered like animals. And for whatever reason, the gods spared me that day. I have been searching for the reason ever since.

Some wounds simply remain. I once knew a soldier who injured his ankle on his very first campaign, and eighteen years of service later, the nasty bugger still gave him trouble. And I can tell you from experience, the wounds of the soul last just as long. Perhaps longer. The memory of Arausio stayed with me, and with those few others who survived.

After finishing my first set of scrolls, I decided I would have to quit writing them altogether. Writing and recollecting the men I served with who died that day—my brother, Titus, men like Ax, Flamen, Terence, Pilate—it was too much for me to bear.

But after speaking with those closest to me, I have decided to continue on. I am still at war with Rome, the only nation I have ever loved, and cannot guarantee that I will live long enough to finish this tale, unless the gods see fit to spare me. Regardless, this memoir might be the last contribution I can make to Rome, and therefore I will press on.

When I first went to Rome, I was a naive young boy. Unschooled in all the ways of the world, I was unprepared for what awaited me in both political life and in the military. My father endowed me with principles, with character, and I hope with some modicum of courage, but these attributes were less suited for a life in politics and warfare than I had hoped. After Arausio, I was many things, but naive was not one of them. I had learned about war. I had learned about life, and death, and the terrible things that men can do to one another. I had no desire to relive the experiences by taking up my gladius again, but Fortuna (and Consul Gaius Marius, for that matter) had other plans for me.

My service to Rome was not completed, and perhaps still isn't. So I will continue my story, picking up where I last left off—hiding like animals in a Gallic village, trying to find survivors among the dead, and trying to discover what remained of ourselves.

Before continuing, be sure to JOIN THE LEGION! You'll receive a high-res map, a family tree, and other companion materials for your reading! On top of that, you'll receive Vincent's spinoff, *Son of Mars*, for free!

I

ESPIONAGE

1

SCROLL I

IDES OF AUGUST 650 AB URBE CONDITA

I lost an eye at Arausio. Had the thing ripped out by a slinger's rock. This wound, and the others I had sustained, were mended by Arrea, the girl I had found and fallen in love with during the campaign months prior. After hiding, resting, and recovering for nearly four months, I began to construct a makeshift camp outside the Gallic village Arelate, and waited for other soldiers to join us.

A few poor souls came in slowly at first, most of them having awakened underneath the bloated corpses of their friends on the fields of Arausio, or washing up like I had along the Rhône riverbank. They were all as broken, physical and emotionally, as I was. Lucius was the one exception: strong, focused, and relentlessly positive. Perhaps his cruel fated upbringing, losing both his parents in his childhood, had prepared him in some way for how truly painful the world could be.

I couldn't accept what I had seen, what had happened. There was a structure to the world, I believed. Some system for how things worked, or should work. Now that I had lived through the single most devastating loss in Roman history, or perhaps all of human history, I could not reconcile the experience with the moral codes I had been taught: my conceptualizations, my beliefs about human nature and the notions of cosmic justice through which I understood everything that had happened in my life, up until then.

The world had become petrifying. It refused to be understood and articulated by a mere boy like myself.

Lucius refused to let me wallow, however. I was still recovering from my wounds and attempting to adjust to the difficulties of balance and vision with one of my eyes now gone, Lucius helped me build our makeshift camp outside Arelate. We started by gathering logs from the Gallic woodline and began with a small perimeter defense. It couldn't have protected us from a band of children with a handful of rocks, but it was something. It kept us, in Lucius's mind at least, in the world of soldiers. We weren't yet prepared to live any other life, for that was even more terrifying.

IT TOOK us a long time to finish putting up the camp. I think Arrea and Lucius conspired to delay the process, afraid of when there would be nothing left with which to occupy me with. When the three of us wedged the final log in the earth, Lucius had already devised another plan.

"Good work, boys," Arrea said, smiling at the two of us.

"Thank you, sincerely." I leaned over and squeezed her now callused hands.

"Quintus," Lucius said, and I already knew something was troubling him, "there have to be more survivors. Don't you think?"

I shook my head. "They would have come by now."

"Perhaps they believe they're the only ones still alive, just like we did for a long time. Maybe they don't know how to find us."

I looked to Arrea to determine whether or not she was in agreement as well, and the blush of her cheeks told me it was probable.

"What would you propose we do?"

"The battlefield is about thirty miles north. We can ride out and see if anyone is still there."

"No. I'm not strong enough to return to that place." I turned and wiped my splintered hands on the Gallic tunic I had purchased a few weeks prior.

"You don't give yourself enough credit. You survived the battle, surely you could return if it meant saving more of your men," Arrea said, placing her hand on my forearm. She was encouraging, but I could tell by the shimmer in her eyes that she understood my resistance.

"And where will we get the horses?" I asked.

"I talked to a villager in Arelate. He said he'd be willing to let us take two horses, and guide us there himself," said Lucius.

"I see you've already made up your mind." I licked the sweat from my lips and blocked the sun from my eye to see my friend's face.

"I'll not go without you."

"And what about you?" I turned to Arrea.

"You know I don't mind working with you, my dove, but I could use some rest anyhow." She stepped closer to me.

"Alright." I nodded, realizing that I didn't have enough excuses to combat both of them. "We can leave at first light."

Lucius instantly sighed with relief. I hadn't noticed the lines of worry that had begun to etch themselves on his once youthful face. I was afraid his concern for me might begin to turn his blond hair gray, but I didn't know how to articulate myself properly...how I could tell him that I wasn't fine, but that I was. The strain my condition placed on Arrea and Lucius shamed me, and the shame made my condition worse.

"Excellent. I'll alert our guide immediately. You two get some rest." He patted Arrea and myself on the arm.

I stood still as my friend hurried off toward the village, already panicking as images of the battlefield flashed before my eye.

"Quintus?" Arrea said, craning into view. "Let's lie down."

I allowed her to lead me to our little tent, the one we had held each other in for months now.

"Do you need help?" She leaned forward to balance me as I took the weight off my leg and struggled to the ground.

"I'm fine. Some things a man needs to do himself."

Once I was on my backside, Arrea nestled up next to me and placed her head on my chest. My heartbeat slowed as I smelled her hair.

Somehow I sensed that her eyes were still open.

"Do you want to make love? It's been months," Arrea asked softly.

"I don't think you'd enjoy that much. I'm covered in sweat and smell like a barbarian."

"Well to you Romans, I am a barbarian, so I don't think it would be a problem." She craned her head up at me and smiled.

"I think I'll just hold you, dove," I said, forcing myself to smile back. *Hold you while I still can,* I thought but didn't say it. I knew there would be a time soon when I couldn't. And perhaps never would again if my brother's fate awaited me upon my return to the legion.

THE SKY WAS STILL black when Lucius stirred me from my sleep. Once again, I was drenched in sweat from the night. The first few times I'd feared in embarrassment that I had pissed myself, but no…it was only the nightmares.

"The guide is ready. He's got three horses up near the road."

"Just give me a moment to change my tunic." I crawled out

of bed and tried to rub the sleep from my eye. I had grown up drinking a glass of honey-water and reading something before I began my day, but life in the Colors had broken me of that habit.

I pulled the damp tunic off and threw on one of the only other two that I owned. In the morning starlight I made out Arrea's sleeping face. Braced up against her arm, her cheek scrunched and lips pursed, nothing had ever been so beautiful. There was something about sleep too, that made her hair even more lovely than when she combed it. If there was anything that still gave me hope, it was looking at her.

"Lead the way, *amicus*." I gestured to Lucius.

We walked from the camp and onto the road, following the sound of horse grunts to the guide.

"I almost thought you weren't coming," the burly guide said with a scowl, his eyes barely visible beneath a dark hood.

"It takes me a little while to get around these days." I gestured to my bad eye.

"I get around just fine." He raised his left arm, which ended at a nub, the skin stretched tight and tucked into a deep scar. That put me in my place, and I remained silent as I struggled to climb his horse.

It was a massive beast bred for working the fields rather than riding, but I always enjoyed that type. Burly, tough, and head-strong, but fiercely loyal if you trained them right.

"You alright?" Lucius said as I swung my leg over the big horse's back.

"I'm fine, comrade. Stop worrying so much." I shook my head and he struggled to get onto his horse as well. He didn't have any injuries, but there has never been a less graceful horsemen than my friend Lucius, although it wasn't for lack of trying.

THE GUIDE LED us through the darkness until the sun rose, just in time to keep my hands from growing numb from the cold. Fortunately the guide spoke little Latin, and didn't seem willing to speak in Gallic much either. We rode mostly in silence, which suited me fine, for I was struggling to fight the urge to spin my horse about and gallop back to Arelate.

Before I had truly decided to stay the course, we had arrived. It wasn't the first or last time I'd been lost in my thoughts, as I'm sure my rambling has already revealed to you.

The guide slowed our gallop to a trot, and then to a full halt, as the bodies came into view.

"You can hitch them up here." The guide pointed to a few posts at the edge of a wood line.

After we hitched the horses, Lucius became the guide and led the way.

It's difficult to describe what it feels like when you're so surrounded by the dead that it's all you can take in. I felt like I had awakened in Hades with the souls of many generations withering all around me.

The battle had taken place in October. And now the months between us and them had begun to decay, but the worst of it had been stalled by the heavy snowfall of winter. Most of the snow had melted, but the bodies of my brothers were still cold, their skin tight as leather across the bone, their open, frightened eyes yellow and milky.

I thought of how many coins it would take to lay over their eyes if we wished to send them on their way to the ferryman. It would have taken more than all the coffers of Rome. I reached up to cover my nose from the smell.

I made the mistake of scanning the face of a dead man at my feet. His throat was severed, the ground beneath him still stained black with his lifeblood. Even with his partially decayed cheeks, I felt like I could picture him alive. I had never met him before his death, I don't believe, but I still felt like I knew him. I could imagine him telling jokes over a camp fire, or complaining about being stuck with guard shift or latrine duty.

"We're here to search for the living, not the dead, *amicus*," Lucius said, before continuing to shout for any survivors who may have returned to the battlefield.

I couldn't look away, though. I knelt beside the man and reached down to close his eyes. Unlike the recently deceased, the skin was fixed in place, and wouldn't move. He would perpetually stare off in fear, always seeing his killer before him.

"I'm sorry this happened to you," I said, first to the man beside me and then to the valley of dead Romans before us, still wearing the armor they had once spit-shined and so proudly worn. Arrows were scattered across the battlefield, some wedged into the dirt and others in the cadavers of my comrades.

"Here." The guide approached and threw a bag of coins at me.

"What's this?"

"It's what the boy paid me." He nodded toward Lucius. "I fought a lot of battles"—his gray beard bobbed as his lips quivered before continuing—"but seen nothing like this." He removed his hood and cupped his hands in respect.

I hesitated to remove the denarii until he gestured for me to go ahead. My hands trembled as I spread the coin out over the open, dead eyes of the a few Romans beneath me. It wasn't much, in comparison to the carnage around me, but it was better than nothing.

"I don't see anyone alive here," Lucius said before noticing what I was doing. "There are too many, Quintus."

I stood and wiped the dampness from the tip of my nose.

"I know. But hopefully one man sent well into the afterlife can secure passage for the rest of our brethren." I gestured to the men on all sides. "I wish we could bury or burn them, but I know we can't."

Lucius approached, stepping over piles of corpses in the process.

"When we win...when we punish those bastards for this, perhaps Marius will send all of us back to lay our brothers to rest." Lucius placed a hand on my shoulder and stared into my eye. "Come on. Nothing stirring for miles. We might as well head back to camp." It was true, the battlefield was completely silent. Even the vultures had scurried off when we arrived. Perhaps we frightened them, or they were satiated. I didn't assume they suddenly developed a respect for the dead.

The only thing that moved were the standards wedged into the earth beside their fallen carriers, the standards that the barbarians hadn't taken with them. It was an eerie sight. The silence played tricks on my mind, making me think I could still hear the clash of battle in the distance.

I carved a sign in Latin onto a rock: "30 MILES SOUTH, EAST OF ARELATE. SAFETY FOR ALL ROMANS."

The guide asked if we should give away our location so openly. Lucius and I just shrugged. The Reds had moved on their way, gone off West to enjoy themselves while Rome mourned. They'd be back, but when they did, we doubted a few starving Romans would concern them.

Lucius and the guide helped me gather a few standards and prop the stone up. If anyone came looking for other survivors, at least they had a direction.

But after seeing all the dead, I doubted there were many more of us left.

2

SCROLL II

FOUR DAYS BEFORE THE NONES OF SEPTEMBER 650 AB URBE CONDITA

That rock proved to be useful over the next month. It was true—there weren't many of us left. But a few, a handful, had stumbled back to the wreckage of Arausio and spotted our sign waiting for them there. They trickled in, one or two a week, for the remainder of August.

"How many do we have now?" I asked Lucius. It was early in September now and hot out for a Gallic morning. I was sweating profusely despite moderate exertion, but I didn't care. Luxuries like bathing were of no concern to me now. Water was perhaps available in Arelate, but personal hygiene was no longer important. We had all survived like animals, and so were resigned to smell like them as well.

"Twenty-seven," he said, taking a knee and propping himself up on his shield. Despite our walls and our complete inability to actually fight, Lucius never went anywhere except in his fighting kit.

"It seems like more." I adjusted my eye patch, which at that time still chaffed my brow horribly.

"That's because we had so few, for so long," he said, feigning a smile. He tended to me as a good trainer does to a damaged colt. We talked little of Arausio and all that we had lost, but he was just as aware as anyone that I hadn't ever left the battlefield. How could I? I left my brother, Titus, there to die. He demanded that I do so, and he was bleeding profusely from the nubs of his severed legs…but could I have done more?

"Do you think there are more camps out there? Like ours?" I asked with all the naivety that still remained in me.

He bit his lip and looked away from me. "I don't think so, *amicus*. I've kept my ears open, and the traders say they've visited every city for miles and haven't heard any news about other camps."

The lavender and glasswort swayed with a gentle early-autumn breeze. The white flamingos bobbed for fish in the swampy pond past our camp. Even the mosquitoes, which had been fierce and active previously, were beginning to leave us alone as the weather was cooling. At any other time, for any other person, it would have been picturesque. The kind of landscape a man can sit within and ponder the wonders of life. But it all seemed dead to me. It all seemed like a lie. A facade covering up the truth about the world that had been so poignantly displayed at Arausio.

"This can't be it, Lucius. I can't believe that," I said, gesturing to the soldiers sitting around our little fort. I did believe it, though, I just didn't want to.

"Cheer up, Quintus. That's twenty more Romans who survived than we believed." He patted me on the shoulder. Twenty was more than just the two of us, but it paled significantly in comparison to the ninety thousand mules we had marched with a few months prior.

"Hello, boys. Hungry?" Arrea approached behind me, delicately balancing a few steaming bowls of soup.

"May Juno bless you," Lucius said, helping her with the bowls and wincing when some of it spilled onto his hands.

"Thank you," I said, not bothering to turn to my left to see her, for I no longer had the eye to do so, "but I think I'll wait awhile."

"Quintus, you must eat!" she chided me as my mother had when I was a child, and I loved her for it.

"Make sure the others eat first." It was my standard response for refusing a meal. I was a centurion by rank, and so it was my job to make sure the other men were fed before myself. But, in truth, I simply didn't want to eat. My stomach was perpetually unsettled, and it didn't seem quite fair that I could dine on Arrea's simple stew while my brothers were being dined upon by the carrion birds.

"I've made enough for everyone. Now, if you're their leader, you need to stay strong." She handed me the bowl, and once I caught sight of it with my good eye, I took it and decided to eat, even if it was just for her.

For all the military decorations that can be bestowed on a soldier, all of them should have been awarded to Arrea. Since Arausio, she had systematically tended to the injured and sick among us like a one-woman *medicus* corp. Soldiers are most often inept at cooking, as we had a special century devoted to preparing our meals, and so Arrea did most of our meal preparation too. When she found a rare moment of quiet, she stitched our torn tunics, returning to us a modicum of our honor as soldiers.

"Sit by me." I slid on the log and made room for her. She hesitated, always feeling that there was something else to be done, but after I gave her a look only lovers may extend to one another, she relented.

"You know," Lucius said, waving the heat away from a spoonful of soup, "we should think about moving soon."

"Moving where? We're protected here," I said, only half sarcastically.

"Back to Italy. Somewhere safe. I met a saffron trader who claimed that General Marius has set up camp. The consul told you in that letter he'd be coming after the snows melt. And they've melted. Perhaps it's true?" Lucius said. He wasn't bred to stay in this Gallic shit-hole and sit on his hands. He knew our duty to Rome wasn't completed yet, and we were ready to meet our fate. I knew this, too, but was perhaps less prepared for what lay ahead.

"I don't think so," I said, taking a bite of soup and feeling my stomach churn.

Arrea and Lucius exchanged a look.

"We haven't received any orders. We should stand by our post until word arrives that we're needed elsewhere," I said. We had paid one of the villagers to take a letter to Rome, so Marius knew where to find us. Even knowing this, my case was weak. It was unlikely that Marius would send an orderly several hundred miles to tell us what he had already told us.

By this time, some of the other mules who had heard us talking had begun to gather.

"Talk of leaving, eh?" one said.

"I like the sound of that."

"Anywhere is better than this," another said.

I looked at Lucius as if to say, "See what you have done?" He only shrugged in reply.

"You all feel this way?" I strained to look around. Everyone nodded.

I struggled to my feet, my leg now mended, but improperly.

"Well, if you're all in agreement, then…then we can move." I didn't want to. I knew it was the right decision, but I didn't want to face the rest of the world. Our dreary, dank little camp was a lot less intimidating than returning to the borders of Italy and revealing to the world that I had lived, while all the others had died. Could I face Marius, look him in the eyes, and tell him that I had seen all of our standards taken by the enemy, all of our men butchered? Could I hold my mother and tell her that her son Titus had died in my arms?

"You're the centurion, here. We'll follow your orders," one of them said, and the others nodded. They weren't my men, and I had never met them before Arausio, but they were like any others. They were good legionnaires, and deserved a better leader than I.

"One of the centurion's first priorities is to understand the will of his men, and to act in accordance to that. If you're all ready to move, then we need to deconstruct the camp. We'll leave at first light."

They all seemed to exhale in relief, and Arrea reached for my hand to comfort me. It would be a long journey home, and far more arduous than simply the miles that spanned from here to there.

As the men set about taking down our feeble little walls, I approached the cot where Arrea and I had made our home for the last months. Nothing covered it save a few capes draped over some sticks, leaving us soaked through every time it rained, but it was our little place. When I held Arrea there, it was only the two of us. The war was a memory, a cruel memory. Or perhaps a tragic play I had seen once in the forum. Packing up that little cot meant returning to reality, to see what remained after Arausio.

I rolled up the cot and took down our makeshift tent. Beside it sat a lockbox that Arrea had kept for me since Lucius had dragged me to Arelate dripping wet and still bleeding from the stone lodged in my eye.

She placed every piece of my fighting kit inside, laying each one delicately beside the next to wait for the day I awoke to my duty. I had not touched them since that day.

I took out each piece, one at a time, and tried to remember how to adjust them properly. My feet sank into the leather of my sandals where they had worn grooves into the soles as we marched for miles in formation to the sound of booming cadence and the calls of *buccina* and tubas. I slid my *lorica* on, the chain mail weighing heavier on my shoulders than I remembered. I had lost weight since Arausio, and it showed.

At the bottom of the lockbox sat something I had almost forgotten existed. It was a crown of leaves, which I was given after I'd scaled the walls first at Burdigala. The foliage had been collected from the battlefield that day and presented to me by the consul and my friend Gnaeus Mallius Maximus. I might have once considered that the proudest day of my life. I could stare up at the vast expanse between earth and sky and not have to worry about if my ancestors were proud of me.

Arrea, knowing this, had saved it for me, even when our priorities should have been on sustenance and clothing. That revealed the kind of heart she had. But holding that crown in my hand now, it meant none of the things to me that it once had. Several of the leaves had been plucked off during our travels, and the tendrils were dying and brown. The copper, which bound it all together, was beginning to rust.

The oak leaves seemed to look at me with judgment and condemnation. How trite a military decoration like this seemed now.

I strapped my gladius to my hip and my dagger to my ankle, then stood. I almost walked away, but then I returned to pick up that flimsy little crown.

"I'm taking leave, be back by eleventh hour," I said to Lucius as I passed by to the entrance of our camp. He stared back inquisitively but said nothing.

I DIDN'T KNOW where I was going, but I needed a moment to myself. A brief pause from the duties of leading a band of injured survivors, and a pause from the watchful eyes of Lucius and Arrea.

As I walked, the Gallic villagers stopped what they were

doing. Some of them turned away, some looked down, others scolded their children for staring. Noticing my limp and the cloth over my eye, they must have all thought me risen from the dead, about to die, or both. The citizens of Arelate were used to our presence by now, but they still refused to meet my eye. A curt nod or a sad shrug was all I was afforded.

After walking aimlessly for a while, I found myself at the banks of the Rhône River. It was calm, the water trickling over smooth stones in accordance with a peaceful wind. It was of a cool-blue hue, and I could see the bottom even where the water was deepest.

It had not looked like this previously.

I will always remember the Rhône as violently red with the blood of my men, rotten corpses bobbing up and down the rapids.

I knelt and ladled some water in my cupped hands. Had even nature forgotten our losses? Regardless, I hadn't. I wouldn't.

I took that leafy crown and nearly cast it into the water, as far away from myself as possible, where I hoped it would travel and bury itself wherever the blood of our men had found its resting place. But I couldn't do it.

Filled to the brim with rumination and pointless contemplation, I turned to find a young Gallic boy behind me. He stared with wide, wet eyes, amazed at the monster looking back at him. He took a few steps back in fear but then regained his composure and approached me.

Taking two sticks in his hand, he tossed one to me and hoisted the other, wielding it like a sword.

Teeming with anticipation, he waited to see what I might do.

I studied the boy, and felt that I knew him well. He was like so many others, like I had been once before, so long ago. He had heard tales of war, of bravery. He wanted to be in the legends, the hero in a campfire story, as most young boys do.

I wanted to tell him how foolish he was. How misguided,

how ruinously misguided were those stories. I wanted to tell him that if he was a soldier, his brothers would die, his friends would die, and that he too, eventually, would die. I wanted to tell him that there was nothing good in war, that there was no glory or adventure to be had in it.

When I had lingered just long enough, the boy decided I must be disinterested. He lowered his play-sword as well as his gaze.

As he began to turn away, I picked up the stick and lunged at him.

A look of excitement spread across the boy's face as he lifted his stick to block the attack. He jabbed at me just as ferociously as Achilles at Troy, and I feigned injury when the stick found its mark.

I gestured for him to come close, and I placed him at my side. I picked up the shield that had followed me through so many battles, nearly twice his size.

Together we marched a few paces, and I showed him how to stab over and under the shield, how to keep your balance and find your mark.

His eyes glowed with fascination, his cheeks lighting up as red as his hair in pleased embarrassment.

As we finished our movement drills, I knelt beside him and ruffled his hair.

I looked into his eyes then, and wished that I hadn't. Visions of the pale, dead-fish stares of my fallen comrades swarmed my mind, and I nearly staggered away from him. I lowered my gaze.

Taking the crown of leaves from my hand, I placed it on his head. He knew nothing of what it meant, or what was done to earn it. I couldn't tell him what I had seen, what I had endured. He would have to find out for himself, but I hoped he would never have to.

Returning to camp, I spotted on the ridge above us a figure that was so decrepit as to make the rest of us look like marble statues by comparison. A few of the men who had better eyesight than me hurried up the hill.

"Lucius, who is that? A local?" I said to my friend.

He used his hand to block out the sun's glare.

"I don't think so, comrade," he said, noticing what I had. The tattered scarlet cloak of a soldier hung around the man's neck.

Only after the mules had helped this skeleton man into our partially deconstructed camp did I recognize him. It was the man I had once hailed as my own centurion: Gnaeus Tremellius Scrofa.

I HURRIED toward my old centurion. Despite his obviously tarnished condition, it was good to see him. I couldn't help the smile from splitting across my face. At least one man of my century had lived.

I stopped short of the man and gave him a salute. He did not return it.

"Centurion Scrofa, thank all the gods! You live," I said, extending my hand. When I saw that his hands were now thumbless, my hand dropped, as did the grin on my face.

We helped him to sit on the log around our campfire, and Arrea prepared him a bowl of soup. His eyes shone when he saw it, and it was clear from his shallow cheeks and exposed rib cage that he was starving, but he couldn't hold the bowl and eat as well. Arrea, goddess that she was, sat beside him and helped raise the spoon to his cracked lips.

"Centurion, can you tell me what happened?" I asked, kneeling before him.

His gaze was aimless and empty; he didn't seem to know that I was addressing him.

"Centurion?"

Finally he looked up at me, his mouth open not for a bite but in realization.

"Centurion Sertorius, Third Cohort Second Century—brother of Prefect Titus Sertorius."

"Yes," I nodded, Lucius patting my back, "yes, that's me."

"Does your brother live?" he asked. They had once been great friends. They had served together long before I donned the Colors.

I swallowed and looked down. "He does not, Centurion," I said. He looked away, with no discernible emotion in his eyes.

"Well, that's a shame," he whispered to himself.

"How did you survive? Where have you been?" Lucius asked. I turned to him and shook my head—perhaps now was not the best time for questions. The centurion still seemed to be in his own world, but he answered in his own time.

"I woke in a cage. I died on the battlefield. I did, I swear on the Black Stone of Jupiter that I did. I died, right there, right with my men, beside my standard." He pointed to an imaginary location on the ground, eyes fixed but seeing something entirely different. "I died, but then I came back. The gods, they…they sent me back. To the Reds. I woke up in a cage, with thirty other dead men." His eyes began to water, and his larynx bobbed in his neck as he struggled to swallow.

"You were taken prisoner by the Cimbri?" one of the men asked.

"I was. They kept us there. For years and years, they kept us. Feeding us only the rats that are meant to feed on us." It certainly hadn't been years, but I'm sure it felt like it had been to him.

"And how did you make it here. How did you escape?" I asked. When he did not respond, I leaned in closer and put a hand on his knee. "Centurion?"

He looked at me, right into my only eye, and whispered, "I didn't escape. They sent me away. They burned the rest of our men…in a wicker cage. I—I…they said, would live."

"They let you live?" one of the mules asked.

"Aye. They let me live so that I could tell everyone that this will be the fate of all Romans if we do not submit." A single tear slid down his cheek and through the screen of muck that covered his face, but he didn't seem to notice it. After a brief pause, he raised his mutilated hands. "Cut my thumbs off, though," he said as if unconcerned. "They don't want me holding a sword anymore."

WE DECIDED to stay in our camp for an extra night, to give Centurion Scrofa some time to heal and rest. He slept for most of it, kicking and moaning as he did so, but I'm sure whatever dreams he was having were preferable to his present reality.

When the camp had been properly broken down the next day, and Scrofa had risen at first light, we set off. We headed east toward whatever the gods had planned for us.

AS IT TURNS OUT, what Fate had planned for us was unpleasant.

We move more like a funeral procession than a marching column of soldiers. Those of us who had maintained our armor wore it; those of us who did not, like Scrofa, wore whatever tunics and capes we could find.

The movement was arduous, not because of the heat or the terrain, but because many of us were weak and injured, and we were forced to stop every few hours and rest. My old, grizzled Centurion Scrofa never once asked to stop. He simply followed behind the majority of us, taking each step slowly and deliberately, and kept his eyes on the horizon in the distance.

We passed through areas Rome's finest might have traveled to for a vacation, if they were willing to make the journey. The autumn sun glowed orange and shimmered off the pond marsh waters and the marigolds and orchids that danced atop it. Roving herds of deer would come almost close enough to touch, anxious to store up on the water lilies before winter arrived. Such things had always had a profound impact on me, it was the sights and smells that often reminded me of my father and our walks together. Now I distrusted it. The same world that produced this beauty produced the brutality of Arausio. If I had to take both or none, I was unsure what I would choose.

Along our path, merchants and other travelers passed us by. They tried to keep their eyes away from us, but most were unsuccessful in doing so.

"What news from Italy?" Lucius asked each time they passed. Most of them simply increased their speed and continued on. One heavily bearded rider finally tightened the reins on his horse and pulled to a halt before us.

"Romans?" he asked in Latin with a harsh Gallic accent. He pulled the straw hat from his head and dabbed away the sweat of his brow. The pelts of recently skinned animals were draped over the horse's haunches, and the Gaul peered over his shoulder to ensure they were still hanging on.

"Yes, sir. Survivors of the battle of Arausio," I replied.

The man seemed shocked, but not overly so.

"Tales have spread about your lot."

"Oh?" I asked, not so interested in hearing what they might be.

"That's right. They say an entire Roman army was annihilated." He paused and scanned the faces of our twenty-odd men. "But at least a few of you escaped the barbarians," he said.

It was strange to us to hear a Gaul referring to anyone as a barbarian, but it was true. The Gauls were a civilized and advanced society compared to those demonic hordes that had defeated us at Arausio.

"Do you have any news from Rome?" Lucius asked again. "We're headed for the camp of General Marius."

The man nodded and tugged at the end of his long beard.

"I've word, yes. The Roman force is situated near the Rhône."

He nodded to the east. "I did some trading at the baggage camp there a few days ago."

"Are there any more Roman camps along the way?" I asked. "We need a place to rest."

He spit some kind of seed from his mouth and nodded. "One, not seven leagues that way. You can make it by nightfall if you don't stop."

"Thank you," I said, and gave the half-hearted signal to my men to continue, taking Arrea's hand and leading the way myself.

"Roman," the Gaul addressed me, "you're lucky that the Cimbri moved on. I've a friend coming from the Pyrenees who said they're back in Spain and wreaking havoc. But they'll be back. Let your general know that." He narrowed his eyes, searching to ensure that his words were received.

"No more stops for the remainder of the day, men. We need to make it to that post," I said. The men didn't groan as mules are accustomed to do. Their lot had already been so arduous, how much worse could a few hours be?

We continued on with no more pauses, halting only to allow the weaker among us to shift some of their gear and lean onto the abler-bodied men alongside them. Arrea walked among us like a soldier herself, and offered to carry some of the gear, to which all of the men respectfully declined.

It was a few hours before nightfall when we spotted the walled fortress of our most forward operating post. The sight was as welcomed as an oasis in Egypt.

"Thank the gods," Lucius said with a smile.

"Don't thank them yet. Perhaps it's only an illusion, and they're playing tricks on us," one of the men said.

"Come on, now. Even the Furies couldn't be so cruel," Lucius replied, taking the front and increasing the pace. For once, my friend was wrong, but not about the camp.

When we arrived, the legionaries stationed there lined the walls. They whispered to one another, perhaps wondering whether they should open the gates or if we were bandits who had absconded with Roman armor.

We halted before the gate and stood in silence for a few moments.

"I am Centurion Quintus Sertorius," I shouted, my voice hoarse.

"And where do you hail from?" one of them replied at length.

"I come from Nursia in Italy. But that isn't what you ask, is it?" I answered.

"No"—the soldier shook his head—"it is not."

"We come from Arelate. We few who survived the Battle at Arausio reconvened there." When I said this, their expressions contorted in a strange way. They did not reply but talked among themselves.

At length, the gates opened.

As we sighed in relief and began to move forward, the post's commander stepped out, followed by a handful of his men.

"Tribune," I said, giving a salute.

He saluted in return but did not make eye contact.

"You came from Arausio, you say?" His Latin was polished and refined, and I could tell from the condition of his shiny bronze breastplate that he had not been in the Colors long. A senator's son, perhaps.

"I do. We survived the battle."

The tribune turned to his men, and nodded to pacify them.

"You survived a battle in which thousands of good soldiers died?"

"Tens of thousands, Tribune," Lucius said firmly, his eyes fixed on the tribune's crest.

"And why, then, did you not stay and die with your countrymen?" he asked.

We were all too taken aback to formulate a response.

"And you, a centurion? You let the men of your century die around you, and you yet lived?" He shook his head. I lowered my gaze in shame. "You're a disgrace to the legion. You should have stayed and died or fallen on your sword."

Lucius began to step forward, but I held him back. There was desperation, fear, and anger in his eyes. It was one of the few times I can remember seeing it. He clinched his eyes shut and ran his fingers through the fair mane atop his head, which was far longer than he liked it. I tightened my grip around his grimy forearm, and he stilled.

"I cannot reject what you say. I have wished that I died at Arausio every day since I realized I hadn't. But many of these men awoke on the field of battle, terribly injured. And they need rest. Will you refuse us entry?" I asked, trying to maintain my composure, but failing to do so adequately.

"You are not welcome here," the tribune said without remorse.

"Please." I held out my hands to him. "I beg you to reconsider. One of our men, this man"—I gestured to Scrofa, who remained silent at the back—"was captive to the Cimbri and endured horrible tortures before he was released. We need your help."

"Released? By the Cimbri? Released so that he can be set to spy on us!" one of the tribune's men said.

"Go, cowards. Return to whatever shadows you crept from. The Republic has no use for men like you." The tribune turned, his cape fluttering behind him. As the gates began to close, I rushed forward in desperation.

"I beg you!" I shouted. The men on the walls collected what they could—rocks, sticks, horse shit from the stables—and began assaulting us with them.

"Cowards!"

"You're traitors to your men!" some shouted.

"On your way!"

"Curses, curses on all of you!" others cried.

The projectiles pelted us, but the words cut far deeper. We retreated slowly, hoping that they would change their minds, or that they were only jesting and perhaps fate wasn't so cruel.

When it became clear that all they would give us were jeers, stones, and horse shit, we turned to leave.

Centurion Scrofa alone stood before the gates, staring on and saying nothing. The stones collided into him, but he seemed not to notice.

A vestige. A stain. The echo, the shadow of human life, but the essence of a man, no more. The centurion, who was once the proudest legionnaire I had ever known, was now totally, irreversibly broken.

3

SCROLL III

NONES OF SEPTEMBER 650 AB URBE CONDITA

So we moved on. With nowhere to go, and nowhere to rest our heads, we moved onward around the fort. We continued our trek east toward Marius's camp, but I'm sure I wasn't the only one who wondered whether our arrival would be welcomed just the same.

The same fears compelled us to stay off the road. We didn't march in a column but staggered on like hungry nomads through the forests and wadded through the swamps. The wildlife didn't seem to mind us. This solidified in us the idea that we were merely shades of Hades now, already gone. We were walking with no real destination except one that might refuse us.

"Centurion, I've got to rest my feet. I swear to Dis it's like my ankles are about to rip out of my skin," one of our men said, panting.

I didn't mean to ignore him, but I didn't know what to say. Frogs croaked all around us, filling the silence as I looked into the vast abyss of woodland on either side of our path and the darkness that covered the distance from one tree to the next. I wondered what Gorgons awaited us if we stopped.

"I don't think Galbus will make it much longer," one of the mules in the back said, bearing the weight of his comrade.

"What do you think we should do?" I asked Lucius and Arrea, both of whom I treated as my chief advisors.

"Exhaustion can kill like a sword, my love," Arrea said. It was clear by the pale and clammy texture of her skin that she, too, was exhausted, but I knew she spoke for the men.

"We can construct a hasty camp. Something to cover our flanks," Lucius suggested, but he looked to me to make the final decision. At any other time, I would have deferred to the senior centurion, Scrofa, but he was clearly unable and unwilling to acquiesce on such matters. It was a wonder that he was still keeping pace.

"Alright." I stopped the forward advance and scanned my surroundings. "There's a clearing up ahead. We'll make camp there. I want wood gathered and a shallow trench dug. We'll have guard shifts of four, two patrolling and two by the walls, rotating every other hour," I said. The men nodded but said nothing in response. Such measures were necessary to ensure their survival, but I'm not sure if they prioritized their lives any longer. Perhaps the first objective was just some rest and a momentary lapse from the burden that consciousness had become.

WE ALL GATHERED wood and helped dig the trenches, officers and enlisted men alike. The trenches were only a foot wide and another foot deep, and the walls were only six feet high. Regardless, with only twenty-seven men in our company, the construction of this little camp resulted in several hours of backbreaking labor for each of us. The one man who could not assist was Centurion Scrofa, who stood by with his thumbless hands, helpless. He did volunteer to roll out our cots while we worked. It was clear that he was ashamed, but he took the job seriously, ensuring that each cot was placed equidistant to the next, as he had once arranged his soldiers.

When our camp had the semblance of protection, Lucius called out the guard schedules, and those of us who weren't on first shift lay down on the moist earth for some rest. Arrea nestled up next to me, but I turned away from her. If I wept, I did not want her to see it.

I WOKE a bit early for my shift, which came a few hours before sunrise. I knew it wouldn't make much difference, but I put on my full kit, my body groaning under its weight. When I neared the barricade, Centurion Scrofa was already present.

"You're relieved, Centurion," I said, giving him a salute. He waved it off.

"This is my shift," Scrofa said as the other soldier hurried to find somewhere to sleep.

"You must have arrived early," I said. He remained silent for a moment, staring through the gaps in our defenses to the wood line in the valley beyond us.

"I've taken as many shifts as I can." He rubbed the back of his grimy neck with a thumbless hand.

I approached and plopped down on a log beside him. "You need rest, Centurion. More than any of us."

He nodded but did not stand. "It's the only use I am to anyone now—to let a few other men get rest. The men who can still fight." At last, he turned to me, and in his eyes I saw a brief glimpse of the noble centurion who had protected me in battle after battle, teaching me with his quiet strength and comforting me with kind words when I was too afraid to carry on.

"You're no use to anyone if you're falling asleep." I patted his shoulder. "Go get some rest. I can cover the walls by myself," I said. The patrol shift passed us by with a nod.

"I'm not going to sleep, Sertorius. I slept enough in those cages. It was all there was to do." He rubbed at the poorly healed wounds where his thumbs had once been.

We sat in silence for a while, listening to the buzzing of insects, the howling of wolves, the croaking of frogs.

"How did they do that?" I asked after a moment. It was a rather rude question, I must admit, but my weariness had gotten the best of me.

"Do what?"

"Your thumbs…"

He held out his hands into the moonlight and rotated them for me to see. "A ceremonial knife. A curved blade. Took them both off as easily as a cook chopping up carrots." He seemed fairly detached as he analyzed the wound, more curious than anything. "They poured some kind of black powder over the wounds and touched it with a torch. The powder ignited and the wounds sealed. Still feels like it's burning, on the inside. Beneath the scars." He returned his hands to his lap.

"I'm sorry for your lot, Centurion," I said, my manner much more like a civilian than a soldier.

"Don't ever pity me," he said. "Feel sorry for the men we lost. Feel sorry for the families who lost them. Not me."

The trees in the distance shimmied with the wind, and a light rain pattered down on the ground around us.

"My brother died well," I said half honestly.

"I'm glad to hear it."

"I tried to carry him off, but he wouldn't let me. He wanted to die there."

"Then he died like a true Roman," Scrofa said with a tinge of jealousy.

"He would be pleased to know that you're still here. He thought very highly of you," I said, to which centurion Scrofa did not reply. "I need to use the privy. I'll go by the trees over there. Hold the guard down for me." I stood and stretched my leg. Before I stepped off, Scrofa stopped me.

"Leave your sword," he said.

"Why?" I asked.

"To protect the walls, of course," he said. Rather uncomfortably, I shrugged. We both knew he couldn't use it. "Well, if I can't use it to fight, then what good am I? Eh, Centurion? What good am I to the legion? To Rome? If it's just to alert the others at some intrusion, we can find a mangy dog to do the same."

"Centurion—"

"Save that for the others, Sertorius." He shook his head.

I met his eyes, and in the moonlight I could see a glimmer in them that I didn't understand.

"Then what is the sword for?" I asked.

"Don't be a fool, Centurion." He kept his gazed fixed, like he once had when I stood in his formation.

"You shouldn't be a fool either," I said.

"I'm going to do the only good thing I've done since Arausio, perhaps since long before it."

"My brother would tell you—"

"Your brother would understand. I cannot fight, ever again. I cannot serve my Colors, and what else is there for me? I tried civilian life before, and it doesn't suit me. This is who I am, Centurion Sertorius."

"Have you no family?" I was grasping for something.

A sad smile touched his lips.

"I've served for twenty-odd years, in some foreign corner of the Republic or another. They would barely know me by now."

"I won't believe it, Scrofa. I won't let you do it. You can still serve. You can train the men, you can teach them the way you once taught me. You can raise up a crop of legionaries who can defeat these bastards, once and for all." I was begging, pleading with him as I had with the tribune at the fort.

He stood and approached me, placing a hand on my shoulder.

"No, I can't," he said. "I cannot look a young man in the eye and tell him this is all worth it...because I'm not sure that it is anymore." He was sad but had resigned himself to his decision. I wasn't going to persuade him. "Sertorius, that is why we need men like you. Men who still have a bit of courage left. You are Rome's last hope now." His eyes were wet, but he did not weep. "Now go. And please, leave your sword."

I hesitated for a moment, but I eventually unsheathed my gladius and stabbed it into the dirt. I turned on my heels and made for the trees, hot tears welling up in my eye.

I glanced over my shoulder once as I walked away from him. Scrofa analyzed the gladius as if it were the greatest artifact from Alexandria to the Pillars of Heracles. He wrapped both of his palms around the hilt and pulled it from the earth.

I looked away and continued to walk.

When I stole another glance, he had the hilt tightly pressed between both hands. He held it at his side, as if ready to engage with an enemy, as he had been trained to do his entire life.

Scrofa stabbed forward and flourished the sword before it fell from his grasp. He picked it up again and tried with the other hand, holding it out before him as if he were part of a ceremony. As I turned away again, the moonlight shimmering in my wet eye, I heard the sword drop once more.

I took my time before returning, trying to collect myself. When I did, the proud centurion was lying on the Gallic soil, my gladius wedged in his belly and clutched between his thumbless hands, the same ones that had wielded a sword for Rome most his life and had reared a crop of soldiers like a she-wolf with her pups.

I had to cup my lips to keep them from quivering at the sight. I wouldn't dishonor his death with sentiment. But still, Centurion Scrofa had once been as a pillar of strength to me. A giant among men in the legion. Brave and unwavering, disciplined but always looking after his men before himself or other officers. If so great a man could fall, how could I do any differently?

I CLEANED AND SHAVED SCROFA. I placed my own lorica and centurion's helm on his head and prepared him for cremation. Once I was finished, he was far more familiar to me. Far more like the man who had led me into my first battle. His face appeared more calm than it had at the end of his life. He was at peace now. His honor was restored. In a way, I envied him, but I didn't allow my thoughts to entertain the feeling for long.

Our first objective the following morning was to gather firewood. Then I placed one coin over both of the centurion's eyes, a fee for the ferryman to carry him safely into the afterlife. Lucius placed one between his lips for extra measure.

We used what little oil we still had in our packs, and lit the pyre. The black pitch smoke rose to the heavens as we all stood in a semicircle around our burning centurion.

As the roaring flames reduced to smolders, all the men turned to leave. There was much land to traverse between us and Marius's camp, and there was no sense in stalling.

Arrea kissed my cheek and squeezed my hand. She alone knew how much that man meant to me, as she had seen me become a man under his tutelage.

She lingered for a moment but then turned to follow the men, leaving me alone with my thoughts.

I gave the centurion one final salute.

"Form ranks," I said, returning to my men. "We have a long march."

4

SCROLL IV

IDES OF SEPTEMBER 650 AB URBE CONDITA

We could smell the privies, the livestock, and the recently hewn leather armor for miles. That was always the first sign that we were nearing Marius's camp.

Next was the thunder of a centurion's voice, and the subsequent execution of his marching orders. We hadn't seen a real Roman camp since General Caepio had marched us out to our personal cemetery. Something stirred in my guts as we approached it. The forward operating base we had come across did not compare. The walls rose so high above us we had to crane our necks just to steal a glance at the sentry guards atop it.

We passed through the outskirts of camp as merchants and prostitutes heckled us, all of whom commented on our poor appearance and said that it looked like we could use an upgrade, in one form or another. When we reached the walls, the mules at Marius's camp did not stay still and stare but instead signaled for the gates to be opened, running back into the fort to spread word of our arrival.

their own allotment of grain, cook their own food. This is a different legion, soldiers." He rubbed his rough hands together.

"Adds a new meaning to the name 'mule,'" one of my men said, and for once, I was thankful for Marius's poor hearing.

"These men can do all of this because they've devoted their lives to it. No more fighting in the war season before retiring to the harvest. These are real warriors. They live and die by the sword... unless, of course, they live out their contract. They'll be done with their service in sixteen years, and will then be rewarded by the state for their sacrifice."

"Sixteen years?" I whispered, shocked. It was hard for a young man my age to fathom swearing away sixteen years of his life, but most of the mules around us appeared even younger than I.

"That's right. For the good of the Republic. You saw a bit of the new legion, Sertorius, but now my reforms are complete." He turned to me and smiled. "You know this now, and the Cimbri will too, soon enough."

We walked on for a while, looking around the camp, mostly in silence. This legion felt very foreign to the one I had served in, under Maximus, and I wondered if I was even prepared for it.

"You'll dine with me. We have much to discuss." Marius clasped his hands behind his back as he walked, his shoulders straight and his gaze fixed, displaying a soldierly discipline that we now sorely lacked.

"Dine with you, sir? We cannot," I said. Although we had ceased to care, we were still very aware of our grotesque appearance and worse smell.

"Nonsense. The survivors of Arausio are hailed as heroes," he said without turning to me.

"We did not receive such a warm welcome from our forward camp," I said, more to myself than him. He stopped in his tracks and turned to me.

"I'll send a message to the camp, then. I'll make sure the

tribune is flogged," he said, as carelessly as if he were ordering another cup of wine.

"Can we at least bathe first?" Lucius asked.

"That won't be necessary. No Roman matrons will be in attendance—it's just soldiers, and soldiers smell." He grinned. He turned and noticed Arrea at my side, her hand clutched in mine. "Naevia!" He called to a girl juggling a vase of water, and she set it down and hurried to him.

"Sir?" she replied. I could tell from her skin and accent that she was Numidian, but she was clothed as warm and fine as a Roman lady.

"Take this girl to get a bath. Offer her something of yours to wear and I'll make sure you're compensated."

"Yes, *dominus*," she said, and reached for Arrea's hand.

My love looked at me, afraid to leave my side. After a moment of hesitation, I nodded, and we released hands. She parted from me for the first time since I'd washed up on the bank of the Rhône.

"What should we do, Centurion?" one of the men asked me, too afraid to ask Marius directly.

"You'll dine with me. All of you. I said that the survivors of Arausio will be hailed as heroes, and heroes eat," Marius said with finality. Enlisted men were never allowed to dine with officers. We were keenly aware that we were unfit for such company.

He led the way to his praetorium.

The roaring laughter of a merry feast greeted us, and ceased only when Marius came to a halt before the table.

"Men, these with me are the survivors of the battle of Arausio. Make some room, they will be dining with us." The officers at Marius's table looked perplexed but followed his order regardless. "Bring some more chairs." Marius gestured to his Numidian slave, Volsenio. "Come, Sertorius, Hirtuleius. You'll sit by me. We have much to discuss."

I peered around the table, suddenly keenly aware of my

appearance. These men were perhaps tougher than the Caepiones and their lot, but they were no less noble. Their faces had clearly been oil shaven recently, and their hair was perfectly delineated.

I stopped walking.

"Sir, please allow us to at least shave first."

"No." Marius grabbed my wrist and pulled me forward. "That won't be necessary."

I said nothing more as we followed on the consul's heels, afraid of what might happen if we strayed too far.

"Well," he said, turning to us with a smile as we took our seats, "you've lived."

"It would appear so." I fixed my gaze on the table.

"I'm not sure it appears that way," a man said from across the table. Stealing a glance at the speaker, I was stunned. He was far too handsome to be a soldier. He had striking features—pronounced cheekbones, wavy blond hair, and eyes as icy blue as the Rhône.

"This is my brother-in-law Lucius Cornelius Sulla," Marius said, gesturing to the man.

"It's a pleasure to meet you," Sulla said as jovially as an old farmer. We reached across the table to shake his hand.

"Well, brother-in-law as was… His wife, Ilia, the little sister of my wife, Julia, just passed away this past moon." Marius took a cup of wine from Volsenio.

"I'm sorry for your loss, sir," I said. "I met your wife once. She was as fair as she was respectable," I said, unable to meet the man's eyes but unable to look away completely.

"The will of the gods. They do seem determined to take the young and beautiful, and allow us brutes to live and thrive." Sulla shrugged.

"So, Sertorius"—Marius turned his gaze again to me—"or should I call you 'centurion' now?" He leaned back and crossed his arms.

"You can call me whatever you like, sir," I said somberly, but my words still managed to illicit a laugh from Marius and Sulla.

"I went through a great deal of trouble to acquire you that military tribuneship. I've never had a man refuse such a kind offer." Plates of roasted bird were placed before us.

"I apologize, sir." I searched for something else to say, perhaps a way to explain my decision, but I couldn't find the right words.

Marius leaned over to his former brother-in-law. "After Sertorius helped my son Maximus get elected to the consulship, I secured a military tribuneship for him. He then proceeded to denounce his commission, become a member of the rank-and-file, and earn the title of centurion by scaling the walls first in a pitched battle with the Gauls."

Sulla raised his eyebrows and nodded as if quite impressed. "I know some playwrights in the city who could make a marvelous tale out of that." He tapped his lips with his finger, clearly trying to imagine it.

I said, "I was no real centurion. It was honorary. I've seen real centurions, I've served under them. I did not deserve the title." I picked at my meal. I had dreamed of a fine course like this for months, but I was unable to stomach it.

"You led men into battle, didn't you?" Marius asked, gulping thankfully at his wine.

"I did."

"Then you were a centurion."

"Not for very long, sir. All my men died within a few months of my appointment." Lucius twitched uncomfortably at my side.

"Well, regardless of all that, you are a centurion no longer," he said. "Look at me when I am speaking to you." His voice was quiet and crisp. I hurried to do so. "You are a centurion no longer. I plan to make you, both of you"—he gestured to Lucius—"tribunes in a new unit."

"Tribunes?" Lucius asked, nearly spitting out a bite of food.

"Yes. That's right. And this time, neither of you will be

allowed to resign your commission," he said with a grin, and slapped my shoulder to ensure I matched his expression. "We are forming a new unit to obtain intelligence about the local tribes and the Reds. You two will be leading it."

Marius took a sip of his wine and looked at us over the rim of his cup.

"I'm honored, sir," I said.

"Marius has told me that you have some command of the Gallic language, is that correct?" Sulla asked. It was becoming apparent that the two had discussed my situation previously.

"I do, sir. Although it's been some time since I've used that knowledge properly." That was mostly a lie, as I had been communicating with the villagers of Arelate for months now, but I wasn't sure what I was agreeing to if I acknowledged that.

"I've no understanding of any language but my own, sirs," Lucius hastened to inform them.

"No matter. Sertorius's understanding of Gallic will be enough. We have other uses for you," Marius said. I was forced to lean in closer to hear his words—the table was roaring with laughter over some bawdy joke or another, but I noticed out of the corner of my eye that the other Arausio survivors were as silent as statues, staring at their already empty plates.

THE DINNER CONTINUED for some time, as did the laughter from Marius's officers, and the quiet indifference of our men. When the meal was concluded, Marius dismissed his staff, but requested that Lucius and I stayed for a bit longer. Marius's praetorium dimmed as the light outside faded, and candelabras were lit in the corners of the tent.

"You received the letter I sent you in February, didn't you?" Marius asked.

"I did, sir," I said, recalling the several rolls Marius had sent me explaining his first years in service to Rome. "It was very encouraging."

"Well, that was its purpose. I wanted you to remember that you can seize victory from the jaws of defeat. I'm afraid that the message didn't land, though, judging by the look on your face and the slump of your shoulders." I straightened quickly.

"Both of you, soldiers, listen to me. We will require much from you over the next few months. If Rome is to be victorious, I must be able to count on men like you. Can I do this?" He leaned in closer.

"You can, sir," I said, and Lucius nodded emphatically beside me.

"Look at me with your one good eye, Sertorius. I want to hear you say it again."

"You can count on us, sir." I looked at our consul but found that I couldn't stop blinking.

"Good. I won't have either of you wallowing. Understood? That's an order."

"I have only one request, sir," I said. Lucius seemed to lean away from me in his chair, leery of what I was about to ask. "I'd like only to visit my home before war season begins in March. I want to deliver word of my brother's death to my mother, in person." Marius leaned back in his chair and scratched at his chin.

"No…no, I don't think so. You're too valuable to me here."

"Marius, come now, don't be ridiculous. We can spare the man for a few months," Sulla said from the corner of the tent, where he was pouring himself another cup of wine from a bronze amphora, apparently unwilling to wait on Marius's slaves to do it for him.

Marius inhaled deeply, seemingly displeased at being spoken to in this manner by a subordinate. His face eventually softened, though, and he nodded his head.

"Yes. Fine, you can go. On a few conditions." He held up two fingers. "First that you're back before war season. If the Reds return, they won't wait to initiate battle with us. I'll have need of you, and I'll not be swayed on this. The other condition is that you stop by the city of Massilia on your way."

"Massilia, sir?"

"Yes. We've heard rumors of mutinous behavior there, and I need to confirm or deny it to know if something must be done. Consider it your first mission in collecting intelligence. While there, you can buy a slave and a horse—you're a tribune now, after all, and you'll be required to have them. That will be your explanation for your presence."

"Understood, sir," I said, although I was already uncomfortable about the idea of going into hostile territory.

I WAITED FOR TWO NIGHTS, for Arrea's sake as much as my own, and then we set off once again for Nursia. As hesitant as I was to visit hostile territory, I was far more nervous about going home. I didn't know what to expect, how I would be embraced by my mother or by my brother's widow, or what I could possibly tell them to ease their pain. Regardless, I felt it was my duty. And my duty was all that I had left.

5

SCROLL V

KALENDS OF NOVEMBER 650 AB URBE CONDITA

They were in Nursia's market when I found them. Mother was inspecting the fish someone had caught earlier that day in the spring outside Nursia. My sister-in-law Volesa stood behind her, holding up her hem to avoid collecting mud, a jug of water balanced beneath her arm. Clinging to her other hand was her son, Gavius. He walked properly, like a little man. His father would have been so proud.

I pulled off my hood and tried to collect my thoughts. I watched them for some time from a distance, knowing that as soon as they saw me, their lives would be changed forever. They would know that one of us had lived and the other had died.

"Welcome home, soldier. Can I interest you in some turnips? Fresh and cheap, best price in Nursia!" a merchant said, heckling me. At this, Mother and Volesa turned and saw me.

Mother burst into tears at first sight. Volesa collapsed, the jug of water shattering beside her and mud splattering across her dress. Mother sprinted toward me and fell into my arms, her legs no longer able to support her.

"Oh, Quintus. Oh, Quintus." She wept into my shoulder. I kissed her head but could say nothing. Gavius tried to help his mother up as I lifted the face of my own mother. Her lips quivered as she touched my face. "Your eye. Your eye," she repeated, running her fingers over the frayed thread of my eye patch.

"I'm home, Mother," I said, my voice quivering.

Ignoring the villagers who had gathered around us and were whispering about what might have caused the scene, I made my way to Volesa and tried to help her to her feet. She pulled away from me as violently as if I were infected with the plague. She crawled away for a moment before making it to her feet. The shimmer in her eyes held not just sadness but bitter despair, and a loathing for the world that had taken her husband away.

Gavius only looked at me, startled and in shock. When I approached again, he backed away as well and hid behind his mother's dress.

"He died bravely, Volesa," I said, my voice cracking. She wept harder still when she heard these words, but she had already known the truth. After news of the battle had traveled throughout Italy, they had probably assumed my brother and I were both dead—and seeing me alive confirmed that at least one of us was. We would have returned together otherwise.

Arrea helped bear my mother's weight, her knees unable to maintain it themselves.

"Let's go home," I said. There was no use in allowing all of Nursia to see our torment. The last time I'd returned home, I had delivered a speech preaching the virtues of hope and perseverance. It had paid off for the city, as the grain provided by our new patron, Gaius Marius, had begun to flow amply. But anyone who looked at me long enough would be able to tell I had very little hope left. Scrofa had said I still had some, but I wasn't certain he was right. Perhaps I only hoped he was.

Back in our home, Lucius's younger brother, Aius, and I helped the ladies onto a couch in the *triclinium*.

Looking at Mother, I could tell she had so many questions to ask, but the words caught in her throat. Perhaps she feared the answers.

"This is Arrea. I found her in Gaul, and she has been very good to me. She'll be staying here with you, and I trust you'll be good to her," I said as Arrea sat beside my mother on the couch. I wanted to tell them how deeply I loved her and how she had nursed me back from the grave, but speaking of romance seemed wrong as Volesa stared with cold eyes at the dusty mosaic beneath her.

"But where, where will you go?" Mother asked, her lips beginning to tremor again.

"I must return to Gaul. The war is not over." I spoke as firmly as I could manage. Mother nodded reluctantly but I could tell she had finally realized we no longer had any control of our fates. "Rome is on the brink of destruction, and I cannot leave the Colors until the battle is won," I said, reaching across to my mother and placing a hand on hers. She shivered as if she were cold, and Aius ran his hands over her arms.

"Titus died well, then?" Volesa asked, all of her tears now dried and her face blank and emotionless. Gavius sat beside her and rested his head on her breast, not seeming to comprehend what was happening. How could he miss a father he had never known?

"He did. He died with his men on the field of Arausio, fighting until his last breath."

"And you saw this?" Volesa asked, making eye contact for the first time.

"I did."

"And you did nothing to save him?" Her voice teemed with anger.

"I did all that I could."

"But you're still alive," Volesa said. Mother turned to her and shook her head, trying to dissuade her from continuing. But the words had already been spoken, and they could not be taken back.

"I did. I held him in my arms as he bled, and he demanded that I live. He wanted to ensure that someone would be able to take care of Mother, and you…and Gavius," I said.

Volesa said nothing but lowered her gaze to the boy clutching to her and ruffled his hair.

"Believe me, Volesa, if I could trade places with him, I would. If it were I who died, and he had lived, things would be much easier for you now, I'm sure."

Mother clutched my hands harder, hoping to save herself from more of my poignant words.

"But I cannot. I have lived," I continued. "As much as that fact has haunted me since I awoke in a daze a week later, with only one eye left in my head, and a few *hemina* of blood left in my body… I can do nothing to change it."

"Quintus, stop now. There is no use in—" Mother started.

"No. Let me say my piece. I've practiced it and dreaded it more than I can articulate since the moment Titus breathed his last breath. I am all that this family has now, and I'll do my best to live in such a way that justifies the sacrifice that he made." I stood and paced around the triclinium. I couldn't bear to meet the gaze of anyone present.

Aius kissed my mother's head and whispered something in her ear as she wept softly.

"I prepared your favorite," she said, reaching toward me with a bowl in her trembling hands.

I stared but didn't accept it. I wasn't worthy of my mother's meals while Titus was dead. Volesa had made it clear she would have preferred if we both had died.

"Please," Mother said.

"It's very good, brother," Aius said, the only one attempting to smile.

I took the bowl and immediately smelled the rich spices of

garum. My mother's dip had once been my favorite dish, to be certain.

I grabbed a loaf of bread and broke it, extending it first to Arrea, who shook her head. Her face was noble and calm, but I could see that she was broken over our family's pain as well.

I dipped the bread in the *garum* but was barely able to stomach it. I had to tighten my stomach to keep from vomiting on the floor of my ancestral home.

"It's very good," I said, my voice barely audible.

Mother looked at me with pink-rimmed eyes. She had so many questions, but it was clear she could voice none of them. No mother should have to mourn their child. But she wasn't alone. Ninety thousand other Roman mothers fruitlessly waited for the return of their sons.

I'd meant what I had said—I truly would have traded places with my brother. If I could change it, if the gods would have granted me this strange request, I would have accepted it without blinking my eye. My brother was a Roman hero of the old breed. He would have lived well, he would have rendered Rome safe and protected, and even after he removed his helm, he would have served Rome in whatever capacity available to him. But who was I but the little brother of a once-great man?

I made my way to my childhood bedroom. The walls and tables were still adorned with the trivial adornments of adolescence. The room felt very strange to me now. It was more foreign than my tent in Gaul.

I approached the dresser to the right of my bed. Atop it sat several wax figurines. A few elephants, a handful of chariots, and then Scipio and Hannibal themselves. Only a handful of years before I left for Rome I had sat outside under our oldest oak tree and played with them. But it felt like a different lifetime, one where I possessed such imagination and zeal for adventure, and the belief that there was glory in warfare.

On the other side of the bed was the altar to our household gods, exactly how I left it. Mother and I once prayed fervently every morning, and I recalled approaching it in solitude many times thereafter, tearfully begging my father for guidance. It had been so long since those coals had been kindled. Perhaps that's why my father no longer offered his guidance to me, because I had not been asking him for it.

"Are you hungry? I could prepare something more hardy." Mother approached behind me and placed her delicate hands on my shoulders.

"No…I haven't been able to stomach much food lately. Soldiers are easily sated anyway. Just make sure Arrea eats," I said without turning to my mother. "I've dragged that poor girl all over the Gaul and now into Italy, and she's only seen death and destruction as a result."

"And she's followed you willingly?" Mother asked. Her question was in part rhetorical, but she was still trying to determine who this man before her was. Perhaps her son was not quite how she remembered him.

"Yes, she did."

"Well, then, you have nothing to apologize for."

"She must curse the day the gods led me into her home," I said, sitting down on the corner of my childhood bed.

Mother sat beside me, neither confirming nor denying my claims.

"Will you marry Volesa? Will you accept Gavius as your son?" she asked after a moment. I hadn't even dared to consider it in the last months. Titus had mentioned it as he lay dying in my arms, but my mind had obviously been elsewhere. "Her father may ask for the return of her dowry," she continued.

"He wouldn't." I turned to mother with clinched fists. I would kill the man myself if he were so cruel.

"It's his legal right. He'll have to take her back into his home and find another suitor. He made an investment in the future of his daughter, and that investment is now destroyed… They were married less than the five years required by custom, so it's his right to ask for the return of her dowery."

"How could a man be so selfish?"

"You have obviously not met Volesa's father," Mother said, shaking her head.

"I'll do it. But not for her father. I'll do it because it was Titus's last wish."

Mother leaned over and placed her head on my shoulder.

My heart raced, and my fingers twitched as I considered the look I'd see in Arrea's eyes when I told her about what must be done.

"How are the horses?" I said, trying to distract myself.

"If you won't eat, then you should rest. We'll talk of such things later." She kissed my head and turned to leave.

I lay back on the bed and stared at the ceiling. Sleep was a most unwelcome idea, for I could foresee the contents of my dreams.

HOURS LATER, when the house had stilled and everyone had gone to bed, I rose and went into the *tablinum*, the office where my father had once helped lead our village. More importantly, the place where I had sat on my father's lap and listened to him reading the ancient words of Stoic philosophers, where he taught me to be a man. I poured cup after cup of wine for myself, running my fingers over the scrolls in my father's library but not daring to read a word. In the dim flicker of the tablinum candelabrum, I sat in silence and tried to quiet my thoughts.

I spotted the bust of my father in the corner of the room. Such a fine piece of art would have been rare in most homes, but my father had influenced many and was loved by all. The sculptor had once been crushed under crippling debt, and my father had helped him out of it. The bust was a gift of gratitude.

The lines of his face were etched to perfection, every inch revealing nobility and poise. It was cast at the height of my father's strength and vigor, but it was exactly how I remembered him, even at his dying breath. I considered what a bust of myself might look like, with a grotesque bundle of pink scar tissue for an eye and the sad wrinkles of a man who looked far older than he ought to.

And then, in my drunken stupor, my thoughts carried me to places a sober mind would never venture. I became angry at the man who was sculpted like a god before me. It was a true likeness, not cast in vain or in ego, but he was so admirable there, frozen in eternal strength.

I was angry with him first because, as I slumped into his chair, which was still worn from the endless hours he had once sat there, I considered how his teaching had left me unprepared for a tragedy like Arausio. It was so easy to remain a Stoic when nothing was wrong, but something told me that my father would have known how to handle all this. And Titus too. But I, I had not the slightest clue. It had always seemed so easy for him to know what was right and then do it. Why had I not inherited his strength? Why was it given to the son who had died and not the one who had lived?

Then I was angry at him for leaving me when I still had so much to learn, angry that I could no longer ask him questions and hear his calm, calculated reply. And finally, I simply missed the man, and I wondered if he would see me as a coward as others did if he were still around to make such a judgement.

"You need to sleep, Quintus," Arrea said from the doorway.

"You should already be sleeping, dear," I said, rubbing my eye to ensure that she wasn't in my imagination.

"As should you." She approached my father's desk and looked around the room. "I've never seen an Italian home. It's quite different than a Gallic hut."

"Much good it has done us," I said.

"Let us go to sleep," she said, her voice soothing enough that, for a brief moment, my heart slowed and my mind eased.

"Can I have you tonight?" I said, winging an arm around Arrea's shoulders and allowing her to lead me.

She giggled as I stumbled. Despite her incomprehensible misfortunes in life, suffering had not broken her.

"Why don't we just focus first on getting you into bed."

"Will you hold me, at least?" I asked, with far more vulnerability than I was accustomed to, but wine has a habit of forcing honesty to the surface.

At length she nodded, then helped me to my room as I swayed from the effects of the wine and fatigue. I fell into slumber the moment my head hit the pillow. But she did as she promised, and held me as I shook with the fever of my dreams.

My temples were pulsating when I woke, and my mouth was as dry as the Egyptian desert.

"Feeling the effects now, aren't you?" Arrea smiled as she heard my groaning.

"I feel like I've had a fight with a Minotaur. And lost," I said, smacking my gums and trying to generate some moisture.

"I've not seen you drink that much wine since…well, ever really."

I exhaled. "Yesterday was difficult. I indulged to ease the pain, but I'm afraid it's only compounded." I rolled out of bed and for the first time realized I was drenched in sweat. I sauntered over to an amphora of wine near the doorway to my bedroom.

"Well hold on, now, what are you doing?" Arrea asked playfully.

"Just one cup to set me up. I'm afraid it's the only thing that will keep me out of bed today." I took one sip and vomited into a plant in the atrium.

She was shaking her head and wore a spiteful grin.

"Quintus Sertorius, you're a smarter man than that."

"I'm not so sure about that anymore," I said, breathing heavily and blinking the moisture from my eye.

I sat at the foot of my bed and tried to keep myself from lying back. As my mind returned to me, I recalled the conversation I needed to have with Arrea, and it wasn't going to be pleasant. But the waiting was worse, so I decided to hesitate no longer.

"We need to talk, love," I said, swiveling to see her with my good eye.

She stood and walked over to me, gracefully sitting across my lap. She wrapped an arm around my neck and laid her cheek against my sweaty head.

"Gods, your breath smells awful!" She laughed.

"*Gerrae*, I wonder why!" I tickled her ribs for a moment but then sobered as I remembered the topic at hand. "We need to talk, Arrea," I said again.

She pulled her head away from mine and stared me in the eye. "Well, go on, then, soldier. I'm ready for it," she said.

"I might have to marry another." The words shook as they poured from my mouth.

She remained still. Nothing was heard stirring in the house. The world had careened to a halt.

At length she stood and turned away from me, and my arms reached out for her to return.

"You either do or you don't, Quintus. Not might." Her voice was calm but firm.

"I do," I said, my gaze shifting to my feet.

"It's not someone, it's who."

"Volesa. My brother's wife. It's my duty. It's custom. I…I…I don't want to, Arrea."

For a brief moment, her head sunk and her shoulders slumped. She looked at the ground away from me and thought for a moment.

Although my romantic escapades were quite few in number and in length, I knew that every lover I'd ever had previously would have reacted in one of two ways: run out screaming, or turn and scream at me.

Arrea did neither.

She knelt beside me. Her eyes weren't wet, but they weren't empty either. I was unsure what they were saying.

"Quintus, I'm ashamed to say this. But there was a time when you were wounded that I had hoped you wouldn't recover. In quiet and selfish moments, I had wished that you might always remain that way, not able to go very far. That you'd always have to rely on me."

"Arrea—" She lifted a finger to silence me, and then clutched my fingers in her silk hands.

"From the moment you stumbled into my master's hut, I wanted to be with you. I wanted to feel the stubble of your beard against my cheek, watch you sleep, taste your breath…" She looked down and exhaled. "I wanted you to stay wounded because I knew that your duty would one day take you away from me."

"Arrea, I loved you…I love you so much," I pleaded with her, my head shaking and my eye shimmering.

"The worst part is that I cannot blame you. I just can't have you." She stood then and stepped away from me.

A single tear developed in the corner of her eye. She brushed it aside with the back of her thumb, making it clear that it was no longer my role to do so.

"I'll stay on for a while, Quintus. I have nowhere else to go. But I don't know what the future holds."

I realized I was shaking.

"I don't either," I whispered. She kissed me on the head and then departed, the expression on her face heavy with sadness but absent anger.

WHEN I WAS able to fully compose myself, I wrapped myself in my father's wool cloak and stepped outside.

I spotted Volesa in the pastures, where she was leading one of the horses. I exhaled and worked up the courage to approach her.

As I walked, I saw shades of my past all around. As clear as day, I saw my mother there planting seeds, wiping a bead of sweat from her head and standing with her wrists akimbo on her hips, her dirt-covered and callused hands pointed backward. *"I can finish this, Quintus, go and help your father,"* the shade said.

Walking on, I saw Titus shoveling up horse shit in the heat of summer with the concentration and dedication of a philosopher.

As I opened the creaky old gate to the pastures, I remembered my father leading a horse by the reins there, whispering to her in full sentences all the while, as if the beast spoke Latin.

"How have the horses been?" I asked as I approached Volesa, who was now feeding the horse a few strands of hay from her hand.

"I don't want to remarry," she said.

"Mother said one of the mares is about to foal," I said, not fully hearing her until after I spoke.

She continued to ignore me as she scratched the horse between its eyes, the stallion's ears swaying back and forth with euphoria.

"But I'd sooner kill myself than return to my father," she continued. "The way he looked at me…touched me…"

"Volesa, I—"

"I would stab his eye out with a hairpin if he tried again."

"Volesa, I don't think we should consider suicide. Gavius needs a mother," I said, firmer now to ensure she listened to me.

She turned at last, her face as white as spit on a summer afternoon. Her eyes pink, all out of tears.

"What about Rhea?" she asked.

"My mother is an aging woman with too much grief in her heart to raise a child."

"For Gavius alone, I'll remain. But I'll never love another." She turned back to the horse and rubbed its damp nose. "Titus was so strong, violence coursed through his veins, and yet he touched me tenderly, and spoke to me gently. I will never love another."

"I don't ask you for love, Volesa. I love another..." I said, and I must have posed the latter sentence as a question.

"You can have as many mistresses as you like. I won't cause a fuss." She was completely unconcerned.

The words made me sad and uncomfortable. I didn't want Arrea to be a mistress, the kind respectable men hide from their neighbors, the kind one couldn't fall asleep next to.

"You can even have children with them if you like. I'll have no more."

"There is only one, and her name is Arrea," I said forcefully, unable to endure anymore. "And she is barren."

"Shame," she said, and nothing more.

I stepped closer and forced her to look at me.

"Volesa, I know that you resent me. And I know nothing else about you except that we both loved Titus. That's the only thing we share. The least we can do is work together to raise the boy in the way Titus would have wanted."

She looked away but didn't disagree. Her auburn locks fell naturally across her shoulders but still appeared to be perfectly delineated. She had wide hips and a pronounced bust, the consummate mother, but not only in appearance. She was meek and nurturing but had the fire within her soul to defend her brood violently if necessary.

I believed then that she had inherited Titus's will. She'd first arrived as a slight, timid girl, afraid of her own shadow. Now, I was certain she could have contended with any warrior the Cimbri could throw at me.

"Do you have any idea how to raise a child?" she asked at last.

"No, but I will do my best. I am older now than Titus was when Gavius was born."

"The way Titus spoke, it appears he had the experience of helping to raise you," she said.

I found myself laughing.

"That sounds like something he would say." And for a moment, I forgot everything else and simply missed my brother.

Looking at her, as the breeze swept through her hair and the sunlight reflected off of every eyelash, I found Volesa more beautiful than I ever had before.

But not the kind of beauty that a groom sees in his bride. I thought only of how lucky my brother was to have had her heart, and how perfect they had once looked standing side by side.

We said nothing else, but it was clear that she understood what must be done. We would be married, for the sake of her son and her future, but that didn't make it any easier for either of us.

I wished, now more than ever, that Titus were still alive.

NINE DAYS before the kalends of February 651 ab urbe condita

"WHEN AND WHERE you are Gaia, I, then and there will be Gaius." I recited the ancient lines as the priest waited for Volesa to do the same.

"When and where you are Gaius, I, then and there will be Gaia."

She wore a stark white dress, the same one she'd worn on her wedding day to Titus, which stood in stark contrast to the black we had donned in mourning since Titus was officially declared dead in November.

I told myself that the mourning period should have been extended for years, as I was grieving not only the loss of my brother but all the men I had served with. I rarely rose from my bed. I took meals in my room, and spoke little. This period of bedridden depression was to be cut short, however, by my wedding.

It was here, in the frigid snow of winter, that I walked through our village in the same ceremonial tunic my brother had worn when he'd married Volesa years earlier.

The ceremonial fire and water were brought out before us. We were supposed to meet each other's eyes, but I looked at her yellow shoes and couldn't bring myself to lift my gaze.

Beside us was a bust of Janus, the god of new beginnings, with two faces, one looking to the past and the other to the future. It was supposed to be a joyous day, but even the villagers who joined us knew this was a somber occasion. When the rites were concluded, we walked from the temple to my ancestral home, and the crowds followed us, more like a funeral procession for Titus than a festive wedding march.

As the doors to the home were opened, I picked Volesa up with ease. It was much more difficult to keep from looking to Arrea. She was in attendance but did not cry. My mother was there as well but did not smile.

I carried Volesa over the threshold and shut the door, anxious for our well-wishers to depart.

The rest of the evening was supposed to be a private celebration for our conjoined families, but no one was interested enough to partake. Volesa's father was visibly disgruntled that he was being robbed of the dowry he wished returned, and my family had our own reasons for being downcast.

Instead, we invited the priest over once more to conduct the adoption ritual that would officially make Gavius my son. When he arrived, the gray-bearded priest recited a few lines, but we were hardly listening. We had already had a long day, and most deeply wanted to be alone.

At last the priest instructed for Gavius to take my hand. I reached out to him, but the child quickly hid behind his mother's wedding dress.

"I'm not going to hurt you, Gavius," I said, kneeling to his level. He said nothing, but his eyes were wide with fear. "I know you don't remember me, but I have always loved you very much," I said, unable to articulate myself more clearly.

Volesa ruffled Gavius's auburn hair, which he had inherited from her, and grabbed my palm with the other hand.

"See? He isn't so scary," she said.

Gavius finally smiled and reached toward me, placing his little palm inside my own.

The priest instructed me to lift him up then, and lead him out to the center of our land. He asked us to lie down on the soil, side by side, until the allotted amount of time had passed.

I helped Gavius to the earth and then laid beside him. The boy said nothing, obviously embodying Titus's stern and solemn spirit, even in his youth.

"Your *tata* was the best man I've ever known. But I will try my best," I whispered to him. "I know that you don't understand…" I couldn't find the right words, so I allowed the rest of the ceremony to pass in silence.

When the priest rang his bell, we rose, now father and son. But we both still felt like strangers.

I slept alone that night, neither in my wedding bed nor in the arms of my only love.

I rose early the following morning and left before anyone else woke. There were no more words to say or promises to make that would make anyone feel better. Not true ones, at least.

I left my lover, my mother, my bride, and my child alone to the cold, empty halls of our ancestral home, and began my trek back to the battlefield that I had so recently departed.

6

SCROLL VI

EIGHT DAYS BEFORE THE KALENDS OF FEBRUARY
651 AB URBE CONDITA

I took the coastal route back toward Gaul. I'm still not sure if this was the correct choice. I imagined that if I was to find any warmth on my journey, it would be near the coast, but whatever tinge of heat I received from the Mediterranean winds was compensated for with a freezing humidity.

I slept on a thin bedroll and used my tunic as my blanket. It was the only thing that kept my body temperature regulated until morning, when I'd find my armor covered in fresh snow flurries and my tent starched with ice. I moved so quickly just to get somewhere warm that, by the time I reached Genua, the calluses on my heels had reopened as inflected blisters.

It nearing the end of January, and I still had a full month before war season would begin and Marius would expect my prompt return. Sometimes I regretted leaving Nursia as soon as I had, but there was nothing for me there until my task was complete. In the same way, I couldn't force myself to stay still for very long. I dreaded returning to camp, but it was the only place I belonged now.

In Genua, I walked towards the docks where hundreds of small vessels were approaching with their morning's fresh catch. One boat in particular stood out, large enough to host a small army and shaped like a Roman bireme. I neared the ship and perused the area for a while, flicking bits of bread to the birds who fought each other for them, and watching as sailors haggled over the price for a few freshly caught eel. Eventually a cheerful man approached me. His smile was wide enough to rival the size of his boat, but it was clearly disingenuous. His eyes were at odds as well, as one seemed to swivel away from the other.

"Greetings, sir!" he said gesturing to the large vessel behind him. He had a mane of waning gray hair that reached down to his shoulders, and his arms were covered in old scars.

"Where is she headed? I'm looking for passage to Massilia," I said. As you may remember, I wasn't terribly fond of water, much less sea voyages. Still, a transport via the Tyrrhenian Sea would cut my journey by half or more. The blisters on my feet beckoned me to be brave.

"She can go anywhere, for you," he said with a smile. "Are you a Roman?" He sized me up, attempting to decipher how much spare coin I might have. If I appeared affluent at this point in my journey, then I could hardly imagine how his other customers looked.

"I am."

"Me too. I'm a Roman citizen. My name is Mellus." He held his back straighter and lifted his chin. If he was a Roman, he hadn't been one for long. I could tell by his accent, which was rich with a Sicilian enunciation.

"Quintus Sertorius." I shook his hand and ignored the urge to wipe mine off on my tunic. "Can a Roman use your ship?"

"I am captain of this vessel, and anyone I deem fit can use my ship. For the right price." He rubbed his forefinger and thumb together. I was already tired of talking with him.

Before we had even reached gates, General Marius, the consul, appeared atop his horse.

"Soldiers," he said, blocking out the sun with the back of his hand and analyzing us for some time. "I'm happy to see you." His back was straight and his head high, his bearing as noble and imposing as I remembered him.

He leapt from his horse, shooing away the legionary who knelt to offer him a footstool.

He approached and wiped the sweat from his brow.

"General." I snapped to attention and saluted him, as did the rest of our men.

He craned his head and struggled to count us.

"This is it?" he asked.

"It is, sir," I replied, remaining in the position of attention.

"Well, at least you live."

He spun on his heels, passed off the reins of his horse to an orderly, and strode back through the gate. We remained in place, awaiting the inevitable hurling of feces and insults, but none came.

"Come on, then," he said. We followed him into the fortification, trying to avoid eye contact with the mules who gathered around to watch us. When I felt safe to do so, I stole a glance around the camp. Something struck me immediately. Every piece of armor was identical. Every mule bore the same close haircut. Most of them even seemed to have a similar body weight.

"Things seem different, Consul," I said looking back to Marius.

"They are." He smiled smugly. "This is Marius's camp. You've never seen one like it."

"What about the baggage train? All we saw were merchants and prostitutes."

He shook his head. "We no longer have baggage trains. Look around." He pointed to the mules training on either side of our path. "They carry everything now. They carry all their weaponry,

"Name your price, then, Captain." He cupped his hands behind his back and swayed on his feet, attempting to decide the highest price he might squeeze out of me.

"Fifty denarii," he said.

"*Gerrae!* That much?" A centurion was paid two-thirds of a denarius per day, making this day-long trip more than two months' pay for me.

"Come now, it's a large vessel. It's what we charge all of our travelers."

"Now you're a thief and a liar." I turned my back to him, and he quickly reached out and grabbed my arm.

"Forty-five, then? I'll do you this favor, as a Roman." He shook his head, as if he were making a grave mistake by offering such a low price.

I exhaled and thought about it for a moment. What kind of fool would spend two months' pay like this? But currencies held little meaning for me now, as it tends to lose its value on most soldiers. What would a few denarii count if we were dead this day or the next?

"Alright." I pulled out my coin purse and counted out what he would require, careful to not let him see what else I had on me. "Fine, I'll do it."

He turned to his men and signaled for them to prepare for departure.

"How did you receive your wound?" He gestured to my bad eye as he turned to lead me onto the ship.

"I lost it in battle," I said, following him onto the creaking wood of the old vessel.

"Mine went sideways during a fight with a drunk Thracian at a tavern in Rhegium. Be careful not to turn to drink in Massilia or you might lose your other eye, like I did." Mellus turned and gave me a sinister grin I didn't much care for. I didn't engage.

THE JOURNEY WASN'T LONG, and the seas seemed to be frozen in silence beneath us, but I became sick regardless. I lurched the moldy bread I had eaten into the Tyrrhenian, which the crew found particularly amusing.

"Is it the wine or the sea, Roman?" one sailor asked as some of them laughed.

When we arrived at Massilia the next day, Mellus met me on the port side of the boat.

"It's been a pleasure traveling with you," he said, jingling over two months of my pay in the purse tied to his belt.

"I thank you for passage," I said, honestly just thankful to see my destination moving closer.

"And where do you go now? What is in Massilia for a Roman legionary?"

"That's not your concern, Captain."

"Drink? Woman? I know the finest brothels here—"

"Stop." I turned to him. "I need to acquire a slave and a horse. And then I'll be on my way."

He chuckled to himself and patted my back rather aggressively.

"Well, Mellus can tell you the way. Just through the port, take a left. They keep the slave markets closest to the docks so that travelers can be tempted to…sample their wares." I glared at the captain but deemed that a discussion of ethics wasn't worth my time.

REGARDLESS OF MY distaste for Mellus, I followed his directions to the slave market. I'll admit that it was quite uncomfortable for me to purchase another man. My family had never owned slaves. These days, my father would have been laughed at, but during my childhood, codes of morality were not distasteful. My father taught us that owning another man degrades the owner, as he learned from the great Stoic philosopher Zeno. *"Whether by conquest or purchase, the title to a slave is a bad one. For those who claim to own their fellow man, have looked down into the pit and forgotten that justice should rule the world."* That's what Zeno said, and that's what my father taught me. But Marius had ordered that I purchase someone to help bear my new load as a tribune, and he was not going to be swayed by either Greek philosophies or paternal sentiments.

THE STENCH of the slave markets wafted to greet me before I had even reached sight of it: unwashed or rotting corpses, thick incense burning in candelabrums in a vain attempt to ward off the smell. Next was the sound of vendors shouting out the attributes of their human property, and the hollered bids of those attempting to make a purchase. Then I saw behind the massive throng of Massiliots the wicker cages filled with men, women, and children. I have a clear memory of the locals being wrapped up in cloaks and wearing mittens, while the slaves wore nothing but old, dirty tunics. It was a wonder that they weren't all dying from exposure. Perhaps they were.

The sight was dastardly. Sunken-cheeked children nestled at their mothers' breasts, seemingly unaware of the urine and excrement that pooled beneath them. Some of them wailed out in protest, not speaking but moaning from a place too deep within themselves for words to describe. Most of them remained silent, their eyes like glass, staring through and past me to something invisible in the distance.

In Rome, such markets existed, and were considerably bigger in number of slaves, I'm sure. But still, Rome was large enough that one had to decide to visit it. Massilia's slave market was at the forefront, the cornerstone of the Greek city, and it was impossible to miss.

The breath caught in my lungs as I walked silently past the cages. It was as if I were subconsciously afraid of picking up disease through the air. Everyone, even the slave masters and bidders, looked like they were running a low fever.

The feces must have remained in these cages for days at a time. It clung to the fibers of the slaves' tunics and seeped into the pores of their skin. Their hair was tangled, and more than a few had open wounds that were festering, spewing blood and the puss of infection.

Flies swarmed around happily, feasting like it was their Saturnalia.

I couldn't look away. Certainly, this must be a dream. A nightmare, rather, especially for those within the cages. The majority of the browsers seemed unaffected, and the slave masters were as jolly as if their wares were expensive Parthian jewels rather than rotting flesh.

"Here, sir." A hand shot through one of the wicker cages at my side, a handkerchief dangling from skeletal fingers.

"What?" I asked, woken from the nightmare.

"The smell. I know. It's quite unbearable." The man within the cage was much older than myself, probably nearing his forties. He was balding, but his grey hair still had flecks of black and was curled in thick locks. Even in this cage, the man had been able to maintain the neatness of his beard, and had obviously retained some of his composure as well. He spoke Greek, and his words were refined and smooth. He didn't seem frightened or perturbed by the injustice around him.

A slave master jumped in front of me and rapped his staff against the cage. Short and fat, the slave master's face was glowing red from anger.

"Shut up, you! We've told you to keep your mouth shut. Do we have to beat you again, or will you listen?" the slave master shouted in a Massiliot dialect of Greek. "Never mind him, sir. He isn't worth your time."

"You speak Greek, then?" I asked the man within the cage.

"I speak many languages, sir"—he gave a humble smile —"although Greek is my native tongue."

"Latin as well?" I asked. The slave master stood by, perplexed.

"Yes. And Hebrew, Phoenician, and Aramaic."

"Yeah, Hebrew. He's a damned Jew. A Greek and a Jew, sir. He's not worth your time." The slave master stepped in between us. "What are you, a soldier? I bet you'll need someone strong and tough. Someone who can follow orders?" he asked with a wink. "This one's not been a slave long enough to mind his manners." He hit his staff against the cage again, the man within only leaning back in response. "Or perhaps a pretty young thing to take the stress of soldiering away? We have some virgins available—" he continued to rattle on, but I pushed the bastard aside and stepped closer to the cage.

"How did you become enslaved?" I asked, locking eyes with the man in the cage.

"It's a long story, sir." The slave looked away for the first time. "I inherited some debt from my father, and not debt from legitimate institutions, if you catch my meaning," he said, not seeming to begrudge his lot as much as would be expected of someone in his position.

"I told you to quit talking!" The slave master reached to open the cage.

"Hold." I stuck out a hand to restrain him. "If you only just became a slave, what were you doing before?"

"I was a librarian in Athens." He seemed quite proud of this, but perhaps a bit sad that he was a librarian no longer.

"Good for nothing, sir. Couldn't hold up your sword," the slave master said.

"What are your skills, then?" I asked.

"Transcribing, writing, reading, languages…"

Already my mind was racing with what I could accomplish with a man like him at my side.

"And are you familiar with philosophy?"

"My time in Athens exposed me to many schools of higher thinking, sir," he said.

"If you'll just come right this way, sir, I'll show you some of our other men. Numidians, Celts…strong, tamed beasts!" the slave master pleaded.

"And for double the price, right?" I asked, turning to tower over the fat little slave master.

"Double the value." He gulped but managed to grin.

"I'll take him." I gestured to the man in the cage.

"If you don't, I'm gonna beat him to death. But really, sir. We have better wares."

"I think you know how much this man will sell for if you can tame him properly. To some scholar or Roman noble, right? I'll take him."

"I'm not sure you can afford him, sir." The man analyzed my scratched armor and dirty tunic.

I revealed my stipend from Marius and a letter of intent with the consul's seal.

"I'm a military tribune of the Roman legion under Gaius Marius. And I am leaving here with this man. Do you understand?"

I wasn't normally so forthright, but I was losing my patience with greedy little men who made a fortune on the suffering of others.

"Five thousand sestercii."

"Here's more than that." I tossed him the entire bag. He tested the weight but didn't bother to count it. He unlocked the cage and allowed the man to exit, kicking back the other slaves who were inching closer to their freedom.

"It's your loss, Roman," the slave master said, extending the slave to me as if he were a loaf of bread.

"I'll take my chances."

I HURRIED out of the slave market, thankful that I would never have to return. Only after I had left the premises did I turn to notice that my new slave was lagging behind, struggling with all the power he had to overcome a limp and keep up.

I walked back to him.

"Slow down, we're in no rush. I apologize. I was simply anxious to leave that place, or I might have hurt that little man." The slave looked at me and nodded in thanks.

"It's a strange master who apologizes to his slave," he said.

We walked through Massilia's streets, weaving in and out of the throngs of travelers who had flocked to see the "lovely city by the water."

"It's a strange slave who disobeys his slave master as you did that man."

"As he said, I haven't properly learned my manners." He smiled, and I smiled back. His manners were quite refined.

"Your name? I hadn't asked your name."

"Apollonius. And yours, sir?"

"Quintus. Quintus Sertorius, military tribune," I said, the words feeling strange coming from my lips for the first time. "So, Apollonius is your name. But you're a Jew? Strange name for a Jew."

"My father was Greek. He was a traveling merchant, on the Egyptian route down to Sidon. He met my mother passing through Jerusalem. They married, and here I am."

Out of the corner of my eye, I noticed something strange. There were several cloaked men who were gathered near a storefront and whispering to one another. Beards covered their faces and their hoods were pulled down over their eyes, but I felt as though they were looking at me.

"Well, I'm happy to have you, Apollonius. And just so you know, I won't have you carrying my sword or shield. I can do that myself."

We passed by a theater where a Greek comedy was reaching its climax, judging by the laughter from the intoxicated crowd. In this gathering, I spotted more hooded men. They were the only ones not laughing along with the actors' jokes.

"Apollonius, have you been in Massilia long?"

"Thirty-one days, if I remember correctly."

"Have you noticed anything strange?" I asked. There was a reason Marius had determined that I must go to Massilia—to ensure that there was no activity that was unbefitting of an ally of Rome.

"I'm not sure what you mean, sir."

"Call me Quintus. That feels strange." I placed my hand on his elbow and quickened our pace to a less dense area. "Have you noticed any strange men visiting? Cloaked men."

"It's winter, sir—Quintus. I've seen many cloaked men."

"Perhaps you're right." I ventured to look over my shoulder to see if the bearded men were still looking at me. I couldn't tell if they were. Perhaps combat had frayed my nerves. "I need to purchase a horse. Do you know where I might find one?"

"Near the north gate. I saw stables when they were carting me in." He pointed in the direction we were already moving.

"I'M LOOKING TO ACQUIRE A HORSE," I said, approaching an old man in a straw hat at the stables.

"Male or female?" he said, revealing a toothless mouth.

"No matter."

"For breeding, riding…what is it for?" The man turned and led Apollonius and me into the stalls where several horses were being inspected by other shoppers and stable keepers. The smell of shit was poorly covered up by the oil of crushed rose petals and the cheap perfume worn by the female visitors. It was just familiar enough to remind me of the stable I'd grown up working in, but my father ensured ours was kept far cleaner. By the sweat of our backs, it was cleaner than most Roman *villae*.

"For battle," I said, remembering myself.

The old man squinted and spit a massive glob of saliva.

"You'll want this one, then, I bet." He led us to a black stallion in the middle of the stalls, which was already being admired by others. "He's only been here a few days, and he'll sell as fast as he can run."

"Let me see him," I said. The man pulled back the rope and allowed us to enter. This stallion was separated from the other horses, for what I imagine must have been aggression issues. You could see it in those massive, wet eyes. He wanted to fight.

"Name?"

"Bucephalus," he shrugged. It was the name of Alexander the Great's famous warhorse, and it was fitting for a stead like this, although I imagined that the old man might have made it up on the spot.

"Here, boy." I approached the horse. He swayed his head this way and that, emitting a low grunt every few moments in repressed aggression.

"If you ever put him out to stud, he'll catch you a good price." The old man leaned up on the chipped wood of the stables and spit again.

"What do you think, Apollonius?" I asked.

"A fine steed, sir," he said, admiring the beast but keeping his distance.

"You know, a stallion this size would make me a target in battle," I said, imagining how I might stand out from the rest atop such an animal.

"If coin is your concern, I can cut you a deal," the stable keeper said, appearing as disinterested as he could manage.

"What about that one?" I pointed across the stables to another stall, where one horse stood beside several others. This horse alone remained passive, while the others snorted and vied for attention.

The stable keeper shook his head. "A girl. Too young. No good for battle."

"You mind if I take a closer look?"

The old man threw up his hands in exasperation but led us to her regardless.

"Hey there, girl," I said as I approached. She leaned in curiously, straining her neck to smell my hands. "Hey, girl," I said again, sensing her reaction.

"Something's wrong with that one. She's dull, half brained, or her mind is broken."

"And what makes you say that?" I asked.

"Our trainers have all but stopped working with her. She's useless. Can't learn a damn thing."

I looked into the horse's eyes, and spoke again in a low voice. Something caught my attention.

I lifted my hand and snapped by her perky ears. They did not respond.

"She's not dumb. She's deaf."

"What difference does it make? She's useless," the man said.

She did not respond to sound, but she responded with a swish of her tale each time I touched her wet nose.

"Because a horse that cannot hear the horrors of battle will be less likely to avoid it." I turned to Apollonius, whose eyebrows were raised. He gave me a nod. "How old did you say she is?"

"Four last August. Too young for battle anyhow."

"Young enough that she can still be taught." I didn't bother to inform the man that I had been raised training horses, and I knew how these stables operated. They took their best-looking and most able-bodied horses, taught them a few tricks, and then sold them at a hefty markup. Those tricks, though, made horses harder to train. I much preferred a clean slate.

We haggled on the price for a bit, and whether the reins, saddle, and some feed would be included, but eventually I walked away with that horse for far less than she was actually worth. The man thought I was a fool, and perhaps my fellow tribunes would as well, but I had made my choice.

"This way toward the road to the Po?" I asked the old man as he counted up his coin.

He gave me a nod, and nothing more. "Come on, then," I said to Apollonius. "I'm anxious to leave this place." He didn't know that where we were going was much less pleasant, but he would soon find out.

I led the horse by the reins we had been provided, and Apollonius cleared the way before us.

As the gates came into view in the distance, I spotted more of the hooded men. If I returned to tell Marius that I had only seen Gallic men with long beards and cloaks in the middle of winter, he would have thought me a fool. But something about it unnerved me.

"Apollonius," I called ahead, "see those men there? You're certain you haven't seen anything suspicious?"

He turned and walked back to us so that he could reply in a quieter tone.

"As a matter of fact, sir, now that I think about it...yes. Several of these men... You mean the ones in the olive colored cloaks, right?"

"Yes."

"They arrived less than a week ago. They all look similar, don't they?"

"They do. I wonder what their purpose is."

"I wouldn't inquire about it, sir. They don't look very friendly." He was correct in his assessment. They moved slowly and deliberately, and there was something sinister about the way they whispered to one another and kept looking over their shoulders.

Some small boys noticed my armor as we walked, and began racing alongside us.

"Roman! Roman!" they shouted, and pretended to march along with us into battle.

I kept my gaze on the bearded men.

"Any coin, soldier? Coin?" they asked.

"Go on, now." I tried to shoo them away, but more and more seemed to join.

"Roman! Roman!" they shouted louder still. The bearded men turned and watched us. I could feel the gaze of several eyes as I tried to get the children to leave us.

"Leave us," I said, but my voice was drowned out by their shouts. I tried to pick up our pace, but I could see that the bearded men were beginning to approach. "Apollonius, take the horse. Take the horse." I passed him the reins and placed a hand on the hilt of my gladius.

More of the cloaked men materialized out of the crowd.

My gaze darted as my heart began to race. Marius had been correct. There was some kind of insurgency in Massilia. And he had sent me into the lion's den.

"We need to move." I took the front and tried to clear our path. Apollonius hobbled along as best he could. My new horse snorted anxiously, perceiving my distress.

As the path cleared before us, one woman remained standing where she was. She wore the same olive cloak as the bearded men, and held a babe to her chest wrapped in a wool blanket.

As we approached, she turned at the last moment to meet my gaze.

"Roman? You're a Roman?" she said, as if in desperation. Wide eyed, she demanded my attention. She leaned toward me as if for me to examine or kiss her child. But then she dropped the blankets, which had been empty, save the dagger that she now clutched. She leapt forward with a shout.

At the last moment, I stepped to the side and caught her arm. Drawing my sword, I shoved it into her belly as she stumbled past me.

As quickly as it had begun, the woman collapsed onto the cobblestone path as the crowds scattered, shouting. I held my dripping sword out before me and turned to meet whatever other assailants there might be. There were none.

The hooded men had disappeared. All the children had scattered, horrified.

"Are you alright, Quintus?" Apollonius said, his hand over his mouth. He stared at the woman in horror, and I could tell he was doing all he could to hold back vomit.

"I'm unhurt." I continued to scan the area, trying my best to avoid looking at the twitching corpse before me.

When at last I did, her eyes were still flickering with light, but her breathe had stalled. I knelt beside her and closed her eyes, and only then did I notice the branding on her neck. I tilted her head to the side, and made out the words "VOLC. TECT."

"Volcae Tectosages." I stood and exhaled.

"What?" Apollonius turned his head.

"It's a tribe. To which this girl and her friends must belong." I shook my head.

"Why would they try to kill you?" Apollonius asked in dismay. "They must have thought you were spying on them."

"I was." I took the reins back from Apollonius. "Come on, we need to move." I led our way out of the city and didn't look back.

7

SCROLL VII

TWO DAYS BEFORE THE NONES OF FEBRUARY 651 AB URBE CONDITA

"Does this place look alright?" I asked as we neared a clearing off of the main road. Frogs croaked and creatures rustled in the distance, but this patch of earth was as tame as we could find. I could tell Apollonius was having a hard time riding. A horse's back, which can feel quite natural to some, can make certain men extremely uncomfortable. My new slave was among them.

"It's dry, at least. You're the master, though, so you can decide," he said, breathing heavily. I didn't respond to him, instead hopping from my new horse and helping him do the same. I laid a few tunics out on the ground. "The breeze is nice, but it's a bit cold, don't you think?"

The labor of walking wasn't enough to warm him, as the shivers in his limbs was apparent.

"Give me just a moment and I'll start a fire," I said.

"Oh," he said cheerfully, "a skill taught in the legions?"

"I learned first from my father many years ago. We'd go

hunting in the mountains north of my village. Winter or summer, it was always cold, so knowing how to start a fire was paramount if you wanted to keep your toes from freezing off."

"City dwellers like myself have a harder time with such tasks," he said, rather uncomfortably, as if he didn't know what to do with himself as I prepared the fire. "That must have been very cold," he said eventually.

"It happened to my uncle once, before he died."

Once the sparks were ignited and puffs of smoke began to bellow out from the little fire, Apollonius rested on the tunic beside it.

"I miss my philosophy books," he said. He crossed his arms behind his head and lay back.

"Oh? Who do you prefer?" I asked, splitting a blade of grass in two and throwing both in the fire.

"Plato, Socrates, Aristotle…any of the great thinkers."

"If you had to choose just one?" Content with my fire, I took a step back and lay down as well.

"Socrates, I think. Although it depends on when you ask me. I might tell you something different tomorrow." The way he spoke calmed me, although I didn't know why. I hadn't been much of a conversationalist in some time. "I have a question for you," he asked when I failed to continue the conversation.

"What is it?"

"Would you object if I fast on Saturdays? My mother would be ashamed if I didn't."

"Oh, is she alive?" I asked, guilt suddenly stirring in my gut.

"No, she died…heavens, nearly ten years ago now. You can bet she would rise from the grave to scold me if I didn't, though."

"Apollonius, if your only request of me is that you don't want to eat on a particular day of the week, I don't think we're going to have any problems," I said. He chuckled and nodded his thanks.

"You have sadness in your eye, master," he said at length.

"Don't call me that," I said. The fire crackled as he became silent. "You can say it around others if you'd prefer, to keep up appearances. But I don't like it," I said. I exhaled before continuing. "It hasn't always been this way. Recent events have been rather unfortunate," I said, feeling guilty about how I'd first responded.

"The rains pour on the just and the unjust. I'm sorry to hear that. You can talk about it if you'd like, but don't feel obliged," he said, his words slow and deliberate. I looked over and analyzed him for a moment. I didn't much want to talk about the last year of my life, but if I were to talk to anyone, this man seemed as good as any. Something in his eyes told me he had no false pretensions or alternative reasons for asking me to speak.

"My brother died in combat, along with many of the men I served with. They say that nearly a hundred thousand died in all."

Suddenly Apollonius shot up as quickly as his slender frame would allow.

"You were at the Battle of Arausio?" he asked, wide eyed.

"I was. You've heard of it?"

"Travelers sang sad songs as they passed through Massilia."

"I didn't know there were any songs. How nice," I said sarcastically.

"I'm sorry for your lot." He continued to look at me until I met his gaze with my one good eye. I nodded my appreciation.

"And now that my brother is dead, I have been wed to his widow. The only woman I've ever loved was forced to watch my betrothal." I exhaled. I didn't know why I'd shared so much, but he nodded along in confirmation of my grief, so I continued. "I can't sleep at night. I can't forget the things I saw, the enemies I killed, the men I lost… I'm trapped in my own mind."

He took his time before replying, and for a moment I believed he had lost interest. "Did you know I'm not really a slave?"

"Is that so? I paid a lot of money for nothing if you aren't." I meant this in jest, but it was in poor taste. He didn't seem to be perturbed, though.

"A man can never be free unless he is free unto himself. The man who is freed unto himself, who is in harmony with nature, is always free. It seems that you've been enslaved in a different sort of way." He crossed his legs and touched a finger to his lips as he spoke. His hands trembled slightly, not in a nervous sort of way but as if this were the most important conversation he had ever had.

"And how do I obtain my freedom?"

"Finding a reason for it all. Seeking peace. I don't know, to be honest. But something tells me the answer is already within you." The words were well spoken, and I was thankful for them, but I was regretful that such philosophy had lost its impact on me after Arausio. I was done discussing my weakness anyhow. But given that Apollonius was considerate enough to listen to my woes, I decided to extend the offer to him as well.

"Were you born in Athens?"

"Actually, I was born in a caravan near the Red Sea. My father was a merchant on the route from Memphis to Smyrna. Passing through Judea, he met a young girl who was naive enough to be swayed by his charms and good looks. After she became pregnant with me, her parents disowned her and cast her out. So she left with the merchant, my father." He seemed to lose himself in thought as he spoke. "Or at least that's how the story goes."

"And your father took her?"

"Oh yes. From what mother told me, he had always wanted children. He was delighted when he first heard the news, even if it was unintended. But during my mother's pregnancy, an unfortunate event befell him. Kicked in the face by one of his camels, several of the bones shattering. My mother tended to him as best she could, but it seemed that Egyptian opiates soothed him better. He had become friends of distributors while in Alexandria, who always made sure he had ample supply." Apollonius's voice slowly transformed from nostalgia to sadness. "He had a dependence on it for the rest of his life."

"How did you end up in Greece, then?"

"After my father was disabled, we moved back to his homeland. He inherited the home of his father, who had recently died, and he wasted away there the rest of his life." He looked down and sighed. "And my mother cared for him the rest of hers, I believe as a way to make up for the sins of her youth."

I was content to let the conversation end there, but Apollonius continued. It must have been a long time—before his captivity, at least—since anyone was willing to listen.

"I was tasked with caring for my father too. Namely, in talking down his anger after one of his drinking binges or opiate comas. I helped raise my brothers and sisters too, who all moved as soon as they were able to get away from that man."

"And your mother?" I asked.

"She was…she was my mother." He was at a loss for words. "She was…unstable. The toll of caring for my father weighed heavily on her, especially in her later years. I'll always believe it led to her death. While she lived, though, I was tasked with nurturing her as well, in a different way."

"And you did all this while working in the Athenian libraries? Sounds quite stressful."

He chuckled. "Heavens no. I loved my work. Before I was a librarian, I swept the streets after festivals and cleaned the public latrines. I can honestly say it wasn't much preferable to slavery. But in those libraries…in those dimly lit halls, surrounded by boundless knowledge, the intellectual intensity…" He came alive, squeezing his fists and drifting off to a place at the forefront of his mind. "I very much miss it."

The winds had tampered the fire, so I tended to it.

"How did you become a slave, then? A librarian must be a fine job in Athens. Did it not pay well? You said something about debts?"

The glossy look in his eye dissipated as his mind returned to the present.

"My father's debts, yes. By the time he died, he was ruinously impoverished, but still gambled when he could and was always determined to have his 'fine Egyptian opiates.' A few legitimate institutions came to me about the debts after he died, but the worst were some nasty Phoenician thugs from across the sea. They took everything we had, and when it wasn't enough, they sold me for the sum owed. They sold me and… and…the girl." Tears welled up in his eyes.

"Your child?"

He shook his head.

"Not mine. My brother's, born out of wedlock and abandoned by both mother and father. I was all she had, and she was all I had." He dabbed his nose with the hem of his tunic.

"She was sold too?" I found myself choking as well.

"Yes. Just four years old now. No, five. Five years old."

"Here you are comforting a fool like me… I'm sorry for what has happened to you, Apollonius." I warmed my hands over the fire, and couldn't bring myself to look at him.

"The rains pour on the just and the unjust alike."

"Perhaps you'll find her one day."

"Perhaps." He smiled and nodded, but I could tell from his expression that he didn't believe it.

"We should get some sleep," I said, looking up at the shrouded moon, full and bright in the sky behind the clouds.

"Yes, go ahead. I can stay awake for a while longer if need be."

"Apollonius." I turned to him. "I can't sleep, remember? I'll keep watch for a while. Get some rest. We have a few more miles tomorrow before we're back at camp."

"Are you certain, master?"

I exhaled and shook my head. "Get some sleep."

8

SCROLL VIII

ONE DAYS BEFORE THE NONES OF FEBRUARY 651 AB URBE CONDITA

I had just reentered the camp when I heard Marius's shouts from halfway across the camp. As I approached his praetorium, he was slamming his fist on the desk.

I entered and stood at attention.

"How can they do this? It's a sham! A travesty. Every news report of the battle made it clear what happened. Caepio was at fault for the defeat!" The blue veins in Marius's forehead and neck were bulging.

"Those reports have been silenced," Sulla said, leaning against a wooden post with his arms crossed. He had a look of bemusement at Marius's anger.

"Sertorius here was at the battle. You saw it, Tribune. Tell us…what happened at Arausio?" Marius exhaled and tried to regain his composure.

"Maximus was in the middle of discussions with the Cimbri. Caepio marched us to meet them before the talks were concluded, and placed us against the Reds with our backs to the river," I said.

"See"—Marius held out his hand to me and looked at Sulla —"everyone knows what happened." Marius lowered his head.

"Permission to ask what has happened presently, sir?" I asked.

"At ease." Marius waved at me to relax. "My son-in-law is being brought to trial for the Battle of Arausio." He tossed the scroll he had received across his desk for me to look at it.

"They seek to have him stripped of his rank, fined one million sestercii…and exiled?" I said in disbelief. Marius was right, I did know what had happened at Arausio. Caepio was the real culprit, he and the boundless egos of the nobles.

"Perhaps you could go to Rome and testify in his defense?" Marius said to me with a spark of hope.

"That would never work. If it's mentioned that Maximus was in deliberations with the Cimbri, he'll be painted as a coward and a traitor." Sulla shook his head.

Marius threw up his hands but didn't disagree. He plopped down in his chair and scratched at his balding head.

"Have you purchased your slave and horse?" he asked.

"I have, sir. The mare is in the stables and the slave is preparing my quarters."

"Good. With the stipend I gave you, you should have purchased the finest steed and servant in all of Rome," he said, but it didn't take long for his mind to wander back to the matter at hand. "What shall I do, Sulla? What am I supposed to do? Let my son be persecuted? Allow my daughter to be cast off in disgraced exile alongside him?"

"What other choice do you have?" Sulla replied.

"That is what I am asking, damn it. You're supposed to be the crafty one."

"You could contact your allies in Rome. They could file a counter lawsuit against Caepio. Perhaps they can expose him as the real villain."

"And with a juror of senators? No. They won't convict one of their own. You know better than that. It will only seem that we believe the verdict is already decided."

"The evidence is quite damning, sir," I added. "Even the nobles can't ignore the facts."

"No, Marius is correct. But we *do* already know the verdict. He will be convicted, and exiled," Sulla said.

"Then I do not know what to do." Marius exhaled.

"You could always kill someone," Sulla said with a shrug. I'm still not certain it was a joke, although Marius treated it as one.

"Tribune Sertorius, you're not here for political advice. What did you see in Massilia?" Marius said to me at last.

"There were signs of mutinous behavior. I can't speak to the extent of it, Consul, but there were a group of foreigners in the city who had been there for a few weeks, according to the slave I purchased. They conspire in dark corners and keep to themselves."

"Is that it?"

"There was a woman with them, wearing the same tunic. She tried to kill me. I found on her neck a branding: 'VOLC TECTO.'"

"The Tectosages." Marius leaned back and crossed his arms.

"Our suspicions are confirmed, then," Sulla said, striding across the room to hand me a cup of wine as a thank-you for the intelligence.

"Yes, they are. But what if they managed to win the Massiliots to their cause?" Marius stared at the ground and contemplated the possible outcomes.

"Well"—Sulla sat on the corner of Marius desk and took a sip of his own wine—"we deal with the Tectosages first. We punish them, fully, for their transgressions. Then we'll see if the Massiliots have the stomach to do what the Tectosages could not. A commerce city like that? I doubt it."

Marius stood and began pacing around the room. "You did

quite well, Tribune. This is valuable intelligence," he said, approaching a bust of Scipio Aemilianus, his old commander and mentor, in the back of the tent. He ran his fingers over the contours of the face and admired the features. "Now we have a new mission for you."

"What is it, sir?"

"Nothing you can't handle," Sulla added.

"Given the nature of the assignment, I won't order you to do it. You're only being asked to volunteer."

I didn't like what I was hearing, but I waited patiently.

"We want you to infiltrate the Cimbri camp. To collect intelligence," Marius said, turning to me at last. For a moment, I wondered if I was supposed to laugh. What an absurd proposition? No Roman had ever attempted anything like that before, not since the days of King Tarquinius at least.

But Marius didn't appear to be joking. "Sulla has been the one planning the mission," he said, "so I'll allow him to detail it for you."

"We need to know more about the Cimbri, Tribune," Sulla said. "Desperately. We still do not know enough about how they fight. How they think. What their motives are… You know more than anyone because of your previous experience in combat against them. You are one of the few who has lived. But we also understand that you have a grasp on the Gallic tongue."

"I do, sir. But the Reds do not speak Gallic."

"Right you are, but their allies do." Sulla wagged his pointer finger. "When the Cimbri return from their rapine romp in Spain, they will call for all the tribes of Gaul to meet with them at the base of the Alps. We've already confirmed this through interrogation. When they do this, we want you to be with one of these allied tribes. Then you can return once you've learned all that you need to know."

"Now you understand why we asked you not to shave," Marius added.

"You want me to don Celtic garb, infiltrate a Gallic tribe, and spy on the Cimbri and Teutones?" I asked, poorly disguising my incredulousness.

"Correct," Sulla replied without blinking.

"In all due respect, that sounds like suicide."

"We would not send one of our finest tribunes into the mouth of the wolf if we did not believe he could come back alive. That being said, we are aware of the risks," Sulla said, crossing his arms.

"If it is true that I am not being ordered, I must think on this."

"Take the night," Marius said.

"Let us know by first light," Sulla said. "We have a Gallic prisoner waiting in the brig to tell you what you need to know. If you cannot do this, someone else will. I'm certain we can find another Gallic-speaking man among us. We need more intelligence, Tribune, and that isn't negotiable." Sulla drained the rest of his wine.

"I've dreamed of punishing the Reds since they killed my brother. But this is not how I imagined doing it," I said. What I truly felt was something more than revenge. I wanted to regain my honor. I wanted to prove to myself that I was not a coward. And the baser side of me wanted to prove that to everyone else too. I knew a lot of people believed the survivors of Arausio were traitors, and I wanted to prove them wrong. But this mission would never be recorded. Even if I did return, it would be lost to the sands of the time, leaving my legacy forever marred by the last thing I was known for: surviving a battle where everyone else died.

"Take the night," Marius said again. "If you'll excuse us, we have other important matters to discuss. Namely, finding a way to stick one up the arse of those decrepit old nobles who are trying to destroy my son."

THE TRIBUNES STAYED in a small barracks adjacent to the legion they were assigned to. We had six tribunes assigned to the Seventh Legion, and so within were six beds each precisely four feet apart. Each had a trunk at the foot in which we could store our personal items, and a stand by the head where we could hang our armor. In the back were a few desks for the dreaded paperwork that came with the position.

There were only a few present when I entered, but I was happy that Lucius was among them.

"Is everything to your liking, Quintus?" Apollonius asked, making sure the creases in my blanket were perfect.

"It is. Thank you, Apollonius." I placed a hand on his shoulder. "Go and get some rest."

"Is there nothing else you need?" he said, his sleepy eyes lighting up at the mention of rest.

"No, go on. I'll see you in the morning."

He nodded gratefully and departed. Lucius was smiling coyly when I looked at him.

"What is it?" I asked as I shook his hand, his grin infectious.

"Nothing. You'll find out later."

"If you put anything in my bed…" I inspected my things to ensure they hadn't been tainted by my friend's mischief.

"Nothing like that," he said. "Do you like our new home?" He gestured to the nearly empty barracks around us.

"Not quite as dirty as a mule tent, I'm afraid to say. I'll miss sleeping on a cot under the stars." I didn't really mean it, but there was a strange sensation of guilt as I touched the soft fabric of my blankets.

"I'm sure there will be less snoring and farting than you are used to. Although, I can promise you that there will be at least *some* farting and snoring."

"If those are marks of a mule, your friend Lucius should be among them, certainly," another tribune said from the back of the tent. He stood from tying his sandals and approached us. "He's been keeping me up for weeks now."

"That's retaliation for waking us up an hour before sunrise with your bloody exercising and morning prayers," Lucius said. It was apparent that they had become friends.

"My name is Cinna, Tribune. Everyone calls me Equus, though," he said. I shook his hand and introduced myself. He was a young man, no more than seventeen years of age. The fact that it seemed unlikely that he would be able to grow facial hair made his mornings a bit easier, I'm sure.

"Because he's as calm as a cup of water," Lucius said. "No matter what camp life throws at him, I've yet to see him react with anything but a nod of the head."

Equus gave us a display by nodding along with what Lucius was saying.

"Growing up around Gaius Marius can have that effect. He sucked out all my anger so he could use it for himself," Equus said.

"You know the consul well?" I asked.

"I do. My father, the elder Cinna, is a good friend of his. Father is in Rome protecting Marius's interests now. Marius did me the great favor of getting me out of my father's hair…what little of it remains…by bringing me here."

"First year with the legion." Lucius ruffled Equus's hair like a toddler's. "We'll have to teach him quickly."

"I'll teach you something about manners in the process." Equus freed himself and punched Lucius in the stomach. "I'd better be leaving. I have to give report to Sulla about the blasted grain provisions. It was nice meeting you, Tribune." He shook my hand and turned to leave, then paused. "I could show you around first, if you'd like?"

Lucius and I shrugged and followed him outside.

"Where to begin?" he said, analyzing the camp before raising a finger and carrying on. "To the front of camp you'll find the main gate, where the standards are on display. Around it we have a *veterinarium* for the horses and a *fabrica* workshop for clothing needs. Just beside it we have the *valetudinarium*." He stretched his finger in each direction.

"A *valetudinarium*?" I asked.

"Yes. A hospital," he replied.

"I know what it means..." I analyzed the large building crafted with brick and covered in plaster, with arches and columns adorning the outside. "We just never had a hospital. We had a tent with a few untrained soldiers tending to the wounded."

"I'd say there are a great many things in camp you'll be unused to," Lucius said with a wink.

"Well the medici are still enlisted men, with as much medical training as a sack of grapes, but it's something. When we start seeing battle, they'll receive a fast education." Equus's demeanor was calm and endearing, and I found myself impressed at the young man's poise. "Follow me this way," he said.

He stretched out his arms, one to the left and the other to the right.

"To the sides, you'll find the *arae* sacrificial altars, the tribunal for court-martial trials and a bit of free entertainment, as well as the grain and meat storehouses." He turned to the right. "Down that path, you'll find the forum, where the men can spend some of their leisure time and all of their money on drink, food, and a bit of gambling."

"There's a forum in camp?" I asked, perplexed. Marius seemed more of a prodigy than ever.

"That's right. These men signed up for years, not just the duration of the war, so they need a modicum of normality. The legionaries need a place to wind down anyhow, and those dirty shopkeepers need a way to take their money. On either side, you'll find additional gates." He pointed into the far distance where I could see smaller exits, both still fortified with towers. I had already witnessed the brutality of the Cimbri in combat, but this camp seemed impenetrable, even for them. It was a small city, by any means of measurement.

"There's the *armamentarium,* where we house the heavy weaponry and artillery that isn't placed on the wall."

"We have heavy weaponry?" I asked with wide eyes.

"Well...no. But it's where we'd keep them if we did." He shrugged.

"Ah, one last thing," he said, leading the way around our quarters and onto another paved path.

A few young soldiers saluted us nervously as we passed them by.

"To the rear, you'll find the prison. Here also we have the plunder stores. Beyond that, you'll see where the *auxilia* are garrisoned." He pointed to the rows of even tents in the distance, each with baggage carts and rows of stacked swords and shields. "And beyond that, in the back of the camp, we have the *quaestorium,* where you can visit for any supply needs." He exhaled as an orator does after finishing a speech and turned to me with a smile. "And that is where I'm heading now to meet with His Highness Sulla. Unless you have any questions?"

"No...I'm a bit perplexed by the complexity of it all, but I'd wager I can figure out the rest on my own."

He saluted and headed off toward the *quaestorium.*

"Keep that one in line!" he shouted back at me, referring to Lucius, who shook his head like an aggravated older brother.

LUCIUS and I walked and talked for a while. I told him about marrying Volesa, leaving Arrea behind, and the little episode in Massilia. He filled me in on what I had missed in camp while I was gone, and updated me on the various camp political disputes, such as two centurions vying for a position as a first spear.

"But how are the men? How is morale?" I asked him, already guessing my answer from what I had seen in my brief walk through camp.

"Not well. Most of them are scared. They're very green... Most of our veterans are dead or too old to fight."

"I can understand why they're frightened. The tales of the savage Cimbri are quickly spinning into myth."

"The senate passed a law last market day to ban any vessel from giving passage to any man of fighting age," Lucius said.

"I left just in time, then. I took a boat from Genua to Massilia."

"Either that, or the captain was hurting from lack of coin." Lucius shrugged.

I told Lucius of my horse, and we found ourselves sauntering to the stables to see her.

"She's a beautiful animal," he said, petting her snout. "Shhh, it's alright, girl."

"She's deaf, I think. It will be interesting to see how she'll perform in battle." I reclined against the wood of the stall and allowed myself to shimmy into the hay-covered mud.

"There's no better horse trainer in the legion. I'd wager any amount of coin," he said. "I'm sure she'll do just fine."

"Lucius," I said before pausing to exhale, "Marius wants me to infiltrate the Cimbri camp to collect intelligence." I ensured my voice was quiet enough that I wouldn't be overheard.

He nodded and took a seat beside me.

"Marius mentioned something about that. I even volunteered, but he knew I don't know a damn word of Gallic, and I've no talent for acting."

"You volunteered?" I asked, my eyebrows burrowing. I suddenly felt ashamed for not immediately accepting the mission.

"Eh," he said, and shrugged. "I knew he wouldn't allow it. Only felt right to try."

"I envy you," I said, looking away from him.

"You envy me? Why?"

"Your bravery. Toughness...that you still believe in our

fight," I said. Out of the corner of my eye, I could see him shaking his head.

"Don't start all that. You were the first man to scale the wa—"

"Please, Lucius...spare me the antidotes of Burdigala. I cannot rest on that feat of stupidity for the rest of my life. To be honest," I said, turning to him again, "I don't even know why I did it."

"If you want a friend to confirm your cowardice or to allow you to wallow, you'll have to look elsewhere, *amicus*. I'm no good at acting, remember?" He clapped my neck and pulled me closer to him. "You're one of the toughest, bravest soldiers of Rome that I know. And you haven't lost your belief in Rome's cause, Quintus. Lie to yourself if you want, but don't lie to me. You wouldn't have returned if you had no hope left."

"I was following orders, Lucius. Just doing my duty," I said. My horse seemed to sense my distress, and lightened the mood by nudging my head with her massive, soaking nose.

"I don't believe that," he said, pushing himself up to his feet. "I think in time you'll remember yourself. You've endured a lot. It's only natural that you've questions to ask and answers to find."

"And you? Why aren't you asking and seeking?" He extended a hand to help me to my feet.

"I am, Quintus. In my own way." His tone was far more serious than it usually was.

"Do you think I should go, then? Accept Marius's mission?"

He placed his hands akimbo on his hips and considered it.

"No."

"Why not? You volunteered, right? Think you're tougher than me, is that it?" I flexed my arms at him as he roared with laughter, the mare seeming to join in with a few grunts herself.

"I only volunteered because I thought that meant you wouldn't have to go," he said, turning to me. "It was pragmatism, Quintus. You have a wife and child now, and a mother to look after."

"And you have a little brother."

"Yes, one that your family is currently caring for." He placed a hand on my shoulder. "I didn't want you to go, because it is reckless and foolish and will likely get you killed."

"But the intelligence is valuable. We need to know how the Cimbri conduct themselves so we can defeat them. Without understanding these strange invaders, we'll likely be slaughtered again." I shuddered at the thought.

He shook his head.

"Have some faith! We have Marius leading us now," he said with a coy grin. It was no secret that he worshipped the ground General Marius walked on. The consul was perhaps the only thing keeping the entire state from declining into outright panic.

"And Marius is the one asking me to do this. He said I have until tomorrow morning to inform him of my decision."

"'Return at first light. Dismissed, Tribune.'" Lucius mocked Marius's gruff voice, with the utmost respect, of course. I couldn't help but laugh. This was why I talked to Lucius. He was the remedy to stress and fear, more effective than wine and he didn't come with a hangover. He was Rome's best-kept secret.

"Come on, then, Tribune. I need some sleep." I opened the stall door and bid my mare goodbye with a kiss between her eyes.

"Hold on, now. You have to name her first," Lucius said.

Naming a horse is always a bad idea as a trainer. It makes it that much harder to give them up. I wouldn't be selling her after she was trained but leading her into battle. The thought of losing a horse was sad, but losing a friend was devastating. And a horse with a name is a friend, my father always used to say.

"You always were a sentimental one, *amicus*," I said.

"You deserve a name, don't you, girl?" he said in a voice reserved for infants and animals.

"I'll call her..."

"What about Sura? After my mother," he said.

"That's her name." I patted him on the shoulder and turned to leave.

"It's a pretty name for a pretty girl. You know, I've got a male a few stalls down. We could get them together and see what happens?"

"You keep your beast away from my girl, or you'll be wearing an eye patch too."

Stallions were typically gelded before war season. This was a precaution so that, lest the horses be taken during battle, the enemy couldn't improve their breeding stock. Marius had ordered the stallions to be left alone, I assume as a gesture that he believed we would ultimately be victorious. Either that, or, if we failed and they took our stallions, it wouldn't really matter anymore.

We departed, and as we walked under the setting Gallic sun back to the tribunes' tent, Lucius did not mention my mission, or ask whether I planned to accept it. Perhaps he knew that it was a decision I alone could make, and it was no use to talk about it any further. Or, more likely, he believed the situation was already settled, and my mind already set on declining. I, however, was not so sure about that.

9

SCROLL IX

NONES OF FEBRUARY 651 AB URBE CONDITA

Lucius hadn't been lying. Equus rose before the sun to exercise while the rest of the tribunes rested on their pillows. He said nothing as he got ready, but he didn't work to keep himself silent either. I was restless anyhow, so I strapped on my armor and threw a cape over my shoulders and exited into the cold morning air.

The Gallic sun was shining orange as it rose in the east, each blade of grass in our camp sparkling with the crystal white frost of the night prior.

"Morning, Equus." I saluted as I walked by, slapping a fist to my chest and extending it forward. We weren't required to salute our equals, but most of us did, out of respect.

"Care to join me on a run?" He stretched to touch his toes.

"I'm barely past crawling. I'm exhausted. Perhaps tomorrow." He smiled at my response, saluted again, and began his run.

I followed the dirt path past the sleeping tent of our mules to the praetorium that lay within the little city our army had constructed.

I entered to find Marius, awake and alert, at his desk. I had heard rumor that Marius prided himself on being the earliest riser in the camp, but I was still surprised. From the look of him, he had shaved, bathed, and already completed a stack of paperwork.

Sulla, Marius's second-in-command, reclined on a couch across the room from him, and appeared far less alert.

"Good morning, Tribune."

"Sir," I said, saluting, "good morning."

"How did you like your barracks? Meet any of the other tribunes?"

"A few of them, sir. Cinna minor, for one," I replied, following the gesture to approach his desk and take a seat.

"That's a good lad. He'll be a powerful figure in Rome one day," Marius said.

"Our consul is a prophet, didn't you know?" Sulla said, rubbing his temples.

"No, but he knows character when he sees it. Otherwise I wouldn't have plucked you from the gutter, Sulla," Marius said. For a moment, I felt tension rise in the room, but both men smiled. "Don't mind him," Marius said to me. "He has no personality at all until he's had his fifth cup of wine."

"Give me a few hours. I'll get there." Sulla leaned back and closed his eyes.

"Have you news for us?" Marius asked, gesturing with his finger for a slave to bring me a warm glass of honey water.

"I do. I accept the mission," I said. Sulla suddenly shot up erect on the couch, and Marius's eyebrows rose to his receding hairline.

"You do?"

"I'll go, if it is how I can best serve Rome," I answered. If I had had more time to decide, perhaps I would have chosen not to go. Perhaps that was why Marius gave me one day, and one day only, to make my decision. I couldn't overthink it.

"I assure you that it is," Marius said, standing to his feet. I stood also, and shook his hand.

"Perhaps you do know character when you see it, Consul," Sulla said with a grin. I tried to shake his hand as well, but instead he pulled me closer and wrapped his arms around my shoulders. He was a strong man, stronger than he appeared. His fingernails were so clean and his hands so soft, you might have thought otherwise, but within the clothes of a sheep was the strength of a lion. And, perhaps, the cunning of a fox.

"You understand that there will be no record of this event? If you succeed, or fail, it makes no difference. You will not win any decoration or be praised by citizens in the streets." Marius seemed genuinely surprised that I had accepted.

"I understand this, Consul. That isn't my goal," I said.

"May I ask you what is your goal, Tribune?" Sulla said, accepting his first wine of the morning.

"To do my duty, sir." The only man's respect I was trying to earn was my own. I needed to prove I was no coward. That I was who Lucius said I was, who my brother believed I would be.

"A man cut from your cloth, Marius," Sulla said with a coy grin.

"Volsenio," Marius called for his massive Numidian slave, who arrived promptly, "take the tribune to the brig. Show him the man he is to interrogate."

I didn't much like the use of that word, but I assumed the prisoner had been groomed for the task.

"Yes, *dominus*."

"Do you know how I became Marius's slave?" Volsenio asked as he led me toward the camp prison.

"I do not. What happened?"

"I was a noble in the house of Jugurtha, Rome's enemy. He was my cousin. I had no aspirations for power, but by name alone I should have been strangled in the *carnifex*. But I went to the consul directly, and asked him to spare my life, and that of my wife and children." Volsenio's accent was thick, but his words were deliberate and his demeanor compelling. He nodded at the guards as we entered and led the way into the dark, damp prison. "I told him that I would serve him if he let my family live."

"And he did?"

"He did much more than that. He made them Roman citizens, paid for their passage to Rome, and arranged for tutors to give them a proper education."

"Jupiter's beard," I said. That was quite a shocking tale. It would explain why Volsenio was so devoted to his master.

"It is true what they say about the consul." Volsenio took a torch from the wall and helped lead me to the back of the building. "He is a great man. And I thank the gods that he has a man like you to serve him." He led the way further. "Here we are," he said, pointing to a door barred with iron.

"Does he let you see your family?" I asked.

"Whenever we're in Rome, yes. Marius demands that I write them often and visit when I can. But unfortunately we aren't in Rome very often. There are many battles to fight." Volsenio looked down. "But I won't leave Marius, not for the rest of my life. I hope that you won't either."

He met my gaze with all the dignity of a free man, and in a way, he was. He nodded as he handed me the iron key, and stepped off.

As I entered, I strained my eye to see the figure of the man in iron shackles before me. For a moment, I thought him dead, as I could hear nothing but the scurrying of mice and the drip of melting ice.

His eyes were closed, his head resting on his chest. His long hair and beard were matted with something thick and sticky, and

I could see unwashed blood on his face and chest. His shirt and trousers were covered in holes, as if moths had already gotten ahold of them.

"Roman?" he said, to my surprise, without looking up.

"I am. Your name?" I stepped in a bit farther but made sure to keep my distance until I was sure he was properly restrained. He was.

"Barrus." He sat up and laid his head against the wall.

"That's an odd name for a Gaul."

"Well, from what I gather, every Roman is named either Quintus, Gaius, Lucius, or Marcus. We Gauls have more freedom with what we call ourselves," he said, already irritated with me.

"That is true." I already found his honesty refreshing. "I meant no offense. My name is… Would you like to guess?"

"Quintus, Gaius, Lucius, or Marcus? Right?" he said with furrowed brows, finally meeting my eye.

"Quintus. You are correct." He smiled in victory. "I am a tribune of the Roman Republic. I was told that you can help me."

"You can help me too, Roman. I need bread and water, or my mind doesn't work right."

I shrugged. A reasonable request.

"Guard. Bring us some bread and water," I said, calling down the corridor. "Can we begin talking while we wait?" I asked.

He thought for a moment and then nodded. He was a prisoner, sure, but he hadn't been one for long. I wouldn't be able to get two words out of him if I tried to force his hand. No man can allow his pride to be damaged for too long, even one living among the rats in a Roman military prison. "Why don't you tell me about yourself?"

"And that will help you destroy the Cimbri?" he said, scoffing at me.

"I need to know the nature of your relation with the Cimbri, and how you can help me."

He exhaled and deliberated for a moment. "I'm a man of the

Tigurini tribe. An ally of the Cimbri. I served in their cavalry at Arausio."

"And this is where you were taken prisoner?" I asked, recollecting the proper words in Gallic.

"Yes. And you better not laugh either."

"I had no intentions of laughing."

"You are a fool, then. What kind of man gets captured in a battle where his army slaughters thousands of the enemy?" His face contorted with disgust.

"I'm sure it could have happened to any of you."

"An arrow caught my horse, and down it went. Landed on top of me leg, and here we are. Some fleeing Romans took the time to graciously free me before they scurried off. I'm a crippled prisoner now."

He stared at the dark earth beneath him and shook his head, reliving the memory in his head.

"I'm sorry for your lot."

"Sorry? Ha! I'm sorry for yours. It was all your men who died."

I took a moment to calm myself before speaking again. I didn't want to end deliberations before they began.

The guard arrived at the door with a cup of freezing water and some stale bread. The Gaul reached out for it, but the guard looked him in the eyes as he passed the cup and loaf to me. After the guard departed, I handed it to the prisoner. Now, perhaps, he would be more prepared to talk.

"If you still call yourself Tigurini, why are you willing to help me?" I asked in as pleasing a tone as I could muster.

He looked up at me, a mouthful of bread still wedged in his gums. He lunged forward, but the shackles restrained him.

"Because I hate the Cimbri more than any man. That I swear," he said, returning to his feast.

"But you were willing to fight with them?" I asked.

He stared at me in disbelief of my ignorance.

"I'm just a man. I herd cattle. What say do you think I have in the war meetings of our elders?"

"I understand. Why do you hate the Cimbri, then?"

His aggressive nature faded, and his shoulders slumped. He took another bite of bread before replying.

"Do not ask me that again, Roman."

"Fine. I won't ask you again. Your willingness to help me is all that truly matters," I said. My eye now adjusted to the darkness of the room, I spotted a wooden stool and sat on it across from him.

"I'll help you. Oh, I'll help you," he said.

"What do I need to do?" I leaned in closer.

"You'll have to dress like a Gaul, talk like a Gaul, act like a Gaul. Following? You'll have to be one of us. You'll have to go to the Tigurini camp, join our army, and meet with the Cimbri. From there you can collect your information."

"Can I not go directly to the Cimbri?"

He laughed. "No. By the gods, no. You're half their height and a third of their weight. They'd pick you out as an imposter from a league away."

He washed down some of the stale bread with a huge gulp of water.

"Can you teach me their language?"

He shook his head. "It would take a few dozen years and a team of experts to explain their mongrel tongue. I spent six months in their camp and can still barely understand it."

"So, I must infiltrate the Tigurini. And they'll take me to the Cimbri?"

He nodded. "They'll take you to them. Don't take any womenfolk or valuables with you. As soon as you enter their camp, it belongs to the Cimbri." His jaw flexed as if he were tasting something putrid. I did not think it was the bread.

WE DELIBERATED FOR SOME TIME. He explained to me the ways of the Tigurini, and what I would need to know to blend in with them, and how I should conduct myself. As with many barbaric languages, there were many different dialects, so he helped refine my Gallic vocabulary and instructed me on the words I should and should not use. It was a productive meeting, but I'll admit my head was pounding by the time we concluded. The more I learned about my mission, the more I realized how foolhardy it really was.

I wasn't a coward after all. Or perhaps I was just stupid.

10

SCROLL X

FOUR DAYS BEFORE THE IDES OF FEBRUARY 651 AB URBE CONDITA

Life as a tribune was nothing if not repetitive. The ten days following my first meeting with the prisoner were followed by the same procedure. The other tribunes and I rose before the buccina's call and convened at Marius's praetorium for our daily orders. Marius told us what he wanted our men drilled on and Sulla informed us of that day's watchwords, making it clear that anyone who left the gates would be expected to deliver them upon reentry or there would be consequences.

We then disseminated and delivered the orders to the centurions under our command. Afterward, I would depart for the prisoner's cell and submit myself to more of his scrutiny about the way I phrased certain things, or the manner in which I carried myself.

What made the fourth day from the ides unique was that I was ordered to reconvene with Marius at the tribunal by the end of second watch.

From a distance, I could hear the snap of a whip. As I turned off the *via principalis* to the tribunal, I saw a shirtless soldier tied to a post, blood already seeping over his trousers and purple welts stretching across his back.

Marius was standing a few feet in front of him, his chin in his hand, shaking his head sardonically.

"What did he do?" I asked as I approached his side.

"He was leading his men on a road march and allowed some of them to steal a local's chickens," Marius said without looking away.

"How sinister," I said with a grin, but I quickly retired it when Marius didn't return the gesture.

"I have no intention of making enemies of our friends or friends of our enemies. So this won't happen again, will it, Centurion Opimius?" Marius said, addressing the soldier.

"No, General," the centurion replied with labored breaths. The whip cracked again and he grimaced.

It seemed a bit foolish to worry about a few chickens when we were waging a war in which thousands of lives hung in the balance, but Marius was nothing if not a man of discipline.

Marius took a step forward to pat the centurion's face, as if to say there would be no more problems when the punishment had concluded. Then he stepped away and bade me to follow him.

"How many meetings have you had with our prisoner?" he asked.

"Once a day since the first, maybe around ten?"

"And how are they going?" He clasped his hands behind his back as he walked, and nodded at the mules we passed by.

"I'm learning a great deal, General. I have a good grasp of the Gallic language as a whole, but the Tigurini have formalities all their own. He's helped—" Marius raised a hand to cut me off.

"I've had several officers come to me lately and say 'why is that Tribune Sertorius of yours so morose?'"

"Is that so?" I asked, a bit stunned.

"It is. I can't recall how many times, actually."

"And what did you tell them?" I asked. I was hoping he would have replied something to the effect of, "because his brother and all of his friends died," but I didn't dare say it.

"I told them it's just your way." Marius shrugged. "But I think we both know that isn't true." He shaded his eyes with the back of his hand and looked deeply into mine. "I'm afraid it will affect morale, Tribune."

I exhaled and nodded. "I'll work on it, General. I didn't realize I was being perceived that way."

"I want you to go talk to Martha."

"Who?" He spoke as if I should already know, but I couldn't place the name.

"My prophetess," he said with a grin, knowing that there were already several camp jokes about her. I recalled hearing of her now.

"You want me to speak with her?"

"I think she'll be able to be of some value to you. She has a tent near the sacrificial altars. Go and see her."

I scratched at some flesh beneath the crest of my helm.

"I haven't spent much time communing with the gods in some time. Is that a suggestion or an order?"

He tilted his head and placed a hand on my shoulder. "I never make suggestions, Tribune."

I took my time getting there, sulking over being forced to talk to the witch Marius had found sometime during his campaign in Africa. I passed by the priests and the sacrificial altars, as well as the frightened or homesick mules who were praying there.

It was easy to differentiate the tent of Marius's priestess from the rest. It was black rather than maroon, and the curtain barring the entrance was made of beads and tiny seashells.

I hesitated at the threshold, hoping that I would hear her speaking with someone else and have an excuse to leave.

"Come, then, warrior. Don't be shy," a raspy voice came from inside.

I closed my eye and shook my head, but I did as she asked and entered.

Stepping in, I was met with the overwhelming and distinct aroma of incense and burning hemp, a smog wafting past me to the exit. There were two candelabras in the corner containing fire-red coals and whatever Numidian spices she had brought with her.

"Come closer." She waved me forward.

Once the smog had cleared, I made her out on the other end of the tent reclining on a dozen pillows.

She looked up at me and tilted her head back. Martha's skin was the color of aged papyrus, and she had dark eyes that shinned golden in the light of her incense. She gestured with a finger for me to step forward, the nails so long that they curled back and pointed to her. Her eyelashes were even longer, and the black that lined her eyelids was so dark and complete that she looked as wild as a Numidian lion.

"I'm nearly blind now, I need you closer." Her skin had been baked for decades in the African sun, and it was wrinkled at the forehead and atop her high cheekbones. Her lips were slim and pursed but colored purple, making them stand out from the rest of her face. "I need to touch you."

I was relieved that she was blind, as I was afraid I might have offended her by the look in my eye. At length, I unbuckled my helm and sat it by my feet. I stepped forward and stretched out my hand to meet hers.

The moment she touched it, she recoiled. The breath seemed to catch in her lungs.

"Such sadness," she said, her voice hoarse and harsh, but not unsympathetic.

When she had at last collected herself, she took hold of my palms again. "Such pain. Tell me, why have you come?" She analyzed my face with those sparkling eyes, which never seemed to settle on one particular place.

"General Marius ordered me," I said. I hadn't realized until I spoke just how uncomfortable I was, even more than I had anticipated. I was used to the family gods and the altars at which my mother and I had once greeted each morning, but foreigners and their odd practices unnerved me.

"Ah," she said, "compelled or not, I have much to tell you." She rolled my hands over in her own and patted them. "There will be a child, I think. Perhaps greater than his father."

I thought of Arrea for a moment before remembering that she was barren. And the thought of having a child with Volesa seemed as impossible as Arrea conceiving. It surprised me just how long it took me to remember Gavius, and that I already had a son by law.

"Has he already been born?"

She craned her head as if lending an ear to the gods.

"And perhaps even greater than you. There is a wife too. One you'll love until the day your body is interred."

I stopped believing the magician's tricks as soon as she said that.

"I am married, but not for love. I love another." Even though I'd volunteered the information, I didn't know why.

"The next time you look upon your wife, you will love her more dearly than the fire of Neith's sun. And you will love only her."

I balked and shook my head. I considered how angry Marius might become if I walked away now.

"May I touch your face?" she asked. I didn't reply but leaned in until she could do so.

She ran her bone-thin fingers over every contour, lingering over every bump and crease. At last she made it to my eye patch.

I recoiled immediately when she touched it, which didn't seem to bother her. She kept her hand poised midair until I leaned back in.

Much to my dislike, she removed the eye patch and ran her fingers over the scarred tissue beneath.

"Does it hurt?" she asked.

"Not anymore," I said, my tone fringing on anger.

"Yes, but that cloth covers more than just a scar, doesn't it?"

I didn't reply. She closed her eyes, and underneath the lids, I could see that they rolled back in her head. Something about this made my anger dissipate and my breath quicken.

"Have you begun to see more, now that you've lost part of your vision?" she asked, her fingers still fixed there on the tissue of my eye socket.

"Yes," I said in a weak voice, although I didn't know why.

"Are you afraid?"

"Yes," I said, and again I didn't know why. I wasn't afraid of her, but I didn't think that's what she meant.

"But of what? You're afraid of many things."

"Afraid of some things," I corrected.

"You cannot truly know a man until you know what he is most afraid of. For this alone reveals the quality of his heart and the contents of his dreams." She removed her hand from my face, sitting up erect for the first time. The burning incense shimmered in her eyes, and for the first time, I wondered if she truly could commune with the gods.

She took hold of my hands again.

"You aren't afraid of being forgotten."

"No," I replied.

"You know that you won't be. You played the simple man for a time but have since discovered that you're destined for greater things."

"I liked being a simple man," I said.

She let out a raspy laugh then, something between the giggle of a girl and the chortle of a dying man.

"You liked it, but you know it's not what the gods created you for."

I did not reply.

Her fingers fixated on my calluses then.

"You were a shepherd once…no…a horseman!" she said with a tilt of the head, her thin eyebrows raised. I felt compromised, as if this prophetess truly did know more than I was comfortable with. "You once trained horses, but you'll soon train men. And not just soldiers for battle but the hearts and minds of your countrymen. No, you will not be forgotten."

Her eyes shut again, and seemed to completely disappear beneath those wrinkled lids.

"No," she said as if she had discovered something fascinating, "you're afraid of being remembered. But remembered poorly. By your men, your mother, friends, lover...your fellow Romans."

"Of course I want to be remembered as a good man. All do, or should," I replied.

"You're living for your epitaph. You're a man already dead, at least in your own mind. You must live in the present, warrior. In this world, not the next. Each day you do not, you miss an opportunity to write your legacy."

My heart beat quicker still, and I wondered what she meant. I don't think she was referring to my memoir.

"Legacies aren't written on scrolls or iron tablets, but in the hearts and memories of men. Every day you waste an opportunity to speak into the lives of the men you serve with, your legacy wanes away."

I started to reply, but she opened her eyes again, and this time with a piercing glare.

"For that is why you are here, is it not? For your men? For those who have already died beside you, and for those who may yet still die?"

"Some men think I'm a coward for surviving a great battle. Some in my own family feel the same," I blurted out without thinking. I was under her spell.

"How can you be a coward, when you have given the greater sacrifice? They sacrificed but a moment and now will commune with their loves ones in a hall of heroes. But you linger on, losing sleep and the ability to eat, to reconcile with your conscience."

"It isn't the same. Not in my mind, or in anyone else's."

She ignored me and continued. "The great general himself once struggled to sleep at night."

"He told you this?" I said, straining to imagine Marius saying those words to a prophetess.

"No." She looked away. "But he didn't have to. The great general no longer kills with the sword but with the wave of a hand and the point of a finger. So now he doesn't sleep at all. And sometime, warrior, the same may be asked of you."

She looked at me again, and for the first time, her eyes fixed into mine, searching deeply. I was afraid of what she found.

"I would rather train horses," I said with a gulp.

A frown creased her purple lips.

"And the dead would rather be alive, but it isn't the right of a man to determine his sacrifices. They did not choose, and neither do you."

I was transfixed, unable to look away from those deep pools of her eyes, when suddenly she struck my forehead with her palm. And then again, harder.

When I collected myself, stricken and perplexed, her thin brows were burrowed and her cracked lips were formed in a menacing snarl.

"So do what the gods command! Be the man you must be!" She released my hand, and only then did I realize how intense her grip had become.

She stood and tossed more incense on the fire, which was followed by a puff of smoke and fresh crackling.

"Go, I must rest," she said.

I stood and picked up my helmet as Martha sank back into her pillows, a hand over her eyes.

"YOU LOOK STRICKEN, FRIEND," Lucius said as I entered our quarters. "Have you seen a Gorgon?"

"Something much more frightening, in my estimation," I replied, sitting on the chest at the foot of my bed.

"There's no blood in your face. What is it, then?" he asked.

I returned the most serious look I could muster.

"A woman who could see right through me." Lucius erupted with laughter before I finished speaking.

"Now don't make me write a letter to Arrea, *amicus*!"

"No, no, it was Marius's prophetess. That Numidian woman we hear so many whispers about." I unbuckled my helm and scratched at my chin. "I don't know if she's sent from Mount Olympus or Hades, but she seems to know all about me."

"I can answer that one for you: she's from Africa! All sorts of conjurers and magicians down there. And you always called me the superstitious one!" He plopped down on my bed.

"Damn it, Lucius, what have I told you about sitting on my bed? You're covered in mud!" I felt very juvenile for a moment, but old friends have a habit of bringing that sort of thing out of you. In response to my complaining, he messed up the blankets and ruffled the pillow, forcing me to pick it up and hit him with it. We laughed for a moment, ignoring the confused and slightly embarrassed glances of the other tribunes in the tent.

Then I remembered all that Martha had said.

"Lucius," I said, interrupting our playtime, "have I been an infernal grump since we arrived here?"

His brows burrowed as he pulled his own trunk nearer and took a seat.

"What do you mean?"

"Marius says I'm demoralizing the men," I said, ignoring the fact that the ears of the other tribunes were perking up.

Lucius exhaled. "He's just worried about you, as I am."

"I'm certain the consul is worried about many things, but I doubt that my well-being is one of them," I said. Lucius didn't reply. If he had nothing positive to say, he'd rather not speak; it was just his way. But his silence told me everything I needed to know.

"Come on, then." I stood and fastened my helmet.

"Where to?" Lucius looked up with wide eyes, as if I were talking about deserting.

"To spar."

"To spar?"

"That prisoner says I need to know how to fight single-handedly, and all I know is unit tactics. So…let's spar." It took him a moment, but eventually a grin split across his lips.

"You don't have to ask twice to get me to beat up on you a bit." He grabbed his helmet and ensured his lorica was tight. As we exited, the grin vanished from his face. "What about your leg?"

"I don't think that will stop the Cimbri, do you, *amicus*?" I said with a grin. "I'm fine. You're not getting scared, are you?"

"I'll get the wooden swords, then."

We gathered a few practice gladii and shields and met in the road between the praetorium and our quarters.

"Here?" I asked as I looked around.

"I don't see any chariots racing through, do you?" he said, steadying himself behind his shield.

"As you wish."

Some of the mules who were just finishing up with their second watch gathered around.

"Aye, what's going on 'ere?" one shouted.

"I've got six denarii on Tribune Hirtuleius!"

"I'll bet a skin of wine on Tribune One Eye!" said another, laughing.

"We never had quite an audience growing up, did we, brother?" I asked as we began to circle one another.

He lunged forward but then stepped back as I approached. We continued to wheel about.

"Remember how I used to whip you when we played with sticks out in your grandfather's pastures?" I said, noticing more and more mules gather to watch us.

"I believe I was a bit smaller than you then."

"I think I still have a few inches on—" Before I finished speaking, he swung high. I deflected it with my shield at the last possible moment. I didn't remember swordplay moving so quickly with two eyes.

He already had the advantage. I was on the defensive and felt unable to attack. My sword arm was paralyzed as I fixed my one eye on the movements of his feet.

He lunged forward, but this time planted his feet and pivoted to the side. He struck a decisive blow to my shoulder with the tip of the wooden gladius.

"Come on, brother, you can do better than that," he said, giving me enough time to reposition myself.

He came again, this time from my blind side. I shifted my shield in time to deflect the initial blow, but he recoiled quickly and cut at my ankle.

"Anyone could do better than this," he said with a smirk, looking away for only a moment to nod triumphantly at the spectators.

I was frustrated and felt my hands start to tremble. I wanted to drop the weapon and tackle him like we did when we were boys, but I denied the impulse.

"You've been practicing," I said, forcing a smile.

"I've waited a long time to get my revenge."

He shuffled forward now, swinging savagely from left to right. As I followed the movement of the wooden tip, trying to match it with my shield, Lucius brought the crest of his own toward my nose, causing the light of my eye to vanish for a moment.

I stepped back with a grunt and immediately felt the iron taste of blood on my lips.

"Ready to end it for the day?"

"I had no idea you were such a showman, Lucius," I said, but I repositioned myself to let him know I wasn't done.

As the blood settled on my tongue, the prophetess's rolling eyes returned to my mind. The chatter of the soldiers circling us faded away, as did the stinging of my nose. The focus of my eye seemed to fade a bit, but the sound of Lucius's sandals in the dirt became crisp. I heard the jingling of his chain-mail lorica.

This time when he attacked from my blindside, I met the wooden blade with a bash of the shield, and then shoved my own into his rib cage.

He stumbled back and shot me a look of surprise.

"That might leave a bruise," he said with a cough.

I puffed out my bleeding nose and smiled at him.

He approached more carefully now. This time, I approached him as well. I swung, he deflected. But I kneed him in the thigh while he was off-balance, sending him to a knee. Before he could readjust, I placed the tip of my practice sword against his neck.

He looked up and we both cackled.

"Well, who wins, then?" one of the mules asked anyone listening.

"The one with the sword to the other's neck, half brain!" shouted another.

"The other's bleeding, that's got to count for something."

I shoved the wooden tip of the sword into the dirt and offered Lucius a hand.

"You just intimidated me with that one-eyed and mean scowl. It's not quite fair, you know?" Lucius smiled. "I'm a much more pleasing target."

Before I could debate Lucius's boasting, a cry sounded from across the camp. It echoed off the walls and in our helms. It took a moment for us to determine where it originated from.

As it continued, it became clear that the wailing belonged to our general. Marius's voice was unmistakable.

We dropped our sparing gear and sprinted though the crowd of soldiers.

The frozen mud had been converted into liquid by the efforts of marching soldiers, and it splashed along our feet as we ran.

Lucius and I arrived along with several other officers and

mules, to see Marius down on a knee with a hand over his face. Sulla was trying to help him to his feet.

"I will kill them all! I swear by Jupiter, Mars, and all the gods...*I will kill them all*!" he shouted, revealing a face swollen with anger, veins bursting on his forehead.

"Come, now," Sulla said.

"No!" Marius pulled away from Sulla's grip and stumbled a few steps. He approached the terrified orderly who had delivered the letter and grabbed him by the lorica before thrusting him to the dirt. He raised his fist to strike him, but Sulla quickly coiled his arm around Marius's to stop him.

At last he relented and looked around the camp, breathing heavily, his lips only beginning to quiver. Such a display was unbefitting of the general, and Sulla knew this. He tried to pull him in and lead him back inside the tent, but the righteous anger in Marius's eyes was not to be dimmed.

"When I am done with the Cimbri, I'll go back to Rome and kill them all!" Marius shouted, his voice now hoarse. Sulla knelt beside him and whispered quietly. I was barely able to hear him.

"Marius, perhaps we should return to the praetorium. We can grieve for him privately," he said. Marius rubbed a forearm over his lips rather forcefully and blinked rapidly.

My heart began to pound as I thought of the possibilities. I look at Lucius, whose brows were burrowed and his chest heaving. He shook his head at me as if to say he had no idea what that letter might have contained.

Marius finally stood and allowed Sulla to lead him away, his eyes still fixed on the scribblings before him.

"Back to your training, soldiers!" Sulla shouted over his shoulder. He met eyes with me and gestured for me to follow.

When I arrived at the praetorium behind the consul, he let his tears flow freely. In all my years, I had never seen a man appear so contrary to his nature. He laid his head down on his desk, pushing scrolls and provisioning documents aside.

"Have a look." Sulla pried the letter from Marius's grip and extended it to me.

"They killed…they killed my boy," Marius said and then moaned into the wood of his desk.

I read the words carefully, over and over, to ensure I had understood it correctly. Marius's son-in-law, Maximus, the former consul and close ally of Marius, was indeed dead. The letter contained no real information, and certainly no condolences. All it said was that the man was dead, and that he'd been struck by lightning.

"Tribune, go out there and tell no one else to enter. The two of you can stay, but this is no time for a social gathering," Sulla ordered. Lucius nodded and turned before he had finished reading the words.

"Maximus was in the prime of his health," I said, almost to myself.

"Struck by lightning. The ancient way of saying that he was murdered, and for just causes. No doubt they spread such lies about Romulus when they finally smothered him." Sulla exhaled. Marius was weeping more softly now.

"Why would they do this? Who would have anything to gain from Maximus's death?" I asked. It didn't seem real. I thought of Maximus and his infectious laughter, and how he had so bravely led us into battle. He had been a friend and a leader to me, and he still seemed very much alive. If there was ever an honorable man, Maximus was one of them. It seemed as though the gods had completely ignored justice, instead allowing cruel men to prosper.

"He was on trial for Arausio. As the evidence was being collected, the prosecution must have concluded that they could not win—that Caepio was the real culprit. If they dragged him through the courts and allowed him to testify before the people, it would have shamed Caepio—but more importantly, all of his family allies. They could not allow that to happen," Sulla said.

"So they killed my boy. To save face." Marius raised his head.

His cheeks were still damp from the tears, but they had dried in his eyes. Now all that remained was a quiet hatred.

"Who, then? The lawyers? The leading families? Caepio himself? Who? Who would have done this?" I asked.

Lucius entered again, eyes wide.

"What has happened?" he asked. Sulla handed him the letter.

"It does not matter who did it. I will make them all pay. They'll soon know that Gaius Marius is no man to be trifled with," the consul said.

"I wouldn't talk like that if I were you, Marius," Sulla said. "You might find a lawsuit of your own upon your return to Rome." Marius stood abruptly, allowing his chair to clatter to the ground behind him.

"You will call me 'Consul,'" he said, pointing a finger at Sulla.

"Apologies, Consul," Sulla said, defiantly meeting Marius's eyes. He waited until the general's anger dissipated. Marius picked up the chair and returned to his seat.

"Quintus Caepio will be the first to go," Marius said to himself. "Volsenio! Bring me pen and parchment," Marius barked.

Sulla threw up his hands in exasperation.

"I'll have his body rotting in the Tiber by the time we begin campaigning." Marius now lifted his eyes and looked directly at each of us. There would be no lawsuit. No one would ever know. "Out with you. All of you. Leave me be," he said as he began his scribbling. Sulla was the first to leave, and Lucius followed him. I lingered for a moment, searching for anything to say that might dissuade Marius from this mad pass. I could think of nothing.

I departed in time to grab Lucius by the arm. I nodded for him to follow me back to the tribunes' barracks.

"Did you hear what he was saying?" I said, doing all I could to tamper my fear and keep my voice quiet.

"I did." Lucius looked over his shoulder to ensure we were

alone. We were, save for Apollonius, who was tidying up my quarters.

"What are we supposed to do?" I pleaded.

"What can we do?" Lucius asked.

Apollonius stopped his sweeping and looked to see if we were in need of help, but inferred from our disposition that it was better to leave us alone.

"No, Apollonius, join us," I said, and patted the bed for him to sit down beside us.

"Lucius, he plans to assassinate a Roman citizen!" I said through gritted teeth. Apollonius's eyes spread with fear. "Tell no one what you've heard," I said, and Apollonius nodded, already knowing this.

"Just as they assassinated his son," Lucius said.

I shook my head, fury rising.

"That does not make it right. And we do not know who did it."

"There is nothing for us to do, Quintus," Lucius said.

"Caepio has a son and a wife, Lucius."

"After all that he did to me…after all he did to you, you want to do something to save him?" Lucius asked, perplexed.

I stood and paced for a moment.

The Caepiones had taken me into their home. Despite the corruption that they deliberately involved themselves in, and tried to embroil me in as well, they had taken me in. They'd eventually threatened my life and sent henchmen to attack Lucius and the consul elect, Maximus, whom he was protecting. I was just as aware of all this as Lucius, but they had taken me in none the less. I had dined on their bread and shared their wine. I had walked with Quintus Caepio's son, Marcus, to the forum, and listened to his wife, Junia, read poetry.

I did want to see their family's downfall. I wanted to see power in the hands of those who deserved it, like Marius, but I couldn't stand by and allow one of them to be butchered.

"After Arausio, even? He caused all those men…he caused

your brother to die," Lucius said, but I could see that he was beginning to waver.

"I'd like nothing more than to see him eaten by worms. But Quintus Caepio was a consul of Rome, not some ruffian to be eliminated in the night," I said, shaking my head.

"I have no knowledge of the man or the events that you speak of," Apollonius said quietly, carefully selecting each of his words as he placed a forefinger to his lips, "but the death of one more man will not bring any of them back."

"Perhaps you are right." Lucius exhaled. "Doesn't feel like justice for Maximus."

"Justice will be served, Lucius. The gods will serve justice."

For the first time, I saw doubt in Lucius' eyes. "Do you really still believe that?" he asked.

We all glanced at the entrance as several other tribunes entered, laughing among themselves.

"Do what you must," Lucius said before turning to leave. I never questioned whether he would be discreet. I knew that, although he adored and worshipped Marius, he was my friend. And that mattered more than anything.

"Bring me a scroll, Apollonius," I said.

I BEGAN TO WRITE A LETTER. I addressed it to the former consul, Quintus Caepio. I told him in plain words that he was going to be killed if he remained in Rome. That he would be killed in the night before he even made it to court for his pending trial. He would not be allowed to give his false testimony and restore his honor. He would die, and perhaps his family alongside him. I reminded him that I wished to see him dead, but that honor bade me to warn him. I told him that he must leave Rome immediately, and never return. If he chose his pride, if he chose to save face, he would certainly lose his life. I asked him, finally, to do this for his wife and son. Although he deserved this fate for the catastrophe at Arausio, they did not.

I sealed the letter with hot wax and the stamp of my father's signet ring. I might have been crucified if the letter was found, but I knew honor demanded it. Maybe I was just soft or stupid, or maybe I had some hope left, after all. It was becoming difficult to tell. Arausio had blurred the lines.

11

SCROLL XI

IDES OF FEBRUARY 651 AB URBE CONDITA

The worst part about being on campaign was when you ran out of friends to talk to, wine to drink, or tasks to attend to. The Cimbri were terrifying in their way, but nothing was more disturbing than silence.

Each day I continued to visit the prisoner for linguistic training, and I sparred with Lucius when I could. But inevitably there were times when everyone else was preoccupied with various tasks, and mine were completed.

I tried to make myself useful and busy in any way I could. I was tasked with overseeing the training of the new recruits in *the Seventh Legion*, and I found myself approaching the mules during their leisure and asking for a weapons check or gear inspection. As soon as everything was accounted for, I would be on my way, looking for something else with which I could bide my time. I had always resented officers doing this sort of useless assessing, but remaining still no longer felt natural.

Despite my best efforts, I couldn't stave off silence entirely. Going to bed was the worst. The visions that visited me in my sleep were excruciating enough, but the worst part was the tossing, turning, sweating. In those dark moments, I thought most often of Arrea. Did she miss me the way I missed her? Did she reach out to find me in bed beside her, as I searched for her? Did she long for my touch? Did she feel empty and listless and confused without hearing my voice?

I never knew the answers. Perhaps she had replaced me with a friendly neighbor in Nursia. She had every right to do so; after all, I had been married to another. But it was Arrea that I loved. Not my "wife," as the prophetess had incorrectly suggested.

Life in the Colors was fulfilling, most of the time. The camaraderie was deep and meaningful, more so than anything I've experienced in civilian life or politics. But the affection of a lover is different as well. Whether I was brave or cowardly, strong or weak, competent or foolish…regardless of my conduct or my performance, Arrea would still love me. Life was much colder without her, even without the winter winds of the north.

And the thought of her with another man sent me spiraling. The feeling crept up, swept around, and seeped into my head. My stomach swirled until I couldn't bear it any longer. I did all that I could to remove her from my mind.

And I was relieved when Arrea would leave my thoughts for a while, but my mind would generally drift to darker things in her absence. War. I thought of war and all that came with it.

When the silence crept in, and I tried to close my eye at night, I swear on the Black Stone, I could hear it. The pitiful screams of the wounded and the dying. The clash of iron that refused to stop no matter how much you begged, and begged, and begged. Not a moment to collect your thoughts, to recollect your training.

Then I could feel it, even as I lay underneath my linen sheets. The earth trembling, hundreds of thousands marching to claim my life, the very soil beneath my feet crying out against the injustice. I could feel the blood of a foe splattered across my face like an errant sneeze, feel the last breath leave the lungs of someone I had called a brother. My feet were tangled in a web of viscera belonging to the butchered soldiers beneath me.

I could taste the salt of tears and the snot that pours freely as you cry holding a friend in mutual grieving. The mist of blood that, once it touches the tongue, does not go away no matter how much you scrub, and wash, and clean.

I could smell the battlefield. Putrid trash mixed with rancid meat and a whore's perfume; that's what the dead smell like. Feces, blood, burned flesh, and decay. The stench is so powerful, it clings to every hair in your nostrils and doesn't go away entirely for weeks. Perhaps it still hasn't. I don't remember what the world smelled like before death.

Then I could see it, as clear as day before me, the battlefield stretched out for miles every time I closed my eye. I could see what I, myself, had wrought. The things that had previously belonged to the world, to the living, which I stole and destroyed. Analyzing the dead, it was as if every slain enemy were a man I personally killed, every fallen comrade a man I was responsible for.

And so I experienced that profound sense of guilt that only a soldier knows, each and every night when laid down and when I ran out of pointless chores to distract myself with.

Often times, I would get up in the middle of the night and dress myself, and move to the slave quarters, where I would wake Apollonius. One time in particular, on the ides of February, I believe, he shot up like a dozing mule on guard duty.

"Yes? What's wrong?" he asked, his eyes wide and shining with fear.

"Will you have a little wine with me?"

"Eh, what time is it?" He looked around with sleepy eyes, straining to see if the sun had peaked out of the darkness yet.

"Third hour. I can't sleep," I replied. The slaves around us shuffled in rebellion against the disruption, but Apollonius nodded dutifully and followed me.

I grabbed a jug of wine and a cup or two, and proceeded out into the freezing, still air.

Apollonius hadn't spent a day outside of Greece in the first fifty years of his life, and was unused to the cold. He had the snivels constantly.

"Here." I extended to him the warmest cloak I was issued. When he refused, as he always did, I insisted, "No, take it. I was raised in the cold. It's what suits me. And I need you at full strength." Eventually, he accepted, and, as always, he was much more cheerful once wrapped in something warm.

He followed me through the maze of tents where mules slept that I was far more accustomed to than the tribunes' quarters. We walked up the guard tower to the sentry post, where the mules posted there stirred to attention.

"At ease. How goes your shift?"

"Frightfully cold, sir. And we're awfully tired," one answered.

"Nothing stirring, and no problems, sir," the more senior of the two responded, shaking his head at the other for such a response.

"Go on to bed, then, soldiers," I said. They looked at me, and then back and forth to one another. Their eyes shined with excitement at the idea of gaining a bit of sleep, but they seemed reluctant, as if it were a test.

"Sir, we can't allow that. We must stay by our post."

"You just received an order from a military tribune of the Roman Republic," I said, and they scurried off, pausing only to salute. "Have a seat." I gestured to Apollonius.

He clutched the cloak around him and shivered as he sat. "Winter quarters wouldn't be so bad if it didn't have to be winter," he said with a smile. I nodded but didn't reply. "You seem troubled, Quintus." I did not hear him at first, pleased only that he called me by my name. I poured us both some wine and sat beside him.

"I am. And I cannot sleep."

"Perhaps you can tell me what's caused this insomnia?" he said, considering his words carefully.

"Let us speak in Greek," I said. Latin may have been my native tongue, but I preferred Greek regardless. The language flourishes in such a way that allows the speaker to illuminate himself more accurately. "I am troubled by many things, Apollonius of Athens."

"Such as?" He spoke more freely now.

"War. Being away from my home. Away from the woman I love. Remembering the men who have died in my care." I finished my cup and refilled it quickly.

"The only men who praise war are those who have never experienced it," he said.

"Those who have never heard the screams of the dying, smelled the rotting corpses, tasted the blood, heard the clash of iron, seen the limp and bloated bodies," I said, looking away from him.

"Yes," he said, no further words of wisdom at the ready.

I turned to him for the first time. "I do not know if I can do it anymore, Apollonius."

Then he spoke in a strange manner. "Praise be to the Lord, my rock, who trains my hands for war and my fingers for battle."

"Who said that? I've not heard him." I thought he spoke of a philosopher. My learned slave knew much more about the wise thinkers than I.

"It is from the Tanach, a Hebrew text. I've translated it many times," he said.

"Ah"—I nodded—"words about your one god, then?" I asked.

"Yes."

"And you think he will fight for me?" I finished my cup of wine.

Apollonius stood and placed a hand on my shoulder.

"You are a good man, Quintus. I believe that he will protect you. And I will pray that it be so."

"But I am not worried about dying," I replied.

"What do you fear, then?"

"It's hard to articulate. Especially in Greek," I said with a smile, which he mirrored.

We talked for several more hours, until the light crept up over the Gallic pines. I sent away each guard shift team that arrived. I drank so much wine I can't recall the remainder of the conversation. Drink was all that could calm my ambling mind at that time.

Apollonius comforted me with the words of philosophers and his Hebrew scriptures. I listened intently, but I wasn't then ready to accept them.

"I believe it's time for you to reconvene at the consul's tent, correct?" Apollonius asked as the sun had fully appeared and I had begun to sober up.

"You are right. A long day is ahead of me," I said with a hopeless chuckle. "I won't be requiring your services for the rest of the day, Apollonius. So go and make up for the sleep I have cost you," I said, patting him on the shoulder and handing him the empty jug of wine for him to return to the slave quarters.

"If you have need of me, please…wake me," he said.

"You've already rendered the only service I needed right now. Go on." I gestured toward the barracks.

As the next watch arrived, I stepped down from the tower and onto Marius's praetorium, more dehydrated and dilapidated now than tired.

The general was outside the tent when I arrived, shirtless and on the ground, exercising.

"Forty-one, forty-two," Equus counted beside him, still sweating from the push-ups he had recently completed. Each time the general seemed like he might have nothing left, he pushed out three or four more repetitions.

Once the number was too high to keep track of, Marius

bounced to his toes. He wiped the sweat from his head, appearing normal in every other way. Not many men his age could have thrived under such effort, but he did. He had been in pain since the death of Maximus, but he had refocused his mind on the task at hand.

"You wanted to see me, sir?" I asked, at attention.

"I did, but not like this. You look like you barely slept." Marius stepped within a few inches from my face and analyzed me.

"Barely, sir."

"You reek of wine."

"I drank my fill last night, but I'm sober and ready for orders now, Consul."

He deliberated a moment before responding. "We all have nights like that." He stepped away from me, to my relief. He grabbed a towel and dried his flesh. "I wanted to let you know what's coming." He waved for me to follow him into the praetorium.

"Thank you for your trust in me, sir," I said as he leaned against the desk.

"You need to know because, as soon as we attack, you'll need to leave quickly on your mission," he said, the defined muscles of his hairy chest still rising and falling from the exertion.

"Attack, sir?" I asked, still a bit groggy.

"Yes. That's right." He turned and gestured to a map on the desk behind him. "We're going to obliterate those Tectosage bastards. The annals of history will forget they ever existed," Marius said, lifting his head high. Now that he had sent out orders for Quintus Caepio to be killed, he was content. He wanted all our enemies in Gaul to feel his wrath.

"The Tectosages, sir?"

"The Tectosages. You reported that they were the insurgents in Massilia, correct?" he replied, irritated at my surprise.

"Yes, but they could have been rebels. We have no intelligence that the entire tribe is against us."

He shrugged. "I don't really care, to be honest. If those fools ended up making it to the Massilia courts, and poured honey in their ears, this will force the Massiliots' hand. They will either be for us, or against us. They've been an ally of Rome for generations, and it is their allegiance I'm most concerned about."

"Understood, sir," I replied. His logic was sound, but the thought of battle brought back all the nightmares I had tried in vain to forget.

"You will lead our left wing of cavalry. You and Tribune Hirtulius," he said, accepting some water from Volsenio.

"Lead the left?" I said, finally unable to hide my exasperation. I had been a lowly mule a few years before, and now the consul wanted me to lead an entire flank?

"The cavalry, yes. A few thousand head of horse, no more. Sulla will take the right. And we will slaughter them, no doubt," he said, taking his water gratefully, his heavy breathing finally slowing.

"Understood, sir."

"Dismissed." He saluted and turned before I could do the same. I departed, suddenly wishing I still had Apollonius to talk with.

12

SCROLL XII

FIVE DAYS BEFORE THE KALENDS OF MARCH 651 AB URBE CONDITA

When word arrived of our marching against them, the Tectosages sallied forth to meet us. They had no hope of victory that I could tell, as their Cimbri and Teutone allies were on the far side of the Alps, but we were there before them. They could not wait. And so they arrayed themselves atop a hill before their villages in the valley.

I led from the front of the left wing, Lucius alongside me.

"How is she doing?" Lucius gestured to the horse beneath me.

"Sura's much calmer than I am," I said, directing my gaze to the chanting enemy in the distance.

"We'll be fine. I've sacrificed twenty-one pigeons this morning."

"Is that the correct number?" I said, jesting. Lucius was always precise about such sacrificial measures.

"It is, according to the camp priests," he said, but he held out his left palm, which was wrapped in a cloth soaked with scarlet, "but I spent some of my own blood as an added measure."

The Tectosage war chief stood at the front of his forces, his back to us. I could not understand the Gallic that traveled over the bitter morning winds to greet us, but there was fire and venom in the chieftain's words. His warriors chanted a response each time he paused.

The centurions of the center blew their whistles, and our forces snapped to a halt. I wheeled Sura around to look at our horseman. There were 2,189 in number, if my records are correct. Thanks to Apollonius's diligent note-taking and record keeping, I'm certain they are.

"Who has fought in a battle before?" I asked. A few hands shot up. I strained my eye to count them. The number was few. "Let me ask a different way. How many of you have never seen battle before?"

They fidgeted, embarrassed, until a few brave horsemen raised their hands, followed by most of the rest.

Lucius and I exchanged a glance.

"That's alright. You have prepared for this moment. You must forget now all you have expected of warfare. You have only two tasks: to kill or maim the enemy in front of you, and to protect the man beside you. We require nothing more. And not a man among us shall die this day. Tribune Hirtuleius here has ensured that by the sacrifice of twenty-one pigeons."

The men chuckled nervously, as did Lucius. It was important to laugh before battle. It reminded a man who he really is. Centurion Scrofa once taught me that.

I forced a smile, but knowing what lay ahead, I couldn't bring myself to laugh with the rest.

"Our objective is very simple. When the Tectosages engage our cohorts in the center, and we are given our signal, we are to wheel about and flank them. They have no cavalry of their own to repel us, and their men will scatter like whipped dogs."

The chants of our enemy increased in volume, sounding far more like the howls of wolves than pups.

"When the order is given, halt your advance," Lucius added. We had been given express orders by General Marius to remain with the center, even if the enemy fled. The Tectosages would meet their demise, but not at the cost of Roman lives.

"Remember who you are, men." I turned again to face our enemy. I unsheathed my gladius and hoisted it into the air. As the command to march was given to the center once more, slow and deliberate now, encroaching the base of the hill with the Tectosages atop it, I directed our cavalry to follow me away from Marius, creating a larger gap between us and the center.

I leaned down closer to Sura, and placed my left hand on her mane. I eased her into a gallop, and our men followed.

The Tectosages, in a blood lust, charged down the hill to meet the Roman center. Our mules marched as silently as ghosts, the Tectosages howling as they crashed against our line like a strong current on jagged rocks.

"Steady, men," I shouted over the stampede, unsure if I could be heard. I said this to calm myself as much as them.

Yellow flags from the center rose and dropped in quick succession. This was our signal. Typically, general orders were given audibly and unit orders were given via the centurion's whistle, but Marius had ordered our line stretched as thin as possible. He knew they couldn't beat us man-to-man, and felt that the sooner they felt surrounded, the sooner they'd surrender.

I lifted my sword to the heavens, to Mars and all of my ancestors, and then dropped it toward the enemy.

"Now, men, now!" Lucius shouted, kicking his stallion to a full sprint.

The sharp winds whistled in our helms. This was my first time riding to meet an enemy on horseback. It was even more exhilarating, and terrifying, than I had previously imagined.

We careened toward them like a stone rolling down a hill,

picking up speed as we went. They shifted from a shapeless blob to defined men with facial features. When they spotted us, we were close enough to see the terror in their eyes.

I could feel Sura resisting beneath me, even as the velocity of her body carried her on.

"Come on, girl. Come on, girl!" I cried. She could not hear me, but she felt it in my heels and the hand on her mane, and obeyed.

We crashed into the enemy, our horses jumping over and onto them like a skipping stone on top of the water.

Limbs were splintered under the weight of our hooves. We cut savagely, left and right, to meet them, our swords knocking off their loose-fitting bronze helms and slicing their faces deep.

Our center gave the order to advance, and they pushed farther into the enemy, capitalizing on the panic and chaos we created in the Tectosage ranks.

Across the battlefield, I could see that Sulla was meeting the enemy with equal force, himself tall and visible atop his horse, a distinguished purple plume on his helm and a uniquely crafted black breastplate with silver etching.

My vision spiraled when I looked down at my enemy. My depth perception had been skewed since the moment I lost my eye, but in the heat of battle, I could hardly tell how close or far my opponent was. I swung violently regardless, and tried to look away when I could. The horse gave me a bit of distance that most warriors coveted, but I could still feel when my sword sliced through flesh.

Sura bucked and roared beneath me. Such an innocent beast. But I held fast to her, and even as men fell in piles beside and behind us, she did not turn and run.

The Tectosages were broken, their undisciplined lines faltering. The bravest among them charged into our center and were swallowed up. The rest scattered, stumbling up the hill, their eyes set on the feigned safety of their villages below.

"Halt men, halt!" I shouted, seeing the red flags waving from the center.

"Halt, damn it!" Lucius shouted with me, some of our men not hearing me over the chaos. That, or their first taste of blood had suited them. They wouldn't experience the residual effects until afterward.

Shouts carried out from our center, and the red flags continued to wave furiously. I looked back and forth between Marius's guard and Lucius, trying to interpret what was wrong. It was then that I noticed that Sulla was leading his men forward.

In hot pursuit of the fleeing enemy, they rolled them up like a carpet, slicing through their backs and trampling over them like tilled earth.

I still believe I could hear Marius himself over the tumult, shouting for Sulla to obey his orders and return to line.

If that were so, Marius's second-in-command did not heed the order. He advanced with reckless abandon, into the villages, sacking the baggage carts. His men chopped down any in their path, and soon the smoke of fires rose from the huts.

Marius at last had no other option. He gave the order to advance, and we moved among them. We progressed at a brisk pace, but by the time we had arrived, Sulla's work had been completed. The Tectosages were annihilated and Sulla's men were already enjoying the spoils.

MARIUS WAS INFURIATED with Sulla's insubordination. Sulla had been victorious, hailed as a hero by his own men. Marius had little room to criticize him, so he did so only with irritated glances and grunts when Sulla spoke.

The battle had been an overwhelming success. Our enemy had been punished for their transgressions, and the alliance of the Massiliots had been solidified by their lack of support for the vanquished. Few Romans fell that day, and only three from our left flank. I proceeded to tell Lucius that we must sacrifice twenty-two pigeons, the next time. He didn't find this humorous, but neither did I.

MOST OF THE TIME, it took longer to reconvene after a battle than the fighting itself. We had to form up, which was difficult after a battle when everyone's out of breath and patting themselves to make sure they aren't bleeding. Then the centurions must take their counts. The enemy survivors must be secured and transported.

But when we arrived back in camp, and were freed for the evening, even the most morose soldiers become quite conversational.

Equus found Lucius and I, or perhaps stumbled upon us, as his eyes were wild and darting all about.

"Are you well, comrade?" Lucius said with a chuckle.

"Wow… That was… My father would…" He pivoted and emptied his stomach onto the dirt. He turned to us again, holding up a finger, seemingly obvious to the string of bile that hung from his lips. "Don't let that sully your image of me. I'm quite…euphoric."

"That sensation in your gut will dissipate once you fill it with wine. Come on, then." Lucius threw an arm around Equus's neck and led him on.

As was custom, Marius hosted a meal for the officers who had helped accomplish the victory that day. Marius kept a rather boorish cook, but we were all thankful for a nice meal, and for the fact that we were all still alive to partake of it.

The general himself sat at the head of the table. He was mostly silent as the rest of the officers swapped stories, laughing and embellishing as they did so. Sulla was clearly the most jovial among us all, and Marius watched him with suspicion the entire evening.

As Volsenio and the rest of Marius's slaves collected our dishes, the wine began to flow more freely. We were celebrating, after all. Marius was ahead of all of us at that point. He had finished his first few cups before the meals were even prepared. And just as his cook was uncouth, whoever prepared his wine had made it quite strong.

Marius's eyes were glossed over and his head was slightly swaying by the time our meal was concluded.

"Alright," Marius's gruff voice boomed. It caught our attention because he had spoken so little that night. "I believe my daughter's mourning for Maximus has concluded," he said. All of us cringed and looked down at the table when Maximus's name was mentioned. Maximus's death had only been declared a month prior, and so we wondered what Marius was getting at. "She will be needing a new husband."

His eyes were fixed on Sulla as he spoke, who held his cup of wine between his hands and swirled it around.

"Sulla, I would like you to marry my daughter," Marius said. It seemed more like a command than an offer, but I assumed it was the wine. Perhaps it was more of a test than either one.

Sulla continued to stare down for some time, but he finally looked up and clicked his tongue.

"My apologies, Consul. But I am already engaged to be married to another," he said. Everyone at the table shifted uncomfortably, except for Sulla himself.

"And you were not going to tell me?" Marius said, his words slightly slurred from the wine.

Sulla shrugged. "I'm focused on the war right now, Marius. I hadn't even thought of it." He acted as if he had simply forgotten to update Marius on a chariot race or a new food he had tried in the forum.

"Well, you should break off the engagement." Marius placed his elbows on the table with force, leaning in toward his second-in-command.

Sulla hesitated for a moment. "I will not."

The tension in the room was rising to choke us. We tried not even to breath, to blink.

All that was heard was the heavy breathing from Marius's nostrils.

"I am the consul of Rome."

"And I have the utmost respect for you and your position."

"I drew you from the gutter and built your career! I saved your milk-drinking life more than a few times in Numidia too." Marius voice rose and carried through the praetorium.

"And I have tried to honor that, Marius. And you know I do not drink milk," Sulla said, meeting the general's eyes. "I am sorry. But I will not call off the engagement."

"And who is this trollop you are to marry, that you should shun my daughter?" Marius asked, his chest heaving with poorly restrained anger. Sulla did not answer but returned his attention again to his cup of wine. "Tell me, Sulla, is it I or my daughter who do not meet your standards?"

"Marius, be reasonable!" Sulla finally shouted. "I need a patrician marriage to further my career. It's not personal. It's pragmatic." He lowered his voice as he spoke. Everyone knew this was the one thing Marius did not want to hear. His plebeian origins were both a source of pride and sore embarrassment to him. To be rejected by his protégé for it was the ultimate betrayal.

"A patrician? Your…career?" Marius's voice was suddenly light, in total disbelief. He could hardly catch his breath. In a flash, he pounced to his feet and sent his chair clattering to the ground. He paced out of the praetorium.

We all remained as still as statues, unsure of what to do. Sulla alone stirred, finishing his wine and asking for another cup.

Finally, Sulla smiled, and looked around the table at each of us.

"Have you seen how hairy his backside is? I can only imagine what his daughter feels like, if she takes after him."

Fortunately, Marius wasn't around to hear him.

13

SCROLL XIII

KALENDS OF MARCH 651 AB URBE CONDITA

I tried to return my attention to training the men. Now that they had tasted battle for the first time, they approached weapon's drills quite differently. As each of them took their turns approaching the dummies, there was something different in their eyes, as if they now saw a long-haired Gaul before them instead of a lifeless wooden post.

"Maintain your balance, Galbus," I said to one of the nearby legionaries as I passed in between the training lanes.

"Left high. Right low. Right high," the first spear centurion of the Seventh Legion called out. His name was Gnaeus Herennius and he was the kind of leader I had confidence in rearing a good crop of soldiers. He was a grizzled old veteran, having seen a dozen campaigns or more in his time.

In many ways, he reminded me of Scrofa in how he approached the discipline of the men under him, although they looked nothing alike. Herennius was rotund but solid as a rock, while Scrofa had been lean and agile. Scrofa had always ensured his face was clean shaven and his hair properly maintained—

before his capture, at least. Herennius, on the other hand, always maintained the gray shadow of a growing beard across his face, but I assumed this was simply because of the swiftness of its growth rather than a lack of tending to it.

"They look good, Centurion," I said. The mules seemed to increase their speed and accuracy as they heard the compliment.

"They've tasted blood now, Tribune. And you're ready for more, aren't you, boys?" he asked.

The men shouted in response and stabbed harder at the posts.

"Left low."

The men continued with fresh vigor for a moment until they came to a halt. All of their eyes rose and looked behind me.

"Oh, continue, men. Don't mind me. Just inspecting." In a camp of rough accents and urban dialects, the voice of Lucius Cornelius Sulla was unmistakable, each word polished like an orator's.

I turned and nodded to him but hoped he wouldn't engage in conversation. I felt him approaching. Chills crawled down my arms as I heard the crunch of his sandals behind me.

"It's a totally different legion than the one we first joined, isn't it?" he asked, jovial and smiling like we were old pals.

"It is," I said, although he didn't join the same legion as I did either. How could his experience resemble mine when he never wore anything but an officer's crest?

"Marius has his faults, but these reforms were quite remarkable. I'm inclined to believe his associate Publius Rutilius Rufus has more to do with it than Marius's pundits like to admit; regardless, I'll give the man his due." I remained silent, eyes fixed on the training soldiers, hoping that if I didn't engage, he might saunter on. "He has certainly been sour lately, hasn't he? Like a spoiled apple."

"He's under enormous pressure," I said.

He stepped into my line of view so that I was forced to meet his gaze. His bronze skin glistened with sweat, but his blue eyes shone brighter. His silklike skin and the slightness of his waist made him appear effeminate, but his chest and arms were built like a Greek wrestler's. His jaw was thick and imposing too, so no one would ever call him feminine to his face.

"Marius throws so many baseless accusations at me, it's difficult to keep count," Sulla said.

"Like what?" I said. I tried to keep my face passive, but I balked at this. I had begun to adore Marius the way Lucius did, even though I remained cognizant of his faults.

"Well, for one, he keeps shouting about rescuing me from the gutter." He brought a hand to his face and waved it to cool himself off. The smell of perfume on his freshly pressed tunic clung in my nostrils. I didn't say anything. "I was, for certain, born in the gutter. When your daddy is the most hated drunk in the Suburra, that tends to be the case. But by the time Marius was introduced to me, I was rich as Croesus. My father's second wife left me a fortune when she died, and my first lover did as well."

"That was fortunate." I stepped away, but he followed alongside me, matching my stride.

"I've so much money, I hardly know what to do with it. I could also give you a loan if you'd like?" His eyes locked on mine, and I suddenly felt the impulse to step farther away from him.

"I appreciate the offer, Legate, but that won't be necessary," I said. He shrugged, unconcerned.

He placed a hand on my arm and led me a few paces from the trainees. When we stopped, he turned and smiled. The grin was friendly and unassuming, reminding me why Sulla was so well liked, by everyone from the lowliest slave to the highest-ranking officers, with the potential exception of Marius, at least at the current moment.

"Are you afraid of leaving for your mission?"

I was too taken aback to respond for a moment.

"No. No, I don't think so. I just want to ensure I have all the information I'll need before I depart."

He nodded but continued to look into my eye to see if I was being honest.

"I wouldn't blame you if you were afraid. It is quite the thing you're doing."

"I thought I was going to die at Arausio. That seems to make death a little bit less imposing." I found some fresh resolve and met his eyes. I didn't know if I really believed this, but I found it easy to say.

"Gods bless you. I feel the same. I've never encountered death, not closely, but I do not fear death. The gods speak to me. They tell me I'll be safe."

"Oh?" I tried to keep my eyebrow from raising and my lips from smirking.

"Yes, they do." He looked down for the first time, and for a moment he seemed embarrassed. "Marius keeps the Harpy priestess around to get a glimpse of what it's like to commune with the gods. But I really talk to them. Apollo guides everything I do. I don't expect anyone to understand that, though."

"The next time you talk to him, put in a good word for me. Perhaps he can help me return safely," I said. I meant it seriously, but I'm afraid anything I said in reply to a man who claimed to speak with the gods was going to sound insulting.

Regardless, he leaned his head back and laughter bellowed out. He slapped me on the back rather forcefully.

"Very good, Tribune," he said after he composed himself. "I'll ask him for guidance. Mostly he tells me about the future, though."

"Am I in it?"

He shrugged, a charming smile still stretched across his face. "I don't know yet, young tribune, but I hope. He tells me that I'll one day be the first man in Rome." Every inking of humor disappeared from his face. "He tells me I'll be the greatest Roman to have ever lived. That I'll usher in a new era, one that harkens back to Rome's finest hour. Strength and prosperity."

I concluded several things in that moment. It suddenly made sense why he had this peculiar look in his eye, as if Rome, the war, the whole world, were absurd, and he was somehow above it all. As if everything was a game or a play he was simply witnessing. If he believed he already knew the ending, how could he feel otherwise?

"Apollo never promised me I would walk into greatness, though. The only companions I have in Rome now are courtesans, actors, and eunuch playwrights. I'll need more than political allies and a patrician wife, too, if I am to be Rome's finest. I'll need a man of action such as yourself. I hope I'll be able to call on you for support when the time comes."

My chest tightened under the breastplate as my heart began to race. I felt like Marius was watching and that I'd soon be greeted with the same suspicion he now offered Sulla.

The words caught in my mouth for a moment, but he allowed the silence to persist until I spoke.

"I just want to make it back alive."

"Of course you do." He patted me on the back again, and smiled, seemingly oblivious to the fact that I wasn't matching the expression. "I'll let you return to your duties, Tribune."

He turned to leave, taking each step slowly and deliberately, in no rush to go anywhere. I took a moment to compose myself before returning to the mules.

"Alright, men, another round!" I shouted.

MARIUS TURNED his attention to the task at hand, as best he could. With the Tectosages dispatched, and the remainder of our enemy on the far end of the Alps, we were able to focus on levying troops from the allied tribes. The Massiliots, Allobroges, and Sequani were the first to join us. They all had just as much to fear of the Reds as we did.

Marius made sure I was at the front of our negotiations with the allied tribes. My knowledge of their languages was useful to him, and I was thankful for something to distract myself with.

It was through this process that we learned about the Cimbri and Teutones, and their plans for the future.

Some of the tribal elders had been contacted by the Reds, who made it known that they were about to begin their departure from the wild lands of Spain, back into Gaul and onward to Italy. We had to act with haste. We were still vastly outnumbered. Some reports stated that the Reds had half a million men between them. So it was paramount that we raise a larger army, but for me it meant that my time was running short. The beginning of my mission was at hand, and I would have to be leaving now.

There was an air in the camp that was familiar from my time serving under Caepio. Every mule I saw had wide eyes, a slight tremor of the hands. Puking was the least of our worries but always seemed to be near at hand. Everyone felt sick and unsettled, even if they couldn't articulate why.

I met one last time with the Gallic prisoner and asked for some parting advice.

"You'll have to earn their respect," he said. It was clear that I hadn't earned his, so that task seemed difficult. "You'll have to prove yourself."

"And how should I go about doing that?" I asked, passing him some more bread and water from the guard.

He chewed gratefully.

"You're short, you're an outsider…so, if I had to say"—even as he munched, a grin split across his face—"you'll have to fight someone in single combat."

"Single combat?" I asked, exasperated. Such foolishness was the stuff of Greek legend. It was more a fairy tale to a Roman than Gorgons and the Harpies combined.

"To the death, if I'd have to wager." He shrugged. "They're a tough lot, my people."

That was all he had to say, so I did not linger.

As I hurried across the camp to inform Marius and seek his approval on my leaving, I heard snarling and the gnashing of teeth. Startled, I ran to find the cause of the disturbance.

Our two camp dogs, Romulus and Remus, were circling each other. The hair on their backs stood up like the plumes of a Spartan's helm, and their razor-sharp teeth glistened with drool.

"Hey, boys, quit that now! No sense in it!" some of the mules shouted.

"Damn it, someone stop that," another yelled.

The dogs lunged back and forth at each other, chomping and scratching, before pulling back.

As I neared, I spotted Sulla just beside them, crouched and analyzing the fight with intense curiosity.

"What is the meaning of this?" Marius's gruff voice rose above the rest. The consul, hard though he was, had a softness for dogs.

"Hold." Sulla held back his arm to keep anyone from approaching. "Just wait now."

The dogs bit at each other, one finally drawing blood. Romulus grabbed Remus by the neck and wrung it like a scrap of meat.

"What is the meaning of this?" I yelled to Sulla.

It became clear when I saw the food that had been placed between the two fighting animals.

Remus turned his head and tried desperately to free himself, but could not. As a last resort, he flopped to the ground and rolled to his back. Romulus let go in response and stepped away from him, the growl in his throat dissipating.

"It is marvelous, don't you think?" Sulla turned to us with amazement in his eyes.

"Marvelous?" I questioned, my gaze fixed on Remus, who remained still and silent on the ground.

"What was the point of that?" Marius asked. The mules lost interest and walked away.

"Could you not see?" Sulla asked. "The battle began with the raising of the hair, the chomping and growling. They did not want to fight; they wanted to intimidate the other into submission. When that option was exhausted on them, then they attacked. At first, with small bites and scratches. When that settled nothing, Romulus did as he must and took his foe by the neck." Sulla gestured as if he had discovered the cure for a disease. "And when Remus submitted, what did Romulus do?" We remained silent, not wanting to be a contributor in this experiment. "He allowed him to live. The posturing, mock battle, and fawning submission tell us everything we need to know. They do not want to kill one another. No matter how weak Remus here is, Romulus might need a hunting partner one day, and so he lets him live."

"Is this why you caused this commotion? To explain the minds of dogs?" Marius asked.

"It is important to the survival of their species. An unspoken rule that if one submits, and exposes the most vulnerable portion of himself to the enemy, that he'll let him live."

"This is bullocks." Marius threw up his hands and began to walk away.

"The Cimbri have won the posturing battle," Sulla said at last. Marius and I both turned and looked at Sulla. "They won the battle of intimidation. Now, every soldier in our ranks wants to roll onto their backs and submit. You can see it in their eyes. One victory against the pitiful Tectosages cannot undo that. But unlike these gracious beasts, the Cimbri will not spare us. They will butcher us to the last man, and rape and enslave every woman and child, in every distant corner of the Republic."

"You think I don't know this? Rome will never surrender," Marius replied, personally offended.

"I know that you do. But we do not have to officially roll on our bellies for our men to submit in their hearts. If they do, the front ranks will roll up like a carpet, the reserves will crumble, and we will have another Arausio on our hands."

"We did not submit at Arausio," I said.

"You did not have a chance to do so. But the effects of that defeat are carrying over. Look around, you must see it." We resisted at first but eventually peered around the camp. We didn't need the additional confirmation of seeing the fear in their eyes, but it helped prove his point.

"Then what are we do to?" Marius asked. He meant the question as mockery, but there was a tinge of genuine curiosity in his voice.

"We have to show our men that the Reds aren't so scary after all. And if we believe we can defeat them, then we can."

I said nothing, but I balked internally. Sulla had not yet faced the Reds in combat. His posing esoteric theories of combat did not measure up with my experience. The Cimbri were, in fact, just as terrifying as these soldiers around me believed. But he made one point that I agreed with. If our men knew this, if they knew what it would be like, the battle would be lost before it began.

As I thought, Sulla approached me. He placed a hand on my shoulder.

"That's why you must leave. Immediately. We need to determine the soft underbelly of these savages, if one exists, so that we can expose it to our men. If not, we will need to invent one. Right now, all we can see are walls of shields."

"I'm preparing for movement, sir," I replied, looking to Marius, who gave me a faint nod.

"Sulla, join me in my quarters," Marius said. "We can continue talking about the philosophy of beasts if you'd like. Tribune Sertorius, I would finish whatever needs done, and leave as soon as you are able. I know you needed to learn what you could from that Gallic prisoner, but time is running short."

"Moving, sir." I saluted, and left for my tent.

Inside, Apollonius was seated at a stool by my bed. He didn't notice me at first, his mind entrenched in a book on philosophy in his hand.

"Quintus." He stood, concerned by the look on my face.

"Apollonius, I need to be leaving. The time has come."

"What are my instructions?" he asked.

"Only that you care for Sura. If I die, there is no reason that my steed should as well. I'll be traveling by foot."

"Anything else?"

"I need you to take down my final will and testament before I leave. I have not updated it since my brother died and I became the father of my family." As I spoke, I lowered my eye. I did not want Apollonius to see the tears welling up, or the trembling of my lip. "Gather pen and paper."

My gaze remained on my sandals as he stood and placed a hand on my shoulder.

"I am much better at receiving dictation in the open air." I met his eyes, and he was smiling. It was infectious, and it dried my eye a bit.

We made for the stables, then rode Sura a mile or so out of camp to the clearing on a grassy knoll surrounded by ancient pines.

"Will this work for you?" I asked.

"It's perfect," he said.

We found a single tree on the hill and leaned up against it. I helped Sura to the ground, and she nestled in alongside us.

"Everything I have shall be left to my heir, Gavius Sertorius," I said, allowing him time to take it down. "Until my heir dons his *toga virilis,* Lucius Hirtuleius will be the steward of my estate. If he also dies, then his brother, Aius Hirtuleius, will be left to lead our family," I said. The number of our male clan members was dwindling steadily.

I was about to continue when I realized that Apollonius had set down his pen and had scooped up some soil in his hands.

"What are you doing?" I asked, thoughtlessly stroking Sura's mane.

"It's amazing, when you think about it. Before the first man and woman roamed the earth, before our oldest ancestors, before Greece or Rome or Babylon…this earth was here." He had noticed the tears in my eye and the choke in my words. "When all seems lost, it is helpful to remember all that you're doing it for. And be grateful," he said. I nodded, and he waited until I could compose myself.

"I apologize," I said at length.

"My friend," he said, "if you were not concerned, you would not be human. Just remember that nothing can ruin your life if it doesn't ruin your character. Otherwise, it cannot truly harm you. I am ready when you are."

"If I am to die, I want you to write to each member of my family directly. To my mother, Rhea, tell her that I love her dearly, and that I am very grateful for her tutelage and care for me. Tell her that I am with Titus and our father, and that I will prepare a feast for her in Elysium. To Volesa, I want you to write an apology. Tell her that I am sorry for the trouble I have caused by getting myself killed, and that everything I have that remains will be to support her and Gavius, as long as they live. To Gavius, tell him to be strong. Tell him to always conduct himself as a Roman, to live as his father once did. Tell him to always place our family first, before all else, and to remember the kind of men he is descended from. To Arrea…to Arrea…" When I at last reached my love, I could not get the words out.

"Quintus," Apollonius said, his voice gentle but instructive, "it is important to remember that we are taking this down as a precaution. You may die, yes. But you may yet live."

I wasn't willing to except that possibility. It seemed like a foolish thing to hope for.

"Tell Arrea that I love her. More than myself. More than Rome. Tell her thank you for all that she has done for me, and that I died a healthy and strong man because of her."

I found myself scooping up the soil beneath us and letting it sift through my fingers.

"Here is to hoping that I will never be forced to write these letters," Apollonius said, lifting his wineskin and taking a pull before passing it to me. We sat in silence for a moment, the only sound that of the wind rustling in the trees and the gentle sway of the grass beneath us.

"Is there anything else?" he asked.

"Yes. If I am to die, my shield bearer—that is you—is to be given unconditional freedom," I said.

"Quintus, I could travel to your home and serve your family."

"And he is to be given a stipend of three hundred denarii and a letter bearing my seal to ensure he is given safe passage back to Greece." Now it was his turn to hide his tears.

"I hope this is not the case, sir."

"I told you to call me by my name," I said firmly, and we both grinned. "Come on, then. Let's get back to camp."

I stood and helped Sura to her feet. I had uncinched her saddle so that she could be as comfortable as the rest of us. As I fastened it back on, Apollonius continued to share his philosophy.

"In death, all we lose is the present moment. Nothing man does can ever take away our past, and we cannot lose the future. How can we lose what we do not, and have never, had?" Apollonius asked. I stopped and turned to him.

"But I would be losing what I *thought* I would have," I said.

"Then stop thinking it. Live in the present moment, and remember the soil beneath us."

I stopped to consider his words for a moment before bursting into laughter.

"Come on"—I helped him onto Sura behind me—"you are wise beyond your years, Apollonius. And that is saying something, as you are about as old as 'the soil beneath us.'" We both laughed as Sura carried us back to camp.

The next morning, I shook Lucius awake and bid him farewell. Leaving behind my armor, my sword, and everything considered to be Roman, I left with only a Spanish spear and a Gallic tunic. I set off west to the Tigurini and whatever fate had in store for me.

14

SCROLL XIV

NONES OF MARCH 651 AB URBE CONDITA

I traveled with the cool morning air, while it was still dark out, to the northern tribal confederacy of the Helvetii, to which the Tigurini belonged. In total, our ledgers counted some four hundred villages in their control. If they all joined, Rome would be in even greater danger, but our intelligence claimed that only the Tigurini would be adding their forces to the Reds' for battle.

I slept on the earth. I ignored the worms and spiders around me, and the bugs that crawled across my skin and embedded themselves in my hair. I stunk, and I knew it. My beard was long and my hair unkempt. When I would rest every few miles, I would drink my fill. By the time I arrived, I was determined to be as much like the barbarians in spirit as I was in appearance: rough, drunk, and full of hatred.

Although I was forced to leave camp in a hurry, I was in no hurry to arrive at theirs. I took my time, stopping in some of the small villages I passed by. I said little, but purchased a few things at the market. A fur cape, a Gallic shield, a ring that had once belonged to a Helvetian warrior. I paid with the Roman denarius, and the shopkeepers took them with glee, not asking why or how I had acquired them.

After several weeks of traveling by foot, I offered a few coins to a caravan merchant to give me passage on a wagon to the northwest of the Helvetian territory, to the villages of the Tigurini. He agreed, and we rode side by side for several days, sharing drink but sparing our words. When we at last arrived, I paid the man well and departed with a fraction of what I had departed with.

When I arrived, I wandered around aimlessly for a while, trying to find someone who could point me toward the gathering forces. The village, I don't remember what they called it, was small, but I was still surprised by the lack of men present. All gone off to fight, I assumed. The one place that still garnered activity was inside a large hut made out of stone, with a giant phallus etched into the exterior wall pointing to the entrance. It was clearly a brothel. Those few men who had remained behind seemed more than happy to take advantage of the decreased demand for this service.

I entered the hut, instantly warming. The moans of the girls and the sweat of thrusting barbarians rose through the hut to create a hot air that was hard to breath.

I plopped down on a chair, very tired from my journey. As I waited, I rubbed at the soreness of my leg. The wounds had long since healed and been replaced with tight, stretched purple flesh, but my leg still irritated me when I walked too far.

"Hello," a girl said, approaching from my side. She was wearing nothing but a shear tunic and a wide smile. She played the game well, and pretended to enjoy what she saw. "You like?" She gestured to herself. My eyes did like what they saw. She had the rustic beauty that Greek statues only hoped to emulate. But although nature demanded that a man appreciate the exposed curves of a woman such as this, I wanted none of it. My mind was fixed on one objective.

"Very pleasing," I said in Gallic, making sure my inflections matched my prisoner's instructions, and looked away.

"You can have me."

"I don't want to have you. I want to fight." I looked up and made eye contact with the girl. Her sharp wit was apparent despite her confusion.

"Then you are in the wrong place."

"I need to know where the Tigurini are gathering for battle."

"I don't give away information for free," she replied, a shrewd business woman, as I'd expected. Someone who offers a service and a product as one must have a keen understanding of economics.

"How about this, then"—I stood, towering over her—"we go back to your cot or tent or whatever it is, I pay you for information, and you get a break from your 'work'?"

"It's a shame. You don't know what you're missing." She looked around the room and exhaled. Suddenly she covered herself and crossed her arms, modest enough not to expose herself without a purpose. "Come, then," she said.

I followed her through a dark and narrow hallway that was not unlike the brig we kept our prisoners in. Every few steps, there were small rooms on the left and right, filled with Gaul's finest women, laboring intensely.

She pulled back a beaded curtain and stepped aside for me to enter her personal work space. A single bedroll was spread out on ground, some hemp burning in a candelabrum in the corner.

"What do you need to know, again?" she asked.

I assumed she remembered, but I repeated myself anyway. "I need to know where the Tigurini warriors are gathering. I mean to join them."

"And why would you do that? You aren't from around here."

"Do you solicit all your customers about *why* they visit you?" I asked. She thought for a moment and then shrugged. "Go ahead, then."

"The customer pays first." She snapped her fingers and held out her hands.

I pulled out my dwindling coin purse and tossed most of what I had left, sparing only a few denarii for emergencies.

"They are massing in the west, twenty leagues or so. Most of our men have left to join them. It has made work difficult. Those that remain are old or crippled."

"Sacrifices of the job?" I asked, calculating the distance in my head. "Thank you."

"Denarii? The coin of the Romans?" She analyzed her payment with a raised eyebrow. "What would someone with Roman coin need to do with information about the location of our warriors?"

I thought for a moment and then exhaled. I pulled the coin purse from my belt and tossed the rest to her. I wouldn't need it for the remainder of my journey.

"No need to serve the elderly and cripples for a few days. Just don't mention my passing through."

"What is to stop me from telling anyway?" she asked rather promiscuously.

"I don't think you will," I said with feigned confidence. "Buy yourself something less revealing." I pointed to her dress. Her laughter followed me as I departed the hut. Perhaps she would spread news of her mysterious visitor, but by then I would be long gone, and so would the Tirgurini.

I TRAVELED the rest of the way on foot. Along the way, I passed, and was passed by, several Gauls with spear and shield, most of them traveling in small groups. More men to join the fight.

When I found it, I wasn't sure it was actually a camp. It was so unlike a Roman camp that I spent some time trying to decide if I had wandered off my path. There were no walls, guard towers, praetoriums, or temples. In a Roman camp, the tents were lined up in rows like orderly soldiers. Here, the Tigurini made bed wherever they pleased, the camp seeming to stretch for miles. The few horses they had among them were not placed in stables but hitched to logs beside cots. The warriors didn't seem to be given meat and grain allotments; instead, they had personally constructed fires beside their collective beds, each cluster with a deer or a boar roasting above it.

It was only midday when I arrived, but most of the soldiers were already drunk. I had expected the Tigurini to operate quite differently than a Roman army, but I was quite shocked at the degree. Roman soldiers were not allowed to indulge in much wine without being given liberty and express consent from their centurions. These men seemed to do as they liked.

I ambled through the "camp" and tried to analyze the enemy. I would need all of the intelligence I could collect if I was to earn myself a place among them. They were a hardy bunch. Most of them bided their time with foolish competitions, like bouts of brawling or attempting to see who could hurl rocks the farthest. They were jovial, even amusing, to watch. Unlike a Roman camp where the mules complained constantly of missing their civilian lives and the ability to have a woman on demand, these Gauls seemed to revel in the opposite. There were no prostitutes soliciting them on the outskirts of the camp. They were away from the pressures of their farms and the nagging of their wives. It was clear that war was what these men lived for.

I did all that I could not to attract attention to myself. I would have liked to find a solitary warrior to approach and introduce myself to, but it was clear that all of these men were well acquainted, perhaps not with the body at large, but at least with other clan members.

Eventually, though, I was bound to make a mistake.

The temperatures began to drop with the sun so I approached a fire pit, upon which a few rabbits were roasting, to warm myself.

I heard a call. "Ay, you." I did not dare turn to the noise but continued to stretch my hands over the glowing embers of the log. "You! I'm talking to you." Soon I heard heavy footsteps approaching behind me.

I turned to find an old man with silver hair down to his shoulders towering over me by at least a head. He, too, was missing an eye. Instead of covering it with a patch, however, he bore the milky-white dead flesh to the world as a war trophy. The rest of his face was scarred and some of the teeth behind his snarl were missing. His breath stank of ale.

"You must not be Tigurini." He breathed heavily through his nose, which whistled from a previous break.

My knees nearly buckled. Had I really already made a mistake? One that would cost me my life? I had been so careful and had prepared for so long.

"Oh? And what makes you say that?" I met his gaze.

"No Tigurini would stand there without a drink in his hand." His companions chuckled behind him. Most of them were younger, possibly sons or junior clan members.

I smiled along with them. "You are right to say that I am not Tigurini. I am a drifter."

"Drifters don't drink?" the clan father asked again, to more laughter.

"I haven't been offered one," I said. I felt a desire for intoxication that was uncommon to me, but I knew I had to keep my wits about me. If I refused him outright, though, their suspicions would be confirmed.

"Get him a drink, boys," the father said without averting his dead eye's gaze.

One of them scooped up some ale from a large barrel and brought it to me. A few others approached as well, the amusement drained from their faces.

"A drifter, you say?" one of them asked.

"Drifters must be from somewhere," another said.

"Where are you from? And why do you join the Tigurini?" someone else asked.

They approached closer still. In the peripheral of my good eye, I could see that they were beginning to surround me. The hair on the back of my neck stood to attention like a Roman century.

I did all I could to maintain my composure.

"It doesn't matter where I'm from. I heard that the Tigurini are joining the Cimbri. Right? And I want to kill Romans," I said, the words stinging in my mouth. They all exchanged a good laugh, and for a moment, their postures relaxed.

"You're too short to kill Romans," one said as his companions guffawed. I found the statement fairly ironic, but I obviously kept that to myself.

The father stepped closer still, close enough to feel the warmth his portly flesh put off like a furnace.

He reached up to my face, I started to move away but then resigned to remain still. His grimy fingers slipped under my eye patch and slowly removed it from my face.

"Why would you hide such a trophy?" he asked. I struggled to swallow and felt my body begin to tremble with anger. I squeezed my fists but released them once the others noticed.

"You've clearly seen battle. But perhaps you weren't victorious?" one of his sons added.

I felt naked before them. Romans did not prize such wounds. To display it marred my honor. I had never felt farther from Italy in my life.

"It's best you leave before you get yourself hurt," the father said, his drunk sons cackling behind him. It was clear that they weren't concerned for my safety.

"I'll fight any man here to prove I'm able," I said, spitting out the words before I could stop myself. As they turned around and sized me up, I immediately regretted my words. The Gallic prisoner had told me I must do this, but I wondered if I could have avoided it, if only for a bit longer. Too late now, though.

"Is that right?" the father said.

"Any man among you," I said again, doubling down on my stupidity.

All eyes turned to one of the younger men, and it made sense why. As tall as all the other barbarians, this man was larger than the rest. His calves were thicker than my thighs, and the muscles of his back extended so that his arms hung out like wings. He had a single scar across his cheek, but the rest of him was flawless. He was old enough to have seen many battles but had clearly been victorious.

"And if you lose, will you beg for your life?" the father asked, feigning concern.

"I will not." They turned to one another. "I will not lose, I mean. I will not lose against him." I gestured toward the big one. All of them gasped in mock surprise.

"It's your death, then, little man," my challenger said, grabbing his club. If victory in battle was determined only on the size of a man, then I would certainly lose. Then again, the Romans would have lost against the barbarians in battle every time we met them. But that wasn't the case. That being said, I didn't have the shield wall of my comrades to protect myself either. My odds weren't good.

The large man stepped toward me, then paused a few paces away. Then he charged forward with surprising quickness. Caught off guard, I held my shield before me. The club smashed into it, shattering the shield I had so recently purchased and sending a quake of pain through my fingers and into my chest. I crashed into the ground.

I scuttled across the dirt and rolled over.

I recalled my sparring with Lucius. I stopped focusing on where my challenger was, and began to look for the signs about where he was about to be.

By the time the barbarian swung his club to crush my skull, I had rolled out of the way. He stumbled for a moment, in his drunkenness, and I took advantage by sweeping his leg out from under him. He shook the earth beneath us as he collapsed. A big man like that is like a tortoise on its back. He struggled to rise, but before he could, the edge of my spear was pressed against his neck. I put just enough pressure to puncture the skin. A single thrust and his life would be extinguished.

I looked him in the eye and shouted, "You are dead, Roman!"

Once he raised his hands in surrender, I turned to analyze the reaction of his clanmates. Their eyes were wide and there were no smiles on their faces.

"Anyone else?" I asked. When no one moved forward, I pulled my spear away from the giant's throat.

After a moment, the father spoke. "Alright, lad." Nothing else needed to be said. The rest of them relaxed.

The wounded man rose to his feet and walked away for a moment, taking a second to nurse his pride.

The father tried to lighten the mood. "So you can fight like a Tigurini. Can you drink like one?" he said, a toothless grin stretching across his face.

"I'll drink you under the table, old man," I said, trying my best to play the part. Finally, the Gauls laughed with me, rather than at me.

"Give him that cup, then," the father said, and gestured for me to sit on a log across from him.

Without hesitation, I emptied the cup into my stomach. That foul ale burned into my nostrils and all the way into my belly, but I didn't let it show. They smiled and nodded to each other.

The father finished his cup in the same manner.

"You hungry? The meat should be ready soon." He gestured to the rabbits. They were a simple kind of people, the Gauls. Easy to anger, easy to befriend.

"Aye," I said like one of them, and for a moment, as the effects of the ale warmed my belly and rushed through my head, I felt like one of them.

The father gestured. "Fill 'im up, lads."

Confident of my display, and that I had proved myself, I ate their meat and drank ale with them the rest of the evening. I even clanked my cup of mead against that of the giant I had defeated. There were no hard feelings. I was the newest member of their clan, even if an unspoken one.

In another life, perhaps I could have been like them. I could have eaten and drank alongside them, and charged furiously into battle. But in this life, they were just men who wanted to kill Romans. And because of that, they were just another enemy I would one day roast above a fire like the meat they gave me.

15

SCROLL XV

SEVEN DAYS BEFORE THE KALENDS OF JUNE 651 AB URBE CONDITA

After a few months of "training" with the Tigurini, which felt more like a seaside vacation, the Tigurini elders received word from the Cimbri that their forces were massing west of the Alps, and gave order for us to pack up our things and march to meet them.

In the interim, I stayed with the clan that had accepted me. We drank until late into the dark, and rose early to hunt during the day. Luckily, I had some experience with a bow growing up in Nursia, for they handed me one and expected me to be a contributor on their hunting expeditions. We brought back plenty of deer and boar, and to be honest I much preferred this meal to the allotment of grain and watery soups we received in a Roman camp.

As the Tigurini force marched loosely through the savage passes north of the Alps, I traveled with these men as well. They still seemed to revel in being away from home. They were hungry for war, and so told old tales, much embellished, the entire journey.

"What about you, Stallion?" the father asked me. When they asked me my name, I answered with the Gallic word for a male horse. It was what my comrades had once called me before they all died, and it seemed fitting that the name should continue a mission to avenge them.

"What about me?" I asked, shouldering my shield and spear.

"Tell us a war story. You've clearly seen a battle or two," one of the sons said.

"I've seen many battles. But none so great as you brave warriors," I said, the sarcasm not lost on them.

"What about your eye?" the giant I had defeated asked.

"And your leg too. We've noticed the hobble. You hide it well, but we have an eye for such things."

We walked a few paces farther before I ventured to reply. "I lost it in battle with the Romans."

"And your leg?" the father asked.

"Same."

They exchanged a confused glance, and for a moment I feared that my phrasing had tipped them off.

"And so this is why you want revenge? This is why you want to kill Romans?" one of the sons asked, a mischievous grin on his lips.

"That is exactly why I want revenge," I said. Afterward, I returned to silence, allowing the bards among us to spread tales of their personal heroism.

We marched on for a few weeks, taking a direct path to the Cimbri camp rather than sticking to the roads. We marched knee deep in swampland and crept over thick thornbushes in the middle of forests. The only thing better about marching with the Gauls than the Romans was the fact that we didn't have to keep ranks, so at least we could go at our own pace. Father was a fat, old man, so he set the pace and we stuck by him.

When the Cimbri camp crept into view, we all gathered atop

the precipice to gaze down on the Tigurini's allies. Their forces were as boundless as the sea.

"The Romans don't know what is about to befall them." The father grinned. I was inclined to agree with him.

We approached their walls at a slow pace, allowing messengers to announce our arrival and seek approval for our entrance. I call them walls, but they were nothing like the fortresses the Romans were capable of building. Unlike the Gauls, the Cimbri at least had something to repel attackers, but they were not high walls of solid wood but massive logs sewn to a sharp point, driven into the ground and facing out to meet attackers like a defensive tortoiseshell.

After a moment of waiting, the Cimbri gave word for us to enter.

"Are you nervous, Stallion?" the giant asked, slapping me on the shoulder.

"I'm just ready to fight," I said.

Upon entering, I was surprised to see that the camp was swarming with not only warriors but women and children as well. I expected some civilians, of course, but it was nearly one woman to every man, and a child to match them at least. And this fact, and how it would affect their mobilization capabilities, didn't seem to disturb them.

There were plots of soil already laid and being tilled. Mothers carried jugs of water as well as babes slung in satchels around their chests. If there was ever a nomad society, this was it. Heracles had not a tenth of the infrastructure these Cimbri had managed to gain. They had been a traveling people for some time now, so it made sense that they could make their homes anywhere available to them.

The father of our clan went to convene with the other clan elders, and returned to tell us to rest for a while, and to find something to eat, while they conferred with the Cimbri king, Boiorix.

He didn't have to tell me twice.

I distanced myself from my comrades and found somewhere to sit down. I didn't want to let anyone know, but my leg was throbbing under the strain of so much walking. Marching under the Roman standard was a much quicker pace, but something about keeping cadence seemed to stifle the swelling around my old wound.

While I massaged the area tenderly, I tried to take in everything I could see, the kind of intelligence Marius would want if I returned: infantry size, number of cavalry, infrastructure, capabilities for movement and supply, quality of arms and armor.

It was impossible to understand the scope of things while seated on my arse massaging my leg, but I knew immediately that the Romans had every right to be scared. Although I had faced them in battle, I was still shocked to see the size of each warrior as he passed me by. What did these people eat, that they grew as tall and broad as Nursian trees? Their children had the hair of old men, so fair it was almost white.

A shadow approached and stretched over me. As I looked up, I saw a massive Cimbri warrior standing before me. He pushed a cup of mead into my hand forcefully. I accepted it and nodded my head. To my chagrin, he plopped down beside me, still a head or two taller than me even while seated.

His hair was fire red and his eyes were as blue as the Alpine caps. There was something wild and savage in them, something hungry for blood. I knew he couldn't see through my disguise, but I was intimidated regardless.

We sat beside each other in silence for a time. Occasionally, he would say something and look at me sidelong, but I couldn't understand him. I had picked up bits and pieces of the Cimbri tongue from the Tigurini who had already encountered them, but not enough to make conversation.

At length, I gave my best effort.

"Where from?" I asked with a shrug.

"Cold north," he said, or so I believed. That was enough for me, and we were both pleased to be communicating with a foreigner.

Not long afterward, the Cimbri king and the Tigurini elders exited their meeting hut. Silence befell the camp and everyone stood at attention facing them.

King Boioroix peered out at his combined army for some time, gazing into the eyes of the men, women, and children closest to him. A smile creased his face and he lifted his arms up in exultation. Everyone erupted in applause. The men beat their shields and stomped their feet, the earth trembling beneath them. The women let out a piercing screech to rival it.

Boioroix began gesticulating wildly, his long hair in thick braids flying freely around him, shouting rapidly in his foreign tongue. When he concluded, there was another eruption of applause. I feigned excitement as well, but I had no idea what was happening.

The red-haired Cimbri beside me was smiling like a hungry man who had been presented with a feast. The king gestured to someone I couldn't see in the distance, and loud drums began to reverberate throughout the camp.

As the Cimbri began to chant rhythmically, and let out howls to the gods like wolves on the hunt, I became frightened.

"What?" I asked the man beside me, not knowing how else to phrase my confusion.

He turned and slapped me on the back, as if he were about to bestow a great gift unto me.

"Almost time for war," he said before turning away to join in the chant.

Cimbri warriors brought out massive caldrons, heavy enough that it demanded a man on either side to bear the load.

I caught sight of Father and my clan to my right, and they appeared as confused as I was, but far more excited.

Father saw me looking at him and approached, followed by the others, as usual.

"Are you ready?" he asked.

"For what, exactly?" I replied. "But yes."

"I'm not certain. But I like the fire in their eyes." Father slapped his chest and shouted over the chanting.

One of the cauldrons was placed a few feet in front of us, and I followed everyone else to gather around it.

As I neared, I peered in and noticed that the barrels were nearly teeming with scarlet blood. The smell of iron reeked in my nose, but there had been scents and various herbs added in as well. I wasn't sure as to their purpose, but judging by the even faces of the Cimbri, this wasn't an uncommon occurrence.

The red-haired Cimbri placed an arm around my shoulder and led me through the crowd directly to the barrel, gesturing to the rest of my clan to follow.

When we took the nearest position to the caldron, the warrior held out his hand for us to stop. After a moment, the chanting stalled, and even the birds in the sky seemed to fall silent, as a woman in black stepped out beside the king at the center of camp.

With a hunched back and a cane, she stepped forward, clicking her tongue and shaking her head wildly like an opium user in the Suburra. She raised the cane to the sky, as well as her head, revealing the whites of her eyes.

She let out a shriek and shook wildly, the black rags flowing from her arms flapping against the wind.

The chanting began again. I couldn't understand their language but felt myself becoming carried away by it. The Tigurini and I smacked our chests, playing our role as best we could despite our confusion.

The ancient priestess continued to lead the chant as the king took second place and walked up and down the line, beating his chest and those of his men to incite their combined rage.

Finally, the shrieking priestesses continued at one pitch, and the crowd erupted.

Before I could assess the situation, the Cimbri warrior had

pulled me in close to him with one hand while the other dipped into the thick barrel of blood.

For a moment, I feared he might ask me to drink it, but then he splashed the blood onto my face, smearing it forcefully over every feature. He slapped a handful over both ears and on both my good eye and my patch, as well as on my lips, and let a scoop drizzle onto my hair.

When he was finished, he grabbed me by my shoulders and head butted me, hard enough that the light disappeared for a moment. When I pulled back to analyze him, in case this was borne of aggression, there was a smile stretched across his face, and the blood from my forehead had transferred to his and dripped over his cheeks.

He nodded and then pushed me aside, grabbing Father and doing the same to him.

For better or worse, I was ingratiated as a Cimbri now. This was my new home. I was a warrior among the enemies of Rome. And if I made one false move, I knew it would be my blood in that cauldron next.

16

SCROLL XVI

IDES OF AUGUST 651 AB URBE CONDITA

I leaned against a tree and analyzed my surroundings. I couldn't see many of the other hunters, but I knew there were six to my left and seven to my right. The Cimbri had taught me much about becoming one with my surroundings, and that was never more important than when we hunted.

The Cimbri language hadn't been easy to pick up, but thankfully the Reds were a people of few words. When we hunted, very little, if anything, was said. To communicate, they used a series of grunts and squawks that mimicked birds or various woodland creatures.

I heard a few of these noises to my left.

I craned my head to see the nearest Cimbri hunter in the distance. He was looking at me, and when we made eye contact, he nodded his head for me to come.

As I neared, he pointed into the distance, where I saw Father with his back to a tree.

I hurried, but took each step on the ball of my foot, careful not to snap any twigs. This, too, the Cimbri had taught me. I felt

I could move as silently as a shade of Hades after we had been going out every day for a few months.

When I reached Father, he nodded in the direction of a deer in the distance, only the antlers visible over a berm of leaves and twigs. It was likely that Father had only heard him. We had become much more attuned to nature.

Father nodded and stepped away. We rotated days on the hunts; every day, someone else would be responsible for making the kill. The Cimbri, not so dissimilar from the Romans, believed each man should carry his own weight.

I knew that if I made a mistake and missed the buck, we would return to camp empty-handed and would go to bed hungry. I might also be beaten by my Cimbri and Tigurini comrades, if a few previous failures proved to be any indication. I had been forced to take part in the beatings as well, but they weren't as violent as one might think. The failed hunter didn't fight back, and he was only beaten enough to leave him bruised and puffy for a few days, a warning not to make the same mistake again.

Regardless of the severity, I wanted to avoid it.

I moved out from behind the tree, nearing the berm, behind which the buck was nibbling on a few roots.

I instinctually pulled an arrow from my quiver and notched it, focusing more on my footsteps.

I was close enough to smell the buck's coat. It was a peculiar smell I would never have been able to identify beforehand. I had two options: I could attempt to flank the berm and get a clean shot on the deer, but if I did so, he might hear me and flee. Otherwise, I could wait for him to raise his head.

Both options concerned me.

Instead, I clicked my tongue. The buck raised his head to scan the surroundings. Before I had even noticed, I had sent my arrow whistling through the wind. The Cimbri had practiced with us for a long time to improve our marksmanship. They said we had to allow the arrow to release itself. When we released the arrow intentionally, it strayed right or left, and inches could make the difference between eating and not eating—or living and dying.

Their teaching proved to be effective as the arrow found its mark at the base of the beast's neck. The buck collapsed to the earth immediately, but began bawling and blatting, a truly horrific cry.

I hurried around the berm and slid my dagger into the beast's throat, a few inches from the arrow, to silence it.

It let out a sigh and fell still, it's wide, wet eyes studying me with surprise.

I got the deer. I won our prize for the evening. I exhaled with relief and then strained to pick up the massive buck. Before I could, I felt the whip of a tree branch against my neck.

I yelped and turned to see the fire-haired Cimbri, who I now knew as Carverix.

"Kill him first next time. We get two." He pointed at a few fleeing does in the distance. I nursed my pride for a moment, and managed a nod. After a moment, the scowl on his face dissipated and he patted me on the shoulder.

The rest of our hunting party, made up of my Tigurini clan and a handful of Cimbri warriors, approached and all congratulated me with a slap on the arm or a head butt. No one said anything.

I slung the buck over my shoulders, and we moved on back to camp. As we passed through the gates, I found myself as prideful of the bloody deer atop me as a father of a newborn. I had earned my keep.

Those near us eyed us with jealousy, some of the women slapping their husbands for not bringing in such a bounty.

"I'll cook it," Father said. Even he had begun to speak sparingly since we had arrived in the Cimbri camp. It was a habit I didn't mind much, especially since I remained fearful that I might say the wrong thing.

I dropped the deer in the center of our group of tents, where my Tigurini clan and Carverix's people had set up. I never fully understood the nature of our relationship to the fire-haired Cimbri, but I believe he functioned as some sort of sponsor for us, responsible for showing us the ways of the Cimbri and ensuring we followed them to the letter.

Carverix and another Cimbri gathered a bowl of grog. We usually returned from our hunt with something, a few rabbits perhaps, but a buck this size was something to celebrate. One of the Tigurini clansmen brought me a cup as Father began to flay the beast, another striking up a fire.

I drained the cup and asked for more as Father slapped the bloody skin of the buck over my shoulders.

"It's yours. We'll tan it tomorrow," he said with pride in his eyes as if I were one of his sons. And in a way, I had become one.

As we waited for the roast venison to be prepared, our behavior quickly devolved into degeneracy. This was quite normal, and I had actually begun to enjoy it. One might assume that espionage requires a sober mind, and perhaps that's true, but I fit in better with a mug of ale in hand, and intoxication was the only thing that kept me from fidgeting nervously and peering over my shoulders in the fear that someone was eyeing me with suspicion.

Before long, my head was heavy and my vision was swirled. I smiled perpetually and swayed with the effects of the grog, as a few of our more rambunctious clansmen attempted to see who could hold their heads under the ale the longest, ignoring the fact that they left hair and grime in our community bowl of grog. They asked me to do it, but I laughed and declined, playing to their ego that they were much better at it than I would be so that they left me alone.

About that time, I noticed King Boiorix and his companions in the stable corral, analyzing a bucking stallion.

Ignoring my heckling companions, I approached and leaned up against the corral fence with drunken fixation.

The stable keeper was chasing after the horse, obviously embarrassed at his failure.

"Useless man!" the king called.

Spurred on by the insults, the stable keeper whipped the back of the fleeing stallion with renewed vigor. That is, until the beast stopped in its tracks and kicked him in the face with the lightning-fast hoof of its hind leg.

He hit the dirt, blood spilling over his shattered cheeks and gums instantly, a few teeth falling out and catching in his beard.

The king shook his head in disappointment and kicked dirt and hay at the weeping stable keeper.

"Useless man." Boiorix scowled.

A few of the king's men stepped forward to try, but the majority stepped away and said the horse was broken.

"The meanest horse I've ever seen." Carverix approached behind me. "We took it from a tribe in the Pyrenees. The king claimed it for his own. Months have passed and he still can't ride it."

The stallion, as black as coal and with limbs as thick as tree trunks, maintained eye contact with those closest to him, daring them to step forward.

I hopped the fence and reached my hands out for the reins. My vision still swirling, I caught a glimpse of one of the king's men approaching, trying to dissuade me.

Before I could address the man's concern, Boiorix himself pushed him aside and buried a finger in my chest.

"What you doing?" he asked, his voice as deep as the stallion's roar.

Carverix had joined me in the corral now, as well, and was trying to pull me away. I assumed he would be held responsible if I insulted the king in some way. Regardless, I couldn't take my gaze off the king of the Cimbri, believing that if I did so, he might strike me. He towered over me, the heat of his breath burning on my forehead. Only a menacing man such as this could have lead such a people.

"You really think you can tame this horse?" the king asked.

"I'm not sure," I said as softly as I could muster, "but I'm drunk enough to try."

Boiorix roared with laughter and turned to his companions with mock admiration. He patted my face twice with big, meaty palms, hard enough most Romans might consider it a slap. Content with my answer, he threw up his arms and stepped away so that I could try.

Everyone else in the corral stepped back, including Carverix, who wore a look of grim resignation.

I moved toward the horse, considering each step carefully. Its black ears were pinned back, and it stamped its feet into the earth with a crack of thunder each time, leaving hoofprints the size of a Roman trench.

We locked eyes. Smoke billowed from its nostrils into the cool evening air with each grunt and exhale. The stallion appeared to be possessed by a demon. But I had seen horses like this. And unfortunately, I knew what came next.

The horse neighed, the sound blood curdling and piercing, and charged toward me. Few horses ever show this kind of aggression, but the ones that do are deadly.

I stood no chance of outrunning the beast, unless I hopped the fence and ran away. But doing so would result in the horse losing all respect for me, and obliterate my chances of earning it, as well as the king's patience in allowing me to try. Instead, I pivoted laterally, staying just a step or two ahead of it each time.

Eventually, it stopped, lowering its massive head, pointed directly at me. It seemed to say the next move was mine.

The stallion wouldn't rest long, though. I had a split second to decide why it was being so violent. My actions would be predicated on that answer. Horses aren't aggressive by nature—aggression attracts predators, risks injury, and burns precious energy the steed might later need. So for it to behave this way, there must have been a good reason.

Was it weaned too soon? Did it lack adequate socialization in its youth? Did it feel threatened? Was it in pain?

The horse patted its foot against the earth and waited impatiently for my answer.

It couldn't have been weaned too soon. It was too robust, too filled out. It probably did feel threatened with so many wandering eyes and bodies approaching it, but it was too controlled for this to be the cause. I spotted fresh welts and old scars along its haunches, so it could have been in pain, but if that were the case, I would expect to see its nostrils flaring a bit more, and it to be more aggressive with its grunts and whinnying.

Could it be the presence of a mare in season? Doubtful. It seemed they kept the stallion isolated, and Carverix explained that it had been this way for months.

It was tired of waiting. The beast bucked its head wildly, chomping at the bit, bared its gums and snorted, two streams of white steam pouring out as if from a furnace.

Was it trying to control resources? Afraid it wouldn't eat? No, I doubted it. For all its lack of training, the stallion appeared to be well nourished.

Boiorix was laughing and gesturing for his friends to do the same. I stole a glance at Carverix, who stood by with downcast eyes. If I failed, I would be dishonored for the remainder of my time in the Cimbri camp. In fact, my entire hunting party might be dishonored alongside me, and that might have been the reason they had all sauntered off. For this reason, I briefly considered how foolish I was to risk such a venture after having drained my fair share of ale.

But it was too late.

The stallion took a few steps forward, thrashing its head wildly side to side.

The cause of its aggression could have been a thousand reasons, but I could only choose one. The beast had a look in its large, wet eyes that reminded me of my own. It had lost someone it loved. It felt pain, but not the kind that resulted from the trainer's whip.

Most horses don't have deep bonds with humans, like dogs do. They are generally more like workmen or servants, and accept their role dutifully. But not this stallion. It had loved its owner, one who had never broken him, but rode with him, almost as equals. And when a steed loses that kind of companion, this kind of hostility can be the result.

It had lost that man, and perhaps the stallion had seen it happen. Perhaps the man had died riding atop it. Now these brutes were trying to break it without earning its trust.

My heart beat in my throat, but I dropped my arms as the stallion approached. I cast my gaze to the dirt beneath me, and waited as it placed its massive head over my shoulder, letting me know that one false move and I'd end up bloody and toothless like the man who'd tried before me.

The steed completely dwarfed me, as it remained there breathing heavily and pawing at the dirt.

"It's alright, boy," I said in Latin, quiet enough so that only the animal could hear me.

I could see from the corner of my eye that the king's companions had wide eyes of mock concern, but Boiorix himself seemed unimpressed.

I looked down into the stallion's eye, and spoke to it again as if it could understand me, just like my father once had.

We shared a moment of intimacy, the beast and I, as I realized it was the only one in that entire camp who knew my true identity, and it seemed to know it too. It ceased its stomping and its snorting slowed.

I maintained eye contact as I took the reins in one hand and stretched out my other arm.

"Hand me that stick," I said, careful to switch my words back to the Red language. One of the king's men stretched forward nervously to do so.

I gripped the reins tighter and whipped the beast's haunches softly.

It bucked like spiders were crawling across his back, and kicked out its left leg wildly to meet the unseen assailant. I maintained eye contact all the while.

"Shh, it's alright, boy," I said. The stallion didn't seem to notice I was holding the whip. I patted its neck and mane with the few free fingers I had on my left hand.

We continued this sacred dance for a long moment, as the stallion rotated away from the whip but didn't remove its head from my side. I noticed briefly that the king's expression was now intensely curious, and the humor had drained from his companions' faces.

As soon as I whipped the beast and it didn't kick out its left leg, I hoisted myself up and threw my own leg over its back. Even drunk, the motion was fluid and instinctual.

Immediately, the stallion charged forward, turning and twisting around the corral, kicking up a storm of dirt. I held the reins tight, and leaned down close to its head, careful to let it know that I was undisturbed.

"Open that gate," I said to Carverix, who did so without a moment's delay.

I loosened my hold on the reins as the stallion charged forth from the corral. I did nothing to contain the steed. It led us straight for the camp exit, and out into wild woodlands of Transalpine Gaul.

It bucked, reared, and charged, but all the while I was patting its neck and speaking to it softly.

I allowed it to run where it pleased, and eventually its anger dissipated until it became more like a calf loosed from its stall than a bull looking to fight.

When the beast's energy was at last spent, it slowed and allowed me to pull it to a halt.

"That's my boy," I said, and gave him extra affection.

We remained there for a moment before I peered out into the

vast, open expanse beyond us. It occurred to me for the first time that I could continue riding. I could return to Marius and never look back. Here was my chance at freedom. And how much more intelligence could I really gain?

"Good boy," I said again as the horse snorted with glee rather than aggression, its tail swooshing audibly behind me.

But perhaps I wasn't ready to leave. All I really wanted in that moment was another cut of venison and another cup of ale.

I continued to debate with myself for a moment, but before I really made a decision, I wheeled the horse around and started back to the Cimbri camp, this time the stallion allowing me to lead.

When I arrived back at the corral, Boiorix and all his men were watching with wide eyes and open mouths. The king himself cheered wildly and slapped his nearest companion on the back.

I hopped off and lead the stallion step by step to King Boiorix's side. I handed him the reins as the king extended a hand for the beast to smell.

"It is a king too. A king of horses. Don't let them whip it like that," I said, pointing to the stallion's scarred haunches. "It won't accept it, just as you wouldn't."

The king turned his attention from the stallion to me, instantly towering over me like the Roman fort walls. Atop that horse, I imagined he would stand ten feet tall or more, a truly terrifying and awe-inspiring sight.

Looking into the king's dark, empty eyes, I feared I had spoken with too much familiarity and would be punished for it. My fears dissolved, however, when he wrapped me in a tight hug and clapped the back of my head forcefully.

"We drink!" the king shouted as he moved off toward his quarters, leading me step by step with an arm over my shoulders. Carverix crossed his arms and looked at me with a mixture of relief, admiration, and irritation. He smiled and shrugged at what a lucky man I was.

When we arrived, I found that there were no tables or chairs but rather cushions situated in a circle around the king's tent.

"Sit," he said, gesturing to a pillow to the left of his own. A servant of Spanish origin brought us a few mugs of ale each, surprisingly of the same quality that the rest of us had access to. Another slave brought me a bowl of boiled cabbage, carrots, and artichokes, as well as Gallic bread, a strange conglomeration of stolen produce. Atop it all was a cut of choice meat that I presumed was veal.

I was fascinated by the king, hardly able to take my gaze off of him, but this time it wasn't because I feared his massive fists. His bare arms had thick maroon scars up and down them, and if I recall correctly, he was missing a few knuckles on his left index fingers. His eyes were dark but not altogether menacing, unless he desired them to be, and the face beneath his long, braided beard was not nearly as old and devious as I had previously assumed. He probably wasn't but ten years older than myself, but even the elders in the room seemed to watch him with intense admiration and affection. As far as I could tell, Boiorix had won over the hearts and minds of every Cimbri warrior in the camp.

The king gestured for me to eat as he scooped up some of the stew in his massive hands and funneled it into his mouth. Juice dripped over his beard and onto the deer pelt he wore over his shoulders. I assumed he had won that pelt the same way I had won mine a few hours earlier. I felt close to him for a moment, as I knew how he must have felt on that day, and how his companions must have been proud of him and drank to celebrate his victory. The feeling of similarity and—I dread to say it—admiration frightened me.

I ate gratefully, but my stomach dropped when I believed I thought I tasted olive oil, the kind a soldier becomes quite accustomed to because it is included in his rations. I already knew how the Reds had acquired it, and this tampered my joy at being included in this merry feast and returned my drunken musings to reality.

I was included in this kingly meal but rarely addressed. Much like when the Cimbri hunt, these men spoke little but seemed to understand each other on a deeper level.

As I ate in silence, I watched them closely. It was clear to see that the king's men loved him as much as they feared him, for they leaned over on his breast and he hugged them tightly. He cut slivers of his meat with a knife and parceled it out around the room to allow the others to taste the best portions. When the king was finished with his cup, some of the men would hurry to their feet and scuttle to refill it, not waiting on the servants. The king did the same for others a few times.

It appeared to me that the Cimbri royalty were just as dirty and smelly as the rest of their men, just as rough and ready to fight or kill. These men, and the king in particular, possessed the kind of violence that had been bred into them since long before Rome was even founded. Yet they had a simple love for one another, like a dog has for her pups—unconditional.

Watching them, it reminded me of the relationship I once had with my *contubernium*. We once sat around each other like this, eating and joking, and teasing each other about our idiosyncrasies or mocking the leadership. Their faces sobered me, for it was the Cimbri who had killed them all.

"I should be going. I feel peculiar," I said, handing what little remained of my food to the man at my left.

I received glares from around the room, but I stood regardless. My stomach was starting to churn, and I feared I might lose the delicious meal all over the king's tent.

Boiorix himself was the only one who did not eye me with suspicion. He stood, towering over me once again.

"You drink my drink anytime," he said, looking into my eye. I nodded my thanks and quickly looked away, fearful that if he gazed into it long enough he might discover my duplicity.

17

SCROLL XVII

TWO DAYS BEFORE THE IDES OF JANUARY 652 AB URBE CONDITA

So summer turned into autumn, and autumn quickly spiraled into winter. The longer I stayed in the Cimbri camp, the faster time moved. I was well aware that my time there was swiftly expiring, but I could never find the gumption to leave. There always seemed to be something left unsaid, some piece of intelligence left undiscovered.

My time there was both dreadful and exciting, exhausting and liberating. Outside of our daily hunting ventures, there was little to do, few chores to tend to, and life was mostly sitting and waiting, or eating and drinking. Unlike the Roman forces, the Cimbri and Tigurini soldiers never asked questions, and were rarely given information. They would simply depart for battle when they were told to do so, and that was adequate for them. For that reason, I feared that each day I'd awake to a battle horn and war would be upon us, and it might be too late for me to leave and get intelligence to Marius.

I feared constantly for my life, that I might be exposed and killed for it. I had made companions and associates in the Cimbri camp who would vouch for me in any other circumstance, but if I were discovered as a Roman infiltrator, the best poets and playwrights would have a harder time creating something more sinister than what they would do to me. Even having won the king's appreciation, I was certain my body would be dismembered in the most grotesque way imaginable, so that I would never be found, never identified dead.

It was hard to imagine this when I sat and joked with my clanmates and my Cimbri associates. I had come to look on Father and Carverix as friends, and it took a great deal of effort to constantly recollect what the outcome would be if they discovered who I truly was.

But as the months passed, I continued to spend time with these warriors, collecting as much intelligence about the Cimbri as possible. I could write nothing down, for fear of being discovered, so I made mental notes of everything I saw. If this were a Roman camp, I would have simply stolen their ledgers, but the Cimbri kept no records and didn't document their numbers.

Fortunately, we did nearly everything with our Cimbri associates. The one thing we separated for was battle assembly drills, as the Romans would have called them. It was made clear that the Tigurini would fight on their own flank, and the Cimbri theirs, so we trained for battle apart from each other. The majority of the Tigurini training consisted of sparring and hand-to-hand duels, although we occasionally marched together, but with much less form and regulation than I was accustomed to as a Roman. But we trained in this manner far less often than our Cimbri allies, to say the least. So occasionally I would linger nearby and watch them as they trained.

The most important thing I discovered was the way in which the Cimbri positioned itself for battle. It was ingenious. I was amazed that I hadn't noticed it in the heat of battle, but as I spied on them here, I discovered the method they used that made them so impenetrable.

Each man's breastplate had two rings hanging from either side. During battle, the Cimbri would link these rings beforehand, to ensure that no man could turn and flee, or falter behind. As long as there was a brave man among them (and of the Cimbri, there were many), their lines would continue to advance. This made it impossible for them to be routed. The Cimbri knew because of this that they must fight, fight to win or fight to die. The Colors have tried to emulate this, but in theory only. We have solid lines of close men, ranks that should act as a barrier to fleeing. But the moment one man routes, unless another quickly takes his place, there is a hole in the line and the whole century collapses in upon itself.

These Cimbri were brave indeed, because they had no other choice.

AS DIFFICULT AS boredom had become, constantly performing like an actor in a Greek tragedy was much more draining. It left me lethargic and weak, which of course I then had to hide—a vicious cycle. The free-flowing ale was the only thing that helped.

When I wasn't with my clan or sauntering on my own, I spent time with Carverix and his Cimbri companions.

The fire-headed man was drilling some of the younger Cimbri on weapons use when I found him that day. He was sweating profusely despite the cool temperatures of the Alpine foothills. He took a break and chugged a cup of mead thankfully.

"How do they look?" I asked, pointing to the young men.

"Ready to kill." He nodded. He passed me a cup, and I took a gulp, savoring the ale I once had despised.

"As am I," I said, acting the part of a bloodthirsty barbarian.

"Not much longer now," he said.

My senses heightened. "Oh?"

"We'll battle soon enough," he said, and my hopes of finding more concrete intelligence were dashed.

"When?" I asked.

"We leave in two days," he said matter-of-factly. Perhaps this was common news by this point, but I had remained unaware.

"Not soon enough," I said.

"Cimbri go south, Teutones go north," he said. I had hardly thought about the Teutones, the powerful ally of the Cimbri who had helped crush us at Arausio. I had heard rumor of their camp just a few miles away from us, but the numbers of the Cimbri were so vast it was difficult to fathom another force equal to it in size.

"We're splitting up?" I asked, stumbling on my words for a moment.

"We crush the Romans," Carverix said, making a gesture with both of his fists, slowly closing in until they crashed against one another. "But first we feast." He smiled.

"Feast?"

"Before we leave"—he drained more of his ale—"big feast."

"To celebrate war?"

"Yes."

My mind began to swim with ideas. If the Cimbri were departing for battle two days hence, my window of getting away was swiftly shrinking. The feast, with the Cimbri drunk and distracted, would be my last chance to escape unnoticed.

My only concern was a nagging one: Had I uncovered enough information to really make a difference?

"Cimbri take no slaves. Too many mouths to feed. We kill Romans before we leave." He gestured to the young Cimbri. "Then they have to kill more Romans to appease the gods, since we will be out of sacrifices."

"We have Romans?" I asked, trying and failing to appear disinterested.

"Yes, plenty. Enough to satisfy the gods."

"'Till the fight," I said. He raised his cup as I turned to leave, feeling my feet go numb.

I WANDERED AIMLESSLY around the camp, heart pounding in my chest, hands trembling. I returned to my tent and sat with Father and my Tigurini clan, draining a cup of ale and pretending I wasn't about to burst.

Not long afterward, Boiorix exited his tent along with a few of the other Cimbri elders. Silence befell the camp, and everyone stood to attention facing them.

Boiorix waited as the men, women, and children gathered around. In a sudden burst of rage, he began howling like a wolf, followed by his army. The friendly, familiar face of the king who had shared his dinner with me previously was all but transformed into the caricature the Romans had always believed him to be: a savage, bloodthirsty killer, worthy only of death.

Like the day of my arrival, the Cimbri began to chant wildly, the ancient priestess leading with her own piercing cry.

"I told you," Carverix said. "Time to kill Romans." Drums echoed throughout the camp, but they couldn't drown out the grunting of nearly a hundred Cimbri warriors who struggled to roll a massive wicker cage to the center of us all. Within were dozens of naked, bone-thin Romans clutching to the bars of their cage and screaming for their lives. Most of them were young men, barely old enough to grow a beard. Their eyes wept for mercy, but the savage Cimbri chants promised that there would be none.

The Cimbri cheered as the Romans rolled into view, some rushing forward to spit on the prisoners, others hurling rocks or horse shit. The pitiful Romans reminded me of the slaves I saw in the Massilia markets, but their fate, I feared, was about to be even worse.

As wood was piled hastily alongside the cage, my heart

dropped into my stomach, and I feared I might audibly moan and give myself away. Romans were about to be slaughtered before my very eyes. My mind coursed with foolish ideas of what I might do to save them, but there was nothing I could think of. I'm haunted each night by the visions of that moment, and still dream of some alternative to standing silently and watching their deaths.

When the wood was piled to their satisfaction, the fire was lit.

Black pitch rose into the cool air, and the screams of my brethren curdled my blood. I looked down and squeezed the tears from my eye as the cheers of the Cimbri rose to challenge the screams.

As the Romans writhed on the floor, struggling in vain to pat out the flames, one man stood with his hands gripped on the wicker bars of the cage.

"My name is Marcus Aurelius Scaurus, a legate under Consul Gnaeus Mallius Maximus," he shouted as the flesh of his feet and shins began to char. "Turn back now! You bring only your doom. The Romans will kill you all."

His strength bid me to look up, and gaze upon what these barbarians had wrought. The charred bodies of the Roman captives thrashed on the smoldering floor of the wicker cage. Aurelius alone stood in silence, inhaling the toxic fumes as the flesh of his legs melted beneath him.

"We burn the rest tomorrow. Then war," Carverix said with a victorious smile, slapping my back. I forced a grin and nodded as if it weren't soon enough, but a more perceptive people would have noticed the trembling of my hands. Whatever respect or admiration I had once held for this savage people had dissolving with the smoke. I was resolved to do what I must. Nothing could have served as a better reminder.

The fires continued for some time. Their death was a slow one.

I cannot bear to continue the description.

18

SCROLL XVIII

ONE DAY BEFORE THE IDES OF JANUARY 652 AB URBE CONDITA

I've spoke of nightmares previously, but nothing rivaled the ones I endured that night. My mind's eye never left that wicker cage, where I saw the faces of my brother and comrades smoldering like a roasted chicken. I saw myself inside the cage too, but rather than burn, I remained alive but unable to do anything to help those around me.

I woke early, fitfully, only to find reality was worse than the dreams. It had all really happened. Dozens of Roman lives vanquished in an instant.

I was drenched in sweat, and I dreaded pulling back my blankets and revealing the wetness to the frigid morning air.

To my surprise, Father was sitting over me, sharpening the tip of his spear on a stone and staring at me with a piercing gaze.

"Morning," I said, stretching, pretending I was just roused from an adequate night's rest.

"You sleep badly?" he asked.

I shook my head. "I don't believe so."

"You spoke in your sleep." He put the spear aside and leaned in closer, as if attempting to smell for prey.

"Did I say anything interesting?" I asked, feigning a chuckle.

"You spoke in a strange tongue." His eyes never left mine as I shook my head and pretended it was a joke.

"I can't imagine what it must have been. Wasn't just grumbling, was it?" I asked.

"They were words I've heard before."

We both fell silent as the jests of our Tigurini clansmen filled our ears.

"You going to tell me what it was?" I asked, still smiling.

"You give me signs that grieve me, boy." He stood, his fingers twisting the wood of his spear.

I quickly rolled from bed but slowed so that I didn't seem suspicious. I threw the deerskin hide over my shoulders and shrugged.

"I'm just ready to fight," I said, and walked away.

He followed me for a few steps but eventually allowed me to proceed and intermingle with my clan. I felt his gaze on me the rest of the day.

THE CARVERIX TOLD me there was to be a feast, but I had no idea what to expect. The festivities began no later than what the Romans would have called second hour. The ale flowed freely, and the finest of local Gallic livestock were slaughtered for consumption. They couldn't take it all with them on the move, so they were determined to drink and eat as much as possible.

The Tigurini joined in gratefully, and I drank among my clansmen as I always did, but I tried to pour out as much as possible when no one was looking. This was difficult, as Father hardly looked away. But this was a time for sober thoughts only, despite how badly I desired to escape them. With Father's suspicions growing and the Cimbri set to depart the following day, I knew my time was short. My mind was already set on leaving.

But somehow I remained frozen beside the fire along with my clansmen. I feared that they already knew my schemes and that their acts of cordiality and attempts at humor were contrived, only to lull me into a false sense of security. Then they might kill me in my sleep or, worse yet, hand me over to the Cimbri to be burned alive alongside today's sacrifices.

But as the day continued, they became more drunk and I became more resolved. Even Father seemed to momentarily forget his suspicions as he sang along with his clansmen some ballads they had been taught in their youth.

By the time the sun began to set, the real feast began. They beat war drums as the Cimbri priestesses swayed rhythmically along with it. Great fires were lit to illuminate the camp, and the smoke hovered around us so thick as to almost block out the man beside you.

I still didn't know what I was to do. I waited anxiously for a moment where my comrades were distracted, but when the times came, I found myself paralyzed.

But after the sun had faded and the men had picked the bones clean, a mass orgy ensued. The priestesses and womenfolk of the Cimbri pleasured their warriors openly in the night air. Such a display made the Roman Saturnalia look like an innocent dinner with the family.

The unwed ladies among them searched hungrily for a warrior of their own, stumbling throughout the camp intoxicated on the ale and whatever inhalants the Cimbri had confiscated from the Spaniards. More than a few times, a woman fell to her knees before me and tried to push up my tunic, determined to perform her service with or without my consent. I stood, too, and moved away as they shrugged and sauntered on to find a more willing participant.

I peered around the camp, and I now found that nearly every

man was engulfed in a drunken ecstasy, even if he had to share with a friend. Now was my time.

As the watchful eyes of Father turned toward the young Cimbri girl who had joined him, I hurried away toward the opening of the walls, careful to follow the cover of the smoke. Even the guards were partaking in the revelry and didn't seem to notice.

As I stood within a handful of yards from the gate, I paused. My legs seemed unwilling to move another step. The memory of the roasting prisoners flashed before my eye in rapid succession: the charred limbs that flickered away in cooling ash, the smell of human flesh that lingered still, the screams and choking coughs of the dying.

I turned on my feet. My mind was at war with itself. Part of me was angry, very angry at myself for what I was about to do. The foolishness, the recklessness. The part of myself I admired most, the part of me that emulated my father and wanted to become the kind of man my brother said I could be as he lay dying in my arms, this side was determined to do the right thing. And this was the side I was determined to listen to.

I hurried through the camp, sticking to the shadows as much as I could. I didn't know where the prisoners were kept, but I remembered clearly where the wicker cage had been brought forth from, so I started my search there.

Thankfully, the Cimbri felt no need to hide their prisoners. It was a wonder I had not seen them before, save that they were in a part of the camp that was designated for Cimbri only and far from our Tigurini tents.

Two guards were standing beside the cages, but just as you might expect, they didn't allow their responsibilities to keep them from enjoying themselves on a night of celebration.

I waited for an opportune time, and while the guardsmen were distracted as they shared a girl, I made my way to the gate of the cage.

I was met with the most foul stench imaginable. The emaciated Romans within were naked and covered in urine and excrement. There was no evidence that they had been fed recently, so one must only wonder how they had stayed alive.

I knelt beside the cage and looked over my shoulder to ensure no one had seen me. The guards were so entrenched in their activities, I'm not sure they would have cared even if they had spotted me.

"My name is Quintus Sertorius," I said in a hushed tone, and by the gods, it felt good to say my own name.

Most of the men didn't move or even look up. They were strewn across the cage atop one another. I thought for a moment that they were already dead but strained my eye in the darkness to make out several heaving chests.

"My name is Quintus Sertorius," I said again, "and I am here to help you. Is there any man among you who can walk?" I asked.

"I," came one voice. The man slowly pulled himself to his knees, then to his feet. He approached the edge of the gate. His cheeks were shallow and his ribs gaunt, but his eyes still shone with a hint of life. A few more of them stood, struggling to do so. "My name is Marcus Marcellus, legate of the Fifth Legion," the first man said, cognizant of the fact that he needed to keep his voice low.

"Well, Legate Marcellus, it's time to get you out of here," I said as a few more men joined him at the edge.

I brandished my spear and began to cut through the ropes binding the exit, looking over my shoulder to ensure I wasn't being too loud as I did so.

At last, the final thread of the rope was severed, and the gates opened. I feared the creak of the wicker would alert the guards, but they didn't seem to hear.

Marcellus and a few others rushed past me as best they could.

"If there is any man among you who may yet still live, pick him up and carry him."

Marcellus and the others reluctantly reentered the cage and helped a few men onto their backs.

"Leave us, go now," someone said.

"It's useless," one of them said.

Dozens of them were still attached to the earth, unable to move, and a few of them were already dead. As fear began to overcome my adrenaline, and I contemplated what I should do, I noticed a man at my feet. Even with sunken cheeks, atrophied limbs, and a dozen infected scars, I recognized him.

It was my friend Ax.

"AX, IT'S ME," I said, kneeling beside my old comrade. He looked up at me, but it didn't seem to register. His breath was shallow and wheezy.

"Stallion," he said at last.

"Yes. Yes, it's me. I thought you were dead," I said.

"It was actually the Cimbri who nursed me back to health. Just so they could keep me here to rot."

"We need to hurry," Marcellus said as the freed prisoners crouched behind me.

"Come on." I lifted Ax up and onto my shoulders, the protruding bone of his hip digging into my shoulder.

"Now—now," Marcellus whispered.

"We need to separate. We'll be caught if we're too close," I said, keeping my eye on the guards, who were no more than a hundred feet away.

"We need swords," Marcellus replied.

"No use. We can't fight them. You're all naked, scarred, and hairy, just like our captors. If you can manage to sway like you're drunk and get an erection, it will help," I said. "Escape is that way."

We spread out from one another like we were given a centurion's order for a wedge formation. We stuck to the shadows and moved carefully.

"Hold on, old friend. Almost home," I said, fearing that Ax's shallow breaths might cease at any moment.

I tried to make a good pace but didn't want to raise any suspicion. The Cimbri were distracted, but even belligerent and in the midst of an orgy, they could be attentive enough to notice us.

As I rounded past the king's hut, I saw the edge of the Cimbri walls in the distance. Only a few minutes' walk but still so far away.

I tried to increase my speed, not venturing to look over my shoulders to see if the others were doing the same.

I continued to churn forward, but the gate never seemed any closer.

When at last the exit was within reach, I heard a Cimbri man bark behind me.

"Hey!" he shouted, but I didn't slow or turn around. "You there!" he bellowed again, his voice closer this time. Knowing I couldn't outrun him, I stopped.

I exhaled and took time turning to meet him. I had failed. And now Rome would likely fail as well because of my stupidity.

"What are you doing?" he asked in suspicion.

"My friend is drunk. I'm taking him back to his tent," I said, trying to force a smile.

He stepped closer.

"Tents are that way." He gestured back to the center of the camp, brandishing an axe from his hip.

Just as he prepared to lunge for me, a spear wedged through his belly. Behind him stood Marcellus, who hastily put a hand over the man's mouth to smother the scream. Where, or from whom, he took that spear, I'll never know.

I nodded my thanks and turned back toward the gate.

"Run!" I said behind gritted teeth.

We sprinted like Zephyr past the exit, bursting out into the cold Alpine snow.

Bodies of fleeing captives collapsed as we ran, unable to take another step.

But I pressed on, with Ax on my shoulders and only a few men at my side, into the darkness, not venturing to look back.

19

SCROLL XIX

IDES OF JANUARY 652 AB URBE CONDITA

Once we had made it a safe distance from the Cimbri camp, I reconvened with the survivors. There were nine of us, the carried and carrier all.

"What are we to do?" one of them asked in sheer terror.

"We have to hurry. As soon as they find those empty cages, they'll send riders after us," another said.

"We have to make for the mountain passes. That's the only place where their horses can't move faster than us," Marcellus said, breathing heavily.

"We can't. We'll freeze to death." I shook my head.

"This is your command," one of them said, looking to me. "What are we to do?"

My eye darted between the men and the black horizon beyond which the Cimbri's camp resided.

"You have to make a decision," another said.

"I know, I know," I said, closing my eye and pouring over every possibility. There was none that seemed adequate.

"We need to do something." Marcellus stepped toward me.

"We go to one of the villages," I said as soon as the thought reached my mind. "We have to go to one of the villages."

"What if they are allied with the Reds? They'll turn us over in exchange for favor with the enemy!" Marcellus shook his head vehemently.

"They might, they might," I said, feeling more confident in my decision. "But we have no other choice. We need clothing and horses. Otherwise, we'll never make it out of here alive."

"And they'll just give them to us?" Marcellus laughed in derision at the foolish plan. But foolish plans had gotten me to this point, so I ignored the laugh and set off for the nearest village I had passed while marching with the Tigurini.

WE MOVED AS QUICKLY as possible but had to match the pace of our least healthy escapee.

"Just a bit farther," I said, catching my breath. "Marcellus, carry him. He can't walk another step." I pointed to the weakest among us, who had grown as pale as the snow beneath us.

I kept imagining that I heard the clamoring hooves of a Cimbri scouting party behind us, but we hadn't seen them yet.

A village crept into view in the distance.

There were no lamps burning in the windows, so it was nearly impossible to see. I thought perhaps my eye was playing a trick on me, but I stayed the course.

When we reached the outskirts of the village, I halted the men and told them to catch their breaths. I knew that it was not air that they needed now but something to cover them. Their bodies were moving only on sheer terror and the blessing of the gods, so I knew they needed food and rest or they would likely die of exhaustion.

The men fell to the snow, letting it engulf them.

I approached the nearest hut. It was larger than the rest, and there was fenced in land behind it. I could see nothing but heard the snores of a few horses in the distance.

What was I to say? Nothing clever came to mind. But it was the only chance I had. The gods had led me this far. Perhaps the gods were protecting me, as Apollonius had suggested.

I banged on the door as forcefully as I could, in total, utter desperation.

I heard nothing stir within the house.

I beat again.

Over my shoulder, I heard some of the men begin to weep.

"Come on, come on. Please," I begged. I spoke to the gods, my ancestors, or anyone listening. "Please."

Finally, the door crept open, a pair of eyes shimmering in the moonlight behind it.

"What do you want?" the gruff voice asked.

"Please, we need help," I said in Gallic.

He inched the door back a bit farther and peered over my shoulder at the emaciated naked Romans behind me.

"Are you Cimbri?" he asked.

"No. No, we aren't. Who we are isn't relevant," I said. "We just need help."

I noticed that he fingered the head of an axe on his hip.

The man was silent for a moment until the crying of a babe echoed throughout the hut.

A young mother, bobbing the sobbing infant on her hip, appeared behind him, her eyes wide with fear and perhaps anger.

"What is the meaning of this?" she cried.

"Please, lady, we need help," I said.

"We do not know you! Get out of here!" She stumbled over her words, but the righteous anger of an indignant mother was still apparent.

"Sir, we need horses and clothing."

"Leave now!" the woman shouted, and then she began to

scream wildly at her husband for even considering it. She stormed off into the house.

"Please, sir. We will all die." I gestured back to the survivors.

"You need to leave," he said quietly as he began to shut the door.

I grabbed at the edge of it and stopped him.

"Please, sir! We will freeze to death out here! We will all die! Do you want this blood on your hands?" I shouted, but even I knew this was in vain. What responsibility did this man have to give away his livelihood to strangers?

The woman appeared again, and shouted at her husband, "We hardly have enough clothing for the winter! Tell that man to leave!" she cried.

I loosened my grip on the door.

"I'm sorry," he said, and shut the door. I heard the lock click shut behind it.

I turned and walked back to the men in total defeat.

They had begun to shiver, their entire bodies trapped in a convulsion.

"We will have to kill them," one of them said.

"Let's just take the horses! Bugger these Gaul bastards. We can take the horses and make like Mercury for the coast," another cried.

"We need to leave, Sertorius. We need to make for the mountain passes. It's our only chance. The Cimbri will be here soon," Marcellus said, looking over his shoulder.

I placed my hands on my hips, and then on my head, praying for the gods to illuminate my mind.

Without thinking, I turned and sprinted back to the house.

Marcellus and the others shouted after me.

"Please! I beg of you! Please help us! The Cimbri will hunt us down!" I shouted, banging against the door with all the might left within my body. "I beg you! We will all die!"

Marcellus and a few others grabbed me by my arms and dragged me away. I fought against them with all my might.

"My name is Quintus Sertorius, a military tribune! I have information about the Cimbri that—" Marcellus tried to cover my mouth. "Information that the consul needs to hear to defeat them!"

They wrapped up my arms and dragged me away, releasing me only once I'd stopped fighting.

I let out a moan and fell to the earth in despair.

And then the door creaked opened. The man stepped out, axe now in hand.

"You said you have information about the Cimbri?" he asked.

"Yes, sir. That's right. I've been spying on them these last eight months. I have enough intelligence to help Rome defeat them!" I nodded vehemently. He shut the door behind him.

"Gods, what have you done?" one of the freed prisoners asked.

"I think you've killed us now, boy," Marcellus said, placing his hands akimbo on his hips.

The door opened again. And this time, the man approached with folded cloaks in his hands.

"How many are there?" he asked.

"Nine," I said, regaining my composure. "I don't need anything."

He handed me the clothes he had gathered.

"Tha… Thank… Thank you, sir." I lost control of myself. I wept, knelt at his feet, as he stepped back, absent the clothing he had brought for us. "I would pay you all that I have, but I have nothing," I said.

His face was stern. He knew what he was doing would cost him a great deal. It was a difficult decision to make.

"There are four paint horses you can take. Don't touch the stallions. Four is all I can afford to give," he said, flinching as he heard his wife screaming inside the hut.

"Thank you," I said, tears flowing freely. I searched for the right words to say but could not find them. He said nothing in reply. "What is your name?" I asked.

"Vallicus," he said, after deliberating.

"Vallicus, I will sacrifice to your health. I will sacrifice for the rest of my life."

He exhaled and nodded.

"You give me hope," I said, my words carried on puffs of breath.

"If you can help destroy the Cimbri, it will be worth it. There is no life here while they exist. Go on, now. Or they'll catch you." He turned again to enter his hut, to face whatever punishment his wife deemed fit.

The men struggled to throw the wool cloaks on, and then hurried to mount the horses. The Cimbri's best riders were likely already searching for us. We had no time to lose.

"Ya!" I kicked the horse into a gallop, Ax bouncing along behind me, the three other overburdened horses to my side.

II

WAR

20

SCROLL XX

To spare you the arduous details of our long trek back to camp, of freezing and starving, I've here included an exert from Sulla's memoir.

It's likely that you own a copy yourself, or have at least borrowed it, as it has been distributed to all ends of the Republic. Just in case you've not come across his writing, it here follows. I have not altered his words or opinions to reflect more kindly on myself, or Consul Marius, which I'm sure you'll be able to tell.

The following took place while I was within the lion's den of the Cimbri camp. Rome didn't sleep while I was gone, and Sulla's account details the political happenings that subsequently took place.

May to Quintilis—Year of the consulship of Marius and Orestes

It was nearly May when we returned to Rome. Just when the weather was becoming bearable in Gaul, Marius was determined to drag me back into the infernal heat of the city. The elections were scheduled for the fifth month, Quintilis, and the great general was fixed on gaining himself another consecutive consulship, despite how illegal it may be. He invited me along, or demanded, rather, not so much because he enjoyed my company but to keep an eye on me.

The moment we stepped onto the Via Appia, Marius was already beginning the skeevy business of campaigning for the election. All sorts of unscrupulous men flocked to his side for a moment with the consul, hoping that they might glean a bit of the prosperity that had followed him for so many years. The men of probity and respect did not greet us, of course, which suited me just fine. By this point, I would rather not be associated with the old general any more than I had to.

As soon as Marius was distracted with shaking hands and casting out prophetic promises, I stepped away on my own business. Namely, satiating my appetites.

I'd take a Gallic trollop whenever I could on campaign, but there's nothing quite like a Roman matron. You know, the type who hates you during and asks you to leverage your position in her favor even before she cleans herself up.

I was a widower now, after all, and free to do as I liked. I took full advantage of my time there, to be certain.

Regardless of my status as a single man, though, Marius looked at me with irritation whenever he saw me about the forum with a mistress. As if my gallivanting somehow dishonored the corpse of my long-dead wife. I didn't see it that way. I was faithful to Ilia. I never communed with a younger woman equal to or above her station the entire time we were married. I didn't believe she would mind now that she was with Hades and Persephone.

Aside from indulging myself in the pleasures of the flesh, I attended plays in the forum whenever I could. I was never happier than when watching actors on the stage. Such grace and beauty, such poise. It was, and remains, incredible to me that, for a moment, one man can become another before your very eyes. It's very much like politics in that way, except politics isn't quite so endearing.

When it was up to me, I'd see plays with Roscius the comedian or Metrobius the impersonator of women. Both were old friends, but I'll admit that it was difficult to pay attention when I attended the plays of the latter, as I could hardly take my eyes off him.

I did take one brief detour while I was there, to the Suburra, where I was reared in utter poverty. I hiked up my toga as I walked, ensuring that the stark white of its fringes wasn't tainted with the muck of my youth. The buildings were much as I remembered, slanted and decaying, overgrowth crawling up the sides of the sunbaked brick, vines and tendrils hanging from the rafters. The people were much the same too, so I wasn't shocked when I found the tenant of my father's old insula, toothless and with one eye that seemed to be running away from the other.

"Greetings, citizens," I said, nodding at him.

He grumbled and concocted some sort of face in greeting. It's hard to tell the purpose when a man has no teeth.

"Are you the owner of this block of insula?" I gestured to the dilapidated apartments behind me.

"Mm-hmm." He nodded and seemed to be chewing on something with his gums.

"Would you sell it?" I asked.

"For the right price." He hawked some bile by his mud-caked toes.

I turned and analyzed the building for a moment. The rapturous cries of children playing carried out from the courtyard within, as well as that of their mothers, who were yelling at them to be careful. Looking at the horse shit and cobblestone paths leading to the insula doorway, I remembered finding my father there once. He had passed out after a night of whoring and gambling. By the time I found him in the morning, the street urchins had stolen every piece of jewelry off him. At least that made it easier for me to drag him up the steps.

"Four thousand denarii?" I asked with cocked eyebrow.

He debated for a moment, his eyes looking thoughtfully in different directions. He made a grumble from deep in his chest before replying, "Couldn't do it."

Something turned in my stomach as my gaze drifted to the slanted doorway, leading to the steps where our beaded door once hung. I had almost forgotten, but then the memory returned to me. A beautiful little cat pouncing up the stairs. I remembered it clearly then. I was just a boy, no more than ten or eleven years old. The cat came to me, choose me, in a way no one else did. He was the first friend I ever had, to be honest. The purring little feline was someone to talk to since my father was too drunk and my mother too dead.

"Never mind, then," I said to the man with the friendliest smile I could conjure. I remembered finding that cat a few weeks later skinned and butchered by the older boys in the insula. They were too poor and too bored to have anything else to do, but I would have killed them all if I had been old enough to do it. If I could go back and kill them, I would. I'd kill them now if I knew how to find them. "No matter. I was just going to burn it."

DESPITE THE ATTEMPTS TO distance myself, I was required to be at the consul's side from time to time. And Marius was a dreadfully boring man to be in Rome with. He kept poor company, for one thing. Reprobate drunken degenerates, the lot of them, which I don't typically mind, but they receive their jollies from scheming for power rather than a lyre and the recitation of good poetry. Not the sort I enjoy dining with. Besides that, the old general refused to attempt a dinner party that wasn't in his own triclinium, where he was most comfortable. And don't get me started on the quality of his cook. Ghastly doesn't begin to describe it. It was a wonder I could keep the food down, especially mixed with the soldier's swill wine he served.

Besides that, Marius never tarried far from his wife's hip. Julia was a prude in the most ancient, respectable sort of way, ensuring that the rest of us didn't enjoy ourselves too much in her presence. I imagine that the majority of the time Marius didn't spend scheming for an election he spent having dull sex with his wife. I imagine it must have been like an old farmer and his nag, who love each other very much but just aren't as creative or passionate as they once were. On the same note, I have to imagine Marius is the kind of man who cries after coitus...one statement from Julia like, "You are a better man than your father," or, "Those mean old patricians just don't understand you," and he'd burst into tears like an old wineskin with new wine. All that bravado and anger must escape sometime, nay?

So there I was, attempting to pass the time as Marius consorted with these profligates, who were spinning webs of the coming victories, not only of the barbarians in the field but his total political conquest once he returned. They all cheered him on and licked their grimy lips as he talked of the spoils he would lavish upon them for their complicity in it. The men most often at his little rallies were Lucius Saturninus and Gaius Glaucia. The latter was a man of little consequence. He was born with some good blood in him, but I'd say there was more good blood on his hands, even by this age. He had a certain look of the eye that was common of rabble-rousers like him, like barbarians really, always looking for a fight. Marius promised him an opportunity to stick one up the arse of the nobles, and that was enough to satisfy him.

Saturninus, on the other hand, rather intrigued him. He was slightly more reserved than the others, and his flatteries seemed to be more calculated and poised. I could tell from the moment Marius introduced us that this young man had more intelligence in his pinky finger than the old general did in his entire body, and that frightened me more than all the rest of their vainglorious boasting.

At least at this moment I had nothing to be afraid of. I was a member of their little alliance for all intents and purposes. Marius may have viewed me with suspicion, but the others didn't seem to. He didn't have a problem inviting me to these dinners, after all, so why should they? I don't think it occurred to Marius at the time that I would ever turn on him. The old general would have never admitted it, to be certain, but I believe, even then, that he looked on me as a son. Marius wasn't a young man at this point, remember, and he had no legitimate heir, at least not after Maximus's death. Some believed he was now impotent or sterile, but I always privately wondered if he just couldn't find the right hole. If knowledge of poetry is correlated to the knowledge of women, and it usually is, then Marius must have been the most clueless man in Rome.

Regardless, I knew his invitations were for a more direct purpose. Now that our alliance had been fractured in some ways, he wanted to show me the scope of his power and tell me about all the things he would soon accomplish, with or without my help. If I had believed that any of it was more than the babbling of second-class men, he would have been right. But I didn't believe a word of it.

I was already searching for a suitable wife. Not among the ladies I was consorting with, mind you, but among the sisters and daughters of Rome's finest. I was forced to tell Marius I was already engaged to another when he offered me the hand of his ill-born daughter, which was false. I simply did not wish to attach myself to Marius any further. As much as I respected him for his discipline in the field, I knew him to be a dimwit in politics. Marius had taken me as far as he could, and it was time to solidify new alliances. It wasn't personal. But I had a mission, one tasked to me by Apollo himself, and I wasn't going to let sentiments for an old soldier like Marius get in the way of that.

It was at this time that I discovered Porcia. She was a tasty young thing with a wild look in her eye, and she came from good stock to boot. With brothers like Lucius and Marcus Porcius Cato, I knew she could help me ascend to the pinnacle of Roman politics. She saw in me someone who could give her a bit more adventure than the dusty old senators who were pining for her hand.

It wasn't quite time for Porcia and I to wed, though. I hoped I'd have long enough to make the political connections necessary for her betrothal, but Marius cut my time short.

He called me to his tablinum the day after he was elected to his fifth consulship, as if I were one of his slaves.

"Your Highness." I dipped low in a bow and then smiled at one of his prettier slaves.

"Leave us." He gestured to all those in attendance. I frowned in mock fear as the doors slammed shut behind us.

"What's wrong, Consul? Shouldn't you be elated on a day like this?"

"You won't be returning with me to Gaul," he said.

The humor drained from my face.

"Why?" I tried to restrain myself but felt my face twitching. I could have squashed the man if I'd desired. But I didn't. Not yet.

"You'll be remaining here in Italy. You'll be assisting in the levying of our soldiers for the upcoming campaign. We'll need more good men for the fight, and I want you to oversee it." He was careful not to meet my eyes.

I began to breath heavily. Despite my best efforts, I couldn't help the intensive breaths from being audible.

"Why?" I asked again, more forcefully this time.

A snarl crossed his face, but again he did not meet my eyes. "I cared for you, Lucius. And you've wounded me gravely. I think it's best if we're no longer around one another."

I choked up for a moment, and not all of it was for show. I'm sure I could have persuaded him to let me stay, but I wasn't sure what I wanted in that moment.

"It wasn't lack of care for you, Marius, but a desire to advance."

"For a year or—"

I cut him off. "As a brother I looked—"

He cut me off. "For a year or more! No more."

I stepped toward his desk, forcefully enough that it drew his attention.

"You weren't born with a drop of good blood in you, Marius, and yet I was still raised more lowly than you. I made a promise as a child, Marius. A promise that I would be nothing like my father. That I would become powerful and great!" For a brief moment of foolishness, I expected him to sympathize with me and understand where I was coming from. I had forgotten what a stubborn old wretch he really was.

He leaned back in his chair and made it clear that he was resigned to end the discussion. He refused to look at me, like a schoolboy in a dispute when the tutor has taken his side. Power was in his hands this day, but I wouldn't allow it to remain so for long.

"I'll be back, Marius," I said, pointing at his side-turned face. "I'll be back with more power and influence." I walked to the door but

paused and turned to him one last time. "Even more power and influence than you."

Up until that point, I had pitied the man. I had pitied him for his boundless ambition and his bounded ability.

But after that day, I always hated him.

21

SCROLL XXI

FOUR DAYS BEFORE THE KALENDS OF MARCH 652 AB URBE CONDITA

Horns sounded and men lined the walls to watch our arrival. Thank the gods we found Marius's camp here, at the confluence of the Rhône and Isère Rivers. We could endure no more traveling. One of us had already died from exposure along the way, and I feared a few others, including Ax, would soon follow him.

Marius himself was the first man through the gates, his guard flanking him on either side. His face was lit up with curiosity and confusion, and perhaps relief that I had finally arrived.

By Jupiter, it was a pleasant sight to see the scarlet flags and plumed helms again. We looked nothing like Romans should, and it was more obvious now as we gazed upon our well-groomed and well-fed brethren than ever.

"Sir." I snapped to attention and gave the best salute I could in my exhaustion. The others did the same.

Marius stood in silence for a moment, analyzing all of us. I wasn't sure if he could tell if the men with me were Romans or not.

"Who are these?" Marius gestured to the escaped prisoners.

"Romans. They were prisoners in the Cimbri camp. I helped them escape." Eyebrows all around us rose.

"Well, then," Marius said with an extended exhale, "we need to discuss some things. Follow me." I hadn't expected Marius to give me any time to rest—I knew him too well by now. But I was surprised at how poised and unaffected he seemed by our arrival. The quickness of his pace alone gave away his concern.

"General," I said before he could turn, "these men need to see the *medicus*. They are badly malnourished."

Marius simply gave a nod, and some of the mules present led the prisoners away from me. I gave Ax a nod of the head before he departed, but his glossy eyes didn't seem to register it.

As I followed Marius through the camp, more and more of the mules stopped their drills and turned to watch the prisoners on their way to the *medicus* tent.

I spotted Lucius among them, a mop of sweaty hair atop his head. His eyes were wet with relief. I was relieved to see him as well. There was certainly a time when I didn't think I would.

"Tell me all that you discovered," Marius said the moment I entered his quarters. Volsenio rolled out a map on the table and slammed *pugio* in the corners to keep it in place.

"The Cimbri are moving. They were leaving two days after we fled, so they are well on their way now. We made the best speed we could, but I can't imagine they are more than a few days behind us."

"Do you know their path of march?"

"The Cimbri and Teutones are splitting up." I stepped toward the map. "I can't be certain, but I understand the Cimbri are going south, where they will attack from the west. The Teutones are moving north of the Alps, where they will circle around and hit us from the east. They mean to flood into Italy with a violent force from either direction."

Marius analyzed my finger's movement over the map as more and more officers joined us.

"And their allies?"

"The Tigurini move with the Cimbri. I heard rumor that the Ambrones were in camp with the Teutones, but I never saw them myself."

"Is that it?"

"I believe so, sir. There could be other tribes that join them on their journey, but they have made many enemies in Gaul."

I then told Marius of the Cimbri method of attaching themselves to one another by their hips. The officers took a collective exhale. It was important to know this, but it didn't make the method any less effective.

I tried my best to recollect all the information I had stored away in my mind—total number of forces, quality of arms and armor, infrastructure, capabilities for movement and supply. I mentioned that I had seen siege equipment, catapults mainly, but very few of them. I finished my brief within only a few moments and then suddenly felt I hadn't presented him with enough. His expression was unreadable.

Marius asked nothing of my time in the Cimbri camp, or how I had attained such intelligence, but simply wanted more, more, more information. He was as stern and contemplative as I had ever seen him.

"That is all I know, sir," I said when I had exhausted every ounce of information I had gathered.

"Well," he said, leaning back from the map for the first time, "as your consul, I could have you crucified for taking such a risk to free those men, jeopardizing all of this intelligence. But as a man, I am proud of you. I commend you, Tribune." He met my eye. "I would give you a military crown if I were able, but to do so would confirm that this mission actually took place. And we can't allow that to happen. Makes us look weak."

"I wouldn't accept it if you did, sir."

"Dismissed," Marius said to me and all the other officers,

making it clear that he wanted to sit alone with his thoughts and the new intelligence for a while.

As I exited, Lucius was the first man to greet me. Apparently, he had been in the consul's tent behind me all along.

"Your tale just seems to get wilder and wilder," he said with a pursed grin.

"We both know my tale would have ended at Arausio if it weren't for you," I said, concealing a smile myself. We embraced.

"I'm glad you're back." He patted my face as he released me. "It's been quite boring without you. I've had to spend far more time with Equus than I would've liked," he said.

"I've tried my best to keep him in line for you, Sertorius, but to no avail," Equus said, extending a handshake.

"I believe it is you who deserves the crown, then, Equus."

"You must be exhausted. Let's go back to the tribunes' quarters and you can rest," Lucius said.

I considered it for a moment.

"I am exhausted, but there is somewhere else I'd much rather be."

Lucius and I walked together to the stables.

As I found the stall where Sura was haltered, my heart warmed for the first time since I'd departed Marius's camp. "Hey, girl." I buried my face in her mane and kissed her forehead. She whinnied and stomped one of her hooves playfully in response. I had missed her as much as anyone while in the camp of barbarians.

"She's been quite rebellious since you left," Lucius said. "She hasn't let anyone else ride her. She only allowed Apollonius to enter the stall without causing a fuss, and only because she knew he came with figs and a brush."

It all felt like a dream. I never imagined I would be here again, with my friend, with my steed. But here I was. All of my senses seemed elevated. I noticed sights, smells, colors I never would have before.

"Tell me, *amicus*, was it bad?" Lucius said, serious for once.

I turned from the horse to him. "I made it back alive. That's all that matters," I said, but I couldn't force out the image of the Roman prisoners burning before my eye.

"And thank the gods for that. I've sacrificed every week since you left."

"How many pigeons?"

"Twenty-two this time. I hadn't forgotten." He smiled.

"How have things been since I left?"

Lucius considered his answer. "Interesting, to say the least."

"How do you mean?" I asked as Sura found her way to the hay-covered earth, looking for a belly scratch.

"Marius departed for quite some time. He was canvasing in Rome for another election."

"Of which he was successful, I'm sure."

"Without question. No one in Rome doubted it, although there were many who opposed it."

"For good reason, I assume. It's quite unconstitutional for a man to have so many consulships in a row," I said, knowing that Lucius would take offense.

"Twelve bloody tables, be damned! We need Marius right now. None of the patricians can defeat the Reds."

"I only jest." I smiled to pacify him.

"Well, he was elected, but it wasn't without cost."

"Cost?"

"He made some unscrupulous friends in the process. He had to have some help within the senate to ensure his election, so he came to some kind of arrangement with a profligate praetor and a rebellious tribune."

"Who were they?"

"The praetor is a man named Gaius Glaucia. The tribune a man named Lucius Saturninus."

I thought about it for a moment. The names both sounded familiar, but I couldn't place them.

"And how did you hear all this?"

"By Mars's balls, man. I'm surprised you didn't hear it in the Cimbri camp. It's all anyone has talked about for months."

"It's a shame I missed out on all the good gossip, then." I shrugged.

"Well, that's not it. Did you see Sulla in Marius's tent earlier?" Lucius asked.

"I've only got the one good eye, Lucius. I'm sure there were many present that I wasn't able to see." I smiled but Lucius did not.

"Well, he wasn't there. Marius sent him home to levy troops."

"An insulting demotion."

"Without question. The tension between them grew as large as the camp before he left. Thing is, though, Sulla already returned with a new command."

"Oh?"

"Yes…as a legate, I believe, under Marius's consular colleague, Catulus."

"I'm sure that caused a commotion."

"Marius hasn't spoken of it"—Lucius shook his head—"but you can tell he is very disturbed. Personally offended, even. Luckily, they're stationed miles east of here; otherwise, we'd have confrontation on our hands, to be certain."

Lucius commenced to fill me in on the rudimentary details of camp life while I was gone, and the various power struggles of the tribunes, most of whom he resented. I pulled an apple from my satchel and fed it to Sura as we talked.

When I summoned up the courage, I told him about finding the men who were set to be human sacrifices and our mad scramble to escape.

"Just to see Ax again…"

"I'm sure that was a surprise."

"I shudder at the thought of my leaving without first taking him with me. I almost left, Lucius. I almost did," I said.

"But you did not."

"I thought all of my companions from the Fourth Legion

were dead. My world seems a bit larger now that one of them is found alive." I blinked the moisture from my eye. I was done with sentimentality for the moment, and there were more important things at hand.

I gave Sura a goodbye kiss, then walked back with Lucius to the tribunes' quarters. Despite my swollen leg and exhaustion, I was walking fine. Lucius didn't seem to care one way or the other, though, as he kept a gentle hand on my elbow as we moved.

As we entered, Apollonius was already rushing to the tent exit.

"Quintus, I just heard you arrived!" He stood still, awkwardly, until I reached out and embraced him.

"I have."

"And I have been waiting anxiously for the moment that I could say, 'I told you so,'" he said.

"And what did you tell me?" I plopped down on my finely pressed linen sheets.

"That you'd make it back alive, of course."

"What about all that talk of dying and only having the present moment?" I tried to recollect our conversation.

"Nonsense! All of it!" We all shared a laugh. "Tribune Cinna told me that you rescued prisoners on your way out? The Greeks could tell a few tales about you, young master," he said, looking me over like a physician.

"I think it's best if those stories fade away," I said honestly, not intending to one day recollect them here.

Apollonius's face lit up and he lifted a finger as if he had made a great discovery.

"I had almost forgotten!" He hurried out of the tent without saying another word.

I had now been away from Apollonius longer than I had known him, but something about his presence felt like home.

He returned far faster than I would have assumed of a man his age, a bundle of letters in his hand.

It was clear that he was as proud of those letters as a man would be of a child.

"I've keep them locked away in the slave quarters. Some of the others said you were dead, and tried to encourage me to break the seals, but I wouldn't do it." He passed them to me delicately.

"I thank you, Apollonius."

"I'll give you some time, then." Apollonius stepped back a few paces and found an empty chair. Lucius was already reclining on his bed and snoring, as was his custom.

I greedily poured over each and every letter. I longed to find the name "Arrea" scribbled on one.

I had a few from Lucius's brother, but most of them were from my mother, who clearly had no idea of my expedition but was angry I hadn't written her in so long.

Two of these letters, thanks to Apollonius's careful stewardship, have remained among my records ever since.

The first was from Junia, the wife of Quintus Caepio.

Hers was certainly a name I did not expect to see.

Dearest Quintus,

I cannot thank you enough for what you did. At great risk to yourself and your reputation, you saved a man in need. We have since fled Rome and are now living in exile on a far-away isle.

So as not to implicate you further, I will not mention where.

Our son, Marcus, is with us, and he is healthy. We are not accustomed to living in these circumstances, and aren't quite comfortable, but we cannot complain. I thank the gods for my husband's life, my child's safety, and for your decent heart. One day, my boy will return to Rome and continue what his father was unable to finish. I don't expect that we will ever be able to repay you for what you've done, but I hope that we shall.

Gnaeus has died, of heartbreak at his son's defeat or of natural causes—we do not know. Since we fled, Caecilia has married again.

I hope that you are well, Quintus Sertorius. And my heart remembers fondly the moments we shared in Gnaeus's domus."

Junia

NEEDLESS TO SAY, I kept this letter private, and shared it with no one save Apollonius until now. It was comforting to see that my decision had benefited Junia and Marcus, but I still wondered if it had been the right choice.

The next was a letter from my mother. It was two months old by the time I read it, but it was the most recent available to me. I could tell that my mother was fearful for my safety, even though word of battle hadn't arrived.

MY SON,

I've long hoped for a message from you. The family waits anxiously each day to see if word has arrived. We all worry about you. We've listened endlessly to the newsreaders in the market. They say you have not met the Cimbri or Teutones in battle. So why have you not written? Perhaps you aren't receiving our letters, or maybe you're too busy with your new responsibilities. Regardless, I pray to the gods that you'll write soon.

I miss you dearly.

Volesa sends her love as well. Gavius is growing like a weed. I'd wager he'll be as tall as I am by the time you return. Aius Hirtuleius has tended to us so well—he has the heart of his brother.

I do not want to alarm you, as I know you have much to worry about already, but your wife has been unwell. Volesa has been confined to her bed for many days now, and has shown no interest in getting out of it, or in speaking with any of us. She has no fever, and displays no signs of sickness. We all care for her, but she refuses to be tended to.

Arrea has taken such good care of Gavius since Volesa became this way. I am very grateful that you brought her here.

I hope to hear from you soon, my son, my hope, my love.

Rhea

And then, written at the bottom of this final letter, was the name I most desired to see.

Postscriptum

This is Arrea. Your mother has been teaching me how to write. I'm improving daily, but don't yet have the words to say to you what I need to.

I want you to return to me. To us, I mean. I still want you to return to all of us safely.

Arrea

AND THAT WAS ALL she'd written. Both joyful and dreadful thoughts seeped into my mind. My head swirled. What did she mean? Was it written in anger? In love?

"Good news from home?" Apollonius asked me as I sat the letters aside and leaned back on my pillows.

"Any news from home is good news, when you thought you were a dead man. But I'm not sure that's what I would call it."

"All hardships are compounded when you are too far away to do anything about them," Apollonius said.

"I believe you're right, my friend." I shook my head. "I wish I could see them now."

He approached my bed and knelt beside it.

"Only a little longer, and perhaps you shall."

22

SCROLL XXII

TWO DAYS BEFORE THE IDES OF MARCH 652 AB URBE CONDITA

I received word from Marius that I was allowed two days' rest before assisting with the construction of a bridge over the Rhône.

The Roman army moved fast, but I'm tempted to say that the Teutones were quicker. We finished building the bridge in two days, and less than a fortnight later, word came of the Teutones' arrival. They would be upon us within two days.

The men collectively exhaled. Battle could be dreadful, but the wait was often worse, especially for those who had actually endured battle before. The green recruits were ready for war, or so they thought. The officers were unsure, Marius among them.

Not long after our scouts returned with word of the Teutones' imminence, barbarian ambassadors also arrived at our gates.

Horns sounded throughout the camp, and the guards along the walls called out.

I was in the middle of overseeing weapons drills when I heard the commotion, and I at once made for the walls.

I peered over the edge to see four riders, all clad in rich gold armor they had likely taken from fallen enemies in Spain. One of them bore a blue flag fringed with gold that flapped violently in the wind.

"We seek word with your master," one of them cried out. He was clearly a Gaul, and one who had spent enough time around Romans to have a firm understanding of Latin.

"You are mistaken," I shouted out. "We are Romans, and we have no master."

Marius arrived below the walls along with his guard, and hollered up at us. "Who is it?"

"The Teutones, I believe, General. They want to talk with you." The Gaul turned to the others and whispered a translation of my words.

Marius deliberated for a moment, and then gave the signal for the gates to be opened.

"Bows at the low ready." I passed the word down the wall to our *auxilia* bowmen, who each notched an arrow but kept it hidden from our enemy.

"Why have you come here?" Marius said, halting before them, several guardsmen on either side with a hand on their swords.

"We wish to offer you one last chance to surrender," one of the Teutones said, his words translated by the Gaul.

"We will not surrender. Have you any other offers?" Marius replied quickly, not pausing to consider.

"King Teutobod would like to meet with you. Will you accept his generous offer?"

Now Marius took a moment to consider his answer.

"When?"

None of us knew why he didn't refuse the offer outright, and perhaps Marius didn't either. Maybe it was simply curiosity.

"This evening. We can share a cup of your wine before we shed your blood," the Teutone ambassador replied.

It might not sound like it, but this was quite an insult. If they had access to our wine, it meant that they had attacked and destroyed one of our allies.

"I will meet with your king," Marius said, and turned at once, his cape whipping in the wind behind him.

"Tell me, Tribune, is it a trap? You know them better than anyone," Marius asked me as I joined him in his quarters.

"I don't know, sir. I wasn't in their camp. I do know they met with Maximus before the battle of Arausio, and showed no signs of betrayal until Caepio attacked them."

Marius sat back in his chair and allowed Volsenio to lather his face with oil and begin shaving him.

"It is risky," one of Marius's legates said, but Marius was already lost in his own thoughts.

"Tribune Sertorius, I'll have you attend the parlay with me. Perhaps the Teutones speak with a tongue similar to the Cimbri."

"I don't believe they do, sir," I said. I hadn't been able to understand a word the barbarian ambassador had spoken.

"Regardless. You survived Arausio, now you've infiltrated the Cimbri camp, saved eight prisoners, and made it back alive… You seem to have powerful gods watching over you. If I am to enter the lion's den, I'd prefer to have someone with friends like that with me," he said as Volsenio finished shaving his neck. "Equus, you too. I want you to command my guard. Your father will be displeased with me for this, but he knew the risks when he allowed you to join me."

"Yes, General," Equus replied, unperturbed.

"Go, all of you." Marius flung his hand toward the exit. "Shit, bathe, and shave. We will leave at the ninth hour."

I FOLLOWED MARIUS'S ORDERS, but took more time to pray than anything. I spoke with my father and brother, and with all our household gods, who now seemed so far away. I feared that soon they would become impatient with my pleading for safety in ludicrous, impossible situations. But they had protected me thus far.

I fixed a saddle on Sura, and led her to the gates for the first time since we'd met the Tectosages in battle. I scratched behind her ear to offer some comfort, but I could tell by her jitters that she expected more of the same.

"Into the mouth of Cerberus, then," Equus said as we met up outside the gates.

"Leave your Greek myths in the city," Marius said. "We enter the Teutone camp. It's much more intimidating than a three-headed dog, if you ask me."

"You don't seem so intimidated, General," Equus said, not dissuaded by the rebuke.

"I am. But not as intimidated as they should be of me," Marius said. "Ya!" he whipped his horse to a gallop, and we hurried to follow after him.

I was shocked by how quickly we arrived. It was no more than an hour or two's ride. The sun was still high in the sky as the Teutones' vast outfit poured into view.

"Should we advance?" Equus asked.

"No. If they want to meet, they'll do so on my terms," Marius replied. "Lift your flag high, boy," Marius said to the banner carrier of his guard.

We waited for some time, wondering whether or not they had spotted us.

"Are you nervous, Tribune?" a member of the guard asked Equus. He himself was visibly shaking in his lorica.

"Not in the slightest. I'll die when I die. I can't add one moment to my life by worrying, any more than I can make hair grow on my head," Equus said, generating a laugh because, even though not yet twenty years old, there was a bald spot atop the crown of his head. "If I had the choice, I think I'd take the hair."

After hours of waiting, we saw a detachment of horsemen separate from the endless throng of Teutone warriors.

"I can't see, is that something?" Marius asked, squinting to make out the shapes in the distance. Even with two operating eyes, his vision was poorer than mine.

"It is, sir. That's them."

Only four riders approached us. They clearly weren't as intimidated as Marius believed they ought to be.

I identified King Teutobod immediately. Although I had never seen him, his authority was undeniable. Even bobbing on his horse, there was a certain swagger that caught my eye. On top of that, the quality of his golden breastplate, which burned orange in the fading sunlight, was finer than all the rest. He clearly took the first and the last of their spoils, whatever suited him best.

Among the others, he stood the largest, his arms sculpted and his legs shaped like tree trunks. I guess, in a culture like theirs, you don't last long as king unless you can defend yourself.

His eyes shone with curiosity and perhaps humor as he sized us up. He was already imagining if he could fit into our breastplates or gauntlets.

"Greetings from King Teutobod," he said. One of his men translated. How he knew Latin, I do not know.

"I am Consul Gaius Marius, leader of the freed people of the Roman Republic." Marius didn't look to the interpreter but kept his eyes fixed on the king.

"Our ambassadors said you will not surrender. Is this true?"

"The Romans never surrender," Marius said. A few of the Teutones chuckled and exchanged playful glances.

"Perhaps you should. The Romans should learn when they are beaten."

"The Romans are never beaten." Marius was unconcerned by their response. I was afraid his tender *dignitas* would be offended, and he might fly into one of his famous rages. But here, atop his black stallion, he remained cool and composed.

"What have you come to propose?" the king asked.

Marius nodded and considered his reply for a moment. "That you return to Spain. Enjoy the spoils of those lesser tribes. Find some land to settle in, plow your fields, and have your women. But do not try to fight Rome again."

The Teutone king tilted his head sidelong as if confused by what he heard, but I felt certain the interpreter had translated Marius properly.

"I plead with you," Marius said again, "return to where you came from. I did not come with trebuchets and war horses. I did not come to kill you. I'll allow you to live this once. But if you come a foot closer, I will kill you all." Marius's eyes were locked with the king's.

The Teutone king now let his head back, allowing his laughter to pour out freely. It echoed across the rolling hills of the Rhône valley.

"I will see you in battle. I'll have your head on the tip of this spear"—Teutobod hoisted the point of his weapon—"then I will plow *your* land, and have *your* women."

Teutobod wheeled his horse around and galloped off toward his army.

We stood still for a few moments.

"Well, that was unproductive," Equus said on an exhale.

"More productive than you might think," Marius said, turning his horse and beginning to trot back toward camp.

"How so?"

"I hope he relays my message." He turned and looked at each one of us. "Now they have a choice."

23

SCROLL XXIII

ONE DAY BEFORE THE IDES OF MARCH 652 AB URBE CONDITA

The Teutones began to move the next day. I couldn't help but climbing to the guard tower to steal a glance. Their numbers were endless: spear tips and golden helms shone farther than my eye could see.

Marius had situated our camp on a narrow hilltop in between the Rhône and Isère Rivers. To most, it would have been a position of strategic value, but as I watched the Teutones massing in the distance—and saw the furious rapids of the Rhône to one side and the Isère on the other—I remembered Arausio, and felt the rush of the cold waters as they engulfed me that day.

An assembly was called for the officers. We meet in Marius's praetorium, as was his custom.

"If they desire battle, they could be upon us by sundown," Marius's new second-in-command, Manius Aquillius said, a grieved look on his face. He had a narrow face with thin, pursed lips as rigid as his posture. Aquillius's eyes were deep set and seemed sad, but I never recall him expressing emotion of any kind. He was a man cut from the same cloth as Marius: discipline and order in all things.

"We shall not give it to them," Marius said, equally as grim.

Lucius and I stood to the back of the room and watched as the men poured over a map, little blue flags indicating the known locations of the enemy, a silver eagle designating our fort.

"All due respect, General," Equus said, "but I'm not sure they require our permission to initiate contact." Tribunes were allowed to attend such meetings, but Equus hadn't yet learned that war councils were for the legates and the generals—we were allowed entry for procedure and ceremony more than anything else. I could see that some of the legates were unhappy, but Equus's point was well taken.

"They can initiate contact all they like. But these walls are strong," Marius retorted.

"So if they assault the walls, we will not retaliate?" Aquillius asked, as concerned as Cinna was.

"No, we will not." Marius's gruff voice boomed out, making it clear that he would receive no pushback on the matter. "We aren't yet prepared to meet them."

I could tell by the faces of others that we all shared the same thoughts: *What are we waiting on, then? If we aren't ready now, when will we be?*

"Where is our quaestor? Somebody find me the damn quaestor!" Marius shouted. Lucius hurried out of the tent to find him.

As we waited for his arrival, Marcus Marcellus appeared. He was still recovering from his time in the Cimbri camp, so he swayed from fatigue as if he were drunk. Regardless, his bone-thin frame was clad in a legate's armor. He'd insisted on being restored to his position, and Marius had eventually agreed.

"Sorry I'm late. The *medicus* was supposed to wake me," Marcellus said.

Marius seemed displeased. Perhaps not as much with Marcellus as with himself for allowing the man to take over a legion in such a condition. But who could refuse the man after he had endured so much?

"Anything?" Marcellus asked again, but no one answered him.

The quaestor entered and gave a panicked salute. "Sir!"

"How is our water supply?" Marius asked.

"Water supply? Adequate, sir."

"Gather all the surplus water we have and take it to the gates. They'll come with fire, and we'll need something to quench it. Leave only enough to last us the week," Marius said.

The quaestor stood by helpless for a moment, wanting further clarification.

"What did I just say? Go!" Marius shouted, and the quaestor sprinted away as if the Reds were after him.

I wondered if Marius had gone mad. Had all of the tales about him been embellished? How could we remain in our fort while a horde of angry warriors careened toward us?

I could see hesitation in the general's eyes. I could tell he, too, was concerned. But his choice had been made. We would wait them out.

"Now, all of you, listen to me. Go to your men. Tell them to array atop the walls. I want them to look into the faces of their enemy and see who it is that we fight. We'll repel the Teutones with arrows and pila, but nothing more," Marius said. "Inspect our men and their weapons and ensure they're prepared for whatever lies ahead. Leave the cavalry in the stables. We have no use for them now."

We could already hear the stamping of a hundred thousand angry Teutones in the distance as we exited the praetorium.

"I hope they don't have siege equipment," I said to Lucius as we walked.

"They don't. They can't. Those barbarians? All they know is

to rush at our walls like water on rock," he said, ever faithful to Marius. I didn't mention the fact that the Teutones had broken through Maximus's walls at Arausio, but I didn't have to. I knew my friend well. And I could tell by his darting glances and the trembling of his hands that he was as concerned as I was.

We split up and I made my way to the Seventh Legion headquarters. I found First Spear Centurion Herennius there receiving the final report from his *optio*.

"Centurion," I said.

"Ready to give report, sir," he replied with a formal salute.

"Give the report."

"Thirty-three men down, sir," he read from the *optio*'s report. "Eight from flux, four from self-inflicted wounds, three in the brig, ten with dysentery, eight with a pox."

"Good, nearly full capacity. Have the centuries line up by rank." I gave a salute. Before I could turn to leave, he leaned in.

"Sir, tell me about the meeting. Is it time to give the Reds one up the arse?" he asked with a sinister grin. He was a grizzled old centurion, and this waiting around didn't suit him.

"No. We will be massing on the walls. Prepare the men," I said. His face scrunched like he had bitten into something sour, but saluted and turned to give the order.

THE RAMPARTS WEREN'T broad enough to fit all of us, so Marius instructed those who hadn't seen battle to take the first rank atop the walls, while the veterans remained in position beneath. I stood with the centurion of the Seventh Legion atop the south wall. We stood silently. All that was heard was the nervous shaking of recruits in their leather sandals, and the pitter of rain on our helms.

The Teutones moved forward methodically as one rhythmic force. Thunder cracked in the distance beneath angry clouds. Every few moments, a strike of Jupiter's lightning illuminated both the gray sky and our enemy before fading back to darkness. It was midday, at the latest, but it felt as if night was descending on us with every stomp of the Teutone front line.

"Everyone understands what we are doing?" I asked. It wasn't rhetorical, but the trembling recruits responded as if it were, with silence. "We stand at attention. We let them know we are Romans and we will not be intimidated. We'll repel them with javelin but will not meet them on the field of battle," I said, turning toward the enemy, attempting to still my own heart. "Your sword will be wet with blood soon enough. Until then, we stand tall, and we stand together." Before I was finished speaking, war drums began to boom in the distance.

"They have siege equipment," Centurion Herennius said, leaning close enough that I alone would hear him.

I strained my eye to make out the enemy machinery in the distance but found nothing.

"Where? How do you know?" I asked.

"I can hear it." He tapped the sagging lobe of his ear. He was old for a soldier but had enough experience that I didn't distrust him.

"Steady, men," I said as the rain poured harder against us, water falling over our helms.

I exhaled as I smelled the stench of urine and terror behind me, but no one said anything. I remembered how overwhelmed I was at Burdigala, and my heart ached for them.

The Teutones now came close enough for us to see the etches of their facial features. Each one wore a scowl, many with missing teeth. Pale scars stretched across their faces and hid beneath thick beards. I stole a moment's glance at the young mules behind me, and realized that we were an army of boys… fighting an army of men.

"The walls will protect us," I said. "Roman engineering will best barbarian steel every time." I spook with feigned confidence. Even as I said this, I spotted the wooden catapults in the distance rolling on massive rocks hewn into wheels.

The men released a collective gasp as they saw it. And then all was silent for a moment of realization and anticipation. The marching Teutones halted, and the war drums ceased.

We looked down at the silent enemy below, hoping it was a bluff.

Then a violent humming stretched through the air. As soon as I spotted it, the massive rock cracked into the walls with a crash to challenge the thunder.

I lost my footing and balanced myself on my shield, the entire fort trembling beneath us.

Then another struck the east wall, and another nearer to us.

The Teutone drums beat three times in succession, and the Teutones roared out as they sprinted forward.

"Pila! Pila, men!" the centurion shouted beside me as he grabbed me by my lorica and pulled me into the ranks of his men. The recruits stepped forward and raised their pila overhead.

The grizzled veteran pushed me as far from the precipice as he could, but strained over the edge to see how close the Teutones were.

We glanced over our shoulders and saw yellow flags waving from the guard towers.

"Bring them down! Let loose!" The centurion's voice was drowned out by the war cry of the Teutones who were now beneath us.

The first rank approached the wall and struggled to balance their shields while they launched their pila at the hordes below. The rain and awkwardness of the wall hindered the men's form, but the tip of a spear is the tip of a spear. After each volley, the barbarians' cries rose to greet us. Their grimy hands scratched at the broken pila in their chests, unable to pry them free. The uninjured Teutones trampled over their fallen brethren to get to the wall.

As the first rank fell back, allowing the second to take its place, their eyes were lit up. They had never been more alive. I knew the feeling well. Terror, sheer terror, but they didn't know if they liked it or not.

"*Auxilia!*" The centurion shouted, hearing the whistles from the guard towers. Our Gallic allies sent down stones and arrows into the Teutones. Hundreds among them collapsed, but more warriors simply pulled the shaft or stone from their flesh and continued hammering against the wall with renewed relish.

I noticed movement in the clouds above us, another massive stone from the catapult.

"Centurion," I managed to say, my voice weak.

"Shields up!" he shouted. The men along the wall hunkered down beneath their shields and crouched together, I along with them. The shadow of the massive stone passed through the light in between our shields. Then, the cry of many Romans carried up from the ranks behind us on the ground.

As we rose again, and our pila volley continued, I stole a glance at the Seventh Legion centuries beneath us. The stone was large enough to clutch a few men beneath it, but it had rolled and taken out several more. Dozens lay mutilated with helmets, limbs, and swords strewn out among them. Romans were flattened like poorly baked bread, unidentifiable even to those closest to them.

The mules around them were shocked and horrified.

"Reform, reform!" the centurion's *optio* shouted, whipping them with his *hastile*. They attempted to reform the line amid the carnage of their friends, just as another stone crashed against the walls.

The force of it sent most of us to the ground. A few of the mules landed on top of me.

I patted myself to make sure I hadn't been a casualty of the rock, still breathing by sheer adrenaline. I was fine, save an inch-long cut from the scabbard of a mule to my forearm. I was grateful that the rock had been down the line from us, but this rock was the first to create a massive hole in our walls.

Like soldiers, wooden walls, no matter how brilliantly

constructed, have their breaking point. The wood splintered and crumbled, taking dozens of men with it. They fell, screaming in sheer terror, into the group of massive Teutone beasts. If they did not die upon impact, they were quickly swarmed and met a far harsher end at the tip of barbarian steel.

"Steady, soldiers! Eyes front!" the centurion barked, seemingly unaffected by the carnage. I knew from experience that it became easier to feign such composure the longer you had been around it.

The last rank approached the edge and sent down their pila, more violently than their predecessors, enraged by the deaths of their comrades.

The cries of the Teutones rose to take the place of their war chants. We were out of pila, and they were out of energy.

The rain continued.

"Reform now, reform along the walls," the centurion said, more softly now.

The *auxilia* continued to notch their arrows, but now the Teutones hoisted their rounded shields to meet them, seeing that their attempt to cut through Roman engineering was futile.

We were close enough now, and the tumult somewhat stilled, so that we could look over the edge into their eyes. They were exhausted and panting but still wore hatred in their eyes and scowls on their lips.

A horn sounded in the distance, and the men began to back up in unison, never taking their eyes off our walls. They wouldn't win this day, but the looks on their faces revealed they believed they would. And soon.

24

SCROLL XXIV

ELEVEN DAYS BEFORE THE KALENDS OF APRIL 652 AB URBE CONDITA

That was the first day of several. The rest were just like it. We continued to mass on the walls, forced to watch our howling enemy approach in silence. The Teutones came with fresh fury every morning and battled until the midday sun wore them out. They taunted us, doing everything they could to provoke us to leave our walls and meet them.

The rain continued to fall in greater and greater quantity. It dripped from our helms, found its way into each crevice of our chain mail, and settled into the leather of our sandals. I can tell you from experience that dampness rusts men like swords, more slowly perhaps, but just as deeply.

At night, we retreated to our tents in an attempt to rest and recover our strength. But how could we, with the Teutones howling at our gates? Even if we could, though, the barbarians didn't give us that chance. Every few hours, just when things would become quiet, the Teutones would send a small force to assail our walls. The bugles would sound, and each legionary would groan as he rolled from his bed and attempted to don his armor in the darkness. After three nights of this, we were painfully aware of what our enemy was doing, but Marius insisted that the entire army amass every time, vowing that his legions would not be butchered in their sleep because the enemy had lulled them into a false sense of security.

"Can't these bastards just give us a little rest?" one of the mules from the Seventh Legion asked, rubbing the exhaustion from his eyes. I was just as irritated as him, but it was good to see that the men were simply exhausted and annoyed, rather than shaken by terror, as they were on the first day.

"They're doing it on purpose, half brain," one of the mule's companions said derisively, "and Marius is determined to let them have their way."

"If they can't break down the walls in the light of day, what makes the old general think they could topple them in the shroud of night?" the first legionary asked. I assumed they couldn't see my rank in the dark. Even so, I didn't care to admonish them for their disrespect. I had been a mule too, not so long ago, and remembered that grumbling was simply part of the culture, and a necessary part.

"A better question is why we haven't met them in battle," a third legionary said, still tightening his lorica at his rib cage.

"Yeah," added another, his voice thick with a southern Italian dialect, "does he think we're weak? Eh? He think we're too green to take them?"

The war cries of the Teutones echoed throughout the camp as they hammered against the base of the walls.

"Some of us are," the first mule added. "I've got nephews tougher than Third Century." The men laughed in unison. That was a positive sign.

"Up the stairs, men." I stopped at the base and directed them up. "Find your positions quickly, and don't say a word when you're on the walls."

"We're getting used to the routine, sir," one of them barked.

The rest fell silent, fearing they had earned themselves an extra guard shift or two for their lack of discretion.

After a few hours of summoning up whatever tumult they could, the small Teutone band, maybe a few thousand strong, would retreat to their camp at a leisurely pace, with enough time to get some good rest before the morning duel.

"Down!" the centurions would shout when the signal was given. We'd wait for some time on the walls, nestled in shoulder to shoulder with the men beside us, until each man descended. In the dull flickering torchlight, I made my way back to the tribunes' quarters.

"I'm looking forward to fighting the Teutones. I believe it will be very enjoyable," Equus said with as much frustration as I had ever seen in him.

"'Fight' doesn't begin to describe it. I'm going to obliterate those bastards," Lucius grunted as he untied his sandals. My old friend could endure hunger, the wind, the rain, bitter cold or blazing heat...but he couldn't handle a lack of sleep.

"By Hera's cunt, do not light that torch!" one of the other tribune's shouted to another, who hung his head and moved away from it. "Undress in the dark, and then everyone shut their mouths." He seemed as ornery as Lucius. I was exhausted too, but I'll admit the absurdity of the situation was a bit humorous. I found myself stifling a smile as I laid my head back on my pillow.

I had learned by then that there was no sense in undressing. I took only my helmet off, and didn't bother to get under the blankets or otherwise make myself comfortable. I crossed my legs and closed my eye. After three days with very little sleep, it didn't take long to drift into a haze, but little time passed before that dreadful bugle sounded again, followed by the moans and curses of a tent full of tribunes.

THIS CONTINUED ON FOR A WEEK. By the end of it, we had men falling asleep in formation, nearly tumbling from the top of the walls until another mule grabbed them.

The mind plays all kinds of tricks when you're that tired. Sometimes I'd strain my eye, during the day as well as at night, to ensure the man across from me wasn't a pelt-wearing Teutone. I heard the war drums and the clashing of rocks against our walls even when there were none. And I believe I experienced the least of these effects. Our *medicus* tent was filled up with those who had been hurt by the catapults or Teutone projectiles, but there were as many or more who were sent there by order of the centurion for showing signs of psychosis.

The water, too, was running short. Orders were given for us to be abstemious with our consumption, but when one is awake nearly all hours of the day, he can consume far more fluids that he would under normal circumstances. We placed empty barrels near the walls to collect the rainfall, and yet we were still short.

Because of all this, we were very pleased when the Teutones approached our walls and didn't attack. There was a narrow strip of land to the east, flanked by the fort on one end and the Rhône on the other. It was here that the Teutones approached and then passed our camp.

As the enemy narrowed down to a few men abreast, their forces stretched back for miles.

"Cowards!" the Reds cried.

"Stand up and fight, Roman dogs!" some of them shouted in crude Latin, which they had presumably picked up from traitors and prisoners.

"Have any word for your wives? We shall soon be with them!" others shouted. This was unequivocally their most common insult, and it had the desired effect. We were furious. The thought of those sweaty barbarians raping and pillaging, sweaty and thrusting in a frantic lust, was enough to turn our stomachs.

The discontent of the men reached new heights.

"Say, Tribune," some of them began to probe me as we were standing atop the walls and watching as the barbarians moved past us, on to Italy.

"No talking on the walls," I said, stifling a yawn.

"Tribune, you lend an ear to Marius, don't you? Why won't he let us fight? Does he think us weak?" These questions had been circulating for a while now, but had usually been spoken in insecurity and shame. Now, it was anger that bore them. They were hungry to fight the Teutones. They wanted to prove themselves.

"Silence, soldier," I said. I believe I would have actually given him an answer if I had one. But I did not. The officers had altogether stopped talking about it. None of us knew what was going on in the old general's mind.

It took six full days for the Teutones to pass us by. Marius ordered that we should not leave the walls until they had had finished passing, but after the first several hours, even he agreed that this was impractical. He allowed different centuries to switch out, allowing others to rest, as if this were simply an extravagant guard shift.

Despite this mercy from the consul, there were Romans atop those walls for six days, watching as the Teutones filed past him, hurling insults about what they would do to his wife and daughters.

When the final barbarian passed us by at last, the bugles sounded and the flags waved again, and for once the orders weren't to rally on the ramparts.

I passed the order along for the men to line up in formation in the center of the camp. All three legions amassed, at close rank so that we could all fit.

"They're finally gone, the bastards?" one of the men who had been sleeping asked.

"The first of them are halfway to Italy by now," one of them grumbled.

"Any sense of what's next, Tribune?" Centurion Herennius asked me.

"No idea, Centurion." I shook my head. The rains continued to pour over us.

"I'm so damned tired of being wet," one of the mules complained.

"You're at attention, soldier," Herennius said, a bit more understanding than he usually was.

We stood in silence for some time, and the longer we remained, the more men began to stumble from their sleep deprivation. At last, the general appeared before us. He alone had eyes that weren't bloodshot with fatigue. He was spry on his feet, appearing as if he had just risen from a good night's rest. We all knew that wasn't true, however. He had slept less than perhaps any of us. General Marius was simply the man who could endure the most, and that was the kind of man we all wanted to follow, even if we doubted his orders.

"The Teutones have departed. It's now time to follow them. We have no time to lose, if we don't want their threats to be made true. Deconstruct the camp," Marius said.

"What?" a few of the men grumbled.

Even the most resolute among the ranks were vocal in their disapproval.

"That's it?" others asked.

Marius did not seem to hear it, although it was impossible that he did not. He moved at a brisk pass back to his praetorium, where he himself would help take it down. No further word was given, and no more rest was allowed either.

Our walls had withstood a weeklong assault from the Cimbri, and we deconstructed it within four hours.

We departed the moment the last plank of wood fell to the ground.

25

SCROLL XXV

TWO DAYS BEFORE THE KALENDS OF APRIL 652 AB URBE CONDITA

We marched just behind the Teutones for a week, following them like a hunting dog on the trail of a doe. Thankfully, I was able to ride Sura, which gave my leg a rest from the rigors of stomping for hours on end. More than a few times, I nodded off to the rhythmic sway of the mare beneath me, allowing her to carry me in step with the rest of the cavalry. Lucius didn't have as much experience riding, so he was far less comfortable. Unable to doze off, he spent most of the time complaining to me about the chaffing of his inner thighs, unconcerned that I didn't reply in my slumber.

Despite our pursuit of the barbarians, we were given time to sleep at night. Even the barbarians stopped for a bit of sleep, drinking, and intercourse. We had no time for the latter two, because Marius ordered that a fort be constructed every night to protect us, but by the gods, we enjoyed the former. We slept like well-fed babes, although well fed we were not. We also weren't adequately hydrated. Our water supply was running dangerously low, and we were rationed a single skin of water per day, despite the thirst that comes from thirty-mile marches.

But the seventh day after we departed our camp proved to be a fateful one.

The tail end of the Teutone army was but a few miles away, and we settled in atop a hill, our enemy in the distance below. We were a handful of miles from the Roman settlement Aquae Sextiae. This heightened our sense of urgency even further, for they could have burned the settlement to the ground at any point, if they so desired, taking Roman ladies and children in the process.

Waterskins were generally passed out upon completion of the day's march, but word spread quickly that there was no more water to be had.

The officers immediately panicked, and the mules let out torrents of discontent. We would all die here, they feared.

But just when we reached the height of our anguish, the order was given to line up in formation—not to construct camp, not to march farther still, but to mass in formation.

The grumbles stilled as the cohorts and centuries lined up abreast atop the hill.

Marius, on his massive black stallion, rode out before us, alone.

His steed bucked with anticipation, the emotion shared by all of Marius's men, but the general himself remained silent for a while, staring over his shoulder down the hill.

"Three paces forward, march!" Marius shouted. The mules took collective steps toward him. "Do you see what I see?" he asked.

"It's the Teutones!"

"It's the Ambrones!" The men among the front ranks pushed word back to those who couldn't see.

At the base of the hill, tens of thousands of the barbarians were wadding in a stream, paddling through the currents in luxurious ecstasy, and drinking freely. I could tell from those still dressed along the banks that it was the Ambrones, the strongest ally of the Teutones. They must have been able to see us atop the hill, but they had grown complacent after being able to see us for so long. Thank the gods Marius hadn't allowed us to do the same.

"You," Marius began, "you men have stared into Pluto's arse for weeks now." Despite his stern tone, the men roared with laughter. "You've looked into the eye of evil, and you've stood tall. At first, you were wary—terrified, even. But you aren't now, are you?"

"No!" everyone shouted in unison.

"I didn't think so. Some of you are tired." He paused so the men could grumble in agreement, which the centurions allowed. "Some of you need sleep. Well, soon you shall have it." His blade sung as he pulled it from the scabbard, pointing it to the base of the hill at the bathing Ambrones. "But we shall not have sleep until we cast our enemy into the eternal sleep!"

After remaining in silence, either standing atop the walls or marching along behind the enemy, the legions roared out.

"Some of you are thirsty," Marius said, nodding in sympathy. He paused for some time, and scanned the faces of his men. "Some of you are thirsty—well, there is your water. Let's go and take it!" The men shouted louder still, and the officers (myself included) stirred in sudden fear that the men might charge forward without the order. "You want sleep, you want water, but the price for it shall be blood. But never fear, comrades, we shed it for Rome. For Rome!"

"Rome!" we shouted in unison, each man hoisting his gladius to the heavens.

"Rome!" Marius shouted again.

"Rome!"

"Let's retrieve what they've taken!" Marius shouted, wheeling his horse about and charging down the hill alone.

The bugles sounded, and we charged after him in reckless abandon.

Caught up in the mania, I pushed Sura harder and harder. I bounced violently atop her but was undeterred. We wouldn't let our general go to battle alone.

Below, the Ambrones caught sight of the thirty-five thousand Romans charging down the hill toward them. Even from a distance, you could see their eyes widen as they struggled against the current to return to the banks with all their might.

But they were too slow, and we charged with too much pent-up fury.

Our cavalry leapt the ford with ease, the hooves beating down on the slowest among them.

The legionaries jumped into the river, rejuvenated simply by the touch of water.

A man before me tried to gather his axe and shield, his mouth agape and eyes wide, but he couldn't ready himself quickly enough. I sliced him from navel to jugular with my long sword as Sura trampled over another before me.

"For Rome!" the shout continued as the water splashed up all around us, mixed with the blood of falling enemies. Their corpses piled up along the riverbanks and slowed our advance, but the rest of their number was trapped. Only a handful of them scurried off toward the Teutones in the distance. The remainder fell quickly.

Only then did we become aware of the horns blowing and the drums beating in the distance. The Teutones were massing.

"Retreat! Retreat!" The order was given, followed rapidly by the cry of centurion whistles.

The cavalry jumped the river again, and the legionaries wadded back across before we sprinted up the hill. By the time the Teutones arrived, we were nearly back to where we'd started. They didn't dare give charge. We had the high ground, and given the thousands of bodies that now bobbed at their feet, they were unwilling to risk such a venture.

When we arrived at the height of the hill, the men were

panting with exhaustion, but a kind completely different than what we'd been experiencing beforehand.

Marius again ordered us to line up.

We formed loose ranks as best we could, but Marius ordered us to break ranks and form around him. The six legions of hungry Romans amassed in a semicircle. Never before or since have I seen a general other than Marius, who was usually a fanatic for regulation and military custom, allow such informality. The men gathered close enough to feel his breath. Ambrones blood was splattered across his face, but his smile was unmistakable.

"Listen closely, men," Marius's voice boomed out, the only voice I've ever heard that could carry far enough for all thirty-five thousand men to have a front-row seat. "The bulk of the Ambrones now lie dead. If you had reason to doubt yourself before, you don't now. Some of you have worried that I don't believe in you…" He smiled after a dramatic but brief pause. "Sons of Dis, you're Romans!"

The men shouted and howled like wolves. We had all been waiting so long to hear this.

"But hear me now"—Marius suddenly took on a serious tone—"within three days, we'll defeat an even greater enemy." He pointed the tip of his sword, still dripping with scarlet blood, toward the Teutones at the base of the hill. "But before that…I know we tainted the water with the blood of our enemies. But that's just fine. For tonight, we drink wine!"

Our cheers must have echoed all the way to whatever shit hole the Teutones hailed from.

War is a brutal and awful thing. In all my years living in it, I have never glorified it. But if there was ever a man to make it bearable, it was Gaius Marius. None of the men sat in silent terror that night considering the men they had killed. Instead, we drank around the campfire with our brothers-in-arms, ate and sang songs, waiting for our next opportunity to fight.

26

SCROLL XXVI

TWO DAYS BEFORE THE KALENDS OF APRIL 652 AB URBE CONDITA

The one stipulation to Marius's declaration of celebration was that we still had to construct a camp. The men were used to it by this point, and they completed the fortifications much faster and jollier than they had before.

"So the general still knows a thing or two about winning a war," Marius said with a grin, his teeth already purple from dark wine. He drank with the men, Manius Aquillius and the other officers doing the same. You would have thought by our disposition that the war was already won. From the guard towers, we could see the Teutones continuing to amass at the bottom of the hill, so I wasn't so sure that was the case. Enraged by the deaths of their brethren, they had decided to halt their march to Italy and stand until we had no choice but to face them.

From the look on Marius's face when the water supply was mentioned, I presumed that we had plenty. It was a clever rouse to encourage the men to fight, and no one seemed to mind because it was successful.

"We never doubted you, General," Aquillius said stoically. It might have been true that Marius's second-in-command always believed him, but I think he was wrong to speak for the rest of us.

"Bullocks," Marius said, draining his wine. "And as I said, the rest of those barbarian scum will lie dead within the week." He spoke with the kind of confidence that inspired it in all of us.

"Here you are, Quintus." Apollonius arrived at my side holding a cup brimming with dark wine. As we marched, he remained in the baggage camp with the other shield bearers, so I hadn't spent as much time with him as I might have liked lately. He was always a welcome presence, though.

"I don't think so, old man. That's yours. I'll get my own." I gestured for one of the mules to bring me a cup from the barrels available to all.

"Nectar of the gods," he said after enjoying his first sip.

Lucius approached us, uninhibited by wine, and I could tell he was distressed.

"What's wrong, comrade?" I asked, patting him on the shoulder.

"The priests have no more pigeons. I have no way to sacrifice before the next battle." He kicked at a rock and shook his head.

"We sacrificed more than enough along those riverbanks today." I pointed past the walls and down the hill. "The gods are appeased, I'm sure. Have a drink." I gestured to the mule to draw up another ladleful of wine. Lucius accepted it reluctantly but seemed to calm the moment the sour wine touched his lips.

"Tribune Hirtuleius, I'm glad you're here," Marius said when he caught sight of him. "Both of you, come here." He gestured for Lucius and I to approach.

"Do you have parchment?" I asked Apollonius as we obeyed the order.

"Yes, sir."

"We're about to receive orders," I said, sensing it from the look in Marius's eyes.

"Tomorrow evening, I want you two to lead our cavalry."

"In battle? We'll fight the Teutones tomorrow?" Lucius asked, a tinge of uncertainty in his voice. As confident as he was in his commander, he relied far more on avian sacrifice to ensure our victories.

"The day following. Those bastards will try to get us to fight tomorrow, and they'll be discouraged when we won't. They haven't been able to entice us yet, and that's the very thing they've done best as they pillaged and raped every village in Spain and Gaul. But the day following, they'll meet their defeat."

"You want us to lead the cavalry, General?" I asked, perplexed. The two of us had shared command of a flank of battle against the Tectosages, maybe five hundred horses at the most, the bulk riding under Sulla on the opposite wing. Leading a cavalry charge against the Teutones was far more intimidating.

"This is all highly irregular, General, if you don't mind my saying so." Legate Marcellus took a step closer to him. Marius's face revealed that he did, in fact, mind. "Having two tribunes lead that many head of horse. I'd like to lead it, if you'll allow me." Marcellus straightened as he put himself forward. He had recovered well since I'd helped him escape the Cimbri camp, but his face was still gaunt and the dark circles under his eyes had never dissipated.

"It would, perhaps, fare better with the newsreaders if an experienced legate is on the wing," Aquillius addressed the consul under his breath.

"Fine," Marius said, hiding a scowl behind his mug of wine. "You can lead the attack. But I want Hirtuleius and Sertorius at your side." He stepped closer to the two of us and pulled us in, but he kept his voice loud enough to be heard by all. "I don't know this man, and he wasn't trained under me. If he does anything 'irregular,' you take charge immediately. You have my permission to do so."

"Yes, Consul," we said in unison. Marius stepped away, followed by the other officers. Marcellus was slighted by

Marius's statement, but he had the command, one I'm sure he'd dreamed of as the Cimbri were starving and torturing him.

I COULD ALREADY HEAR the war drums and the screams of the dying in the recesses of my mind, and judging from the squeaking beds all around me in the tribunes' tent, I wasn't the only one. Did we have what it took to defeat the Teutones? Could we do what our predecessors could not? Or would we be another sad tale in the forum of an entire Roman army swallowed up by the Reds and the sands of time.

After tossing long enough to adequately ruin my firmly tucked bedsheets, I decided the only way I could get some rest was to get up and walk for a while. Sometimes this helped. Other times it did not, but I was out of solutions.

In the dark, I stood and threw my lorica over my shoulders, then slung my sword over my shoulder rather than on my hip. As I exited, I found that the camp was very much still awake. No one was talking, but there was also no snoring. The entire camp seemed to vibrate with nervous energy.

I followed the pale moonlight on the path to the walls. The black night air played tricks on my eye, and I thought for a moment I saw a catapult's rock headed for us. On the ramparts, I reached for the top of the wall to steady myself. I found that my hands were trembling far more than I had previously noticed. My breaths were short and labored, the imaginary catapults having disturbed me a great deal.

"Tribune, how goes it?" one of the guards asked from the tower. He was anxious to speak with me, I could tell. Most likely this was to keep himself awake and alert, or distract himself from his own dark thoughts.

"Just needed some fresh air," I said.

The guard nodded in disappointment when I revealed that I

wasn't interested in engaging in conversation, and returned to his post.

I stared out over the sweeping hills to the Teutone forces amassed at the stream below. Here we were, each and every one of us, trembling in our sandals about what lay ahead, and the Teutones seemed to be resting as easy as babes. As far as I could tell, there were no guards on post or men moving in patrol. Their arrogance exceeded anything I had ever seen. They must have believed the battle was already won, and given recent history, who could blame them?

Just before I turned to descend back to the tribunes' quarters, unsuccessful in my attempt to calm myself, I spotted something I hadn't noticed before. In the distant east, at the foot of the hill we were now situated on, was a thick forest.

I strained my eye to make it out more clearly. The trees were ancient pines and the grass and shrubs grew up around it in unmitigated overgrowth. If there were any creatures of the night hiding in that wood line, I wouldn't have been able to see it.

Before I had even formulated a plan, I found myself running to the praetorium.

"Halt!" the guard shouted, hand fumbling to his hilt as he saw me nearing.

"Tribune Quintus Sertorius," I announced myself to pacify him. "I need to see General Marius."

"The consul is sleeping. You'll have to come by in the morning, sir. He needs his rest," the guard said, stepping between me and the entrance.

"I need to speak with him tonight," I replied, trying to convey the importance of my message with a stern look.

One guard looked to the other, who shrugged.

"Let him know we tried to stop you," he said after a deep exhale, stepping aside and holding back the tent flap.

I stepped into the tent, focusing my eye so that I didn't stumble in the darkness and cause a commotion. Marius's staff was attempting to sleep in their quarters, but each one stirred and looked up at me as I passed through. Marius's quarters were on the far end of the praetorium and hidden by another leather flap.

"General Marius," I said from behind it. It was a great insult to enter without permission, but I considered doing so because of the urgency of the message I was relaying. "Consul?" I said again, raising my voice a bit but still attempting to avoid disturbing Marius's sleeping staff.

I leaned in closer to hear a few grunts and heavy labored breaths from inside. For a moment, my cheeks reddened as I considered the possibility that Marius was attempting to destress the night before battle with one of our camp prostitutes. I decided I could wait a bit longer, but just before I turned to leave, I heard the general's labored voice say, "Come in."

I pulled back the flap, my eye burning as the general's quarters were still well lit by several candelabrum.

The general stood up, his hands akimbo on his hips. He was shirtless, his torso glistening from the perspiration of exercise.

"I thought you were resting, sir," I said, quite surprised to find him like this.

"This is how I rest, Tribune. What do you need? Wine?" He pointed to a jug on his night table.

"No…well, yes, I'll have a cup," I said. He waved me on to help myself, then jumped back to the floor to continue his push-ups.

"I'm assuming you wanted something more than this?" he grunted in between his repetitions.

"I saw something from the walls. There is a thick forest in the foothills." I suddenly realized how foolish this sounded.

"This is Gaul, Tribune. There are trees everywhere."

"Sir, I think we could position our cavalry there. The Teutones wouldn't be able to see us behind the vegetation, and I believe we could flank them." Marius's ears perked up. He pounced to his feet and looked me over. For a man past fifty years on earth, he was still remarkably strong, each muscle rippled and defined from the next.

"You think we could?" he said. I could not tell if he was mocking me.

"I do."

"And they wouldn't notice you moving there?"

"It's quite a distance from their camp, and as far as I can tell, they have no patrols."

"You only have one eye—perhaps you couldn't see them," he said. Now I knew he was jesting, but it was good natured.

"My one eye can see for two. I would have spotted the patrols if there were any to see."

He poured himself a cup of wine and gulped gratefully.

"Alright," he said with a shrug, "do it, then."

"Do it, sir?" I replied. It was not the response I was anticipating.

"Yes. Now, under the cover of night. Alert the rest of your men and get them on horseback before the end of the hour."

"I'll admit I'm surprised at your trust in me, Consul."

"I've spoken with Martha." He turned to me with an uncharacteristic smile. "She said we'll achieve a great victory tomorrow. The gods are on our side."

He must have noticed something in my manor that displeased him.

"*Gerrhae,* Sertorius. What is it?"

"It's good news. I've just come to place my faith in the strength of our arms." Knowing Marius the way I did, I was surprised to see he didn't do the same. "The gods didn't protect us at Arausio." I was also surprised that this prophecy had the opposite effect on me. Hubris always precedes a fall, and I believed that's what auspices of victory could bring.

"I'll pretend I didn't hear that." He poured himself another cup of wine. "Go on, then, go tell your men. And leave now."

"And what about Marcellus? What if he rejects the idea?" I said, finding myself objecting to my own plan.

Marius grunted and snarled. "You tell that man he is being given an express order from a consul of the Roman Republic. If he doesn't like it, I'll have him stripped of rank."

"Yes, sir," I said, finishing my cup and turning to leave.

"Tribune," Marius said before I exited, "ensure that he goes along with it. He has been flogged by the Cimbri enough. I'd rather not make an example of such a man." He set down his cup of wine and returned to the ground to continue his exercise.

I hurried through the camp with the difficult task of alerting our four thousand cavalrymen. Fortunately, the majority of them were billeted together, but finding the officers was another matter entirely. The hour had nearly vanished before I found Legate Marcellus.

He was very much awake, seated at his desk with a small candle burning. As I entered, he seemed not to notice, still scribbling on a scroll quite carefully.

"Legate." I stopped and saluted. He took his time before looking up.

"Tribune, what can I do for you?" he replied, rather disinterested.

"We have new orders. We are to rally the cavalry presently and march for a wood line in the distance to set up an ambush."

He did not react to my words but rather continued to read the letter before him.

"I guess this is as good as I can get it. Tell me, Tribune, what you think of this for a last line?" He began to dictate from his letter: "'I know I have no claim of the gods, but something whispers to me, perhaps it is the prayer of our son, that I shall return to the both of you unharmed. If I do not, beloved Cornelia, never forget how much I've loved you, nor that, when my last breath escapes me on the battlefield, it will whisper your name.'" He looked up, his eyes wet but unafraid. "I've been thinking of something else to say, but it's nearly impossible to determine the correct words."

"Are you writing a letter to inform them of your death? The

battle hasn't yet been fought," I said, attempting to jest. But I knew all too well that this warranted some merit. There was a high probability that we would perish, and sending a touch of love from the grave was the most gracious thing a man could do.

"So, we ride for the trees, then?" he asked, standing from his chair. He folded the letter delicately and sealed it with hot wax that had been heating over a candle.

"Yes, Legate. Our orders are to leave presently," I replied.

He adjusted the ring on his finger and then pressed it hard into the cooling wax, leaving his seal defined upon it.

"Alright, then," he said, his voice soft and thoughtful. "Let's go. It's as good a day to die as any."

Soldiers say such things at times, rather morbidly, but always with the hope that their claims will be proven false. There was no such sarcasm or wit in Marcellus's words. He had faced death for so long in captivity that perhaps he was simply unafraid of what the enemy could do to him now. His voice carried none of the false bravado and reckless daring that generally accompanies such statements—he genuinely meant it. Today was as good a day as any, and I was inclined to agree with him.

27

SCROLL XXVII

ONE DAY BEFORE THE KALENDS OF APRIL 652 AB URBE CONDITA

We set out with a few hours of darkness remaining. Lucius was very displeased. Not because of the danger involved with such a rouse, or because sleep was stolen from him, but because he had been hoping to rise early the next morning to find a fitting sacrifice for the battle. Once again, he was not able to do so, and he seemed more frightened by an angry god than by the Teutones we rode to ambush.

"You know we'll all be butchered to the last man if they spot us," one of the horsemen whispered as the gates closed behind us.

"Well, if Fortuna favors us, they won't. If they do, perhaps it will give Marius enough time to take advantage of the distraction," I replied.

"How very noble of us," the horsemen replied sarcastically.

"Get your spacing," I directed the cavalry behind me, "and make sure to keep your horses quiet."

With one hand, I held the reins tight. With the other, I stroked

Sura behind the ear. From time to time, I leaned over and placed my cheek against her mane and whispered, "It's alright, girl. We'll be alright." She couldn't hear it, but I hoped she could feel it. She brayed a few times but seemed calm enough, so perhaps my soothing worked.

We made the journey last as long as it could. The slower we moved, the less likely we were to be detected, but we also dreaded the hours of waiting once we arrived.

"Direct your horses," I said when we reached the tree line. "Hold them firm. Be careful what you allow them to step on."

Each of us stole a glance over our shoulders to see if there was movement in the distant Teutone camp. There didn't seem to be, as the camp continued to rest on in peaceful slumber.

We wheeled about and stationed ourselves facing where the battle would take place the following morning. It was empty, and so peaceful now. The pale moonlight shimmered on the dew-covered grass, which swayed with a gentle spring wind. The lilies of the field sent a calming aroma wafting to us. The stream passing through the Teutone camp could be heard bubbling up and trickling over smooth stones. A bystander would have had no way of foreseeing the horror that would soon take place here.

We awaited first light in anxious silence. Some of the men tried to talk among themselves, but I had to tell them to keep the volume down more than a few times, so eventually they gave up. The rest of us either prayed to the gods or our ancestors, or imagined what death might feel like: the Elysian fields, the celebration of a warrior entering peace at last, seeing loved ones once more.

It was a great relief to all of us when the sun appeared, and we heard our forces begin to stir in the camp on the distant hilltop.

"Not much longer now," Marcellus said from my right. I assumed at first that he meant the battle, but something in his eyes told me otherwise.

Soon afterward, the Teutones began to wake in the valley. They wasted no time in preparing themselves. They didn't bother with bathing or eating but immediately donned their armor and brandished their swords. We had given no verbal indication that today would be the day, but both sides seemed to sense it.

Marius's forces began to pour out of the gates to the bugle's cadence. It took nearly an hour for them all to exit the fort and form into battle assembly. By this time, the Teutones had arrayed themselves in whatever way suited them best. There didn't seem to be much tact behind how they amassed, but their sheer boundless numbers were enough to make it appear stronger than the solid formation of Roman soldiers.

The Romans, once formed, marched forward a few paces to the crest of the hill, standing directly over their barbarian enemy in the foothills.

I looked to Lucius to see what he was thinking, but his eyes were closed and his lips were moving with rhythmic prayer, not seeming to notice that the battle was among us.

"Here it is, men," Marcellus said over his shoulder, "all of your training, all of your fighting, all of the sacrifices you've made since the day you dawned the colors... It all comes down to this moment. The fate of the Republic is in our hands now."

I struggled to swallow.

The Teutones began to chant, hoisting their spears, axes, and swords into the air. They stomped their feet and gnashed their teeth. If they had been angry the last time we met them in battle, it did not rival the fury they now displayed, since thirty thousand of their allies were now reduced to ash and decay.

The barbarians began their ascent up the hill. My stomach dropped and my head felt light. I adjusted the straps to my helm, ensuring that it wouldn't come loose during the battle. I needed everything to work out in my favor if I were to make it out alive.

To my surprise, whistles blew, and the Romans advanced. So

far, Marius had been reluctant to make any sort of move. We'd stood firm and waited for the enemy to reach us, with the exception of our attack on the Ambrones at the river, but here Marius led his troops farther down the hill.

This enraged the Teutones even further. They thought they had frightened us into utter submission. They thought they had won the posturing battle. Seeing Marius's forces aligned in full array and marching to greet them caused such a bloodlust in the Teutones' war cries that I have yet to forget it. We had the high ground, but the Reds couldn't back away from the fight now. When the order was given, the Teutones broke into a full sprint up the hill, determined to punish us for our arrogance.

Marcellus lifted his hand and prepared to give us the signal for our advance.

"Hold." I quickly reached out and grabbed his wrist. He turned to me with a peculiar look in his eye, and to my surprise, he deferred to my judgement.

The two armies crashed into one another. A sound like an angry storm carried through the valley and echoed in the forest. Thunder, the crack of lightning, heavy rainfall on rocks—it was the violent push of the Teutones against our line, spear jabbing at shield and sword piercing flesh.

Marcellus's eyes were still fixed on me, growing slightly as the cries of the butchered began to echo out. The centurions shouted orders, the bugles blew, and the Teutone drums carried on, shaking everything and echoing in our helms.

"Tribune," Marcellus said, only a touch of haste in his voice, "what are we waiting for?"

"Hold," I said again. Lucius had now finished his prayer, and looked to me with a nod of the head.

The Teutone line was now fully engaged, pivoting and shifting like flood water around a powerful tree. The Roman line remained fixed.

"Now," I said to Marcellus. He lifted his hand and dropped it with a shout.

"Charge!" The words carried out over the treetops. We burst out into the orange sunlight of early morning, whipping the reins as hard as we could.

Marcellus took the front, charging at full speed, his gladius hoisted high and pointing at the Teutones we were careening toward.

The Teutones hacked and slashed at the shield wall of our front ranks, so engaged and enraged that they didn't notice us at first. One by one, the blue eyes of the right most flank looked up at us, widening with terror.

"Charge!" I echoed the call, bouncing atop Sura. The Teutones turned and hoisted their round shields to protect themselves. Marcellus and those at the front crashed into them with the thunder of an angry god. Sura reached their line and suddenly bucked with fear, jumping over the front ranks and crashing down on top of several trembling enemies.

The infantry drove forward now, taking advantage of the momentary panic we created.

Sura reared wildly, kicking and twisting against assailants on all sides. I clutched my legs around her with all the force I could muster to stabilize myself, stabbing down at the stumbling Teutones on either side.

"Bring them down! Kill them all!" Marcellus shouted, his voice carrying above the tumult.

A bearded Teutone with a fur cape approached my flank, a heavy axe hoisted above his head. He let out a lion's roar, giving me just enough time to spin and slice down at him. The tip of my gladius found its mark, carving through tendon and sinew from his collarbone to the opposite pectoral.

Blood sprayed up and covered my face and sweat-drenched arms. The axe dropped from his hands as he stumbled back and fell to a knee. I turned to meet a young Teutone boy who lunged at me with a spear, his teeth gritted and smeared with the blood of the fallen around him. I bashed the spear tip away with my sword, exposing the man's midsection. Without thinking, I thrust my sword like an extension of my body, the blade digging in between his ribs. Blood bubbled from his lips as his legs buckled beneath him.

I turned to find the bearded man returning to his feet. His legs seemed to wobble like rotten wood beneath him, but he was determined to kill me. The axe now buried under the bodies of his allies, he lunged with nothing but his hands. I brought my sword down to pierce his neck, but with the powerful grip of a snake around its prey, he halted the attack and reached with the other hand to pull me from my steed.

I collided with the earth, the air driving out of my body with violent force.

I tried to steady myself as an engaging Teutone tripped over my shoulder and landed atop me. As I tried to shimmy out from under him, the bearded warrior towered over me, axe now in hand. Blood poured from the wound I had inflicted, over his breastplate and down the side of his leg.

In a panic, I patted the earth around me, searching for my fallen sword. The warrior put his boot on my throat and hoisted his axe above his head, for a moment blotting out the morning sun. He snarled, revealing teeth soaked in blood as if he had taken a bite of raw meat.

My fingers grasped something. It wasn't the steel of a gladius but the wood of a spear—presumably owned by the boy I'd just killed. As the axe began careening down for my head, I brought the spear up in a last stroke of desperation, the tip of the spear sinking into the warrior's armpit. He stumbled, a waterfall of blood pouring from his mouth onto my lorica. The axe dropped from his hands, dinging my helmet but nothing more. As the man slowly stumbled back to the earth, I stood and drove the spear deeper and deeper.

When those hate-filled eyes rolled back and his tongue puffed out, I turned to find that the rest of the cavalry had advanced on. They were some distance ahead, hacking and slashing at the panicking Teutones, Marcellus still leading the charge with shouted orders.

I looked left and right but could find Sura nowhere. Beside my feet, I found the gladius that had followed me into so many battles. I wasted no time in grabbing it, along with the discarded shield of some dead Teutone or another, and advanced toward the cavalry. The Teutones around me, too distracted with their own dying or routing, did not notice. Panic was spreading like a disease. Some of them tried to rally their forces with renewed war chants, but the Romans continued to drive forward, silent and impassive, with the exception of Marcellus and the four thousand horsemen.

My heartbeat quickened, suddenly arrhythmic and uncontrollable. Perhaps it was the fall, or the men I had just killed, but all I could think of was Sura. If I was forced to look into those wide, wet eyes as they blinked their last, I knew it would be the end of me. I tried to increase my pace.

An enemy caught sight of me. He approached with a mallet the size of a tree trunk hoisted over his head. I remember it as a massive stone fastened to a log, but my mind was already in a fog by this point. He swung viciously. Still too far away to strike me, the wind alone that it propelled nearly sent me to my backside.

I met his eyes as I tightened my grip around the round shield and brought the top of it to the tip of my nose.

"Agh!" he shouted as the mallet swung again to meet me. I hoisted my shield at the last moment to deflect it. The wooden shield splintered around my arm, but the Teutone recoiled from the deflection. Without thinking, I raised my gladius and brought it down quickly, severing his arm in one swift motion. His cry was bloodcurdling. I still believe that he might have proceeded to kill me if he had another weapon available to him. Without waiting for such an event, I lunged toward him, my bloody blade struggling through his golden breastplate and then gliding through his flesh as if it were nothing but a butcher's cut.

As I dislodged the blade, I brought what fragment of my shield remained into his neck, toppling him to the earth, where he was quickly covered with the bodies of other falling barbarians.

I blinked to keep myself alert and shifted to keep the sun from my eye.

"Sura!" I shouted, or perhaps I only imagined it. So many men collided with the earth at my feet, friend and foe alike, and there wasn't a moment for reflection. The only thing I considered was my innocent stead. She had not asked for war. If the Teutones knew her sweet heart, even they would not dare strike a blow.

The bugles suddenly sounded with a different pitch. My mind was warped, too dazed to realize what it meant. The Teutones were faltering and tripping over each other to escape while the Roman lines advances at double speed. The forward line pushed me with them, but I continued to stumble over the bodies of the fallen toward the advancing cavalry.

My foot caught on the corpse of a rotund Teutone, and I sprung forward to the ground. My head whipped against the mud, and for a moment, the light of my eye dimmed. I don't believe it was long before I shook the haze away, but when I did, there was a man on the ground staring back at me. His eyes were wide but emotionless. Atop his lower body lay his faithful stead, which seemingly had fallen simultaneously.

The mouth of the man was open, as if he were to say something or give me an order, but lifeblood had trickled from the corners of his lips and was already beginning to dry.

Only after staring at the man for some time, as if his death were some beautiful, grotesque work of art, did I realize that it was Legate Marcus Marcellus. I swear I could still hear his cries of "charge" as I gazed into his dead eyes.

When I peered up at the advancing cavalry, the sun burning a spot in my retina, I identified Sura treading along with the rest, just as dutifully as if I were still atop her.

Life surged through my limbs as I bounced to my feet and sprinted toward her.

"Halt, halt!" the centurion's orders were given. The bloodlust of the Teutones seemed to be infectious, as the order was not heeded until it grew in both volume and in number.

I heard Lucius's voice among the tumult, finally ordering our cavalry to tighten their reins and maintain their position.

I didn't consider myself the object of the orders, and continued at the fastest speed I could manage, eye set on my beautiful girl, who continued to buck and whinny with the rest of the cavalry.

When I reached her, I fell on bruised knees and clutched her legs.

"It's alright, girl. I found you. I'm here." I unbuckled my helm and let it slip from my sweat-drenched head. "It's over now," I said to her as much as to myself.

She turned and nuzzled her wet nose against my forehead.

"Up, Tribune. The fight isn't over," I heard a voice say. I would have been embarrassed if it was anyone but my friend Lucius.

I pulled myself back into the saddle and then nodded for Lucius to lead the way.

He directed us to continue to the far flank of the Roman line. Only when we were there was the order given to continue our advance.

Even with my one eye, I could spot the Teutones scrambling in their camp for a last-moment escape. Some of them were successful in doing so, as I could see bodies fading into the morning mist in the hills in the distance. Most didn't have the time and resigned themselves to the fate we Romans had in store for them.

A group nearly the size of our entire army was already beginning to march out, absent swords or shield, but with white cloths hoisted high on makeshift banners.

Once we reached the bottom of the hill, not a hundred yards

from where the Teutone camp had so recently been, Marius and his detachment rode out before the army. If anyone else had been speaking, the rest of the cavalry and I wouldn't have been able to hear him, but Marius's voice had a habit of carrying.

"Men, we've achieved a great victory today. Rome is rendered much safer now than she was last night. Now, we are going to advance on their camp. Anything you find is yours. The city does not need any spoils. You do. Everything these barbarians have either once belonged to you or your fallen comrades. You may now take it back."

The ranks of the men roared with approval. Their energy was still surging. I said nothing, but lowered my head to Sura's mane.

"One last thing, lads," Marius said, hoisting up a finger, "do not touch the bodies of the fallen Teutones. We shall not give them burial as we do by custom." The general grew silent for a moment, as did the ranks, who watched him with utter confusion. "They wanted land, and now they have it."

Marius's legions surged forward into the Teutone camp. Lucius gave a nod for the cavalry to do the same, but I and many others stood in place. I looked up the hill, where thousands of bodies lay atop each other. There were enough writhing bodies of the wounded to give the entire field the look of crawling, scraping movement. Perhaps it was simply the ghosts leaving their bodies.

It was nearly impossible to tell friend from foe, or wounded from the dead. I did surmise that there were nearly three dead Reds to every Roman, but that was still too many comrades who were now in Elysium. If I had been able to comprehend that at the time, I feel certain I would have fallen again from my horse. Luckily, the gods had protected me with a fogged mind. I wouldn't have to reconcile it until the nightmares visited me later.

When at last I sped up into the village, I followed Marius,

who directed the chaos around him. He then pounced from his horse and wiped the blood of his sword off on his shin.

His guard burrowed around him in protection, but he pushed for some space.

"I want that king," I heard him say over the tumult.

There was only one hut that was crafted for a king, one not so different from Boiorix's lodging in the Cimbri camp. I fixed my grip again on the hilt of my sword and followed Marius inside.

As my eye strained to adjust to the darkness, there on the ground were three slain bodies, of two children and a woman in the finest clothing I had seen on a Red thus far. Beside them was the king, who held a sword but didn't move to either attack or to kill himself.

"Hello, old friend." Marius stepped forward. "It seems I've beaten you. Shackle him," Marius ordered the mule closest to him. King Teutobod of the Teutones didn't resist as Marius's guard bound him forcefully. He stared past us with the broken spirit unique to the vanquished, mouth open and blood splattered across his face and kingly garb.

They beat his face and rapped him over the head with the hilt of their gladius, daring him to retaliate. But he did not. He only lay there on the floor, atop the bodies of his fallen wife and children, as they wound rope around his wrist and ankles. His resignation resembled that of his conquered nation. The Teutones were no more.

As they carried him away, ignoring the bodies behind him, he began to weep. He was no longer a king but just another destitute man on the losing side of war. And war was an awful thing. I would have been moved with pity or even compassion if the image of the burning and butchered bodies of my comrades wasn't still so fresh in my mind.

Marius's orders were carried out. The men sacked the Teutone camp, taking anything and everything they had with them. Several men, like myself and Lucius, decided instead to get a head start on closing the eyes of our dead and placing a coin in their mouths for the ferryman.

The bodies of the Teutones were never touched. I've heard tales in the years since that they decayed there for some time before the Massiliots eventually gathered their bones to construct fences. I've also heard that the grapes harvested in that region have been unusually rich ever since.

War can have such unforeseeable effects.

28

SCROLL XXVIII

It is necessary at this point in our narrative to include another exert from Sulla's memoir. While we reveled in our victory over the Teutones and planned for war with the Cimbri, Sulla and Consul Catulus were already engaging them.

April to Quintilis—Year of the consulship of Marius and Catulus

It was three days before we heard of Marius's victory over the Teutones. Tales of the victory had been embellished by the time it reached our camp, no doubt from the honeyed lips of Marius himself. Regardless, it appeared to have been an overwhelming victory.

I'll admit to being very disappointed when I heard the news, not only that Marius had achieved more than his due share of glory from the victory but also that I had been denied mine. I had been instrumental in coordinating his battle strategy before he sent me away at the height of his jealousy. I had also orchestrated and organized a mission to collect intelligence from the Cimbri, sending one of our tribunes, Quintus Sertorius, into the Cimbri camp in a heroic display of espi-

onage. We tried to keep talk of it stifled, but rumors about it spread like an insulae fire within a year or so. It was probably Marius or that tribune, Sertorius, himself who started spreading the tales.

Regardless, it was the stuff of legend, to be certain, but without Sulla it never would have happened. Marius lacked the necessary wit to strategize for such a mission and the tact to convince the young, morose tribune to accept it. I was responsible for that, regardless of whether or not I received the credit.

Although I had been snubbed of my due honor, and inclined to be perturbed, the goddess Venus whispered in my ear that I would soon be given the respect I deserved. I knew it was only a matter of time.

The moment of glory I awaited was to be delayed, however, by the incompetence of my general, Consul Catulus. He wasn't a bad sort of fellow, but he was one of the dullest men Rome ever produced. He was far more inclined to poetry and the couch. Some say that I am, as well, and that may be true, but a real Roman knows how to fight when it's required of him.

The one thing that Catulus did well was trusting his advisors and handing responsibilities to those more capable than himself, unlike Marius. He hadn't wielded a sword since he was a young man, and I'm certain he never took a life, so he made the correct choice and gave me unrequited control of our forces. My word became law in Catulus's camp, which suited the both of us just fine. If we lost, I would be the first to die and he might live. If we won, he would take his share of the glory. I agreed to the arrangement because, in this manner, I could at least ensure the blundering fool didn't allow us to be butchered as the Roman armies before us were.

This strategy was far more suitable to him when the enemy had not arrived, however.

When we first spotted the boundless Cimbri hordes advancing for us via the Brenner Pass, he began to visibly panic. We were entrenched in the Alpine passes, which were difficult to maneuver individually, let alone with a force the size of the Cimbri. Their banners were hardly spotted in the distance when Catulus began to cry out for the centuries to be rallied.

"What are you doing, Consul?" I inquired.

"We must retreat," he said, straining his aged eyes to make out our enemy.

"That is highly ill advised, sir," I said. I'll admit that I began to boil with anger, as this was the first time that Catulus had questioned my authority.

"We cannot defend ourselves here." His blubbery cheeks trembled with fear.

"We have no choice. The mountains are our only means of defending our flanks. They outnumber us too greatly otherwise." It was true. Our ledgers counted twenty thousand men, nearly five legions in limited capacity, but the Cimbri had their hundreds of thousands. If we met them in the open field, they would have swallowed us up like Pluto's shadow.

"It's a tactical retreat, we shall meet them soon enough, young legate," he said, trying to smile as if supremely confident. It wasn't difficult to tell that he was bluffing. Such politicians always sound like children dressing up as soldiers when they use words like "tactical." I would have laughed if the circumstances weren't so dire.

How cruel fate can be sometimes, when she places power into the hands of the inept rather than the able.

I had been in control of strategizing our movements, organizing our supply lines, and forging alliances with the tribal networks surrounding the Alpine hills. But now that battle was imminent, the consul demanded that we retreat. Tactically or not, it was the wrong decision. He said we would meet them later, but I felt confident at that time, and still do, that he simply intended to delay meeting the Cimbri until his term of consulship was over.

The mountain passage now declared indefensible, our camp was deconstructed and we began our retreat. Marius may have been a half-wit whose good luck and abler subordinates earned him far more glory than he was due, but the man certainly knew how to construct a camp and order a march. Catulus's army displayed sloppy tendencies by comparison. We covered very little distance before the Cimbri began to make up ground between us.

We traveled for two days, the Cimbri close enough on our trail that we could hear their Harpy priestesses howling in the night.

In his haste, Catulus had failed to properly scout our line of retreat. We found ourselves with our backs against the Adige River, without a path to maneuver farther.

"Here, here, we shall meet them," Catulus said. It was clear he wasn't confident in his decision, but he wasn't left any other options.

"This is far less defensible than where we were previously dug in, Consul," I said.

"We shall construct a bridge over the Adige, in case we need to retreat," he replied without addressing my concerns.

Only a coward plans for defeat.

The bridge was indeed constructed, within one day's time. Catulus's army was far less capable at building than Marius, perhaps, but by sheer terror, they worked all hours of the night to ensure it was assembled promptly. By the time it was completed, the Cimbri were not but a mile up the path; they could be upon us as quickly as they desired.

"We shall retreat over the bridge," Catulus said at first light. His eyes were weary and his breath stank of recent regurgitation.

"You never really meant to fight them here, did you, Consul?" I asked, not bothering to hide my scorn from such a man.

"We will fight them only when we can be assured of victory, Legate," he said to me. This statement, more than any other, proved that he was undeserving of his authority. Any man who has wetted his sword will know victory is never assured in battle. Venus had imparted her blessings on me, and I knew I was safe from the enemy, but I could not be certain the fate of our men. The farther we retreated, the closer we led the Cimbri to the beating heart of Italy—Rome itself.

We began another "tactical" retreat across the bridge, forced to move four abreast. One legion was to remain on the eastern side of the bridge in defense as the others crossed, and this decision proved fatal.

As the first four legions began their final assent over the bridge, men on both sides of the forge were heard shouting out in terror.

It was then that I looked up to see the massive beams and thick trees careening down the river stream, no doubt sent from the enemy. They collided into the bridge, splintering the wood and sending legionaries cascading into the river and immediately drowning under the weight of their armor.

More and more logs came as the soldiers tried to fish their comrades out of the water, others trying to jump from one bank to the other. The bridge cracked with the clap of thunder, and one of our legions was abandoned.

I searched in haste for the consul. What was his plan now? He had been so apt to retreat himself, but four thousand of his men were now stranded, with no means to retreat themselves.

No order was given. Each man, officer and legionary alike, were confounded about what needed to be done.

"Catulus, we must find a way across the river!" I shouted above the tumult.

Rome had already suffered the defeat of ninety thousand at Arausio. She could suffer no more losses.

"There is no means to do so." Catulus hung his head "The river has been scouted south and there is no means of escape."

"You damned fool!" I shouted, knowing the consul couldn't afford to execute another officer when he was about to lose so many.

It was then that the Cimbri began their descent from the passes, sounding as if all the gods in their four-horsed chariots were riding to greet us.

At length, Catulus conspired with his more like-minded and cowardly subordinates, who collectively decided for the remainder of our army to continue our retreat by land.

The four thousand on the far side of the river cried out for justice. Some took to diving into the river in an attempt to save themselves. None, to my recollection, were successful.

Even from a distance, I could hear one man rallying the men: it was a centurion I knew well. His name was Gnaeus Petreius, the bravest and ablest of their lot. A tribune had taken command of the legion left behind, and had already made it known that he would surrender to the Cimbri. From across the river, I spotted Petreius wedge his sword into the tribune's belly himself and take command. They would not be surrendering.

The cavalry with the abandoned legion whipped their horses away, forsaking their men by taking paths unavailable to foot soldiers. I've heard tale that the man in charge of the cavalry detachment was the son of the father of the senate, Marcus Scaurus. The story has it that Scaurus disowned his son when he arrived at Rome, safe while his men fed the carrion birds. The coward later took his own life in an attempt to redeem himself.

Petreius and the abandoned legion fought like rabid dogs against a lion. They were surrounded but packed in closely together, covering themselves with their shields and fighting to take as many barbarians with them into the afterlife as possible.

I could do nothing but watch in horror. If only I could have been across the forge, if only I had been in command and not the cowardly consul, perhaps fate would have taken a different course. The fact that we lost four thousand men, and a centurion such as Gnaeus Petreius, is a blight on Roman honor to this day.

Catulus led us away from the Adige and our butchered dead to the eastern bank of the Po.

The barbarians now had complete, unrequited access to Italy itself.

29

SCROLL XXIX

SIX DAYS BEFORE THE KALENDS OF AUGUST 653 AB URBE CONDITA

While Catulus and Sulla licked their wounds, we settled in for the long winter ahead. Water and food were no longer a concern for us, as the bounty of the Teutone camp was plentiful. Marius himself had perhaps never seemed more powerful and grandiose, as he became consul of Rome for the fourth consecutive year. This time, rather than sharing his position with a buffoon like Catulus, his subordinate Manius Aquillius was to be his co-consul. Even the nobles had bowed their heads and taken a knee, realizing Marius was their only hope of defeating the northern menace—Catulus's incompetence having already proven that. The nobles had, however, voted to ensure that Catulus maintained his command in Gaul as a proconsul, so that if Marius was successful, at least they could retain some of the credit.

Our winter quarters were settled in along the west coast of Massilia, while Catulus's forces gathered near the banks of the Po in northern Italy. The Cimbri could have marched on Rome if they had so desired, but the snows came in time to force them to consider halting, which they eventually did. It certainly wasn't because of Catulus's meager forces, which remained close enough to keep an eye on them, but not close enough to engage in combat. The Cimbri seemed completely unperturbed by them—and for good reason, given recent events. Perhaps the Cimbri simply liked the land they had earned for themselves among the hills. Some rumors spread around the camp that the Cimbri would remain there, giving us enough time to amass a larger force and repel them back to their homeland. I wasn't so sure.

When those snows melted, I was certain that a battle would soon be upon us.

Marius, too, was determined that this would be the year we would meet the Cimbri. After so many years of using the fear of the northern invaders to win the votes of the people, he knew he must act. One enemy was defeated, yes, but the greater threat remained. If he lingered, who knew when the people's belief in him would wane? Or when they would cry out for another general to be their savior?

He wouldn't allow anyone else to take the glory he so desired.

When the flowers began to blossom, we deconstructed our camp and set out for the Po. We would merge our armies.

Marius was uncomfortable with this, and, in fact, we all were. When living in a Roman camp, you get used to the way things are. You don't want new leadership and new regulations being pushed down the chain of command, but alas, times did not give us the luxury of choosing such things. The Cimbri army was nearly two hundred thousand strong, or so the reports said. Even including our *auxilia* and reinforcements, we had no more than thirty thousand after the loses at Aquae Sextiae, and Catulus some twenty thousand. It would take every last man at full capacity if we had any hopes of repelling our enemy.

"Be careful not to embarrass them, men," Marius said from atop his horse as we marched. "They've had a rough go of it lately. Don't boast too much about our victories or it might make them jealous." It was clear that he was more than comfortable with the idea of our spreading rumors of his greatness, but it made for a good laugh.

We traversed the thawing Po for a few hundred miles before we spotted Catulus's camp along the southern banks.

"Marius is pitching a fit, I'm sure. Look at their walls. Couldn't keep out a band of Sicilian slaves," said Equus, shaking his head as we trotted toward them.

Our army was called to a halt as Marius and the legates sped ahead of us from the back of the column. I and the other tribunes peeled off of the formation and followed them.

It took some time, but eventually a detachment of cavalry was seen exiting Catulus's camp and riding for us at a steady pace.

"Greetings from Rome!" a voice came from one of the riders. He was heavyset and seemed to weigh down the stead beneath him. The thickness of his armor didn't help the matter, but a man of Catulus's stature was certain to protect himself at all costs.

"We are Rome," Marius said, but not loudly enough to be heard by the incoming riders.

"Proconsul Lucius Lutatius Catulus," he introduced himself, as if his former co-consul might not recognize him. I believe the real intent was to remind everyone of his authority, and preemptively protect it from being misappropriated.

There was an awkward silence for a moment as our horses grunted beneath us. I spotted Sulla on a steed to the right of Catulus, his eyes shaded by the cover of his helm. His disposition was no longer jovial, as was his custom, and there was no pursed grin on his lips. The veins in his neck were of a bluish hue, and bulging.

By contrast, General Marius had never seemed more at ease, his chin high and his back straight.

"You understand why we are here?" Marius asked, as if speaking to foreigners or a direct subordinate.

"We received word of your arrival two weeks ago. By senatorial decree, we are to merge our armies," Catulus said. "We expected you some time ago."

"There was much land to traverse, and fresh off a victory such as ours, we had a great deal of spoils and slaves to transport." Marius did not hide his glee well. I believe I spotted a snarl on Sulla's lips.

"How far off are the Cimbri?" Consul Manius Aquillius asked.

Catulus turned and pointed to the hills in the distance. "Not two days that way. You can smell the stench of them if you sniff hard enough."

"Good. We'll meet them soon enough," Marius said with finality.

"We'll meet them?" Catulus balked. "The senate is levying new troops for the upcoming war season."

"My dear friend." Marius separated himself from the rest of us, gracefully swaying on his black warhorse as he approached his former consular colleague. "It is March, if you had not noticed. It is war season. There is no reason to delay."

Catulus peered over his shoulder at Sulla, looking for counsel, but the legate averted his gaze.

"You'll need to deconstruct your camp. We'll form up there," Marius said, pointing to an expanse of land surrounded by the winding river of the Po on either side.

"There? What is wrong with where we are now?" Catulus asked, incredulous.

"It's defenseless, for one. The Cimbri already know these hills better than we do, and they'll pour out of the Alpine passes faster than Jupiter's lightning. They could surround you from all sides within an hour. It's a wonder they haven't done so already."

Catulus's mouth was agape as he shook his head and considered what objection he might make.

"Let us make one thing clear," Marius continued before the

proconsul could speak, "we might be merging armies. But I am supreme commander here." He paused to let the words sink in. "There will be none of the fuss that befell my son, as Caepio tried to take more than his due share of power and winded up losing ninety thousand Roman lives. I am consul. I am Marius. And my word is law."

I was afraid for a moment that Marius had gone too far, but Catulus and his staff remained silent. Sulla was nearly trembling atop his horse, but even he said nothing.

Marius lifted the reins of his horse and swayed around to face us. "Deconstruct the camp," he shouted back to Catulus.

We parted for Marius to pass through. "Move the men forward. Have them begin the construction. These fools don't seem to know how to do it correctly," he said to any of us listening.

THE NEW CAMP THUS BUILT, and with Marius's personal *dignitas* at a new high, we set about with the difficult task of waiting. Once they were constructed, I led Sura to the stables and brushed the muck off of her coat and dug the dirt from her hooves. I combed my fingers through her mane, and she barred her teeth and swished her tail playfully as I did so.

"How, by all the gods, do you keep her so clean?" Lucius said from behind me, attempting to steady his stallion with a tight grip on the reins.

"A little bit of attention, comrade. You could do this, too, if you gave it the time," I said.

"He won't let me! The bastard is as stubborn as I was when I was a child."

"A bit of payback seems appropriate, then." I smiled at my old friend.

"He fights me constantly. When I try to lift his legs, he bucks and spits at me. Who knew horses spit? Gobs of it, all over my freshly cleaned armor."

"Anyone who's spent some time with a horse would know that, friend." I chuckled.

"I've spent more time with horses than I'd like, but I'll admit the bugger is growing on me." Lucius held out his hand for the stallion to sniff before proceeding to scratch his cheeks, but only after getting permission to do so. "Do you like her? Eh, papa found you a girlfriend," Lucius whispered to his beast, gesturing to Sura.

"Don't encourage him." I picked up some hay and tossed it at Lucius.

"You can see it in their eyes, can't you? It's true love." Lucius led the horse to a stall across from me, and then entered mine. "She's a sweet girl," he said, serious for a moment.

"She is. It almost makes me feel guilty."

"Guilty?"

"That I brought her here. That I lead her into battle… In another life, she would have been the best friend in the world to some young boy or girl."

"There are no other lives but this one, Quintus." Lucius allowed Sura to rub her head against him. "The gods led her to you. She's your steed for a reason."

"Always with the gods." I shook my head. I was attempting to jest, but it was lost on my companion. He tried to stifle it, but I could see fear in his eyes.

"You don't believe in the gods anymore?" he asked. I broke eye contact with him and massaged at my leg, which had begun its throbbing again.

"I'll believe in them if we defeat the Cimbri," I said, surprised by my own answer.

"That's not how it works, *amicus*," Lucius replied.

"Don't worry so much, Lucius. I pray, I sacrifice…I do all that's required of me. But it's hard to trust in the gods after all the things we've seen, all the things we've done." I knew it was a sign of weakness, but I couldn't stop staring at the mud beneath us.

"One man's experience can't confirm or disprove the gods."

"It's the only thing I know how to base it on."

Lucius stood and poured some water in his hand for Sura to lap up.

"Well, if you must base it on your own experiences, then recall that you survived Arausio when others did not—found by your friend clutching to driftwood for your very life. You then went on to live within the enemy's camp, free a dozen prisoners—"

I cut him off. "Only eight made it back with me. One died."

"Eight men who would have died a horrible death. The gods may seem cold at times, and they allow the incomprehensible to happen. But where you go, they seem to follow. That should inspire a bit of hope in you, if nothing else," he said.

"Thank you, comrade." I shook his hand. Intellectually, I could not deny what he said. In my heart, though, I could accept none of it. Not until the Cimbri were defeated, at least.

"Come on, I've an idea," Lucius said, opening the stall door for me to exit.

"What is it? I need to receive the report from the Seventh Legion's first spear."

"That can wait until tomorrow. General Marius didn't give us any orders."

"It's regulation, Lucius! You're not one to break the rules." I wagged a finger at him in mock chastisement.

"Well, I know." He took my rebuke far more seriously than I'd intended. "But even officers need a night to themselves, don't they?"

"What do you have in mind, Tribune?"

He considered his words carefully, and his eyes squinted as he began to speak. "I want to get drunk."

I erupted into laughter. At first, he seemed offended, but he eventually joined me.

"What? Come on, I want to drink!"

By the time I got my laughter under control, my gut was aching from the effort. To hear Lucius Hirtuleius speak of getting drunk was like hearing a virgin speak of an orgy. He might have a drink or two from time to time, but he most often preferred to keep a level head. After reaching adulthood, I had, as well—until Arausio.

"You won't receive any complaints from me."

We charged up from the stables to the tribunes' tent, fresh reserves appearing at the prospect of a good time. It was odd, traversing a Roman camp. It felt like we hadn't gone anywhere since I and the other Arausio survivors had arrived at Marius's camp. Everything was constructed in the same location, so it wasn't difficult to find.

Equus was standing holding back the tent flap as our shield bearers carried our mattresses inside.

"Thank you, Apollonius." I gestured to him as he entered.

"Not a problem, sir, I know you need your rest."

"I've told him a thousand times to call me Quintus, by Jupiter's stone," I whispered to Lucius, who was already focused on the task at hand.

"Equus! Would you like to join Tribune Sertorius and me?" Lucius asked, as if making a grand gesture.

"And what does that entail?" he asked with a raised eyebrow.

Lucius leaned in as if he were delivering a message containing quite nefarious details. "We're going to get drunk."

Equus threw up his hands. "You two reprobates go about your business. Some of us have to maintain some discipline in this place."

"Oh, come on, Equus! Lighten up, you bastard," Lucius chided. Our mutual friends, the Insteius twins, and I had often teased Lucius in the same manner growing up, so it was quite humorous to hear.

"We have no idea when the Cimbri will attack," Equus retorted.

"We know they won't tonight," Lucius replied.

"That's true, or otherwise Tribune Hirtuleius would be hunting for pigeons to sacrifice instead of a goblet of wine," I said.

Equus debated it until a smile creased his lips.

"You two are a terrible influence."

"I'll find some wine," Lucius said, scurrying off. "The darkest, most unwatered I can find!"

The three of us set across camp with a few cups and two full vases of wine.

"No, no, no, you're doing it all wrong," we heard some mule saying to a few others as we passed them by. We couldn't help but turn to see what they were discussing.

Some of our legionaries were instructing Catulus's men on the proper use of a gladius.

"You hold your shield like that, and you're liable to get yourself killed," another said, crossing his arms and shaking his head.

"Show them how to do it," one of Marius's mules said.

Lucius, Equus, and I chuckled among ourselves. These same men were likely the ones who had been throwing up and pissing themselves before we met the Teutones a few months prior, but they deserved their moment of pride. None of us knew how long it would last.

We found a relatively quiet spot near the eastern gate and plopped down on the soil, careful only not to spill our wine.

"Now let's drink," Lucius said.

"To the dead and those about to die." Equus lifted up his cup, and we did the same, before draining them. All three of us poured another, and gulped them down like thirsty men stranded in the Sinai.

"The men seem proud," Lucius said after a cup or two.

"That puts it lightly. They're as boastful as gladiators by now.

If you didn't know better, you'd think they had just captured Troy or just conquered Hannibal's forces," Equus said.

"The Teutones are no enemy to despise. They were tough, and our men deserve their moment in the sun," Lucius said before taking another sip.

"*Were* no enemy to despise. They're gone now," Equus reminded him.

"By the gods that's right," I said, lifting my cup.

"Yes, they are," Lucius said.

We drank in silence for a moment, listening to the chorus of insect in the distance and the chatter of mules closer still.

"That really was something, wasn't it? We drove through them like mad," Equus said, staring off at the stars in bewilderment.

"Right?" I shook my head.

"I've never seen anything like it!" Lucius shouted.

"Your cavalry hit them like a lightning bolt from Mount Olympus," Equus said with a laugh of disbelief.

"Rolled them up like parchment! Sealed their fate with hot wax." Lucius shook his head, his eyes cast in the distance, just as surprised by the outcome as Equus.

"You were on the right flank, though, Equus; your men held out the longest. What was it, twelve enemy standards your men captured?" I asked.

"Never seen anything like it." Equus took a sip.

"I'd like to see Scipio's men do that!" Lucius lifted his cup.

"We did lose Legate Marcellus, though," I said, immediately regretting it. His dead eyes flashed before me until I blinked and turned my attention back to the two men beside me.

"Gods protect him," Equus said.

"He died in service to Rome," Lucius said, a bit more contained than before.

"Marius really is the genius they say he is, isn't he?" Equus said as Lucius and I both burst out with agreement.

"I told you all along!" Lucius shouted.

"I never doubted it. But the man is a damned prodigy!" I said, pouring myself another cup.

"It's like the man is a prophet. Like he can see the future," Equus said in amazement.

"He does have that prophetess. Perhaps Martha told him exactly what to do," Lucius said. We all had a good laugh at this, but I wondered for a moment if it was true. Perhaps Marius had an ear to the gods, who instructed him. In the silence that followed, I considered what Lucius had said in the stables, and decided I did still believe in the gods. But perhaps it was just the effects of the wine setting in.

"These Cimbri don't have any idea what's about to hit them," Equus said, breaking the silence. We all laughed and raised our cups.

"They've met Romans but not Marius's mules!" Lucius shouted.

"We'll 'give them their land,' by the gods!" I drained my cup and lay back on the damp earth, staring up at the stars. To my disappointment, silence followed.

"I guess Marius has never met the Cimbri either." Equus spoke what we all were thinking.

"He will soon enough," Lucius said, appearing sober despite the blush in his cheeks and the twinkle in his eye.

"Those men really don't know what to expect," I said, more to Lucius than Equus, because he alone in the camp had experienced it with me.

"No. They do not." Lucius sighed.

"Are you scared?" Equus addressed us both. I believe it was meant to bring some humor back to our growing seriousness, but I could sense the tension in his voice.

"How could we not be?" Lucius answered for the both of us.

I poured myself another cup and lay back on the soil again, wondering who that earth would belong to within the week.

30

SCROLL XXX

FIVE DAYS BEFORE THE KALENDS OF AUGUST 653 AB URBE CONDITA

Lucius and I both awoke to the consequences of our indulgence. Equus claimed to be experiencing the same, but given that he rose at his usual hour and exercised, I assumed that his youth had spared him the worst of it.

Tasks were given to us throughout the day, which we took to with less than our usual vigor. I punished myself with negative thoughts, like why I hadn't steered my friend back to the path of wisdom and told him that indulging in unwatered wine was of no use to a Roman tribune. For I had tried it and he had not. But, ultimately, I did not regret it. If we were to die at the hands of the Cimbri, this was at least a memory I would carry with me to the fields of Elysium. The only thing I regretted was saying things that had encouraged our conversation to turn sour. I might have been suffering, but there was no reason for my two comrades to do the same.

That evening, as I was receiving the report from the first spear of the Seventh Legion, the gates opened.

I did not know why at first, having ignored the initial ruckus it had caused. Only when I dulled out the centurion's voice and looked over my shoulder to see foreigners riding through our camp atop Gaul's best horses did I realize what was happening.

I could have identified that armor anywhere.

I had spent months in the Cimbri camp, after all.

"Very good, Centurion. Tell the men to stay hydrated," I interrupted him and then hurried off toward the praetorium.

If the Cimbri were to meet with our general, I would be with him.

"Consul!" I shouted as I entered, beating the Cimbri ambassadors.

"Yes, I already know," Manius Aquillius said from the right of Marius's desk. I wasn't addressing him, but if he knew, Marius did as well.

"They're a few moments away," I said, suddenly realizing how out of breath I had become.

"I'm glad you're here," Marius gruff voice called out from his quarters. Nothing had ever sounded so sweet. "I'd like you to sit in with us." Marius entered the main room of the praetorium. "Move the desk. Bring out couches for us to recline in a circle. Our Tribune Sertorius has told us how these barbarians like to convene." Marius gestured and Volsenio hurried to obey him.

Catulus and Sulla looked dumbfounded.

"You make Rome look weak," Catulus said. Marius stopped in his tracks and pointed a finger across at his former co-consul.

"You'll let me handle this, Catulus. Perhaps you can learn something," Marius said.

Catulus's cheeks blushed and he looked like he might burst into a fit of rage, but Sulla whispered for him to keep calm.

By the time the praetorium was rearranged to Marius's liking, the tent flaps opened. Everyone paused and looked up as the two Cimbri emissaries stepped in, a Roman guard on either side of them. They stopped to analyze everything from above their lifted chins. They ran their fingers over the bust of Scipio and glared for some time at the gilded bull and ceremonial swords near the entrance, as if none of us were there. They were curious but undisturbed by what they saw.

Marius was the first to stir and approach them.

"Greetings from Rome," Marius said, the gruffness typically in his voice tamed a bit. He seemed as friendly and unassuming as an Italian farmer.

"Greetings," one of the emissaries replied in Latin.

"Would you sit with us?" Marius gestured toward the couch. They said nothing in reply but followed him to take their seats. After they were settled in, Aquillius, Catulus, and Sulla did the same. I remained at the back, behind Marius's couch, never taking my eye off the Cimbri emissaries' smug eyes. "Are you hungry?" Marius asked. When they didn't respond, he mimicked the act of eating.

"We are not hungry, but we will eat with you," one of them replied. Marius snapped his fingers, and Roman delicacies were brought out on golden plates and passed out to those on the couches. Sulla and Catulus never looked down at their plates, keeping their eyes locked on our enemy instead. Marius was the only Roman who began to help himself, seemingly undisturbed by their presence.

One of the Cimbri emissaries picked up some of his food and brought it to his nose to sniff, suddenly appearing like a wolf with an unidentified scrap of meat.

"It's fried eel, very good," Marius said again. These were delicacies that Marius's cook rarely prepared, as Marius preferred something hardier. It was clear that he wanted to impress our guests.

This attempt was spoiled when the emissary took a bite and his face contorted as if he were about to vomit. He placed the remainder on the plate and scooted it away from himself.

Marius did not allow his irritation to be apparent, but I could see Aquillius's eyes twitching.

"Would you like some wine?"

"Yes," one of the emissaries said. They both held out their hands for a slave to bring them Rome's favored drink. They took it without acknowledging Marius or those who handed it to them.

"We have enjoyed drinking your wine," the other Cimbri emissary said. The first was already draining the cup, the purple liquid spilling out over his lips and tricking down his long beard. It must have been quite a sight to the refined Romans in the room, but I was accustomed to seeing this from my time in the Cimbri camp—although it was typically cheap mead and not Falernian-grape wine.

"We want land in the place you call 'Gaul,'" one of the emissaries said as the other lifted his chalice to be refilled.

"No," was Marius's only reply. The jovial smile on his face had now faded. He ignored the food in his lap and looked directly at his guests.

"No?"

"We will not give you land," Marius said again. Tension engulfed the room. The only sound was the Roman standards flapping in the wind outside the praetorium. One of the emissaries was about to stand up, but the other placed a hand on his arm to still him.

"You should reconsider."

"Rome does not give land to her enemies. You are fortunate we gave you food and wine. But that is all Rome shall give you." There was no hesitation in Marius's voice.

"Our cousins will be arriving from the west any day now," one of the emissaries said, a grin creasing his face in triumph. "You will not be able to withstand our combined army."

"Do not let your pride be troubled. No one could withstand us," the other said, more restrained than the first.

"Your cousins?" A smirk crossed Marius's face as well. "The Teutones and Ambrones?" Marius now let his head roll back in careless laughter. The Cimbri emissaries glared at him, but there was more confusion in their eyes than malice. The rest of us looked away, almost unable to keep our feet from tapping. "Volsenio, show them our most honored guest."

Volsenio disappeared for a moment and then returned with the sound of iron shackles dragging along the earth.

Teutobod, king of the Teutones, stood within Volsenio's grasp, his hands restrained behind him. His face was swollen and purple, dried blood covering his lips and his left cheek. His fine robes had been torn, but fine they remained. He was still adorned with the trappings of a king, but covered in mud, blood, and spit; it was clear to the Cimbri emissaries what had happened.

The Cimbri jumped to their feet, shaking with fury. Teutobod didn't look up at them, staring only at his feet in utter humiliation and defeat. It appeared that the Teutone survivors who hadn't been captured had scurried off to safety. Clearly, no one had delivered word of the defeat to their Cimbri allies.

"Your cousins wanted land, emissary. Now they have it."

One of the Cimbri men lunged at Marius, who didn't budge or blink, but the other grabbed his wrist.

"Where do you want to meet your end?" asked the more stable of the two.

"On the Raudine Plain, first light, three days hence," Marius said without pause or hesitation.

The Cimbri emissaries turned on their feet and hurried out of the praetorium without further hesitation.

"That was how you 'honor' them, Marius?" Sulla asked, hand on his chin. I realized then that my heart had been racing the entire time.

Marius reclined on his couch and exhaled deeply. "That went exactly how I intended." He pulled his plate back over and gorged on the remainder of his fried eel.

"Three days? Are we really prepared to meet them, Marius? Or is this some kind of ruse?" Catulus asked.

"That's Consul Marius," he said, picking something from his teeth, "and of course we're ready to meet them. My men are, at least."

"Our legions are ready," Sulla said firmly.

"Then we have no concerns. Send word to Rome that we'll meet the bastards soon." Aquillius stood and handed his untouched food to a slave. "We need to begin preparations immediately."

"The preparations are already completed. We've only to disseminate the orders." Marius gestured for Volsenio to grab the scrolls from his desk.

"You didn't plan on consulting with me on this matter?" Catulus asked.

"You'll receive your share of the credit, Proconsul, I assure you. But the battlefield is mine. And we will crush them."

Three days before the kalends of August 653 ab urbe condita

Marius conferred with the command staff for the next two days, going over the plans for battle and allowing them to make their suggestions. Few were accepted, but Catulus and Sulla seemed to be pacified. The battle would take place the following morning at first light, as Marius had decreed. The night before, Marius had ordered for the tribunes to rally at the south wall, where we were to be briefed about the battle that lay ahead.

We'd waited in silence—only breaking it to shoo away a few mules who were attempting to eavesdrop—for the consuls to arrive. Marius and Aquillius came promptly at the eighth hour. There was a grim presence about them, as well as with us, but one of seriousness rather than fear. We all realized that the fate of the Republic would be decided the following day, but the die had been cast, and there was no uncertainty to fear any longer.

"Good evening, Tribunes," Marius began.

"Evening, sir." We snapped to attention.

"You all realize what will happen tomorrow?"

We nodded with dour approval.

"We will need you all at your best. The men will look to you more than ever, and they should see nothing but bravery and relentlessness in your eyes. Otherwise, we will fail." He reached out and Aquillius handed him a stick. He kicked away some twigs and rocks, creating a clean plot of dirt in front of him. "Gather around." He waited for us to do so, and then began to draw lines in the sand. "Our men will be stationed here, in the center. All three of our legions shoulder to shoulder. We'll meet the bulk of our enemy." Aquillius nodded with approval behind him. "Catulus will take the left wing, and Legate Sulla will take the right." Marius continued to draw out the field of battle as some of the men groaned.

"I know. I feel the same as you. I wanted Consul Aquillius to lead one of the flanks, but we'll need all of our men at the center. We can't stretch ourselves too thin. Our cavalry, however, will be placed here," he said, drawing a circle behind Sulla's flank. "We have no room for trickery or deceit this time, men, no flanking or ambushes. We have to reinforce the flanks, or our less experienced allies might falter," Marius said. "Our horse will be led by Tribune Hirtuleius."

All eyes turned to the left of me where my old comrade stood wide eyed.

"Tribune Sertorius, who has also led the cavalry in recent battles, will be placed here, with the Seventh Legion." He poked directly at the center of our dirt formation as all eyes turned to me.

"Sir, if I may…" Lucius gestured nervously.

"Go ahead," Marius replied without looking up.

"Tribune Sertorius is far better on a horse. I'm not quite as experienced—"

Marius cut him off. "You're as experienced in leading cavalry as any man in this legion. Besides, I want Tribune Sertorius with the Seventh. If First Spear Herennius falls, I want Sertorius to lead the Seventh."

"Perhaps he could lead the cavalry and I—"

Marius raised a finger to silence him up again, "No, Tribune. He has experience leading men as a centurion. I believe you are the right man for this position, and I do not make mistakes." Lucius gulped but the rest of us smiled.

"Equus... Tribune Cinna, rather, you will go with Tribune Hirtuleius. If he dies, you'll take over," Marius said and returned to his dirt battle map. It was necessary to take such precautions in battle, but it was always sobering to hear that your death or the death of a close friend was plausible.

Marius continued to explain the roles of the various tribunes. Many of them attempted, respectfully, of course, to object. All were denied. Marius was quite certain about his decisions, and there was a confidence about him that was undeniable, leaving us all with the conclusion that he actually did know more than we.

"I want everyone to go to sleep. We'll need you rested. Drink willow water if need be, but no strong wine tonight. We'll need you at your best." He paused and scanned our faces. "Don't worry, though, if we win tomorrow, we'll get so drunk we'll have to lay on the battlefield just to hold on."

We laughed, as much in nervous anticipation as in response to the joke, but it was important to do so, considering what lay ahead. It was likely that many of the men to our left and right would be reduced to ash the following evening or, worse yet, rotting under the corpses of their friends.

"Dismissed, Tribunes."

We snapped to attention, saluted, and shouted in unison, "Jupiter!"

"*Optimus et Maximus*," Marius said with the responsive salute.

Before I departed, I approached the Consul alone.

"General Marius. I have a question for you," I began.

"And what is it, Tribune Sertorius?" Marius replied.

"Martha prophesied that we would win the battle at Aquae Sextiae. I doubted her, but she was right." I attempted to smile and signal contrition at my disbelief. "Has she given word about tomorrow?"

Marius looked up and met my eye for a moment. Then he exhaled and stepped away. He said nothing more, leaving me embarrassed and confused. I didn't know how to interpret his response, but none of the ways I attempted were positive.

APOLLONIUS WAS IN THE TRIBUNES' tent when I arrived, a damp towel and my helmet in hand.

"How are you, *amicus*?" I asked.

He stood and hung the helmet on the stand by my bed and approached with a nervous smile on his face. He extended his hand, which I shook in the Roman manner, something he took great pride in since he had begun to do so.

"So tomorrow it will begin?"

"Tomorrow it will end, Apollonius. It will end." I exhaled and plopped down on the trunk at the foot of my bed.

He shrugged his shoulders. "One way or the other, it will end tomorrow."

"That's right. And all I can lose is the present moment," I said as he found a stool and pulled it up alongside me.

"Tribune Sertorius, we're going to visit the *valetudinarium* and attempt to cheer up the men, are you coming?" Equus said as he passed me by.

"I'll join you there in a while." I waved him on and then turned back to Apollonius. "And, one way or another, you'll have your freedom tomorrow."

Apollonius looked down at his feet. "You very well may live."

"Regardless, this war will be over, and you'll have your freedom."

He looked up and met my eye with an indiscernible look.

"Rome will need you sooner or later, and you'll need a 'shield bearer.'" He tried to smile, but I could tell it was difficult for him to do so.

"Well, maybe I will." I pulled up my leg and began to untie my sandals. "But you shouldn't have to be the one to do it. You've put up with me long enough."

"Not good enough at it, ay?" he asked.

"Better than good. But you deserve to find your family. Some other poor fool will put up with me eventually."

He looked down, but a thankful grin, less forced now, covered his face.

"Shall I write something to your family before battle?"

I considered it for a moment. "No. I think I shall do so this time," I said with an exhale. "If you'll grab me some parchment and a pen, that may be the last request I'll ever make of you."

After I prepared my last words to my family, I joined Equus and some of the other tribunes at the valetudinarium.

"I'm looking for Marcus Axius," I said to the highest-ranking *medicus*. It had been a while since I had visited him, and each time he had been resting. Occasionally I feared he might never wake up, and that made it more difficult to return.

"Let me check the rolls." He departed for a moment and then returned. "Nobody here by that name, sir."

"Maybe just Ax? That's what we called him." My heart began to beat faster.

"We don't use nicknames here, sir," he replied.

I tried not to panic but moved quickly through the stalls, peering behind every curtain.

"What are you doing, Sertorius?" Equus laughed, not understanding my task.

"I'll be back in a moment," I replied and hurried on.

Finally, I found him. He was a fraction of the size he once

was. The mallet-like hands he had used to clap me on the back were bone thin, and his barrel chest, which used to give him the hardest time when putting on his armor, was now shallow and recessed. It was a wonder I had recognized him in that cage, and even less so now.

"My old friend," I said as I approached his bed. He didn't stir for a moment, but then his eyes open and he shifted. "Lie still."

"Well, I better salute, you being a tribune now and all." He tried to laugh but ended up coughing. The smile that had once charmed the whole damned legion was filled with broken teeth and splintered lips.

"Shove it up your arse, Ax. We'll always be tentmates, as far as I'm concerned." He shifted in the bed so that I could take a seat beside him. "I really thought you were dead, Ax. I saw you take an arrow."

"Well, that makes two of us." He pulled back his blankets to reveal his bare chest and a thick scar across his sternum. "That's where the arrow got me. I thought I'd be dead too, but apparently it wasn't deep enough, or it didn't hit anything vital." He paused and laughed cynically before coughing once again. "I tried to charge into them so I might die like some sort of hero, but I collapsed before I killed a single one of them."

"I saw what you did." I laughed with him. "Heroic or not, I thought it was foolish."

"Well, that's what I'm known for." He sucked wind through the missing gaps in his teeth. "So the arrow didn't kill me. So old Marcus Axius is going to die from infections and lung congestions."

"Who says you're going to die?" I barked, still attempting to be playful. Ax's face became quite serious, though.

"The *medicus*. Says I'll probably die. Called it an act of the gods that I've made it this far."

"Well, the gods will just have to keep on acting, then, won't they? You're not going anywhere on me, Ax. I'm a tribune now, remember? That's an order."

He smiled and shook his head.

"If I have anything to do with it, I'll keep fighting. I'd really like to see home again." We both sobered.

"We're going to make sure that happens, Ax. And as soon as you're well enough for transport, we'll get you home. We have to win tomorrow first!"

"The battle is tomorrow?" Suddenly his eyes sparkled like they used to. I didn't know why.

"Oh…yes. I assumed you'd heard."

"I'm mostly forgotten about in here. Don't hear much gossip."

I didn't know how to respond to that, so we sat in silence for a moment.

"Want me to light that candelabrum?" I asked.

"No, I'll probably go back to sleep when you leave."

"Oh," I replied. There was so much I wanted to say to Ax, and presumably so much he'd like to say to me. But we didn't have to. After everything we had endured together, we knew each other's hearts.

"I best leave, then. I'll be fighting for you tomorrow, Ax, so you fight for me."

"Order confirmed, Stallion." He leaned up in bed and shook my hand. I met his eyes and he nodded before I turned to leave.

I didn't know if he would still be there when I returned, or if I would be alive to do so.

I saw as many of the other mules as I could on my way out. The men there told us how distraught they were that they wouldn't be marching with us into battle. Some of them might have been feigning it, to be certain, but I could tell that the majority of them meant it. You'd be surprised how brave the soldier's heart can become when he develops love for his brothers. I bid them farewell and told them not to worry, for by midday tomorrow, the Cimbri would be destroyed. I hoped that was true, but I knew we wouldn't have to suffer the consequences of the lie if it wasn't.

I departed the valetudinarium, knowing that many of us would join the dead and dying there soon enough.

31

SCROLL XXXI

TWO DAYS BEFORE THE KALENDS OF AUGUST 653 AB URBE CONDITA

Bugles sounded to wake us far earlier than usual, but not a man among us groaned. We understood what would come this day. The fate of civilization was about to be decided, and the fog that hovered above the earth seemed to tell us the gods were just as aware of this as we were.

"Centurion," I said with a salute as I approached the Seventh Legion tents.

"Tribune Sertorius." He returned the salute and accepted a handshake once I offered it.

"How are the men, Herennius?"

"They're ready, Tribune. They understand what's about to happen." He adjusted the straps of his belt and ensured his sheath was tight.

"And you?" I asked, waiting for him to make eye contact.

"Just another day in the legion, sir."

I smiled. "Just another day."

We didn't bother to deconstruct the camp. Either we would

be victorious and would soon return here to celebrate and burn our dead, or the barbarians would have another obstacle before destroying what remained. There was quite an eerie feeling as we poured through the gates.

"Tribune, stay with me in the battle. But remain behind me. It will damage morale if you fall," Herennius said as he marched his cohort through the gate, myself at his side.

"Don't you worry about me, Centurion. I'll guard your flank and you guard mine," I said.

I adjusted the straps of my helmet. It no longer chaffed me. It seemed to have worn grooves into my face and now fit naturally. I stretched my toes in the leather sandals on my feet. Where there had once been raw blisters, there were now calluses as thick and hard as a soldier's shield. My mind traveled back to the first time I'd held a sword, the wooden one we used in the Fourth Legion as I learned how to hold it properly. I recalled stumbling up the ladder at the Battle of Burdigala, and the first man I killed. I could almost hear the shouts of my *contubernium* beside me as we cried out Mars name under Maximus's rhythmic chant. I saw the Tectosages fall and the Ambrones drowning in the river as our men triumphed over them. I recalled King Teutobod kneeling in defeat before Marius, and the general's booming voice crying out, "Rome!" I remembered Marcellus's sad, dead eyes and the beautiful letter he'd written to his wife. I thought of Centurion Scrofa and his last words to me that I was "Rome's last hope."

I hoped he was right. I said a silent prayer that all of this had prepared me for the battle ahead. But there was no time for doubting now. It either had or hadn't. Either Rome would be victorious and stand alone and supreme above all the earth, or the Republic we had built would crumble. We would know at first light.

We were silent as we marched to the Raudine Plain, a pale-blue light creeping over the Alpine hills in the distance behind us. Even the centurions weren't barking orders at their men.

Centurion Herennius didn't so much as look over his shoulder, trusting that his men were doing as they had been taught.

The signal was given for us to halt. The fog covered the field of battle, and we strained to see the enemy. They were still in the distance, pouring out of a passage in the hills. They moved as one massive, uncontrollable enemy of Rome.

A few of the men behind me threw up what little was in their bellies.

"That's right, men, water the earth—for soon it shall be ours again," I said to a handful nervous chuckles. A friend of mine once said the same thing before the battle in which he died. But in the months that followed, he was proven correct. We defeated the Teutones not sixty miles from where he and ninety thousand Romans were killed.

A few officers sped past the front of our line, ensuring everything was as it ought to be. I took their silence to mean that it was. The battle was at hand.

As the Cimbri hordes materialized in the fog, a voice cried out, "Make some noise, men! Let them hear you!"

The order was passed down the line to every legionary.

We roared as loudly as we could, looking into the faces of those next to us to encourage them to do the same.

"Stomp your feet, let them hear you!" the shout came again. We followed the command and took the initiative to brandish our swords and beat them against our shields as well.

The Cimbri began to posture in the same way in the distance, but I could hear little of it over the war cries of our own men. After years of Romans marching in silence, and after seeing Catulus's men flee from them with tails tucked between their legs, this must have been quite a sight for the northern invaders.

"It's time to end this! It's time to punish them for their crimes!" a commanding voice cried out from the rear.

"Steady, men," Centurion Herennius shouted above the chanting. He had joined in but wanted to ensure that his men didn't get carried away. "Remember your training. Fight for the man beside you, stand fast behind your shield and stab over it. Do not look away. Do not retreat. Do not break the line."

The yellow flags dropped and bugles sounded.

"Advance!" Herennius shouted along with the other first spears before blowing his whistle, his voice hoarse in the way only a centurion's can become.

"Here it is," I said to myself beneath my breath.

I could feel it. The men wanted to run into battle. But we kept the given pace. Toe to heel, toe to heel. Slow and steady. The Cimbri, still a ways out, were charging as fast as two hundred thousand men chained to one another can run.

We remained silent until they were nearly upon us.

"Jupiter!" a voice cried out.

"Optimus!" every Roman replied.

"Jupiter!" the voice came again. It was then that I realized it was our general himself.

"Maximus!"

"Jupiter!"

"Optimus!"

The Cimbri charged through the fog, appearing everywhere around us.

"Pila!" the first spears cried. Herennius turned and grabbed my shoulders, pulling me down with him and covering us both with his shield as the first ranks hoisted their pila and launched them at the surging Cimbri. Hundreds of them crashed into the ground, each screaming and scratching at the shaft in their rib cage, but they were dragged along with the others regardless. "Second rank!"

The first rank ducked and the second let their volley fly.

So many fell that I believe our men paused to see if our enemies would falter. They did not.

A rumble sounded out from the Cimbri side that overcame their chants and cries. My mind didn't perceive it at first, but my heart did. It was a sound I knew well. Charging through the fog, the Cimbri cavalry raced toward us, passing by their infantry to cheers of exultation.

"Shields up!" Herennius's words had barely escaped his lips when the horsemen crashed into our line.

The cavalry lunged over the shield walls, crashing atop men in the second and third ranks. The first were sent to their backs with a kick of the hooves to their shields. Gladii shinned in the morning sun as they stabbed at the horses and horsemen atop them. The horses' cries were deafening as they collapsed, kicking and stirring all the while.

I steadied myself behind my shield as a horseman aimed right at us. I leaned back and braced myself, but Herennius stabbed up into the beast's belly, sending it from its path to the damp soil beneath us.

He turned to me, face drenched in the blood, and nodded.

"Thank you," I said as I repositioned myself.

"Steady! Hold the line, hold the line!" Herennius cried out.

Some of the cavalry wheeled about and darted away as quick as Zephyr. Whether it was the rider or the beast that decided to do so, I do not know. Others charged harder still, crashing into our line and creating wide gaps.

Before we could reform the Cimbri infantry had arrived. The northern invaders towered over us.

"Shields high, men!" Herennius shouted, leading by example from the front of the formation.

Axes, clubs, and broadswords crashed down against Roman shields. I brought my own up, and tried to push forward to the front, but was equally distracted by the severed leg of a man beside me. He was screaming, staring wide eyed at the carnage of his own body as spurts of red blood shot out from the exposed white bone of his femur. Mules on either side were trampling over him until, to my relief, men in the later ranks pulled the man to safety. Just as I was at the height of my distraction, a man in the first rank fell under the slice of an axe to the exposed flesh of his neck. He fell backward like a pine tree cut at its base, his neck dangling on the few remaining ligaments as he did so.

I didn't consider it, just stepped over him to fill the gap.

The Red who had killed him stepped back and hoisted his axe, which was still dripping with the blood of my countrymen.

It crashed into my shield. Splintering the wood, the tip of the axe had pushed through and was inches from my face. But it was wedged. He tried to free it, but he was too slow. I lunged forward with my gladius as an extension of my arm. I slid it into his belly and dug deeper and deeper.

He gurgled blood and screamed like a wounded animal until he toppled back. He dangled from the chains tying him to the men beside him until he was cut loose. In the meantime, I stabbed my sword into the dirt and freed the axe from my shield. Then I pulled back and sent it twirling at the next enemy in line, catching him in the sternum. He made little noise at all, except the sound of his breath being driven from his body, as he spun and fell into the arms of his men.

"Tribune! Get back in line!" Herennius was shouting, bearing his shield against the flurry of attacks of a young Cimbri butcher.

I ignored him.

"Tribune!" Herennius shouted, severing the warrior's arm and kicking him in the chest back into the line of his brethren.

His personal enemy now stalled, he reached across to push me back with his shield. I shoved it away with my own.

I was a soldier too. A tribune, sure, but a soldier first. This was my battle. My fight.

Exasperated, he stepped back in line and blocked another attack from the next man in front of him.

A burly Cimbri with a beard down to his chest, whom I still believe I'd met in their camp, barreled toward me with a lung of the club. The shield absorbed the brunt of it, but the force nearly sent me to my knees. As he recoiled from the block, I stepped forward and bashed my shield into his face. His nose cracked and blood began to flow immediately. As he tried to blink his vision back, I took a stab at his thigh, slicing the flesh, blood spraying out before I returned to position. He writhed on the earth and was trampled by his brethren.

Herennius blew his whistle, and the first rank stepped to the side, and then back, allowing the second rank to take its place. I would have liked to stay there, but habit got the best of me, and I moved along with the rest of the men in the first rank.

We tried to collect our breaths as the men at the front attacked with fresh vigor. The man to my right was standing quite still, in line with the rest of us, but the labor of his breathing caught my attention. Turning to him, I saw that he still bore his shield in position before him, but his sword arm was now severed at the elbow. Blood bubbled out from the wound and poured down the back of his arm to his side. He analyzed it, utterly perplexed.

"Get this man out of my formation!" I shouted, pushing the injured mule back through the ranks. His eyes were glossy and confused as the men behind us carried him away.

The second rank was fighting hard but didn't find the Cimbri as exhausted as they'd expected. We seemed to be at a standstill. We could advance no further, and neither could the enemy.

But then I heard that dreaded hum. Before my mind could place it, rocks smashed into our lines. Catapults.

Men on both sides of the divide, Cimbri and Roman alike, were smashed beneath it. Bodies were flattened like stale bread; legs were torn apart at the knee.

Havoc reigned. The centuries on either side of us, who had been hit by the catapults harder, began to falter. The line was broken. Centurions blew their whistles and *optiones* tried to beat their men back into place, but panic was spreading like a fire.

"Stand fast, men!" Herennius stabbed an assailant and pushed him back into the waves of advancing Cimbri.

The thunder of horse hooves rang out again as I saw the remainder of the cavalry swinging around in the distance and careening toward our right flank. They were being cut down in vast numbers, but still they poured into us like water on rock.

A catapult's rock struck our century, taking out an entire rank of men.

"My leg!" one cried.

"Oh, oh, kill me!" another shouted.

But we couldn't even turn to assist them.

The Cimbri cavalry broke through the ranks of a century a few paces down from us as the Red infantry continued to surge forward. The chains at their hips had begun to snap, and some of them pushed through our line swinging violently in all directions. Holes widened in our ranks as the bodies piled up and legionaries withdrew in fear.

The blurry visions flashing before my eye reminded me of Arausio.

"Don't retreat! Push them back!" I shouted when I found the breath, and hurried to fill the closest opening.

One of the Cimbri warriors had his back to me, and I sunk my blade into his spine.

Casting him aside, I shouted, "Jupiter!"

"Optimus!" a few of the men replied.

"Jupiter!" I cried again, more forcefully, as I held my shield fast before another assailant.

"Maximus!" more of them returned the call as my sword sliced through the exposed flesh of a Cimbri kneecap.

Then all eyes began to swivel to the right.

"Eyes front, men!" Herennius shouted, perceptive enough that he didn't even need to turn around.

But even I couldn't help but steal a glance.

In the distance was a head of cavalry, a wedge formation, with a Roman standard held high.

The legionaries let out a roar that forced the Cimbri to turn as well.

Lucius was at the helm of the cavalry charge, Sulla's flank

following behind him. His sword was lifted to the heavens and his snarled face as angry as Hades.

"Lucius!" I shouted in exultation, although he couldn't hear me, as the cavalry crashed into the Cimbri infantry.

"Steady yourselves, men," Centurion Herennius cried out again when he had the chance to do so. "And, Tribune, get back into line!" His voice reminded me of old Scrofa's, and this time I complied.

I struggled to catch my breath, suddenly burning from the rising sun and drenched in perspiration beneath my lorica.

I blinked sweat from my eye and focused my gaze on the enemy still before us. Those who weren't already smeared with blood were drenched in sweat of their own, and their eyes were squinted. The sun was blazing behind us.

"Push them back!" I shouted, lifting my sword above the century. "Send them to Hades!"

"They're faltering!" cried some of the mules.

"Advance!" Herennius relayed the call, hoisting his shield in front of him and driving with the rest of the men into the Cimbri ranks. The butchered enemy were nearly piled up to our knees as we crossed over them.

The cries of the wounded still rose out through the morning air, but the desperate gasps for air were just as apparent from our living enemy.

"Harder, men, drive them back!" I cried, my voice becoming hoarse like the centurion's.

I could see the heads of our men turning to the right as Lucius and our cavalry were hitting the Cimbri flank around with Sulla's forces.

The Cimbri were turning to run, but couldn't. Crippled by their own linked hips, they stumbled over one another. The bravest among them turned to kill the cowardly before turning back to meet their fate at the tip of Roman steel.

"They're faltering, men!" a shout rang out.

"Advance!" Herennius yelled again and then deferred to his whistle.

As some distance appeared between us and our enemy, I realized the fog had dissipated, only to be replaced by the burning light of the Italian sun. We charged forward, shoulder to shoulder, slicing through and stomping over all the Reds who were too slow to get away.

"Advance! Advance! Advance!" The cries came from behind our forces, and I still believe it was Marius himself. "Double-time!"

We ran, on what reserves of energy I do not know, right into the Alpine passes our enemy had so recently descended from.

I spotted the "walls" I had once dwelled within, the wooden logs driven out to impale us as we approached. But we separated and pushed right through them.

Within, the Cimbri were falling into the arms of their women, who, in fury and disgust, slew them with daggers of their own.

"For Rome!" the men shouted.

"Wipe the bastards from the earth!" Shouts came from all side. The frenzy was let loose.

I saw mothers throwing their children under stampeding horses before cutting their own throats, and old men shouting out in fury until they were consumed by steel.

"Burn it down!"

We ignored all that was around us. If you think this impossible, I can ensure you that in the frenzy of battle you notice nothing but the enemy before you and the task at hand. Only later do you realize what you witnessed.

From the center of the Cimbri camp rode up a few hundred more Red warriors atop the finest steads they could muster.

I spotted King Boiorix, tall and noble atop the stallion I had helped him train, impossible to miss, at the front of them. They rode directly for the Seventh at the center of the Roman line.

"Death! Death!" they shouted in their native tongue.

"Steady, Legionaries!" Herennius shouted, his voice cracking under the pressure.

Absent pila, we had nothing to repel them with, so we blockaded behind our shields and allowed them to vault over and into us with one last furious attempt at revenge.

The barbarian king was thrust from his horse into the Roman formation. The mules around him had likely never seen the king before, but they knew who he was. They hesitated for a long while before stabbing him.

"Burn the camp!" the first spears cried out. Mules on all sides poured around me. The last resistance had been crushed. Now it was time to solidify our victory.

Without meaning to, I dropped my sword and shield. And then I fell to my knees.

I was overcome. I wept with no tears, as only a soldier knows how. I brought a bloody hand to my face and covered my quivering lips, trying to contain the heaving of my chest. Marius had said that the men should see only "bravery and unwavering relentlessness" when they looked at us. But the battle was now won, and I didn't give a damn.

Toughness, Roman *dignitas*...let city dwellers be concerned with such things. The soldier cares not.

I unlatched my helmet and let it fall to the ground, the plume digging into the earth. I laid my head against the dirt and wept without restraint. With blood-soaked fingers, I scooped up some of the soil beneath me. I had never been so grateful for something in my entire life.

Men charged all around me, as we had past the bodies of the wounded before. I ignored it all. We had won. We had won at last.

"Tribune." I felt a hand on my shoulder.

Looking up, I realized some time had passed as the men had spread out around the camp to take their share of the spoils.

"Yes," I said, blinking vision back to my eye.

"I told you to stay behind me." It was Centurion Herennius,

who grabbed me by the forearm and helped me to my feet. His face was splattered with blood like war paint, but he was smiling —the sad but proud smile that often accompanies the victorious.

"I thought we decided I'd watch your flank and you'd watch mine. That's how I remember it," I said, trying to smile, which almost forced me into another fit of thankful weeping.

"We've won," he said.

I looked around the camp. Romans were cheering from every corner of it.

"It appears we have," I said.

"Looks like you've had an injury." He pointed to a gash along my bicep. I don't know why, but I convulsed with laughter.

"I guess I did. I hadn't noticed. I'll use that as my excuse for why I'm shaking so much." I held out my hands, which were trembling uncontrollably.

The centurion smiled and shook his head before lifting his own hand, which was doing the same.

"No need for excuses."

"You did well today, Centurion. I'll be sure to let Marius know." I patted my face to ensure no snot was dripping over it.

"You have to leave it all here, you know?" the centurion said, looking deep into the only eye the Cimbri had left me.

"What?" I asked, perplexed, wondering if there was someone behind me I hadn't seen.

"You have to leave it here. Everything you've seen." I looked around to ensure it actually was me he was addressing. Everyone else was pillaging. No one else was near us. "Centurions… Centurions, we keep fighting. So will the men. But you'll go home. You'll go back to city life," he said. I began to offer some kind of objection, but he waved it away. "You'll go back to city life. Become a politician, raise a family. And then you'll begin to believe it's all a lie." He met my eye and squinted his own. Even in my haze, I believed every word of it. His words, hoarse and strained from the battle, were entrancing. "You'll believe war is reality. All this," he said, gesturing to the chaos around us, "you'll believe this is real, and that is a lie. Don't let it happen, Tribune. Leave the war here, and return to what you fought for."

He patted me on the shoulder.

"I will, Centurion," I said, trying to dissect all he had said.

"This victory will be remembered until the ends of the earth." He exhaled and placed his hands on his hips. "I don't give a damn about glory, but it's comforting to know that these men," he said, nodding to the battlefield our men had just fought and died on, "will be remembered."

"It is." My voice was little above a whisper. I was still wondering if the centurion was a figment of my imagination or a shade of Hades sent by Marius's prophetess, Martha, to comfort me.

"Hail, Tribune." The centurion saluted and then spun on his heels to join his men.

A hundred twenty thousand Cimbri died on the field of battle that day. Another sixty thousand were said to have been taken prisoner. The war was over.

32

SCROLL XXXII

TWO DAYS BEFORE THE KALENDS OF AUGUST 653 AB URBE CONDITA

After the Cimbri camp was destroyed and the captives were gathered up, we marched back together. No amount of rigorous cadence could have stalled the joy of victory. I don't think even the grimmest of centurions would have wanted to either.

When we arrived back in camp, everyone present lined the path to applaud us. There were no rose pedals to throw as in a Triumph, so they tossed handfuls of dirt and roared their approval.

Most of us couldn't help but smile, despite our military bearing. Rome's greatest enemy was vanquished. It was a victory for all. I know, at least, that I was smiling. I wished so badly that my brother had been there to see this moment. He was hard, stern, and dignified to his core, but I know he would have basked in this moment all the same. I smiled more in knowing that he could now find rest, his death avenged and his killers laid low.

I looked for Lucius once we were given orders to disseminate and feast.

His face lit up with joy when he spotted me.

"We made it, you bastard!" He locked his arms around my neck. I hugged him back, struggling for air in his relentless embrace, but I couldn't help but laugh.

"We did, *amicus.* We did," I said, holding my injured arm away from him.

"Gods! I might faint," Lucius said, noticing the wound. "You're alright, aren't you? You need to go to the *medicus.*" If I remember correctly, it really didn't look that serious, to a combat veteran, at least. But Lucius was always more concerned for my safety than for his own. If the gods ever created a better friend, I've not met him.

I laughed and shook my head. "Not yet. There are far more critical patients that need to be tended to. I'm fine."

"Quintus, you should at least tie something at the shoulder. Cut off the flow of blood."

I waved for him to desist, and stepped away.

"What would your mother say, Quintus?" He did his best Marius impression and wagged a finger at me.

"Lucius, I'm fine!" I shouted. "I'm glad that you made it back."

He nodded and kicked some dirt beneath his feet.

"I'm glad too," he said. "Go to the *medicus* when you can!" he called after me as I started to walk away.

"I will!" I hollered back. "This would have never happened if you had sacrificed more pigeons!" His laughter carried out through the camp as I headed straight for the slave quarters.

Apollonius wasn't there when I arrived, but he must have known I was headed to see him, for he returned shortly.

"Quintus," he said, his lips already quivering.

"I'm alive, comrade," I said. He extended his arm for a Roman handshake, which I promptly batted away and embraced him.

"Rome is free of her invaders, and you are free of your servitude," I said, my voice still strained from the events just hours prior.

"I'm free?" he asked.

"Yes, you are," I replied.

"I'm a free man?" he said again.

"You are, *amicus*." He erupted in laughter, and I slapped his chest. Just as we reached the height of our jesting, he sobered and became silent. Taken aback, I did the same.

"I have a proposition for you," he said.

"Alright, let's hear it, then," I replied, curious more than anything else.

"I'll work for you. I have the experience to be Rome's greatest assistant. I'll take your notes, carry what you cannot, write your letters...and I'll do it for half the price of the next man," he said, far more emphatically than was his custom, tapping a finger to his lip and nodding his head.

Rather than replying, I embraced him again.

"I believe I have a task for you, freedman," I said.

EPILOGUE

The day after the victory, word arrived that Marius had been elected to yet another consulship. Of all the men who had ever reigned supreme in Rome, none had ever stood as lofty as Gaius Marius the day before the kalends of August.

And his joy matched the occasion.

"Sertorius, my lad! We did it. We crushed the bastards!" he said as I approached him for the first time since the battle. It had been difficult to find an audience with Rome's most famous individual. He pulled me in close to him and, quite uncharacteristically, kissed me on the head. I could smell wine on his breath but could tell his endearment was genuine.

"We did, Consul. Congratulations on the election."

"Ah"—he waved his hands—"I don't care about that. Just doing my duty to the Republic. What I'm happy about is obliterating those Reds from the face of Gaia's earth."

He took a few steps away, expecting me to follow. I did, along with a few dozen other officers, all anxious to spend time with a man who could now hand out political favors like cups of wine.

"I could see the look in your eye the whole time, Tribune Sertorius. You doubted me, you didn't think we'd win." He smiled and gestured to the victorious celebration all around us to show me that we had.

"I never doubted you, General. Not for a second."

"By Pollux!" He slapped me on the shoulder and gestured for Volsenio to fetch me a cup of wine.

"You earned it, Tribune," the giant man said with a grin to match his height.

"Then I'll drink it." I raised my cup, and Volsenio raised one of his own.

The mules around us were already singing ballads about the victory, improvising lyrics poorly.

"Consul, there was something I wanted to ask you for."

"Whatever it is, I bet I'll give it to you," the general said as he stopped in his tracks and turned to face me. He placed a hand on my shoulder and tried to conjure up the most serious face he could, despite the fact that he was swaying from the effects of the wine.

"I wasn't able to collect much of the spoils after the battle."

"Too busy chasing women, if I know you well enough?" he said to the laughter of the others gathered. He didn't know me very well, I guess, but I laughed along with them and assumed it was the wine.

"No, too busy kissing my own arse and thanking the gods it was still there."

"What do you want, then, Tribune? Coin? Girl? Spoils?"

"Actually, Consul, I had something else in mind." I stepped in and leaned closer so that everyone might not hear my request. "I'd like horses."

"Horses?" he blurted out, ruining any chance of discretion. He turned and squinted at me. "You're not thinking about going back to farming and shoveling up horse shit, are you, lad? The survivor of Arausio, the hero of Aquae Sextiae and Vercellae, can't be shoveling up horse shit. I'm certain we can find a better use for you than that."

I smiled and shook my head.

"That's not it at all, Consul. I have a debt to repay."

He nodded. "How many do you need?"

"How about five? Six?"

"You can have a hundred if you want them." He waved his hand. "Talk to the stable keeper. Those horses lost their riders in the battle yesterday, so I hope their new master will fare better than their last."

"I'll ensure that he does."

"Go with fortune, then." He saluted and began to walk away, before turning to make one last point. "But I order that you return before my Triumph. I want you there with me, drinking every cup of wine in the city. Because you earned it. You hear me, boy?" He spoke now to all the soldiers in earshot, and lifted his voice. "You all earned it! This victory is yours!" He returned his attention to reveling in the adoring applause of his men. And I went to collect my horses.

WITH SIX HORSES trailing behind us, Apollonius and I departed for his first task as a free man. Unlike the many journeys I had taken, riding and marching through the Gallic forests, we took this trip slowly. We swapped tales on the way, and made time to admire the flowers, the breeze, the soil beneath us…all of which I had missed in the panic of war with the Cimbri.

When we arrived at our destination, we were neither tired nor ragged, as I had been after my previous treks. Nay, we were refreshed.

"Let's take them around back, Apollonius," I said, hopping off Sura's back and hitching her near the hut.

"Are you certain this is the right home? They all look the same to me," he asked.

"I'm certain. There was snow up to our knees and it was pitch black outside, but I remember. I couldn't forget."

I unlatched the wooden gate and helped Apollonius round

up the horses. I was leading them to the field when I spotted a man with a rake.

Alerted, he lifted the tool like a weapon and analyzed us with suspicious eyes under a straw hat.

"We come in peace," I said in Gallic, lifting a hand and passing the reins I had to Apollonius.

"Who are you?"

"My name is Quintus Sertorius. I'd guess I look a bit different than the first time we met." He pulled off his hat and stared at me for a moment, the wary look draining from his eyes.

"The runaway?"

"That's right. And you're Vallicus."

"I am." He tossed the rake down and pulled off his gloves before walking over to greet me. "I'm surprised you live. The Cimbri sent riders through every village within a hundred leagues to track you down. I had no idea I was aiding such a notorious getaway."

"Well, we wouldn't have lived if you hadn't." I extended my hand to shake his.

He peered over my shoulder to look at Apollonius and the horses we'd brought with us.

"Those are for you. They aren't the ones you gave to us, but they should perform adequately. Young and healthy, able to work the field, ride, or stud."

His mouth opened but he didn't say anything. Eventually he swallowed and looked down.

"I didn't expect to be repaid."

"I didn't expect to be able to repay you. But I'm glad that I can." He stepped past me and toward the horses. He inspected each one delicately, saying nothing for some time.

"These horses are far more expensive than the hags I gave you."

"Those hags saved my life, and the lives of eight other men. So they were worth more than anything I could offer."

He looked down, and for a moment I thought he might weep, but then he composed himself.

"I'm not a Gaul, you know," he said.

"You're not?"

"I'm a Lusitanian. The Cimbri butchered my people and forced my family from our ancestral land. That's why I gave you those horses. I hoped if what you said was true, you might have had some information to help defeat them. I didn't do it out of goodwill."

I stepped toward him and patted the horse at his side.

"That information did help defeat the Cimbri. But don't forget for a second that an act of charity and selflessness, in the midst of warfare and bloodshed, is goodwill. I cannot thank you enough."

He said nothing more but extended a hand. As I released my grip on his arm, I slid a bag of coin into his palm.

He looked down at it in bewilderment.

"For the clothes you gave us."

"I protest." He extended it back to me, but I stepped away.

"The Cimbri are defeated. Go back to your ancestral land, Vallicus of Lusitania. And go with fortune."

"Perhaps we'll meet again someday."

"I hope under better circumstances." I waved at him as Apollonius and I walked back to Sura, Vallicus watching our every stride, hands trembling on the reins of his new horses.

"You're a good man, Quintus Sertorius," he said as I helped him onto the back of the horse.

"Don't start with that now, old man. I've had enough of sentimentality for one day, or perhaps the whole year."

He laughed. "Well, you're a lousy bastard, then," he said.

"That's more like it."

I eased Sura into a trot, headed for Italy.

AFTER ANY BATTLE, a soldier must check himself to see what he's lost and what remains. After Arausio, I had lost so much. After Vercellae, I analyzed not only to see what I lost but also what I gained. I seemed to possess much more than I had at the moment I washed up on the bank of the Rhône. I had my life, no war to worry about, a horse and a friend alongside me, and a future ahead of me. For the first time in a very long time, I could accept that. I was going back to Rome.

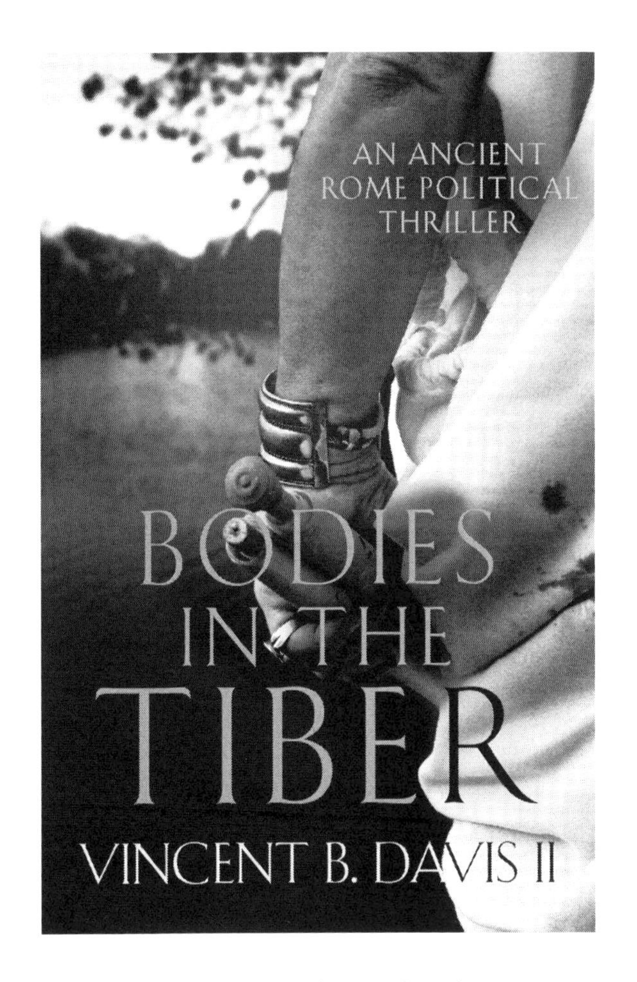

Sertorius' saga continues in *Bodies in the Tiber*!

Did you enjoy :)? Leave a review! For every review at Amazon.com Thirteenth Press, LLC will donate $1 to ASPCA, a nonprofit dedicated to fighting animal abuse.

Didn't enjoy :(? Email the author at Vincent@thirteentpress.com and let him know what he can do better!

Sign up for Vincent's newsletter and receive free Ancient Rome ebooks, family trees, a high-res map, and more!

ABOUT THE AUTHOR

Vincent B. Davis II is an author, entrepreneur, and soldier.

He is a graduate of East Tennessee State University, and has served in the United States Army since 2014.

He's the author of six books, three of which have become international bestsellers. When he's not researching or writing his next book, you can find him watching Carolina Panthers football or playing with his rescued mutt, Buddy. You can connect with the author on Facebook or Twitter @vbdavisii, vincentbdavisii.com, or at Vincent@thirteenthpress.com.

BB bookbub.com/profile/vincent-b-davis-ii
g goodreads.com/vbdavisii
f facebook.com/vbdavisii

Printed in Great Britain
by Amazon